IN THE SILENCE OF THE SNOW

French-born Marie Gabin forms a friendship with Veronica Attwood in their final two years at school, but this is tested when Marie is forced to disclose a secret to her friend. The First World War takes its toll when Marie loses the man she loves. Veronica's husband suffers injuries that eventually leave her a widow, but she finds consolation in her love for the land. Returning to France, Marie marries her childhood sweetheart, but once again life brings involvement in war for the two friends.

IN THE SILENCE OF THE SNOW

IN THE SILENCE OF THE SNOW

by

Jessica Blair

Magna Large Print Books
Long Preston, North Yorkshire,
BD23 4ND, England.

British Library Cataloguing in Publication Data.

Blair, Jessica
    In the silence of the snow.

    A catalogue record of this book is
    available from the British Library

    ISBN   978-0-7505-3823-7

First published in Great Britain in 2013 by Piatkus

Published in Large Print 2013 by arrangement with
Piatkus Books
an imprint of Little Brown Book Group

Magna Large Print is an imprint of Library Magna Books Ltd.

Printed and bound in Great Britain by
T.J. (International) Ltd., Cornwall, PL28 8RW

For Jill who sparked the idea for this book,
and contributes so much to my life,
and remembering Joan
with whom I shared many wonderful years.

And in memory of my Lancaster crew of 44
(Rhodesia) Squadron, 5 Group,
Bomber Command:

Mike (pilot), Eddie (navigator),
Arthur (engineer) Ivor (wireless operator),
Ted (mid-upper gunner)
and Ken (rear-gunner).

PROLOGUE

Marie Gabin left small imprints in the light covering of snow as she stepped across the paved verandah to the stone balustrade that fronted the house known as Rushbrook, on the southern edge of the North Yorkshire Moors near the market town of Helmsley. She shivered, tugged at her long black skirt and automatically tightened the belt on her woollen, calf-length coat, trying to draw comfort from its warmth. She smoothed her close-fitting hat, tugged at the scarf tossed loosely round her neck, held it there with one hand and let her gaze rove over the snow-covered sward shimmering under the moonlight. A tear trickled down her cheek. She brushed it away and sighed.

'If only.' Her lips tightened. She really shouldn't contemplate the meaning behind those two words. The past was the past, the future...

'Ah, there you are.' A pleasant, gentle voice broke into her thoughts.

Marie gathered herself. 'Sorry, Veronica, I should have told you I'd come out.' Marie started to turn to greet her, thankful for the friendship forged at boarding school in 1912, seven years ago when they were sixteen.

'No, Marie, stay there. I'll get a coat and join you. Sylvia is settled with the nursemaid.'

Marie watched her go, wishing she could turn

back the clock to the day in 1918 when she had returned home to France at the end of the war.

A few minutes later, clad in a Burberry trench-coat, Veronica came out of the house and slipped her hand into Marie's.

Lost in the beauty of the night, neither woman spoke until Marie said, quietly, as if she were afraid of breaking the tranquil splendour, 'It is so beautiful.'

'It is,' replied Veronica, as large white flakes began to drift slowly down from a sky that still for the most part displayed the magic of its stars. 'On a night like this you can hear silence in the falling snow. There seems to be peace everywhere. I never thought when Michael and I married that I would be living at Rushbrook so soon. Why did this terrible accident have to happen just when he was getting over the horror of the trenches and his wounds were healing?'

'With your help, I'm sure he'll cope.'

'I hope so. I think he'll be strong enough. His nightmares were becoming less frequent and life was beginning to calm down for us. Working with his father on the estate was good for him, but now...?' A note of doubt entered her tone, which she quickly rectified. 'Of course, the extra responsibility could help keep his mind occupied. He has a good foreman, Crosby, who has been with the family for years, and we are blessed with good friends. I'm so thankful that you were here when this happened. You're a true friend.'

Marie gazed wistfully across the snow-covered scene. 'So are you.' She paused as if she wanted to hold this moment in time, keep it close to her and never let it go. She turned, took hold of Veronica's hands and looked at her friend with an expression of sadness and regret. 'I've some news I wish I didn't have to break to you.'

1

Sixteen-year-old Marie Gabin straightened up from her desk, picked up the letter she had just written, and leaned back in her chair to read it again.

9 September 1912

Dearest Mama,
After two days here I am sure I am going to like the convent where you were educated before me. It is comforting to know that you were once here at St Mary's.
The room I share with an English girl called Veronica Attwood is a little sparsely furnished but comfortable enough and, as you saw, we have a very good view across the playing fields and can see the towers of York Minster in the distance. The headmistress, Sister Loyola, seems a pleasant, considerate woman, but one who will stand no nonsense and be strict when necessary. There are about fifty boarders here.
I am sorry you had to leave without meeting Veronica. I think we will become special friends. Her family has a small country estate near a place called Helmsley about twenty-five miles north of York and

thirty from the coast. She spent last summer holidays in France learning the language, but it is amusing to hear her speak it. I've promised to put her right during the two years we will be here. Maybe then we'll go to finishing school together.

I am writing this in one of our two common rooms. The bell will be going any minute for us to start our first lessons and I need to go upstairs so I will close, dearest Mama. I miss you. Give my love to Papa. I will write again soon.

Your loving and respectful daughter,
Marie

She slipped the letter into the envelope she had already addressed, and sealed it. Grabbing her two books, she hurried to the door. As she stepped out she almost collided with another girl who was rushing along the corridor.

'Watch where you're going!' she snapped, glaring with hostility at Marie. 'Want a detention?'

'I heard that, Monica Beasley, and I know you can't give one, so don't try and take it out on us new girls.'

Monica's glare darkened as she noticed Veronica, who had just arrived. The bullying girl had been caught out, and knew it. She said nothing, but swung round in her tracks and stormed away.

Marie sighed with relief. 'Thank goodness you were here, V.'

The two girls started towards the hall together.

'I'm leaving this letter on the table for posting, as we were told, and then going to our room,' explained Marie.

'So was I,' said Veronica. 'We'll have to hurry –

the bell will be going any minute.'

As they started up the stairs, Marie asked, 'You knew that girl?'

'Yes. She lives near us. Always has had a reputation for thinking she's better than anyone else.'

'But she is a monitor.'

'Take no notice of that blue ribbon pinned to her blouse; she's only a "half monitor". That means she has the authority to help full monitors or staff if called on to do so, but she certainly can't give detentions.'

'Well, thank goodness you knew that.' Marie felt their friendship had deepened in the last few minutes.

The bell for the first class of the day started to ring.

'Better hurry if we want to see if there are any letters,' said Veronica.

They rushed down the stairs together.

'One for me,' cried Veronica.

'From Michael?'

'Who else? Is yours from Jacques?'

'Yes.' They hurried off towards the classroom.

'You don't seem so pleased,' Veronica observed.

'I am, but there are times when he takes so much for granted. He's nearly three years older than me and he thinks that entitles him to boss me. He knows my papa expects us to marry,' Marie explained.

'And you don't view that prospect with favour?'

'Well, I'd like to have some say in the matter, when the time comes.'

There was no chance to say more; they were in the classroom.

Veronica lay on her bed trying to catch up with the passages of *David Copperfield* that the teacher had set the class to read before the evening English lesson. She was thankful that rain had curtailed outdoor activities and had given her this opportunity to read David's first meeting with his great-aunt, something she had neglected to do since the last English lesson. Ten minutes later, when she felt she was getting to grips with the story, the door opened. It did so in a way Veronica would have termed reluctant. That assessment was borne out when she saw a glum-faced Marie step inside as if the whole world were weighing heavily on her shoulders.

'What's wrong with you?' Veronica asked, letting the book slip down beside her on the bed. 'Beastly Beasley been bothering you again?'

'After a month here I can deal with her badgering,' replied Marie, letting the door click shut behind her. 'It's this,' she added, holding out an envelope and a sheet of paper as she crossed to the bed.

Veronica sat up, swung her feet to the floor, and took the paper and envelope. She recognised Marie's mother's writing from previous correspondence.

'Read it,' prompted her friend.

As Veronica scanned the letter, Marie flopped down on the bed and perched on the edge of it beside her friend.

'From the look on your face, I take it you don't want to do this at half-term?'

'I DO NOT!' replied Marie emphatically. 'I had

expected to be at home and I definitely don't want to go to an armaments conference in Switzerland. Papa will be tied up in meetings; Mama will be chatting with other delegates' wives. I'll be left on my own to amuse myself.'

'Won't other people's children be there?'

'If they are, I won't know them,' Marie muttered gloomily.

'What about Jacques, won't he be at home?'

'No. He'll be at the conference too. His father insists Jacques should be there because he'll take over their business one day. My papa agrees that's how it should be; never too young to start learning.' She raised her eyes to heaven.

'Right,' said Veronica in a no-nonsense tone. 'You, M, are coming to spend half-term with me!'

For a moment the room was filled with silence before Marie, her eyes brightening with hope as her friend's meaning sank in, said, 'Oh, V, may I? It would be marvellous.'

Veronica laughed at her reaction. 'Of course you may.'

'But will your parents agree?' asked Marie doubtfully.

'I have ways to wind them round my finger, especially Papa,' replied Veronica with a knowing nod.

'Ah, *mener quelqu'un par le bout du nez*,' smiled Marie. Veronica gave a little laugh. 'I'll have to learn that expression.'

'Seriously, do you think they'll agree?' asked her friend hopefully.

'I'm sure of it. And Jeremy won't object; you'll keep a sister two years younger than he safely out of his hair.'

'Oh, V, that would be wonderful! Truly wonderful!' Marie flung her arms round her friend and they both collapsed in laughter on the bed, only for Veronica to sober them both up with the question, 'What about your parents? Will they agree, M?'

'I'm sure they will. There's no reason for them to object.'

'Good. Then we'll write the necessary letters. When we get their approval we'll inform Sister Loyola and all will be well. Oh, M, we're going to have a wonderful time!'

Six weeks later the spacious entrance hall of St Mary's Convent was filled with the cheerful sound of excited schoolgirls eager to be away for their ten days' mid-term break. The noise rose three storeys high, reverberating from the circular landings above and increasing in volume before bouncing back against the stone-flagged floor below. It would not be stilled until every last girl had departed.

The ten nuns and ten teaching lay-staff were all there with calming, reassuring words, fending off last-minute problems. 'I've lost my purse and it has my railway ticket in it.' 'My hat's gone! I know I put it on that chair, miss.' 'Oh, I've left my bag!' 'Don't forget to bring back the book I loaned you...' Words whirled around the room. The double doors at the front of the building opened, to reveal carriages and traps approaching, and the two 'jack-of-all-trades', who worked for the nuns, ready to help with the bags and luggage.

The activity out in the open helped to ease the turmoil inside. Departures became a steady flow.

Veronica and Marie, each carrying a small valise and handbag, came down the stairs together. Sister Loyola, who had just reassured one of the younger pupils that her elder sister would be there in a minute, saw them and strolled across the hall to reach the bottom of the stairs at the same time.

'I'm pleased to see you two looking neat and tidy for once,' she said in a tone that expressed praise rather than criticism.

'Thank you, Sister,' they chorused.

'I have been pleased with the way you've settled in, and your work has been good on the whole. I hope it will continue so when we resume our studies.'

'We'll try, Sister.'

'Thank you, Sister.'

'Good.'

Any further conversation was halted by the increased buzz of excitement coming from beyond the open doors.

'What's going on?' demanded Sister Loyola, and started for the door.

Veronica and Marie followed in her wake and, with curiosity aroused, the groups of girls still milling about in the hall broke up and headed outside after them. The nuns, who were there to make their usual farewells to the girls bound for the world beyond the convent walls, were swept along in their wake. Chattering girls, surprised by what they were seeing, spread along the length of the stone verandah, leaving the broad steps to the nuns and lay-staff.

The chatter sank to a quiet buzz as if anything louder had no right to intrude on the low hum coming from the motor car that approached the convent at a slow but stately speed. It must be its owner's prize possession. Its white body and gleaming chrome trim, in pristine condition, were meant to catch the onlooker's attention and many of the girls commented on how quiet the engine was, purring as if it did not want to intrude.

Veronica's eyes widened and widened. 'Good heavens!' Though she whispered them in disbelief, the words reached Marie who was standing close to her.

'What's the matter?' she asked quietly.

'That's Moylan driving!'

'Who's he?'

'Josh Moylan. He looks after our carriage and traps.'

'He's doing more than that now,' chuckled Marie.

'He certainly is,' agreed Veronica. 'And he's only a couple of years older than us.'

'Oh!' was all that Marie could say in reply.

'And that's Mama sitting in the back!'

The white car with its shimmering glass and sparkling chrome began to slow down. It stopped. Moylan jumped out and came round to the passenger door.

Silence spread across the scene; even the squeak of the harnesses on the horses champing between the shafts of two traps seemed subdued.

Veronica was even more surprised than her friend. The driver she was seeing now was immaculately dressed in a well-fitting light grey suit; on his head he wore a peaked cap tilted at a slight angle that allowed a glimpse of his jet black hair. She knew the other girls' imaginations would be running riot to see such a personable young man, but wondered how they would have reacted if they had seen Moylan in his working-clothes caring for the Attwood vehicles.

He opened the door and held out one hand in case his passenger required help.

The lady who stepped elegantly from off the car diverted attention away from him and brought whispered gasps of admiration from the crowd of girls. 'Oh, my!' 'She's beautiful!' 'I'd kill to be like her!' 'Those lovely clothes.'

They fitted her to perfection, revealing them to be the work of a very accomplished dress-maker. The open-necked light-brown tunic-coat, with small lapels, flattered her slim waist before falling to mid-thigh over a narrow ankle-length skirt, slit at the front to facilitate ease of movement. The high-necked lace blouse she wore beneath perfectly enhanced the beauty of her oval face, with high cheekbones, full lips and a petite nose. Her eyes sparkled with the joy of life, perfectly offset by a wide-brimmed hat worn with a silk scarf tied in a neat bow on the left-hand side of its low crown.

'Who is she?' Speculation ran rife among the wide-eyed audience.

That speculation was answered when Sister Loyola moved from the steps towards the lady, saying as she did so, 'Mrs Attwood, it is a pleasure to meet you again.'

'And for me also,' replied Catherine, in a low, gentle voice.

'Your arrival has caused something of a sensation,' continued Sister Loyola.

'Oh, my goodness, I never intended...'

'No, Mrs Attwood, there is no need for apology. I should offer you my thanks. It does us all good to see something of the world beyond our convent walls. Now, no doubt you wish to collect your daughter.'

'And Marie Gabin.'

'Of course. It is extremely good of you to have her. I'm sure she and Veronica will enjoy being together. They get on so well together, and all in all have had a successful term. They are both older than their years, but that needn't be a bad thing. I think they will be good for one another.'

'I'm pleased to have your opinion. It gives me a little insight into Marie before I meet her.'

Sister Loyola nodded. 'I reassured Madame and Monsieur Gabin that it would be in Marie's best interests to come to you rather than to stay in the convent during the holidays. Her father was the more concerned; her mother realised the advantages to Marie of being with a friend.'

'I will do my best to entertain both of them.'

'I know you will,' said Sister Loyola. 'Oh, dear, I'm forgetting my manners. Forgive me, I should offer you some refreshment before you set off.'

'No, please, you have enough to do, seeing to all these girls. I'll get my two out of your way. I've caused enough upset as it is.'

'Not at all.' The headmistress cast a glance over at the girls who were still buzzing with excite-

ment, many of them plying Veronica with questions. When she heard Sister Loyola call, Veronica
felt relieved.

'Got to go!' she said. 'Come on, Marie.'

The two girls grabbed their bags and hurried
down the steps.

'Mama!' cried Veronica, and mother and daughter hugged in a way that carried Sister Loyola back
to her own schooldays.

'This is Marie,' said Veronica at length.

'Hello, Marie,' said Catherine. Seeing the girl
look somewhat embarrassed by not knowing how
she should respond, Catherine smiled at her and
said, 'Have you got a hug for me too?' The ice
was broken by her warmth.

As she hugged her, Marie whispered, 'Thank
you for having me.'

'It will be our delight. Now, both of you, say
goodbye to Sister Loyola.'

'Goodbye, Sister,' they said together.

'Goodbye.' Sister Loyola smiled then turned
away to meet some other parents.

'In you get,' said Catherine.

Josh, having stowed the girls' bags, was holding
the door open. On letting Marie get in first,
Veronica said, 'Marie, this is Moylan, Moylan
this is Marie.'

'Pleased to meet you, miss,' he said, touching
his forehead with one finger.

Marie nodded and smiled.

Veronica could not hide her surprise at his
attire. In return Josh revealed he had noticed by
giving her a cheeky wink as she stepped into the
car.

'This is beautiful,' commented Veronica, casting her gaze around the vehicle as they motored down the drive towards the convent gates. 'And so exciting! The whole school was envious. When did you get it?'

'Just after you started at the convent,' replied her mother.

'So you must have known before, and you didn't tell me!'

'We wanted it to be a surprise. Your father wanted to come today but he had the opportunity to view some cattle he's interested in. When the car came, he arranged for Moylan to learn to drive in case another driver were ever needed.'

'So won't he be looking after the other vehicles any more?'

'Oh, yes, that will still be his principal job. He'll be driving this only if necessary, like today. And I'm going to learn to drive as well.'

'You?' uttered Veronica in surprise.

Marie laughed at her astonishment. 'Why not, V? My mother drives.'

'There you are.' Catherine smiled.

'But...'

'It's time ladies were able to do more things for themselves,' said Marie.

'Well said,' agreed Catherine. From what I've read in Veronica's letters and what I've seen already, I'm going to like you, she thought.

Veronica shuffled on her seat. 'This is so comfortable, Mama.'

'And so good to see out of,' added Marie.

'Those are the two reasons why your father chose this model. He has always desired to have

24

a Rolls-Royce so when the chance came, through an unexpected windfall, I encouraged him to buy it.'

'The other reason, Mama?' Veronica asked when her mother paused.

'Because it runs so quietly,' she replied.

'It's quieter than our car. I must tell Papa about this Rolls,' said Marie.

Catherine gave a little smile as she said, 'The manufacturers have called it The Ghost because it is so quiet.'

'Oh, good, now we have a ghost in the family,' laughed Veronica.

'Your house doesn't have one?' asked Marie, showing surprise.

'No.' Catherine smiled. 'I gather yours does?'

'Oh, yes,' replied Marie. 'A Musketeer. It was his home once, but he was killed defending it during the wars of Louis XIV.'

'Have you seen him?' Veronica pressed her, with a tremor of excitement in her voice.

'Of course. He appears kneeling in prayer in our chapel on the anniversary of his death. He's a benevolent ghost, no malice to him.'

'You knew the house had a ghost when your family bought it?'

'Yes. Papa looked into the house's history. It was in a poor condition but he realised it could be made very attractive, especially considering its position with land running down to the river. But you'll see it when you come to visit ... and you, Mrs Attwood, and your husband too. I know Mama and Papa would be delighted to entertain you.'

'That would be very pleasant,' replied Catherine.

The sincerity in Marie's voice and her bubbly personality had greatly impressed her hostess already.

As the journey progressed she became even more delighted that Veronica had found such a friend. Marie, curious about the things she was seeing, asked pertinent questions without overburdening Catherine with them. She, wanting to know more about Marie's family, managed to put some of her own.

'I believe you came to the Convent of St Mary because your mother was educated there?'

'Yes. She's English. Met my father when she was studying in Paris after she'd left the convent. She married him and has lived in France ever since.'

They exchanged the dates of her mother's time at the convent and came to the conclusion that Margaret had left the convent the year Catherine started.

'So there'll be about two years' difference in your ages,' said Veronica quickly.

'That's about it,' agreed her mother. 'What is it your father does, Marie?'

'He has taken over my grandfather's business producing optical instruments.'

'That's a world I know nothing of,' said Catherine.

'I think it's connected to the Army. I've seen high-ranking officers at the château.'

The talk drifted through a number of topics as Veronica pointed out various landmarks and points of interest. As they proceeded through the market town of Helmsley the white Rolls-Royce drew so much attention that people stopped in their daily tasks to watch it go by. Four miles east of the town they turned into a narrow road with a rougher surface, that headed towards rising land.

'If we had kept on the road we have just left we would have come to Scarborough on the coast,' Veronica told Marie. 'Mama, can we go to the seaside while Marie is with us?'

Catherine smiled indulgently. 'I have no doubt you'll be able to persuade your father.'

'Oh, good.' Veronica bounced in her seat with excitement. 'But you'll help, Mama?' Then she turned to Marie. 'We're on our land now.'

In the fields well-fed cattle grazed. They left this road when it began to climb a steady incline. 'To the moors,' Veronica told her friend, and went on to explain what moors were when Marie showed ignorance of the term. They turned through iron gates into a tree-lined roadway that bore recent signs of levelling.

'When was that done?' asked Veronica.

'Your papa had the surface prepared ready for the arrival of this car,' said Catherine. 'By the way, he took Jeremy with him to the Dales; they are staying overnight so you won't meet them until tomorrow, Marie.'

'Something to look forward to,' she replied politely. Then, with her excitement mounting at the prospect of seeing Veronica's home for the first time, asked, 'Where's the house?'

They drove out from beneath an avenue of trees

27

which were obscuring the view. The house appeared as if heavy curtains had just been drawn
aside.

'There!' said Veronica proudly, delighted by the
wonderment that shone in Marie's eyes.

Brunton nestled cosily into the hillside but was
not overpowered by it. It looked contented, settled. Marie sensed it welcoming her, stranger
though she was.

'It looks old,' she said.

'The central section is the oldest,' Catherine explained. 'Seventeenth-century, built as a medium-
sized three-storeyed manor house. The two wings
were added about a hundred years later, making
the frontage more imposing and allowing the
building of those twin flights of stairs giving access
to the balustrade that, as you see, runs the full
width of the frontage. Much renovation work was
carried out before Mr Attwood's grandfather
bought the property. Then his son added an extension on the east side that includes a dining
room with easier access from the kitchens, making
it much more convenient when dining. I'm sure
Veronica will enjoy showing you round.'

'Oh, I will, Mama,' she enthused. 'You'll love it,
Marie.'

Josh manoeuvred the car round the curving
drive towards the front door. Their approach had
already been noted by someone. The double
front doors opened and the butler, housekeeper,
footman and two housemaids stepped out to wait
at the bottom of the steps for Josh to halt the car.
He was out of his seat quickly to open the door
for his passengers.

The butler, immaculate in black trousers, short black coat, white shirt and black tie, stepped forward. 'Welcome back, ma'am. A pleasant journey, I hope?'

'Indeed it was. Thank you, Welham.'

The housekeeper, immaculate in a white blouse, tight across her bosom, and black skirt flaring slightly from her waist, stood straight-backed and sharp-eyed to offer her greetings next.

'Thank you, Mrs Cole,' replied Catherine

'Miss Veronica,' the butler and housekeeper both acknowledged her homecoming.

She returned their smiles. 'Mrs Cole, Welham, this is my dear friend Marie Gabin.'

Their respectful greeting of 'Welcome to Brunton Manor, Miss' made her feel comfortably at home, and when the footman, Sanders, and housemaids, Ruth and Lily, added some courteous words of their own, she was very pleased indeed she had made friends with Veronica Attwood.

2

Marie stirred. As her bewildered mind slowly cleared she became vaguely aware that she was in bed and that somewhere there was a knocking sound that was becoming louder. Was she at St Mary's Convent? No ... somewhere else ... somewhere welcoming and new...

Drowsiness disappearing, Marie grasped the bedclothes to her and sat up in bed. 'Come in.'

The door opened. Veronica peeped round it. 'Hello, sleepyhead.'

'Hello.' Sleep still thickened Marie's voice. 'Oh, dear. Have I slept in? Should I have been up?'

Veronica stepped into the room. 'No, no,' she laughed as she came and sat on the side of the bed. 'It seems you slept well.'

'Oh, I did. This mattress is so comfortable.'

'Good. You'll be fresh for the day then.' Veronica laid some clothes ready on the bed. 'There's one of my riding outfits, with split skirt; we ride astride here. Mother is very forward-looking. I'm sure it will fit you, we're about the same size. It's a beautiful morning so I've asked Storey, our head-groomsman, to have two horses ready in an hour and a half. I thought we'd ride over to Rushbrook so you can meet our neighbours, the Eakins. Their estate is about the same size as ours. We've known them all our lives. So up you get!' As she stood up she jerked the bedclothes off, bringing a scream of protest from her friend. Veronica, laughing, raced from the room to avoid the pillow she knew Marie would throw at her.

Half an hour later, she was tapping on Veronica's door. Answering the call of 'Come in', Marie stepped inside, saying, 'What do you think?' and struck a pose.

'Perfect,' replied Veronica as she cast her eyes over Marie's attire. Down the large black puff sleeves ran a contrasting insert of white fabric, its colour matching the high-necked under-blouse with its wing-tipped collar which Marie wore beneath. The black split-skirt was ankle-length and revealed highly polished black riding boots. Marie carried a small-brimmed hat, which had a bright scarlet ribbon tied around the base of its low crown. She placed it on her head at an eye-catching angle and laughingly asked, 'How's that?'

'Attention-catching!' grinned Veronica. 'What about mine?' She whisked her hat out from behind her back. Its pale blue matched the colour of her skirt, which was cut to the same style as Marie's, and worn with a cream-coloured blouse. The tips of her brown boots peeped out from beneath her riding skirt.

'I think we both look just right,' Veronica announced, and with a flourish, linked arms with her friend. 'Let's have breakfast and ride!'

They fell into step, left the room and negotiated the landing together, tripping lightly down the stairs to enter the dining room.

'Shouldn't we wait for your mother?' Marie asked on seeing the room was empty.

'Oh, no, she'll have had hers. She's always up early for her morning ride, so breakfast is informal.'

Marie realised someone had been listening out for their arrival for, a few moments later, a maid appeared.

The meal was served without any fuss while the two girls speculated what Sister Loyola and their convent friends would say if they could see them now, appropriately clad for their ride.

They were close to finishing their breakfast when Veronica's mother walked in, looking the picture of health and good humour after her early-morning ride. Wind-blown hair tumbled down Catherine's back to just below her shoulders; her cheeks glowed. Marie thought she looked just as beautiful as when she had first seen her, and that her riding outfit in tan and cream subtly complemented the freshness and smoothness of her complexion.

'So you two are riding as well,' Catherine commented as she came to the table. She sat down in her place at one end of it.

'I'm taking Marie to meet the Eakins,' said Veronica.

'Splendid.' She glanced at their guest approvingly. 'I'm sure you'll like them.'

'I'm looking forward to it.'

The door from the kitchen opened and a maid brought some coffee for Catherine.

'You ride at home?' she asked Marie, following the question with a laugh. 'That's a silly question, seeing you appropriately attired and wearing that outfit with such panache. Veronica's looking after you then?'

'She certainly is, Mrs Attwood,' returned Marie, who added with a smile, 'and yes, I do ride at home. All the family does.'

'And they are?'

'Mama and Papa, and my two brothers, Claude and Roland.'

'Your brothers are older than you?'

'Yes, Roland by two years and Claude by four.'

'I hope we will meet them all some day.'

'I do too.'

'Mama, we'll have to go. Storey will have the horses ready,' Veronica broke into their exchange.

'Very well, off you go. Have a nice time.'

Veronica was already on her feet. She went to her mother, kissed her on the cheek, and said, 'Thank you.'

Marie had risen from her chair and seemed hesitant about her next move. Catherine held out her hand and smiled; a gesture for which Marie was grateful. She kissed her hostess on the cheek. 'Thank you,' she said quietly, already feeling great affection for Mrs Attwood.

As she watched them leave the dining room, Catherine hoped the girls' friendship would strengthen and always survive no matter what else came their way. Left alone, she enjoyed her coffee and turned her thoughts next to her husband. She hoped he and Jeremy had purchased the cattle they wanted. She missed Charles when he was away even if it was for only one night. She missed the warmth in his eyes and the feel of his arms around her. The love they had felt for each other at their first meeting had never left them, and had been their strength when Charles' father had been killed, failing to negotiate a fence while out hunting. The strength of their attachment had been tested when the lawyer revealed her father-in-law had left an estate riddled with debt and facing extinction. Rumours of gambling and about the way such a good horseman had been killed piled on the agony to such an extent that the shock had killed Charles' mother.

The dilemma facing Charles and Catherine only strengthened their love, and it carried them through the trying period of clearing his father's debts and getting the estate into profit again.

During that time they found great joy in the birth of their two children, and gained an added incentive to make sure that the estate would continue and be their legacy to the future.

Family memories were dear to Catherine; she regarded them as vital to her life. Now, as her past and her present mingled, she felt at peace with the world. She drained her cup and went upstairs to change.

Veronica led the way along a passage, flanked by a big kitchen and storerooms, to a door that gave admission to a large square cobbled yard. As they headed towards an archway in the centre of the buildings that stretched the width of the yard, Veronica explained, 'The outdoor staff's quarters are above the workshops. The stables and tackroom are in a yard of their own beyond the archway.'

There they found Storey and two groomsmen with their horses, saddled and awaiting their arrival. Veronica introduced Marie to the three men, who paid their respects.

'Miss Veronica, I've put you on your favourite, Amber.'

'Thanks.' She smiled her gratitude and pleasure. 'I don't know when we will be back.'

'There'll be a groom waiting, miss.' Storey turned to Marie. 'I chose Bess for you, miss,' he said, indicating a chestnut mare standing quietly under the soothing touch of a groom.

'Oh, she's beautiful,' said Marie, her voice full of admiration as she stepped close to the horse. She patted its neck and then gently stroked it, all the time speaking softly. 'Bess, you are a beauty, we are going to get on so well.' The horse turned her head and nuzzled Marie, returning the greeting.

'You've made a conquest, miss,' Dick Storey commented, his tone showing a little surprise. 'She's placid enough but I've never before seen her show such interest in a stranger at first meeting. You have a way with her; you must have horses at home?'

'We have,' replied Marie. 'And I do like them.'

Dick helped her into the saddle; Marie took the reins and brought Bess alongside Veronica, who was already settled.

The head-groomsman touched his forehead. 'Have a pleasant ride.'

They left the stable-yard on a track towards low-lying countryside and the wide valley that, Veronica explained, led all the way to the coast. She gave a little smile. 'I'll get round Papa to take us there ... it won't be difficult. He'll jump at the chance to show off his new car!'

They kept the horses to a walk initially, but once the track widened they moved into a trot and finally a steady canter. After three miles they took a right fork, and after another three Veronica slowed the pace when the track entered an oak wood. After half a mile they emerged into open ground and she reined in her horse. As Marie drew up alongside her, Veronica announced, 'There it is, Rushbrook House!'

Long and low, seemingly proud of its isolation, it was a peaceful sight. Smoke curled lazily from the chimneystack on the north side.

'It's like the original part of your house before the rest was built on,' commented Marie.

'Yes. The indoor staff have rooms in that extension you see on the left. Outdoor staff have that row of cottages just beyond the two small fields. Coming back from there towards the main house you can see the fold yard and stables.'

'Someone's noticed us,' said Marie, noting the rider who had turned away from the stables, to which he had been heading, and was coming in their direction.

'Michael,' said Veronica, putting her horse into a walking gait.

'So this is the man you talked about so often at the convent. You were always looking for his letters.' Marie's words were as much a query as a comment. 'Ah, I know it is. You're blushing,' she added with a teasing twinkle in her eyes.

Veronica said nothing but watched Michael, who had put his horse into a gallop. A few minutes later he was pulling to a halt with a flourish, to prevent the animal running further. 'Hello, you two,' he called out. 'Who's, your friend, Smudge?'

'Marie, she's French. Well, half-French.'

'Which half?' asked Michael with a grin.

'Papa's French,' replied Marie. 'And you should handle that horse more gently.'

He pulled a face at the criticism. 'She likes to run.'

'No doubt, but she didn't like the way you pulled her to a halt; you were hurting her.'

Michael winked at Veronica. 'What have you brought us, Smudge?'

'Not what but who, Michael. A very dear friend

36

of mine, so you'd better behave.'

He inclined his head to Marie. 'Whoever is Smudge's friend is a friend of mine,' he said, with a broad smile Marie knew was genuine when their eyes met.

Her own eyes warmed as she said to him, 'I'll be your friend if you'll treat your horses with more consideration.'

'I can only bow to your wishes.' He inclined his head deferentially. 'Now, Smudge, am I inviting you both to luncheon?'

'Will your mother mind?'

'Oh, you know how much Mother adores you. You need never ask such a question.'

'Then your kind offer is accepted. Thank you.'

'Good. Let's go to the stables. The grooms will look after your horses.'

As they moved off Marie queried, 'Why do you call her Smudge?'

Veronica answered quickly, preventing him from elaborating on the explanation which she knew he would do if he had half a chance. 'I accidentally smudged some work he was doing and I've been Smudge to him ever since.'

'And always will be,' he said. 'My own dear Smudge.' A rich nuance of feeling was conveyed in his comment.

Marie glimpsed Veronica's answering blush and raised a questioning eyebrow at her friend, but made no comment. That would have to wait. Marie lodged it in her mind for the time being.

Once the grooms had taken their horses, Michael said, in a serious warning tone and with a meaningful glance at Veronica, 'Come on. Let's introduce Marie to the matriarch.'

'You make that sound as if it is going to be an ordeal for me,' she said.

'Don't take any notice of him,' said Veronica. 'Mrs Eakins is a lovely person. I'm sure you'll like her.'

Marie felt the doubt Michael had momentarily generated in her lifted by her friend's words.

He led the way along a stone-flagged passage from the back door to the hall, where the atmosphere was in marked contrast to the gloom of the passage. Here light streamed in from the double sets of large south-facing windows to either side of the double doors. The hall was spacious, with just the right amount of furniture to make it homely rather than imposing.

'Mama will be in the writing room, as she calls it,' said Michael, heading for a door on the right. 'Dining room that way,' he added, nodding towards the left. He opened the door. 'Yes, here she is,' he said over his shoulder. He stood to one side, holding the door open to allow Veronica and Marie to enter the room. 'Mama, I've brought visitors ... invited them to luncheon.'

Elspeth Eakins rose quickly from the mahogany secretaire at which she had been writing. Her face expressed curiosity and delight; she loved surprises.

'Veronica! It's a pleasure to see you again,' she said with great enthusiasm as she took the girl into her arms and gave her a big hug.

'Mrs Eakins, may I present my friend Marie Gabin,' Veronica said as Elspeth released her hold on her to turn to the stranger.

38

'Marie, I'm so pleased to meet you.' Elspeth opened her arms to her too, in a gesture that was filled with warmth. 'Veronica's mother told me you were coming to stay at Brunton. You are very, very welcome here too.'

'Thank you, Mrs Eakins. I am pleased to be here.' Marie was surprised; she had expected Mrs Eakins to be a similar personality to Mrs Attwood, but that idea had been well and truly confounded, though deep down she felt sure they were both kind and considerate, genuine people. Outwardly, though, they appeared to be so different. The calm stateliness of Veronica's mother held peaceful certainty, whereas even in these few minutes Marie had sensed in Mrs Eakins a bustling whirlwind of a personality.

Elspeth, though dressed in a good-quality ankle-length brown skirt and lace blouse, did not wear clothes with the same natural elegance as Catherine, but nevertheless exuded an air of gentility.

'Let us go through to the drawing room,' said their hostess. 'Michael, I think the first visit of this charming young lady from France should be celebrated with a glass of Marsala.' She turned to Marie. 'I know Veronica is allowed a glass on special occasions. I assume you are too?'

'Yes, I am,' replied Marie.

'Splendid. We like Marsala as an aperitif.'

As they crossed the hall, Michael went to a bell-pull and before he reached the drawing room a maid had appeared.

'Ah, Lucy, a new bottle of Marsala, please.'

She nodded and soon returned with the bottle.

She went over to some glasses that were set on a sideboard close to one corner of the room.

'Just leave it, Lucy,' Michael called, 'I'll see to it.'

'Yes, sir,' said the maid and left the room.

His mother was enthusing to Marie about the view from the drawing-room windows. A well-kept wide grass sward sloped gently away from the house; distant areas of woodland and fields of grazing cattle formed an attractive patchwork scene. Michael waited until his mother had finished expressing her love for Rushbrook and turned back from the windows before he poured the wine.

The half-hour before lunch was only interrupted when the door swept open and a stocky, red-faced man with a beaming smile on his face bustled into the room. 'I'm here!' he announced. 'Oh.' He pulled up short when he saw the stranger. 'Sorry, sorry.'

Marie was startled by the sudden intrusion, but when no one else reacted she realised this was normality in the Eakins household.

'Clive, don't startle our visitor,' Elspeth chided. 'Meet Marie Gabin ... you remember, school-friend of Veronica's? Catherine told us she was coming for half-term.'

'Ah, yes.' He beamed with pleasure. Marie had started to rise from her chair. 'Don't get up, my dear. Well, not unless you have a kiss for me.'

Swept up in the relaxed atmosphere, she smiled and stepped forward, saying, 'It will be my pleasure,' and kissed him on the cheek.

Not having expected her to agree so readily to

his suggestion, he blushed with embarrassment.

Marie quickly lightened it by saying, 'It is a pleasure to meet you, Mr Eakins.'

'I hope everyone has been looking after you.'

'Indeed they have.'

'Splendid, splendid.' He turned to his son. 'Have you a glass for me?'

'You've a beer in your hand already, Father,' Michael pointed out with a smile. 'It seems Marie has flustered you.'

'Oh, yes.' Clive Eakins glanced down at the glass in his hand. 'I collected it as I came in via the kitchens.'

Elspeth patted the seat of the sofa on which she was sitting. 'Come, sit here, Clive, and finish your beer. Luncheon will soon be ready.'

He did as he was bidden, then, as if remembering he had neglected their other guest, said, 'Oh, Veronica, hello. How are you?'

'Very well, Mr Eakins, thank you.'

'Good, good. Er, Michael, did you go to the Fifty Acre?'

'I did, Father.' He added an explanation to Marie. 'That's what we call one of our fields.' He turned back to his father. 'I think we can turn some of the cattle in there.'

'Good. Tell Crosby tomorrow.'

'Now you've got that out of the way,' said Elspeth, 'no more business talk, we have guests.'

The talk continued with pleasantries, and did so throughout an enjoyable luncheon.

As it neared its end, Michael announced, 'This afternoon I'll take Veronica and Marie to the two lakes.'

'A good idea,' approved his mother. 'We keep them for trout,' she explained to the newcomer.

'And that makes for fishing,' Clive added, his enthusiasm evident at the mention of the fish.

'And that keeps men happy,' commented Elspeth as if she were passing on advice to the two girls. 'Now let us relax in the drawing room with coffee.'

An hour later Veronica and Marie held their horses steady in the stable-yard as Michael took the reins from one of the groomsmen and swung into the saddle. He led the way out of the yard and, once clear of the buildings, allowed Veronica and Marie to draw up on either side of him.

'We'll have to ride single-file for about half a mile through the wood,' he explained to Marie, 'but it is an easy ride.'

She found this to be so, and as they all emerged from the trees the girls pulled to a halt on either side of him.

Marie gasped at the view before her. The open ground dropped smoothly to two lakes, the water's gentle movement sending shimmering sunlight dancing across the surface. Beyond, the rolling farmland's many shades of green mingled with browns and yellows, foretastes of the coming autumn, making a picture that would stir many an artist to pick up their brushes. 'It's beautiful,' she half-whispered. 'Why didn't you tell me, V?'

'Because I didn't want to influence your judgment. I wanted it to be a surprise, and to see your reaction,' replied her friend.

'You are so lucky to have this on your land, Michael,' said Marie. 'We are still on Rushbrook

42

land, aren't we?' she asked.

'Oh, yes. We go three fields beyond the lakes and four on either side.'

'And with all the land we have ridden through it is a big estate,' observed Marie.

'Yes,' he agreed, 'Brunton will be a similar size; it has no lakes but has more land on the flat.' He paused and then added, 'We like it here, don't we, Smudge?'

Marie caught an unmistakable expression in his eyes as he looked at Veronica and received her unfeigned agreement. Marie had no opportunity to comment on it, however, until she and Veronica parted from Michael on the way back.

'He's in love with you,' she said then.

'He's not,' replied Veronica, a little sharply.

'Ah.' Marie gave a little laugh. 'And you are with him.'

'Nonsense! We're too young.'

'The quickness of your replies and your blushes betray you.'

'Rubbish.'

'V, there's nothing wrong with it. You're never too young or too old to fall in love. I think the French recognise and deal with affairs of the heart more readily than you English do. You always seem to want to hide your feelings.'

Veronica remained silent. She would remember Marie's words for a long time afterwards, but for now she pushed them to the back of her mind; there was school and then finishing school to think of before the lure of love.

3

Veronica and Marie were enjoying a cup of tea in the drawing room with Veronica's mother when they heard the sound of horse's hoofs and of wheels crunching on the gravel driveway.

Veronica jumped to her feet and ran to the window. 'Papa and Jeremy,' she called. 'Storey must have heard them; he's come round the end of the house.' She hurried back across the room, calling, 'Marie, come and meet them.'

Catherine was already on her feet and hurrying across the room. She led the way to the front door and flung it open. Stepping outside, she skipped quickly down the steps, her face wreathed in a smile of joy. 'Charles!' was all she said, but the way she expressed that one word told everything of her love for him.

He turned from handing the reins to Storey, held his arms wide, and greeted her with a smile to match hers. 'My love,' he said, taking her in an embrace that said so much more.

They kissed, desiring to prolong it, but knowing they should not do so in front of the two girls and Jeremy; the groom was already leading the horse and trap away. With their arms round each other's waist, they turned to the two girls.

'Papa!' Veronica came to him and kissed him on the cheek before adding, 'This is Marie.'

'I guessed as much. Marie, I'm so glad you

could visit us. I was sorry not to be here when you arrived but I am sure you will have been well looked after.'

'I have, Mr Attwood. I thank you for your hospitality.'

'It is our pleasure,' he replied. 'And this is Jeremy.'

Even though Jeremy's pleasantly delivered greetings were outwardly reserved, Marie sensed a hidden self-assurance in this handsome young man.

He was dressed in tweeds like Charles and had assumed his father's trait of looking immaculately dressed. Seeing them together, she could easily imagine Jeremy taking over the estate one day. Both men were slim but well-built, tall, with Charles maybe two inches more than his son's six foot. The father had a teasing twinkle in his eyes whereas Jeremy's seemed to hold a cautious light, awaiting his assessment of the stranger. Even as she was aware of this, Marie saw it change, and, as they exchanged polite conversation while walking up the steps to the house, sensed he had made his decision about her.

They reached the door and the younger ones held back. Jeremy waited for his sister, then he turned to Marie, gave a slight bow and said, 'May I add my personal welcome to Brunton Manor? I hope you are enjoying your time with us?' Now she knew his conclusion had been favourable,

'Thank you, Jeremy,' she said graciously, and her warm smile received one in return. She felt even more comfortable with the family after this.

Knowing that Charles and Jeremy would be

back, Catherine had consulted with the house-keeper and cook about having a special evening meal to welcome them home, and to greet their guest into the family.

'Do you dress for dinner?' asked Marie when she and Veronica learned of Catherine's plan.

'Not every evening,' Veronica replied, 'but we do for special occasions and when we have guests.'

'Oh, dear. Then I have nothing appropriate to wear,' said Marie with a troubled frown.

'Don't worry, I'll fix you up. You managed my riding outfit, I'm sure you'll get into one of my evening gowns. We'll have fun getting ready.'

The two sixteen-year-olds enjoyed choosing what they would wear and how they should do their hair. They primped and posed in front of the cheval glass in Veronica's bedroom.

'Well, what do you think?' Marie finally asked.

'Suits you,' replied Veronica approvingly, after casting a critical eye over the pale blue dress that flowed from a tightfitting waist to Marie's ankles. It was complemented by a waist-length jacket of similar material worn loosely over a lace blouse. Marie's short dark hair had been parted to one side to allow the natural waves to dictate its flow and enhance her round face, petite nose and Cupid's bow lips.

'You think so?' queried Marie, apprehensively.

'I'm certain,' replied Veronica. 'What about me?'

'Delightful,' returned Marie. 'Red suits you,' she commented, eyeing Veronica's outfit which was similar to hers except for the length of the sleeves and the cream silk blouse.

A clock chimed in the distance. 'Half an hour before we eat. Come on, let's go down.'

Reaching the stairs, they paused and grinned at one another; without a word exchanged each knew what the other was thinking. They put on a graceful air and took each step down with exaggerated poise.

Jeremy came hurrying into the hall. Suddenly aware of someone on the stairs he came sharply to a halt, turned and looked up. His astonished expression stopped the girls mid-step, awaiting his comment.

'Gosh!' He swallowed. 'I didn't know I was going to have to escort two beauties to the dining table!'

Relieved at the complimentary observation, the girls smiled at each other and then continued down the stairs.

Reaching the bottom, they both said in unison, 'Good evening, Jeremy.'

He gave a little bow as he replied, 'Good evening. May I say how lovely you both look?' He stepped over to them with his arms crooked in readiness. 'May I have the honour of escorting you to the drawing room?'

They acknowledged his offer with an inclination of their heads, and slipped their arms under his.

'He doesn't look too bad himself, does he?' Veronica put the question to Marie.

'He certainly doesn't,' she replied, with an approving glance at Jeremy, elegantly dressed in thigh-length black jacket, black trousers, white shirt and black bow-tie. Everything fitted to perfection, emphasising his athletic figure.

Their entry into the room froze the conversation between Catherine and Charles, leaving in its place admiring approval of the three young people.

Charles, as immaculately dressed as his son, sprang to his feet from the sofa on which he had been sitting with his wife. 'Young ladies, you look wonderful.'

'Thank you,' they both said together.

'Don't you think so, Catherine?' he said.

'I certainly do, my dear,' she replied rising gracefully to her feet and displaying the sinous lines of her own figure-fitting silver-grey dress with the fashionable neck looping low to reveal a long-sleeved pink lace blouse worn beneath.

'Mrs Attwood, you look lovely. We pale beside you,' said Marie in all sincerity.

Catherine accepted the compliment with a smile as she said, 'You are too kind, my dear.' She turned to her husband then. 'I think the girls deserve a drink.'

'Of course.' He crossed quickly to the sideboard where he poured some Marsala into five glasses. As they were filled Jeremy passed them round.

When they were all seated, Veronica said, 'Mama, as we came in I heard you mention the word suffragette.'

'Yes, there have been several reports of them in the newspapers lately.'

'You aren't thinking of joining them, are you?' asked Veronica, a touch of alarm in her voice.

'I sympathise with them. I'm in favour of votes

for women, but I don't approve of some of the things the militants do. I don't believe smashing windows and similar acts of destruction help to achieve anything. Demonstrations, yes, but not destructive demonstrations.'

'Do you agree, Papa, or are you against Votes for Women?' asked Jeremy.

Charles paused thoughtfully for a moment. 'You will have seen reports in the newspapers, and you two girls will have heard talk at school. To answer your question, Jeremy, I think women should have a right to the vote, but I agree with your mother about the demonstrations. When militancy gets out of hand, and it seems to at times in London, then you can expect punishment to be meted out. But I don't condone the severity of the sentences or what happens to the women in prison.'

'Mama, you won't ever demonstrate, will you?' Veronica asked with marked concern.

'We are far from London here, but if the chance came for me to make a peaceful demonstration I would do so. I would never become involved in any act of destruction however. I prefer to support the movement in other ways. It is a just cause and I'm sure it will prevail some day.' She noted the relief in Veronica's eyes. Seeing Marie somewhat bewildered by the conversation, and knowing suffrage was not a prominent debate in France, Catherine changed the subject then.

Conversation flowed easily and continued to do so throughout the meal during which plans were made for the rest of the girls' school holiday.

St Mary's Convent
Near York
Yorkshire
England

10 October 1912

Dear Mama and Papa,
I have had a lovely time with Veronica's family who were most kind to me. We rode around their estate and visited their neighbours, Mr and Mrs Eakins, and their son Michael, who are long-standing family friends. I had a nice quiet horse called Bess. Veronica and I explored their estate on foot. Veronica's brother, Jeremy, was most attentive when he accompanied us. Mr and Mrs Eakins took us in their brand new car to Whitby and Scarborough, which are both on the coast.
I get on so well with Veronica, and I have to say she has come on extremely well with her French. I'll have her talking like one of us before we leave St Mary's.
I hope we can invite them back, maybe next Easter holidays rather than Christmas when the weather might be bad for travelling.
I will write again soon.
Love,
Marie

The result of this letter was that Marie's mother wrote to Catherine Attwood.

Château Gabin
Rue du Paris
Senlis
France

25 October 1912

Dear Mrs Attwood,
I must thank you for all your kindness to Marie during the recent holiday. It was a comfort to know that she was with good friends during that time. I am very pleased that our daughters get on so well. I can sense in them a friendship that should last a lifetime. I am sure that will be confirmed when I see them together. I hope that can be arranged during their Easter holiday.
With that in mind, I extend to you, your husband, your son and of course Veronica, an invitation to visit us from Wednesday 27 March until 3 April.
I await your answer and look forward to meeting you.
Yours sincerely,
Margaret Gabin

Catherine noted that the signature was written in the firm flowing hand of a confident person. When Charles and Jeremy came in from dealing with a problem raised by Storey concerning two recently purchased horses, she read them the letter while they were being served luncheon.

'What do you think, Charles?' she concluded.

'It would be good to establish a friendly relationship with Marie's parents since the two girls get on so well together.'

'You and Jeremy'd be able to spare the time?'

'Easter seems far off. We have Christmas to consider first. Marie's mother must like to plan ahead. But as far as I'm concerned, I'll manage it. What about you, Jeremy? Want to come?'

'Yes, I'll come. It will be a new experience for me, going abroad.'

Catherine smiled to herself at the quick response from her son. Perhaps he wanted to meet Marie again.

'Good. That's settled,' said Charles. 'I'll warn Simpson and he can plan to be in sole charge,' he added, knowing the entire working of the estate could be entrusted to the capable hands of his manager. 'You and I will go into York tomorrow, Catherine, and make the travel arrangements.'

'I'll write to Madame Gabin, thanking her and saying I'll let her have the details when we finalise them. I've been thinking about the dates she suggests. The third of April is just a week before the girls start at the convent again. I'll suggest Marie travels back with us.'

'A splendid idea, if that suits the Gabins.'

Catherine penned the letter immediately so that it could be dispatched that day.

A week later they received a brief reply from Madame Gabin, expressing her delight, and that of her family, at the forthcoming visit. It also contained an appreciative reply to Catherine's offer to escort Marie back to England ready for the new school term.

It left them all with something to look forward to during the remainder of the year and into 1913.

4

Veronica was woken by the brighter than usual morning light streaming into her bedroom. Captured by its unusual intensity, she glanced towards the window. Then, with excitement, she threw back the bedclothes, swung out of bed and moved quickly to the window. Snow! There had been snow during the night.

As she dressed quickly, and pulled on her outdoor clothes, she thought it was a good thing the snow hadn't come three days sooner; that would have meant staying at the convent until travel was possible once more – and goodness knows how long that would have been. As it was, she felt sure that all the girls would have reached home by now, even the five pupils from abroad, though she had no knowledge of the weather conditions they might have met on the way. She believed from reports in yesterday's newspaper that Marie would have had little trouble reaching Senlis.

When she entered the dining room her father and brother were close to finishing their breakfast. Veronica had hardly made her 'good mornings' when her mother came in.

'A good job you brought the cattle in,' commented Catherine as she sat down at the table where, as usual, a maid was already moving towards her with some porridge and another was hovering nearby with a jug of coffee before they

53

turned to serve Veronica.

'It was Simpson's intuition,' replied Charles. 'Jeremy and I are going to see that they have settled all right. Has the snow changed your plans?'

'No,' Catherine replied. 'I was going to write some letters. Snow doesn't alter that.' She looked at Veronica. 'What do you plan to do?'

'I'll take Thor and Hector for a walk, see how they like their first snow,' she replied.

'I think they'll love it.'

Though they were cautious when brought from the kennels, the young dogs were soon revelling in chasing each other, sending the snow swirling around them, and, urged on by her laughter, leaping at the snowballs she threw in their direction.

They raced up an incline with Veronica trying to keep up with them. The dogs disappeared over the top. Knowing there was a small wood on the other side, she urged herself on to keep them in sight, but in her attempt to do so she lost her footing and rolled down the slope towards the trees. Before reaching them she came to a stop and lay, gasping air into her lungs, feeling none the worse for her fall. Thor and Hector, thinking her escapade was part of a game, swung round and raced towards her. Reaching her, they fussed excitedly around her, licking her face and pawing at her. Their antics brought laughter to her lips as she rolled with them in the snow.

Her hilarity stopped when she became aware of a figure leading a horse out of the wood. She grappled with the dogs, trying to calm their exuberance with gentle words. Relief swept over

54

her when she recognised the horseman muffled up against the cold. Michael! Veronica struggled to sit up.

'You all right, mi...' He stopped as if puzzled. 'Is that you, Smudge?'

'Of course it is,' she replied, and added teasingly, 'Are you blind?'

'I am not,' he rapped back as he hastened towards her, 'but I didn't expect to find anyone out here rolling in the snow.'

She lay laughing at his expression while cuddling the dogs to her. They broke away as Michael neared them, wary for Veronica's sake, until they detected friendliness in the approaching figure.

She took hold of the hand Michael held out to her, to help her to her feet. 'Thanks,' she said, and started slapping the snow from her clothes.

'You all right?' he asked with concern. 'What happened?'

'I slipped at the top and rolled down. No damage done.'

'You are sure you're all right?'

She smiled, reached out and touched his cheek. 'Don't look so bothered. I'm unhurt.'

'But I am bothered. I don't want anything to happen to you.' The words were out almost before he realised he had said them.

'That's sweet of you,' she said, flattered by his anxiety. 'Thank you.' She stretched up on her toes and kissed him lightly and quickly on the cheek.

He touched the spot where her lips had been. 'I'll remember that for ever,' he whispered as if to himself, but Veronica caught the words. She said nothing but smiled to herself, seeing his reddening cheeks. Then the spell was broken when he said, 'I'd better get you home ... you need dry clothes. Get up on my horse.'

'No. I'll be warmer walking.'

'Then I'll walk with you.' He swept up the reins of the horse which had stood quietly by after the initial inspection by the dogs, now lying patiently in the snow.

Veronica read Michael's action as an indication he would brook no further protests from her.

They set off, he giving her a helping hand as they climbed the slope together.

Once on the level ground they fell into step and he endeavoured to keep the pace as brisk as he possibly could in the snow.

'Have you got all your plans made for visiting the Gabins at Easter?' he asked.

'Yes.'

'Looking forward to it?'

'Yes, I am. It will be interesting to visit them and see their way of life.'

'Give you a good chance to see how your French goes down with the natives. Jeremy tells me he's trying to learn the language from you.'

Veronica laughed. 'Trying! That's about it. He's hopeless.'

'That'll disappoint him. I think he took a shine to Marie when she was here.'

'Jeremy?'

'Yes.'

'Oh, well, that explains why he was so keen to go to France then. Well, jolly good luck to him.'

'Suppose so. But hey, don't let it give you any

ideas about getting a French boyfriend.'

'As if I would,' Veronica replied.

He said no more but she noted his blush again and locked it away among her treasured moments.

Once they reached Brunton Manor, she and her mother insisted that Michael stay for luncheon; a small reward for his gallantry in escorting Veronica safely back to the house. Once the meal was over he decided it was best to leave for home as the brightness of the morning was disappearing and gathering clouds threatened more snow.

Veronica sat in the bay window of her room, watching the snowflakes drifting slowly down and letting her mind wander back to what had happened in the snow earlier that day. She linked that with the observation Marie had made about Michael's feelings when she had stayed at Brunton Manor in October. Was there truth in what she had said, Veronica wondered, and if there was, how did she feel about Michael? At that moment her heart skipped a little beat. Was it an indication of the feelings she had not examined closely up to now?

During the rest of the holiday the question of her feelings for Michael kept recurring. At times she would chide herself: You're too young. At others she would warn herself: There's a whole life ahead. Was this only a crush or was it something deeper?

Over the Christmas and New Year period the two families spent a great deal of time in the rap-

port that only comes from long and close friendship. They dined, walked, had fun in the snow,
attended church services together, and the New
Year saw them all herald in 1913 at Brunton.

As the hands of the clock in the drawing room
slipped near to midnight silence came over the
group of friends, leaving only the measured tick-
ing to intrude on their thoughts. Then came the
first chime that heralded in the New Year.

'Happy New Year!' 'Happy New Year!' resounded from everyone at the same time. Jeremy responded to his sister's good wishes but his thoughts
were on her friend, far away in Senlis, wishing she
were here.

'Happy New Year, Michael!' Veronica let her
eyes meet his with a meaning he couldn't quite
interpret, but he didn't allow that to interfere
with the touch of his lips on hers and the tone of
his voice that put much more into 'A Happy New
Year, may it bring all you wish yourself' than the
usual greeting. It was another moment Veronica
kept locked in her heart and mind ten days later
when she returned to boarding school.

Noise swirled around her when she walked
through the main doorway to the convent. Excited
greetings were resounding off the walls as girls
called out to each other. Quick snippets of news
were exchanged as pupils hurried off to dump
their luggage. Veronica threaded her way among
the throng looking for Marie, but her search was
in vain. She hurried up the stairs, expecting to find
her friend in their room, but disappointment filled
her when there was no sign of her, not even a suit-

case. She wondered if Marie were all right. Then chided herself for her own concern; she had no idea what time Marie was meant to arrive from France.

She had left the door open and the familiar sounds of returning girls rose and subsided, laughter and comment all around. Veronica was closing her empty case when a shout of 'V!' filled the room.

She spun round and straightened up. 'M!' She was across the room in a flash and falling into the open arms of the girl who had just dropped two cases and was standing in the doorway. They whirled each other across the room, eyes brimming with pleasure and laughter ringing off the walls. They collapsed on their backs on Marie's bed.

'*Phew!*' Veronica took a deep breath. 'Have a good time, M?'

'*Oui*. Lots of fun. A long Midnight Mass, the priest preached far too long, great food, lots of nice presents. Jacques gave me some beautiful earrings and I saw the better side of him.'

'So he didn't boss you about?'

'No. He can be really kind. Maybe the festivities brought out the best in him. Hey, that's a nice necklace,' Marie said, eyeing the delicate turquoise beads that hung round Veronica's neck. 'A present?'

'Yes. From Michael.'

'Ah!' said Marie, bending over to have a closer look at them. 'Very nice,' she emphasised. 'Then it must be right what I said when I stayed with you in October. Michael's in love with you. What about you? And don't give me any sloppy answers.'

'Well...' Veronica paused for a moment, then added, 'He is rather nice.'

'Good,' laughed Marie, 'be happy.'

'I intend to be. Maybe you'd better make that resolution too. Michael told me Jeremy had taken a shine to you.'

'Jeremy?'

'Yes. Now it's your turn to blush. And I can tell you, he was enthusiastic about coming to visit you when the invitation came. Looks like you are going to have a choice; I don't need one. So how do you feel about my brother?'

'Don't ask me. It's not wise to discuss feelings for someone with his sister.'

'All right, a pact of silence on love affairs?' queried Veronica.

'Yes, for this term. Who knows what may happen when you visit during the Easter break.'

'It would be so good to have you as a sister-in-law,' mused Veronica.

Marie made no comment, though the remark had made her think; instead she came back to more mundane considerations. 'I think you had better take that necklace off, Sister Loyola won't permit it.'

'I know, but I did want you to see it.' A twinkle came to Veronica's eyes as she paused then added, 'Maybe Jeremy will get one for you.'

Pleased to be together again, they settled well to the new term and their progress satisfied Sister Loyola, though at the end of it the headmistress had to point out that mathematics was still Veronica's weakest subject and she should set herself targets to improve her grasp of the subject.

'So what?' was her comment to Marie. 'I'm never going to need it.'

'You'll always need it, especially if you are going to help Michael run that estate one day,' Marie pointed out.

'And who says that will happen?'

'I do. I've seen you mooning over his words whenever you receive a letter from him. And don't tell me we made a pact – term's over now.'

'Not until we leave tomorrow.'

'Well, as good as.'

'Ah, and then maybe the truth will come out about you and my brother.'

'Jeremy, I've never seen you so enthusiastic about something as you are about going to the Gabins,' commented his mother the day after the Easter services were over.

'He can't wait to see Marie again,' explained Veronica casually, a comment that brought a look of reproach from her brother.

'I suspected it was something like that,' said Catherine.

Jeremy blushed; he had never thought that the cause of his eagerness was so obvious.

Catherine gave a sympathetic smile. 'There's nothing wrong with it, Jeremy; Marie's a lovely girl. And, Veronica, don't tease him. It might rebound on you one day.'

'Can't,' she said. 'I know where my heart lies.'

'We've all known that for a long time, ever since

61

you were a kid,' said Jeremy. 'You were always goggle-eyed about Michael.'

'So you can't tease me,' mocked Veronica triumphantly. 'I'm off to see him now.'

'Are you all packed?' asked Catherine.

'Yes, Mama.'

'All right. Don't be late back. Your papa wants an early start.'

'I won't be, Mama.'

Catherine, admiring her daughter's light-hearted casualness and her certainty of where her love lay, watched Veronica walk from the room.

'Are you packed?' she asked her son.

'Bar last-minute bits and pieces,' he replied.

'Good,' she said. He turned to go but she stopped him. 'I don't want to see you hurt. Remember, Marie has French blood in her, and her father's outlook on a relationship developing between you two may well be different from mine.'

He came over to his mother, kissed her on the cheek and said, 'Don't worry about me, Mama.'

She smiled and patted his arm. 'I always worry about my children, but I have confidence in them too.' She felt a touch of pride as he walked from the room.

'Is the car in good order, Moylan?' asked Charles as he came over to Josh who had just brought the Rolls-Royce to the front door.

'Yes, sir. Running as soft as a whisper.'

'Full of petrol?'

'To the brim, sir.'

'Good. Have you got the route worked out?'

'Yes, sir. Largely as you planned it, to take in

the two stops, the second leaving us good time to make Dover for the morning crossing.'

'Splendid. Then you'll return home and be back in Dover in ten days' time to collect us.'

An hour later Moylan eased the Rolls-Royce away from Brunton Manor, its four passengers viewing the coming ten days differently but all with eager anticipation. Charles was quite confident that his new car would impress and outshine whatever vehicle Monsieur Henri Gabin owned.

5

'Monsieur Attwood?' The young Frenchman, smart in chauffeur's livery, put his query when Charles led his family past the Customs post.

'Yes.'

'I am Alain and I am here on Monsieur Henri Gabin's instructions to drive you to Senlis.'

'Thank you,' said Charles, relieved that the chauffeur spoke English well-enough, though with a marked accent. 'My family,' he added.

Alain gave them all respectful smiles. 'Madame, Mam'selle, Monsieur. The car is over there,' he added, indicating a red car parked nearby. 'Let me take your luggage, Madame.' He took Catherine's suitcase and placed it on a luggage trolley he had commandeered for their arrival. Once it was loaded, he led the way to the car where he quickly arranged the cases and bags and strapped them in place, making sure there would be no movement during the journey.

'Would you mind riding in front beside me, sir? It will be more comfortable for everyone that way.'

'That will suit me,' replied Charles, pleased that it would give him a better chance to assess the car and compare it with his own.

Once he saw that his passengers were comfortable, Alain guided the car away from the docks and into the open countryside. Unsure whether they would want to talk or not, he put one query. 'I hope you had a good crossing and no...' he left a slight hesitation '...*mal de mer?*'

'No, not at all. We found we were all good sailors,' replied Charles.

The uneasy silence that settled on them then was disturbed only by low exchanges from those in the back, but was finally broken when Charles enquired about the car and Alain latched on enthusiastically to his passenger's obvious interest. Apart from answering Charles's questions, he readily replied to the queries from the rest of the family about sights visible along the way.

'Monsieur Gabin gave me instructions to make a stop at a small hotel in a village near Amiens for refreshments. The Gabin family is well known there. You will find excellent food and service,' the chauffeur told them.

They were greeted by a rotund, red-faced man with a ready smile that was matched by the friendly light in his wife's bright eyes. Shepherded into a cosy dining room after refreshing themselves, they were charmed by its low oak beams and rustic furniture. Two maids served a meal of partridge, fried apple slices and a rich butter and cream sauce. A plate of fresh fruit followed, with an assortment of local cheeses and breads baked by the landlord's wife.

The landlord shunned Charles's attempt to pay. 'It has all been taken care of by Monsieur Gabin.'

As they walked to the car feeling highly satisfied, Jeremy whispered to Veronica, 'If we are dining like this all the time, I'm going to enjoy myself.'

'I think we are about halfway to our destination in Senlis,' commented Catherine when they had settled in their seats and were waiting for Alain to check the security of their luggage. 'Monsieur Gabin's influence seems to extend for a considerable distance.'

Alain drove at a comfortable speed until he finally announced, 'We are not far from Senlis. You can see the church tower ahead.'

The tall spire cast a protective shadow over the small town. Their curiosity about what the place was like had to be curbed until later because Alain turned the car through open iron gates suspended from stone columns at the entrance to a drive lined with poplar trees, which for a while hid the house from sight. The curves in the drive allowed the house gradually to reveal itself until there were no more trees, only an open expanse of well-cut grass that heralded a well-ordered estate and house.

'I like that tower,' Veronica whispered to her mother, referring to the three-storeyed addition to the west end of the long main building. The sharply rising roof of the tower gave it the appearance of wearing a hat while the two windows on its top floor seemed to be peering at them, seeking to assess the merits of any new arrival.

Alain swung the car round the drive, which looped in front of the stone building, to bring the vehicle to a halt at the main entrance, which was centrally placed with four large windows to either side, their shutters folded back against the wall. Matching windows without shutters stretched along the upper storey.

Alain was out of his seat quickly to attend to his passengers. He was helping Catherine when the double doors opened from the inside. Two footmen, simply but neatly attired in dark blue trousers and jacket and white shirt, came forward to attend to the newcomers' needs and take charge of their luggage.

'Welcome to our home.' The greeting was uttered with warmth and sincerity by a slim, elegant, upright man who stood at the entrance.

'Monsieur Gabin!' Charles came forward with outstretched hand. When he felt his hand taken he realised the lithe appearance of Henri Gabin hid an unexpected strength.

'Monsieur Attwood, you and your family are most welcome.' Henri's glance embraced them all before his wife emerged from the house to add her greetings.

Any further formalities were shattered by the sound of clattering feet speeding out of the house and Marie shouting, 'V! V! Why didn't someone tell me you were here?' She flung her arms round her friend who responded as loudly to the enthusiastic greeting.

66

'You weren't slow in finding out!' laughed her mother.

The ice was broken, and Christian names agreed on as the rest of the introductions were quickly made.

'You'll meet our sons, Claude and Roland, later; they were needed to check on the suitability of some timber from a recent felling in Vauban Wood.' Henri waved a hand in its general direction.

'Vauban?' queried Charles.

'The previous owner of this property, who apparently claimed to be descended from the great seventeenth-century French military engineer,' Henri explained as he started to lead everyone into the house.

'This is an elegant hall,' commented Catherine, admiring its spacious proportions.

'Let us show you to your rooms. When you've freshened up, come and join us in the drawing room for a cup of tea,' said Margaret. She added with a smile, 'That's an English habit I haven't lost since coming here. I don't think I ever will.'

'I'm pleased to hear it,' replied Catherine in a tone of approval.

As Marie and Veronica, lost in their chattering, reached the stairs behind their parents, Marie stopped and turned to Jeremy, who had been bringing up the rear. 'I'm so sorry, you are being neglected. I got so engrossed on seeing V again.'

'Think nothing of it. Just being here is sufficient reward,' he said quietly, but there was no mistaking the meaning that lay behind his polite words.

Marie caught it and was troubled.

Half an hour later, when the new arrivals entered the drawing room, Margaret tugged the bell-pull beside the ornate fireplace. A few minutes later two maids appeared, each carrying a tray which they took to the long table that stood against one wall. One of them proceeded to pour the tea into the cups which had been placed ready for the arrival of the guests. The other handed them round and, after everyone had been served, left Marie and Veronica to offer the patisseries that had been set out.

Conversation flowed generally for a while, but gradually smaller groups formed.

'Would you like to see the rest of the house?' Margaret asked Catherine.

'I'd love to. It has such a welcoming atmosphere, which I am sure is due to you and Henri.'

'I think we will have left our mark on it, but we found it friendly ourselves when we were first interested in buying it.' Margaret rose from her seat as she was speaking. 'Are you two coming?' she asked, eyeing Marie and Veronica.

'No, Mama, I'm going to show Veronica the tower.'

'Very well. Perhaps we'll see you there.'

'We'll take Jeremy,' Marie suggested. 'Otherwise he'll be subjected to boring old business.'

Her suggestion relieved Jeremy who feared he could easily be isolated until he met Marie's brothers. Even then he couldn't be sure how he would fit in with their interests.

Once he was alone with Henri, Charles enquired, 'If you don't mind my asking, have you much acreage? As I'm sure you know, I am a landowner in Yorkshire and run much of it as a productive estate.'

'Oh, yes, Marie described it all to us; she was charmed by it. I have a considerable acreage but it isn't all close by.'

'Isn't that inconvenient?'

'Not really. You see, the farm and woodland are run from here. I'll show you around tomorrow. We have extensive vineyards a short distance south-east of here. I'll take you there another day. Are you a wine drinker?'

'Yes, but I'm no connoisseur.'

'Ah! Then I shall make you one. Well, as far as I can in the short time you are here. But you will come again. And I'll give you a bottle of the best wine we produce, for you to enjoy in your own surroundings.'

'You are being most kind.'

Henri gave a dismissive gesture with his hand. 'You were more than kind to Marie. I appreciate that, and I know without a doubt that Margaret does too.'

'So, like myself, you are a man of the land?'

'Not really. The farm and the vineyard are of interest, naturally, but my main concern is the family business on the outskirts of Paris. It is a small firm manufacturing optical instruments for commercial use, but we also produce, in a small way, items for the Army and Navy. I'm rather proud of it.

'My grandfather founded it. He realised the

69

potential of developing optical apparatus for industry and warfare. He was scientifically minded and had an inventive bent, attributes he passed on to my father and to me. The firm thrived. I took charge when my father died suddenly when he was fifty.'

His voice took on a note that revealed his obsession with his inheritance. 'I am determined it will continue to thrive, as a memorial to them. There were times, particularly prior to the 1880s, when demand for our goods was small. We, along with a British firm, Ridley Brothers, provided private clients' needs only. Then scientific research in the 1880s changed the optical glass industry. For a number of years now we have been producing special instruments for the Army and Navy, and I know Ridley's have been doing the same for your military.'

'Do I detect from what you say that both our governments believe war is inevitable?' Charles asked.

'I wouldn't put it as bluntly as that but you probably know as well as I do...' Henri paused thoughtfully. 'No, maybe not. I'm nearer this sort of speculation than you are. You don't see everything reported in newspapers,' he said, and then took up his conjecture again. 'You'll be aware of rumblings in the halls of power that are symptomatic of war. Leading dynasties are jealous of each other's influence; their subjects are uneasy and want to exert more control over their own destinies. It only needs a single spark, a hot-head, a fanatic, to set the powder-barrel alight and plunge Europe into turmoil.'

'Oh, yes, I've read these things in the newspapers but, as you imply, being a farmer I am not so close as you to political thought and military strategy. But surely we men will have more sense than to light a torch that could cost so many lives?'

Henri gave a small smile that conveyed a hint of sadness. 'Ah, if only men were always reasonable,' he sighed. 'But we have to be aware of and prepare for such possibilities. My government and yours are quietly encouraging armaments firms to be alert to the situation, without over-stretching themselves financially in case war does not break out. My company and Ridley's realise the type of warfare that will develop, and that will necessitate and increase the production of various optical instruments and the invention of new and better ones; optical munitions, as they are being called.

'Although our governments are reluctant to place large orders, because hopefully these instruments may never be needed, we are given the go-ahead as far as is viable without substantial official investment. I have close contact with Ridley's; we confer about future commercial developments that could be beneficial to us both. And military developments? We have to be very careful there, but should our governments give us permission for an exchange of information hinging on the military, then both firms will have a better understanding of where the future may lead.'

'It all sounds very intriguing.' Charles gave a little chuckle. 'Much more so than farming and land management.'

'Ah, but what you do is just as important. War

could bring a blockade, affecting food imports; you would play an important part in your country's survival.'

Charles gave a little nod, accepting Henri's observation. 'Does your connection to this firm, Ridley's, ever necessitate your visiting England?'

'Yes. Nothing regular, but occasionally – whenever we think it could be advantageous. We both jealously guard our own research and development, but we are prepared to exchange research and do whatever is necessary should war come.'

Charles nodded his understanding and added in the friendliest of tones, 'May I offer you hospitality at Brunton Manor whenever you are in England?'

'That is most kind of you. I will certainly bear it in mind.' Henri smiled his appreciation as he pushed himself up from his chair, saying, 'Let us take a stroll outside and then you can relax before dinner this evening.'

Charles rose to his feet and stretched himself. 'I'm looking forward to seeing your farm and the vineyards.'

'You shall, and before you leave I'll take you to my factory – give you some idea of what we do there without revealing anything you shouldn't know, of course.'

'Margaret, this is a delightful house. It wears its age with such dignity and you have modernised it in a way that updates it without breaking from the past,' commented Catherine as they settled in the drawing room after the tour of the house.

'It is kind of you to say so. Henri is so forward-looking; it comes from the inventive mind that is applied not only to his work. Please make yourselves at home, treat the house and the gardens as your own during your stay.'

'It is most kind of you. I know we all appreciate your goodwill.'

'Although I had no apprehensions about sending Marie to St Mary's Convent, having been there myself, I was worried about how she would settle. It was a great relief when her first letter told me about Veronica. I could tell immediately that she had found a friend, and I have been comforted by the way their friendship has developed. Now that I have met Veronica, I can see how lucky Marie is.'

'I am sure it works both ways. They have benefited from both starting there at the same time, and from Sister Loyola's perceptiveness in putting them together.'

They fell into easy talk and reminiscences about their own time at St Mary's until they decided it was time to change for dinner.

Just as Catherine reached the stairs, Margaret having departed to check that all was in hand for the evening meal, Marie, Veronica and Jeremy burst in, breathless and red-faced.

'Oh, Mama, you should see the tower,' gasped Veronica. 'It's a magical place.'

'I have,' said Catherine, 'Marie's mother showed me. We didn't see you.'

'So many hidey-holes, nooks and crannies,' said Marie. 'I got lost in there when I was little.'

'It is enchanting,' agreed Catherine. She glanced

enquiringly at her son. 'You look as though you've been run off your feet?'

'After Marie showed us round, the girls insisted on hiding and I had to find them. It took some doing. I thought I wasn't going to, and I knew we should be getting back.'

'Well, here you are now, just in time to get changed.'

'Now you know why we let you find us,' said Marie with a teasing smile that Jeremy thought about while he dressed for the evening.

They came down to find Roland and Claude awaiting them with their hosts. As Charles introduced them, the Attwoods learned that twenty-one-year-old Claude's main interest was the farm and vineyard while Roland was absorbed by the optical business.

'Very convenient,' as their father put it.

With introductions over, the two easy-mannered young men were attentive to their guests, showing a lively interest in the English and England, which neither of them had visited since their maternal grandparents had died several years ago. They helped to engender an easy atmosphere throughout the meal, something the Gabin family managed to maintain during the rest of their stay.

Apart from relaxing in the colourful gardens around the house, they explored Senlis and were much taken by the old-world charm of its narrow cobbled streets and its tranquil atmosphere. Jeremy spent an interesting time with Claude when he was supervising the felling of some more trees. Henri also accompanied his son when he took Charles on a tour of the farm, which ended with an interesting exchange of ideas about the prospects for new farming methods in both countries. When Catherine showed doubt about accompanying Margaret to dine with her and several of the town's ladies, her apprehension about intruding on their enjoyment was brushed aside. The welcome Catherine received could not have been warmer. On horseback, Marie and Veronica, sometimes accompanied by Jeremy, enjoyed some of the nearby attractions of the countryside. Sight-seeing in Paris was a must, as was a shopping expedition there for Catherine, Margaret, Veronica and Marie, the two young ladies having an exciting time helping their mothers choose new dresses and then being told to choose one for themselves, which was made all the more exciting when they entered one of the most exclusive salons in Paris.

Henri chose that day for himself and Roland to take Charles to see the Gabin factory, while Jeremy had gone fishing with Claude.

Henri drove the car thirty kilometres south-east of Paris before he halted before some closed iron gates situated in a high hedge that flanked the quiet road in both directions.

'Your factory is here?' asked Charles with surprise.

Henri laughed. 'You expected to see a large factory and smoking chimneys? Sorry to disappoint you. First, our business does not require that. Our sort of manufacturing requires more delicacy. Also the nature of our work, both commercial and military, needs to be kept secret so we like our land and buildings to be out of sight.'

'Don't local people know of you?' queried Charles.

'Yes, but very few realise what we really do here, and those who do are loyal employees, carefully vetted. We put it about that we conduct special research for the commercial world. Even if anyone got an inkling of our connection to the military, they would need intimate knowledge of certain aspects of that work before they could appropriate it.'

While they had been speaking a uniformed man had appeared. On recognising the car and its driver, he opened the gates. As they passed through, Henri acknowledged the guard's salute with a cheery, 'Good morning.'

'You make it sound most intriguing,' said Charles as the car rolled forward along a road that climbed away from the gates for half a mile. Henri slowed at the top of the rise.

Charles found himself looking down into a bowl-shaped valley surrounded by hills no steeper than the one they had just climbed. At the centre of the depression was a series of one-storeyed buildings linked by covered paths.

'The factory?' asked Charles.

'Yes, and our research unit.'

'Very nicely hidden,' observed Charles, 'and with lookout posts for extra security.'

'According to recent government orders.'

'Mmmm, so alarm bells are definitely ringing in the higher echelons of government.'

'You would be told, "Merely precautionary measures." I suppose the thinking is, better safe than sorry.'

76

'I am curious about one thing, Henri. Why show me all this?'

Roland chuckled. 'Papa will only show you what he lets you see, and will only tell you what he thinks you should know.'

'In the time you have been here, I have come to know you, Charles, probably better than you are aware,' Henri explained. 'I pride myself on being a good judge of men. You are the quintessential Englishman. I am sure I could trust you with all our secrets but as yet I won't. Nevertheless, our families have become close, so I will show you and tell you as much as Roland indicated and no more. But I think you will find it interesting.'

6

'You look to be deep in thought, Charles,' commented Henri as they drove back to Senlis.

Charles started. 'I'm sorry,' he replied, and then added, 'I was far away.'

'Where were you?'

Charles gave a little laugh. 'Not far, really. I was thinking about all you have shown and told me. Though naturally you can reveal little of your defence projects, I realise the ways in which your commercial work can help your military work, especially in producing top-quality lenses.'

'That is true, but I can say no more than that,' replied Henri cautiously.

'I wouldn't expect you to.' Charles left a little

pause then asked, 'Does it lead you to believe that war is inevitable?'

'Not inevitable, but with so much unrest between the countries of Europe, who are all suspicious of each other's territorial ambitions, and increasing military expansion, it does make me wonder at times.' Henri pulled a face. 'Charles,' he went on brightly, 'don't let us think of such things ... they may never happen. If they do, we'll deal with them then. Now, we must plan your remaining days with us. I think Margaret has something in mind. Hopefully, when we get home she will have some news for us.'

Margaret kept her 'secret' until everyone was seated for dinner. She then announced that she had arranged a visit to Paris, principally to go to the Louvre. 'I'm afraid you won't see the *Mona Lisa* – she was stolen two years ago.'

'We heard about it,' said Jeremy. 'I'm disappointed, but it can't be helped.'

'But you will see many other wonderful paintings,' said Margaret. 'In particular, *The Oath of the Horatii*, painted by David in 1784. Although it shows a dramatic Roman scene, it is popularly interpreted as a depiction of the traumas of the French Revolution.'

'What about the sculptures?' asked Jeremy.

'There are many of those, but in my opinion the most beautiful is *Nike of Samothrace*, also known as *Winged Victory*. It is from the Hellenistic Period, about 190 BC. Although it is headless and without arms, the wings are wonderfully carved. Even more beautiful is the depiction of the drapery around the body. Have you a particular interest in sculpture, Jeremy?'

'No more so than in other aspects of art, but I do wonder at the talent of those who can shape human forms out of stone, wood, and particularly marble.'

'Then the Louvre will be a joy to you. We will dine at an exclusive restaurant and, if the weather is good, sail down the Seine.' Margaret glanced across the table at her husband. 'You, my dear, are excused.'

'Do pardon my absence,' he said, glancing round at everyone, 'I have an important meeting tomorrow. I know you will all have a splendid day. I believe the weather promises to be good.'

'But you will not be excused four evenings from now. I have accepted an invitation from Victor and Josette Martineau to dine with them. They are keen to meet our English friends,' Margaret announced.

'Splendid,' replied Henri enthusiastically. 'I'm sure you will like them. He too is in the armaments trade.' His lips twitched into a little smile as he added, 'We term ourselves "friendly rivals". Seriously, though, we do collaborate quite a lot.'

'Have they any children?' asked Catherine.

'One son, Jacques, who is the same age as Claude,' replied Margaret. 'Sadly, after his birth they were told they should have no more children.'

'So Jacques would receive all their attention?'

'Yes, but they were careful not to spoil him.'

'He and Marie became very good friends. As they grew up together, Marie filled the place of the second child Josette could never have. I think she hopes that one day...' Margaret left the implication unspoken.

It was not lost on Jeremy who caught Marie's eye. His raised eyebrows caused her to blush and she lowered her eyes. But he wondered if he had caught in her expression a touch of annoyance or even defiance at what her mother had just hinted.

'Jacques has grown into a fine young man,' put in Henri. 'Very intelligent and sharp. He will easily take over the business when his father decides to retire. You will see that for yourselves when we visit them. Now, I see we have all finished so the young ones may be excused. But, may I ask, will they please leave the small drawing room vacant?'

Marie rose from the table and was followed by Veronica, Jeremy and her brothers. As they entered the large drawing room, Marie said quietly to Jeremy, 'You kept your interest in art hidden from me.'

'You didn't ask, and anyway I thought you wouldn't be interested.'

'I'd not say no to hearing about any of your pursuits.'

He detected a note of genuine interest in her voice and said, 'I'm not only flattered but pleased,' with a wide smile that it pleased her to have caused.

The topic was prevented from going any further when Veronica joined them while Claude and Roland poured the coffee which had been awaiting them on the sideboard.

Once the young folk had left the dining room, Henri gave an explanation to Catherine and Charles. 'I asked them to leave this particular room vacant because Margaret and I have something we would like to discuss with you.' Catherine's and Charles's surprised expressions brought a suggestion from Henri. 'Let's make ourselves comfortable there and talk over a glass of wine?'

Catherine liked that room with its delicate mahogany furniture, the armchairs drawn in a semi-circle in front of the richly carved fireplace where flames danced cheerily, and the country scenes depicted in the water-colour paintings on the walls.

'That sounds tempting,' she said. 'No doubt we'll try another of your own wines?'

'Of course,' replied Henri, 'but I think I will make this an extra-special one.'

'This sounds as if it is linked to the matter you wish to consult us upon,' said Charles.

'Well, it could be, but no matter what the outcome, we can still enjoy the wine.' Henri had gone to the mahogany sideboard on which four cut-glass wine glasses had been set out on a silver tray. A matching tray held two bottles of red wine.

While he opened a bottle, the two ladies enlightened the men on their visit to an afternoon tea party in Senlis especially organised for 'Margaret's English friend'. Henri filled four glasses and distributed them before resuming his seat. He raised his glass. 'To our dear friends, Catherine and Charles.'

They accepted the toast and made one in return. 'Margaret and Henri. May our friendship, brought about by our daughters, blossom through the coming years.'

They drank, and then Henri said, 'It is about those daughters that we wish to speak to you. They will soon be entering their last term at the convent and Margaret and I wonder if you have considered what Veronica will do then?'

'We are thinking of sending her to a finishing school. We have made tentative enquiries with Sister Loyola, asking if she has any recommendations.'

'A good idea. I'm sure wherever she suggests will be good,' commented Margaret, glancing enthusiastically at her husband but receiving a frown in return.

'I had a school in Switzerland in mind,' said Henri, a sharp note entering his voice.

'I told you I had spoken to Marie about her future, as you requested, and that her answer was she would like to go with Veronica, wherever that might be,' said his wife.

'We would be delighted if they could stay together. I think it would be easier for them both, especially in a new environment,' put in Catherine.

'With the unstable political situation in Europe, we would rather Veronica stayed on our side of the Channel,' put in Charles.

'England might be the best solution, Henri,' said Margaret, quickly seizing on Charles's observation. 'Marie would be out of harm's way there should the worst happen because of all the recent unrest.'

'And we would always be there for her. Our home is Marie's home,' Charles confirmed.

'That's very reassuring and comforting,' added Margaret. 'Thank you.' Her tone of voice bound their friendship even closer. She sensed Henri's displeasure at being out-manoeuvred in this way and grasped the opportunity to settle their daughter's future the way she wanted it. 'I think we should see what Marie and Veronica themselves have to say.' With that she was on her feet. She went to the bell-pull and in a few moments was instructing a maid, 'Tell Miss Marie and Miss Veronica, who are in the drawing room, that we would like to see them.'

The girls were curious about why they had been summoned, but when they heard about the possibilities for their future education there were excited smiles and they accepted, without hesitation, the chance of staying together.

In spite of facing one more term at the convent, Marie and Veronica both felt as if adulthood was drawing close.

'I think you could have given my idea of Switzerland more consideration,' said Henri peevishly as he and Margaret were getting ready for bed later that night.

'Don't look like that,' she countered. 'You don't have to have your own way about everything, do you? You should be happy that your daughter is happy.'

'I am, but I don't like being shown up by my own wife.' His voice had turned cold.

'You weren't shown up, and you know it! It's

just that your ego doesn't like being thwarted.' She eyed him challengingly. 'That trait in you has become more marked recently; particularly with me, and I don't like it. Don't spoil the rest of the Attwoods' visit by trying to change their minds or Marie's. The girls' education is settled!'

The visit to Paris, with its boat trip down the Seine and time spent in the Louvre, was a great success, enjoyed by all, but especially by Jeremy who took the opportunity, when others drifted off to view their own interests, to spend some time with Marie.

He felt they were becoming closer, but that was dealt a blow when they visited the Martineau estate ten miles south of Paris. The Martineau family gave them a warm reception and the whole evening passed off well, with fine dining in pleasant surroundings in a house that revealed the elegance and good taste of Victor and Josette. Conversation flowed across many topics, and the host and hostess and their son saw that no one was left out. But Jeremy, though he hid the feeling, was jealous of Jacques. He was handsome, with clean-cut features that Jeremy felt could have been carved by one of the Greek sculptors whose work he had recently seen in the Louvre. Jacques had a poise and charm that Jeremy envied, especially when they were turned on Marie. He tempered his feelings and attitude with the knowledge that she would be travelling back to England with his family soon, and she would share some time with him then.

The final two days at Senlis were hectic with everyone wanting to use the time to the best advantage, but inevitably the moment came when goodbyes had to be made. Because Marie was returning with the Attwoods there was more luggage to be packed into the car. Alain's skill in stowing it brought praise for the chauffeur from Charles. The farewells they made were warm and genuine and laced with the hope that they would all meet again before long. Parting from Marie was not easy for Margaret and Henri, but they drew comfort from the fact that their daughter, while sad to be leaving, was happy to be returning with Veronica, and would be in the good hands of her family.

Their return journey to Calais had been organised by Henri who had issued specific instructions to Alain not to leave the port until he had seen their ship sail.

Approaching Dover, Charles announced that he had decided they would have a leisurely journey north and would stay overnight on the way. This made travelling much more agreeable and resulted in their arriving at Brunton Manor in the early afternoon two days later.

'Has everything been in order?' Catherine asked Mrs Cole after being greeted by her housekeeper

'Yes, ma' am,' replied Mrs Cole. 'There are one or two things to mention, but maybe we can do that over a cup of tea?'

'Splendid idea,' Catherine approved, familiar with the ritual of having tea in the housekeeper's sitting room when there were household matters to discuss.

'I'm away into Kirkbymoorside,' announced Charles. 'I'll see if Fred Swan's heard any more about the two horses he was keeping an eye on for me. Jeremy, check with Bert Simpson that all has been well on the farm while we've been away.'

'Right-ho, Father,' he replied. As he went upstairs to change he overheard an exchange between Veronica and Marie.

'I'm going for a ride. Want to come, Marie?'

'If I know your horse it will find its way to Rushbrook,' she teased in reply.

'So?' said Veronica.

'Well, you won't want a gooseberry along with you. I'll stay here and write to Mama.'

'Just as you wish,' replied Veronica, but there was no mistaking her relief at her friend's decision. 'I'll get ready.'

She hurried to her room and Marie went to climb the stairs. She reached the top at the same time as Jeremy.

'I heard that. No need for you to be on your own. I'm going to check on a few farm things, do you want to come along?'

'Why not? It will be good to be out in the fresh air in pleasant company,' she replied with enthusiasm. She smiled to herself when she saw his cheeks redden, but at the same time felt flattered by his reaction. 'I'll get my jacket and see you in the hall in five minutes.'

'Where first?' Marie asked as she rejoined him.

'Fifty Acre field,' he replied. 'There are some cattle there I want to look at before I see our farm manager.' He paused outside the front door, standing at the top of the four steps.

Marie saw his gaze fixed on the scene before them. An expanse of lawn stretched before them, giving way to a neatly trimmed hedge beyond which lush green fields supported grazing cattle and sheep. Thick hedges and fine stands of trees, oaks, elms and chestnuts, completed the view that held his attention.

'You love it here, don't you?' Marie said quietly, as if breaking the silence would shatter his moment of reflection.

'I do,' he replied, 'I really do.'

'So it will be your life in the future?'

'I see no other for me.' He started briskly down the steps.

'One day you'll take over from your father. Or will you find a place of your own?' she asked, matching his stride.

'I'll not move from here. There is no need. I'll follow Father. I know it is what he wishes too. Mother and Veronica are well provided for, and I would always welcome them at Brunton.'

'And if you marry?'

'Then the girl would have to love me truly and be of like mind.'

'You think you can find someone who matches that description?'

'I'm sure of it. She would know she would not be a slave to my expectations.'

'But an equal partner?'

'Yes.'

'Goodness me! Then you're standing out against present convention – men generally do expect their women to be subservient to their wishes.'

'Those attitudes will die out soon. Look at the suffragette movement. We aren't really affected by militant demonstrations here, as they are in London and other cities, but women do make their opinions known in other ways. I think it's only right men and women should be equal partners in life.'

'How surprising. Your radical views would not go down well in present-day France. There's little talk of votes for women there.'

'Well, time will tell,' he said with finality in his tone.

Realising this, Marie asked, 'Which is Fifty Acres?'

'Two fields further on.'

They fell into the sort of pleasant, non-committal chatter that both realised signified they were enjoying each other's company.

Veronica, enjoying the feel of the breeze through her hair, kept her horse to a steady trot. It was good to be in the Yorkshire countryside again. As much as she had enjoyed being with Marie and the Gabin family in France, she realized now how much Brunton Manor meant to her. Here she lived in harmony with her mother and father and Jeremy; she felt safe. She pulled her thoughts up short and slowed her horse. Why safe? What had caused her to consider feeling otherwise? It was as if she wanted to lock away this time in her life in her heart and never let it go.

Veronica shuddered. Maybe her life was *too* idyllic – did that mean tragedy loomed near? With such ideas came a sensation of girlhood finally cast aside, gone for ever. After one more term at school she would step into the adult world. Overcome by a sudden intense desire to see Michael, she put her horse to the gallop and urged it towards Rushbrook.

At the house she slowed to turn her mount towards the stable-block. When she did so, she saw Mrs Eakins come from the yard.

'Hello,' she called brightly when she saw Veronica. 'Have you had a nice time?'

'Oh, yes, splendid.'

'Mother and Father well?'

'In topping form.'

'When did you get back?'

'Just a short while ago.'

'And Marie? Did she return with you?'

'Yes,' replied Veronica. Seeing the query in Elspeth Eakins's expression, she added, 'She decided to remain at Brunton this afternoon and write home.'

Elspeth nodded and, noting that Veronica had been glancing around during their exchange added, 'Michael's down by the river, fishing.'

'Thanks, Mrs Eakins,' answered Veronica, and immediately turned her horse to gallop away in the direction of what she knew to be Michael's favourite stretch of water.

Elspeth gave a little smile of understanding as she watched the dust spurt under the horse's hooves. 'That girl's in love,' she commented to herself.

She strolled thoughtfully back to the house, pleased with the prospect of having Veronica as her daughter-in-law. But what of Michael? It was more difficult to tell. He was apt to keep emotion out of his liaisons with women, but lately his mother had wondered if self-imposed barriers were beginning to crumble.

Nearing the river, Veronica slowed her horse. She guided it through a stand of beech along a path that led to the river bank. When it came in sight she stopped. Michael, rod in hand, was in the gently flowing water. She watched for a few moments, drinking in the sight of him and realizing that her feelings for him were undeniable.

She slid from the saddle, secured her horse to a branch, and then stepped slowly into the open, to stand close to the waterside.

Michael, concentrating on his line, did not see her until he suddenly felt himself observed. He turned sharply, lost his footing, and with arms flailing, ended up sitting down in the water. He gasped and turned angrily on the intruder, but the reprimand froze on his lips when he saw a girl, her face aglow, laughing at him.

'Smudge!' His cry was a mixture of surprise, joy and criticism, but the latter was quickly dismissed in the knowledge that Veronica was here.

He pushed himself to his feet, grasping his rod as he did so, and splashed quickly over to the bank. As he stepped on to firmer ground he dropped his rod and, ignoring the water dripping from him, grasped her in his arms.

'Hey, you're wet!' she protested, but made no attempt to free herself.

'I know. You were the cause of it so you can be wet too.' He grinned, and held her closer. 'You're home and...' He left the words unspoken as he looked down into her upturned face and saw there something he had never seen before. His hopes were answered. The time had finally come. He bent his head to Veronica's and met her lips with his. After a moment he would have stepped back, but she clutched him to her and kissed him again.

Their lips parted and she said, 'Yes, I'm home.'

'So it seems,' he replied, in a tone that told her he was overjoyed to have her back where she belonged.

7

Late-morning the following day the Attwoods' butler brought the mail to Charles, who was busy in his study perusing the milk returns. He flicked through the envelopes and, seeing 'St Mary's Convent' printed in small letters in the top left-hand corner of one, he immediately left his desk and looked for his wife. He found her returning from the rose garden.

He held up the envelope and called, 'It's here, Catherine.'

'Good,' she answered, and quickened her step to join him.

Meticulous about opening envelopes, Charles took a penknife from his pocket and carefully slit the envelope. He handed it to her and she withdrew Sister Loyola's letter.

Dear Mr and Mrs Attwood,
I received your enquiry about finishing schools for Veronica and am pleased to know that she is to continue her education in this way. I believe it is the right step for her and that she will benefit greatly from the two years she will spend at whichever school you choose.

I am grateful that you sought my advice on a suitable place for her, though I am afraid I cannot give you any strong recommendation because I have a vested interest in one of the establishments I will mention and it would be unfair of me to direct my pupils to that particular school. However, what I will do is give you a list of four schools at which I believe Veronica would be happy and receive the necessary advancement to her education and broadening of her views before her entry into the wider world. The final choice from that list must be yours. I hope you understand and appreciate my position.

I look forward to meeting you when Veronica returns to school for her last term with us.
Yours sincerely,
Sister Loyola

'She encloses the names and a page of notes on each school,' Catherine concluded.

'Let us deal with this at once and send them off to Henri and Margaret today,' said Charles, leading the way to a seat beside the front door.

They read Sister Loyola's notes.

'The school that impresses me most is Mrs Latimer's Academy for Young Ladies in Kelso,' said Catherine.

'I agree,' replied Charles. 'The courses she offers

would suit Veronica admirably.'

'I particularly like Mrs Latimer's emphasis on self-reliance while encouraging the ability to make friends and mix socially,' commented Catherine.

'She also states that the study of a foreign language, particularly French, is of primary importance to the development of her young ladies,' Charles pointed out. 'That will suit Veronica, and be easy for Marie.'

'True. But first we must contact the Gabins. I'll compose a letter explaining the reasons for our choice,' Catherine said. 'We'll tell the girls...'

'Young ladies,' interrupted her husband with a smile.

Catherine sighed. 'Why do they have to grow up?'

'We've all had to do that,' he said sympathetically. 'We can still give them our love and be there if needed.'

Catherine nodded, squeezed his hand. 'You are so right and I love you for being you.' She leaned close and kissed him, then sprang to her feet and hurried to the front door, calling over her shoulder, 'We'll tell them over luncheon.'

'Right, then I'll drive you into Helmsley to post the letter.'

Satisfied that they had both selected the same place, Charles remained seated, contemplating where that choice might lead.

Over lunch Catherine explained to Veronica and Marie the decision they had made about the finishing school.

'I have written to your mother and father, Marie, telling them of our preference. I hope they will approve of our choice and follow suit.'

'I am sure they will, Mrs Attwood, and I personally thank you for the trouble you are taking on my behalf. I shall write to Mother and tell her I am in full agreement with your choice; it sounds just the place for us both.'

Approval from Marie's mother and father came the day the two girls were to return to school. Charles, accompanied by his wife, drove them in his Rolls-Royce. None of them interpreted the dark clouds that hung over York and its surrounding area as in any way ominous. They viewed this journey as marking the end of one era and the start of a new one, filled with hope for their future which they all saw as starting with the autumn move to Mrs Latimer's Academy for Young Ladies.

When Catherine and Charles told Sister Loyola of their choice, she expressed approval, saying that she was sure the two 'young ladies', as she now termed them, would do well under a staff she knew had a gift for preparing their wards for the adult world.

As they drove home Catherine revealed a thought that had come to her during their chat with Sister Loyola. 'Though she did not say so, I think we chose the finishing school she herself would have recommended.'

'You think so?'

'When we told her our choice, I caught a glimmer of relief in her eyes.'

'Then let us hope the girls do well and live up to Sister's expectations.'

Rumours and stories ran rife among the students at the convent, speculating about the reason Sister Loyola had called a special assembly in the main hall of all the students, teaching staff and other employees. No one could remember such a gathering ever taking place before or being called so quickly.

Questioning glances were exchanged between the girls when Sister Loyola, looking grave-faced, walked in. The rumble of conversation died to silence as she mounted the stage at one end of the hall. She drew herself up, hands clasped in front of her.

'I have called this assembly because of some serious news that was relayed to me just twenty minutes ago. Today, the fourth June, will always be linked with the suffragette movement of which you have all heard through your classwork on current affairs. Whether we agree that women should have the vote or not, whether we agree with militant protests or not, I am sure we will all be alarmed and saddened by the action of the suffragette Emily Davison who ran out in front of the King's horse during the Derby.' For a moment there was a stunned silence then a buzz of shocked remarks filled the hall.

Sister Loyola held up her hands and called for silence. When the assembly had settled again she continued, 'Miss Davison was badly injured and it is not known if she will live. I decided I would break this news to you personally to bring to your notice that, in my opinion, such reckless actions, while bringing the cause to the notice of the public, do nothing to advance it. There are many ways in which causes can be promoted but actions of an extreme nature do not help. May in fact do harm. I fear this poor woman's misguided action may soon be yesterday's news as the suffragette movement peacefully carries the day on votes for women.' She paused to allow her words to sink in then said, 'Now, let us bow our heads and pray for Miss Davison.'

The assembly broke up quietly, but a shadow hung over the convent while Miss Davison's life hung in the balance. Four days later prayers were said again to mark her death. The following month a peaceful gathering in Hyde Park, organised by the National Union of Women's Societies, brought together 50,000 women, an event which Sister Loyola also brought to the notice of the school in support of her belief in non-violent protest.

The same theme was echoed in Catherine's letters to various organisations and Members of Parliament, written and sent with more frequency since the Derby tragedy.

With their education at the convent nearing its end and a new world awaiting them outside, Veronica and Marie agreed that they should stop using their initials as their names. 'V and M are too girlish and must be confined to the past,' Veronica announced, an observation that was readily agreed with by Marie.

They finished their education at St Mary's Convent with good reports from their teachers, with special praise from the French teacher.

'It was only natural that Marie should shine at

this subject, but her influence on the rest of the class has brought an improvement all round. Due to her close friendship with Veronica Attwood, Veronica's fluency in the language is almost indistinguishable from that of a French native.'

That ability was to stand Veronica in good stead when she and Marie settled into Mrs Latimer's Academy for Young Ladies, where the mastery of another language was seen as essential for any young lady stepping out into the world.

But first there was the summer to enjoy.

Because Marie's father was in America on business and her mother had accompanied him, the first three weeks of her summer holiday were spent at Brunton Manor. It was an idyllic time, when all seemed well with the world. The girls rode and played tennis at Rushbrook; Michael and Jeremy played cricket for the local village team and were ably supported by Veronica and Marie who had to have the mysteries of the game explained to her. They picnicked by the river, strolled by the sea, visited Helmsley, Pickering, Whitby, Scarborough and York, danced to music from their new gramophone on the lawn at Brunton, and then performed more gracefully at a Hunt Ball. The girls never lacked for male company in any of these activities; Michael and Jeremy were ever ready to be their partners or escorts.

They gave little thought to the dark clouds gathering over Europe.

8

'Marie, I have accepted Mr and Mrs Attwood's choice of finishing school, given Sister Loyola's endorsement of the establishment,' said Henri, leaning forward over his desk in his book-lined study. 'See that you don't disappoint us. When you return to England next week, your mother will accompany you so that we will learn for ourselves what this school is like and be able to picture you there.'

'Won't you be coming, Papa?' asked Marie, sitting straight-backed on the chair opposite his.

'I had intended to accept the Attwoods' invitation to stay with them, but I have heard this morning that, because of our government's concern that the unrest in Europe could spread, I am required to meet political and military bodies to discuss the situation.'

Marie gave a grimace of disappointment but knew it was no good protesting. Her father's obsession with his business was coloured by his zeal to serve his country in what he saw as the fullest way possible.

'I have implicit faith in the way you will conduct yourself in your new environment, and in the relationships you will develop during your passage to adulthood. But I would like you to remember that you have grown up with Jacques, you know him well, and that his mother and father think highly of you.'

Marie bristled at the hint of interference behind her father's words. She stopped her lips from tightening and betraying her feelings. She'd thought her special friendship with Jeremy Attwood had not been obvious, but she had overlooked the fact that parents know their children better than the younger generation realises. It also irked her that she was sure her father was hinting at a future marriage, which he would view as enhancing his business. After all, Jacques would inherit a thriving company and there was the prospect of a profitable amalgamation for them both. Her desire to be in control of her own future was strong, but to rebel openly at this juncture would be unwise. Her father would not hesitate to cancel her place at the school and to end any further connection with the Attwood family. Better she should keep quiet for now.

On the day of her departure for England her father wished her well. 'These are two important years for you, Marie, use them well. Be careful in the friends you make, and remember what I said to you the other day.'

'Yes, Father. I hope I will be a credit to you.'

'I am sure you will.' He kissed her on both cheeks, helped her and her mother into the car and said to Alain, 'Drive carefully, you carry a precious load.'

'Yes, sir.'

Henri, wondering what the future held for them all, watched the car until it was out of sight.

Veronica and her mother were on the quay at

Dover to meet Marie and her mother. The reunion of the two young ladies was fun, while their parents slotted comfortably into their own relationship.

As they settled in the car, driven by Josh, Catherine enquired after Henri.

'He's well,' replied Margaret. 'He was sorry that business forced him to change his plans, but he sends his respects and good wishes.'

With one overnight stop, their journey to Brunton Manor was pleasant in spite of ten miles of torrential rain brought by a storm sweeping east across the country.

When the car approached the house, Marie's heart beat a little faster at the thought of seeing Jeremy again and she wondered if his last words to her still held true? Her father's hints about the future intruded on her mind but she pushed them away when Jeremy and his father came out to meet them. Jeremy took both her hands, gave her a kiss on the cheek and said quietly, 'I'm pleased to see you back at Brunton.'

Marie blushed in reply. 'It's nice to be back and to see you again.'

Though there was little chance of their being alone together during the four days before Veronica and Marie left for Kelso, when they did manage it, the subject of their developing relationship was not discussed between Marie and Jeremy. It was as if both of them sensed there might be obstacles ahead and neither wanted to acknowledge them; let what would be come about. They would deal with it. So it was that with words unsaid they parted. In the future they would speak them.

Veronica and Michael had no need to discuss the coming years when they said goodbye; an understanding was already there between them. They expected their future to lie together in the Yorkshire countryside they both loved.

Charles drove them north to stay in the best hotel in Kelso. At mid-morning the following day, after obtaining directions to Mrs Latimer's Academy for Young Ladies, he drove along a road on the south bank of the Tweed, which every so often gave them tantalising views of the placid river winding through the farmland and parkland that enhanced the two attractive Georgian houses that they passed. Finding a noticeboard, beside open wrought-iron gates, declaring this to be Mrs Latimer's Academy for Young Ladies, Charles turned off the road.

Well-established oaks and horse chestnuts dotted the manicured grassland leading to the granite building. Its square and solid appearance was relieved by carved window frames and a more extensive use of glass than was usual in buildings of this era. Charles judged by these and other architectural alterations that a previous occupant had wanted to live in the light rather than perpetual gloom.

'If the alterations inside match those on the outside,' he observed, 'I think this house will have much to offer the young ladies destined to live here.'

'I think you are right,' agreed Margaret as she stepped out of the car, 'I can already feel its friendly atmosphere.'

'So can I,' concurred Catherine, 'and we haven't been inside yet. What do you two think?' she asked, looking at Veronica and Marie who were eyeing the building and its immediate vicinity.

'I think I'm going to like it here,' said Veronica.

'So do I,' agreed Marie. 'This is a lovely valley, so gentle, tranquil and peaceful. I hope Mrs Latimer isn't an old battleaxe!'

As if on cue the front door opened, but instead of the person Marie had visualised there emerged a young woman who was probably no more than thirty-five. She was slim, and immaculately dressed in a black skirt and white blouse with puff sleeves that were fastened tight at the wrists. Holding herself straight, she exuded natural authority but without any hint of severity; in its place were gentleness and serenity and a love of life.

In the few minutes while greetings were exchanged Veronica felt that Mrs Latimer had assessed both her and Marie and their parents as well.

'Mr and Mrs Attwood and Madame Gabin, welcome to Teviot Manor, my Academy for Young Ladies. I hope your daughters will be happy here and gain much to prepare them for their entry into the wider world. And I hope, when I show you round and you see the facilities I have developed, you will be pleased you chose my school. Now, enough of our chatting. Come in and partake of a cup of tea and some scones.' She led the way into the house, leaving two handymen to deal with the luggage.

Their entry into the house elicited an immediate remark from Margaret: 'What a wonderfully spacious hall. Not big or overwhelming but so comfortable. I suspect that is the style throughout the house.'

Mrs Latimer smiled her appreciation of the comment as she said, 'Thank you, Madame Gabin. That is the effect I tried to achieve when my husband and I took over the property.'

They had reached an elegant yet comfortable drawing room. A neatly dressed maid was standing beside a table set against one wall. Cups, saucers and plates were already laid out beside plates of scones and sponge cakes. She left them to go and fetch the tea.

A smiling Mrs Latimer, continued the conversation effortlessly. 'I noted you showed surprise when you met me. No doubt you expected to see an older woman. Someone in charge of an Academy for Young Ladies conjures up that impression certainly. I can promise you, age makes no difference to the running and organising of my academy. In fact, I have found that being closer to the age of my young ladies brings me nearer to their way of thinking than is the case in most other such establishments.'

'Your staff ... are they of much the same age?' queried Catherine.

'Yes, except for two of them. There are ten members of staff in all, able to communicate easily with my young ladies thanks to their skill and experience.'

'And does your husband play a part in the establishment?' asked Charles, taking another scone offered to him by Mrs Latimer.

'No, he plays no part in it, he looks after the

estate only, but I must say that if it were not for his efficiency in doing so, the academy might not exist. We bought this property for its potential as a farm. It was rundown but my husband was sure he could revive it and maintain an ongoing profit. The house was in a parlous state and the original intention was to revitalise it as a home. Then I saw the possibility of turning it into a small academy for young ladies. I felt I had something to pass on that might be of value to inexperienced females. I am pleased to say that within four years of establishing it I could say it was a success, but I could never have managed it without my husband's support, the backing of his working farm and his constant attention to the needs of the estate.'

Their hostess noted that everyone had finished their refreshments. She looked at Veronica and Marie. 'Have the young ladies any questions?' she asked, but almost immediately added with an understanding smile, 'Ah, no, they'll probably come pouring out once your parents have left. First let me show you round the house.' She rose from her chair and led the way out of the room.

Everyone was impressed by what they saw. The rooms were tastefully decorated and appointed, but Mrs Latimer explained, 'I like my flock, as I sometimes call them, to put something of their own individual stamp on their rooms, without going to excess. And, of course, there has to be compatibility of taste when two girls share a room. When designing the academy, I did think of individual rooms but that would have meant a considerable isolation for the young ladies and less time for them to share their daily experiences and exchange ideas, which I believe are essential for their personal and social development.'

When they returned to the drawing room Mrs Latimer said, 'As you know, I asked you to come today before the rest of the young ladies return tomorrow so that we would suffer no interruption. I presume you are staying in Kelso?'

'Yes,' confirmed Catherine.

'For two more nights,' added Charles.

'And you?' queried Mrs Latimer, looking at Margaret.

'Oh, I'm in the capable hands of my friends.'

'Then your daughters have a choice: they can stay here now or leave with you and return tomorrow.'

'It's their choice,' said Catherine, and was pleased to receive a nod of agreement from Margaret and Charles.

Mrs Latimer made no comment but thought it quite right that the young ladies were allowed to choose for themselves.

'Well, what is it to be?' Charles asked.

Veronica and Marie exchanged a glance, each knowing the other's thoughts. 'We'll stay here tonight, if that is all right?'

'Of course it is,' replied Mrs Latimer. 'It will give me a chance to get to know you better. Well, in that case,' she addressed the three adults, 'why don't you come to lunch tomorrow? My other young ladies won't be returning until the afternoon.' She sensed hesitation in them so said, 'I won't take no for an answer. Unless you have something else planned?'

'Not at all,' replied Catherine.

'Then lunch it is. Shall we say twelve o'clock?'

When Mrs Latimer took them to see their room, Veronica and Marie both expressed delight.

Mrs Latimer made no comment but, satisfied by their reaction, said, 'I will leave you to settle in then. You'll find your luggage in there.' She indicated a door to the right. 'Please explore the house. A light lunch will be set for you in the dining room and you'll dine with me this evening at six-thirty. If our paths don't cross before, I'll see you then.'

'Thank you, Mrs Latimer,' they both chorused.

When the door closed behind her, they turned to each other and whooped. Grinning, they flung their arms round each other.

'This is wonderful!' said Marie.

'Couldn't be better,' agreed Veronica. 'Try the beds!'

They each flung themselves on to a bed and bounced. 'Territory claimed,' laughed Marie.

'And so soft. I'll never wake up in the morning!'

'Nor will I.'

'How lucky are we?'

They both raised their heads and looked about them. Besides the two beds and bedside tables, the room contained a large wardrobe and a window-seat, to the left of which stood a dressing table.

'Did you see that view when we came in?' asked Marie, delight permeating her voice.

'Only glimpsed it,' replied Veronica. She swung herself off the bed and strode to the window.

Marie was quickly beside her.

'Oh, my, just look at that!' Veronica exclaimed, eyes enthusiastically taking in the scene before them. A long lawn stretched down to the river which at this point made a big loop around the property creating the impression that on this side the buildings were protected by a moat. Beyond the water, they could see equally well-tended grounds, leading to an impressive Georgian house.

'This is a beautiful part of the country,' commented Veronica.

'I like it,' agreed Marie. 'I'm so glad our parents picked this place.'

They sorted out their luggage, each girl claiming wardrobe and drawer space, and arranged toiletries in the bathroom.

'I expect each double room has its own,' commented Marie. 'I think Mrs Latimer is a forward-looking person who embraces new ideas.'

'And I think you are right.' Veronica gave a little chuckle as she added, 'I wonder what the girls at the convent would say to all this luxury?'

'They'd be dumbfounded. Come on, let's find that light lunch and then explore.'

The next day their parents arrived in time to spend an hour with their daughters before lunch. All three of them were pleased by the enthusiasm with which Marie and Veronica described life at the academy. They had no doubt that the girls would settle here and enjoy the two years ahead. They were also pleased with Mrs Latimer's hospitality and views, which seemed exactly suited to the life they wanted for their daughters. They left the school, feeling they had chosen wisely.

Veronica and Marie settled quickly into the community of twenty-five pupils plus the staff. They were encouraged to develop consideration for others, no matter what their social standing; taught the etiquette appropriate to the world in which they were likely to live after leaving the academy; encouraged to devote time to interests that attracted them personally, and above all, while they were not directed specifically to a particular faith, encouraged towards a Christian outlook, with tolerance for and understanding of other faiths and respect the beliefs of others.

9

'Marie ... Marie, wake up, wake up!' Veronica shook her friend's shoulder, which was still buried beneath the blankets.

Marie gave a sleepy moan.

'What?'

'There's snow!'

'Ugh!'

'Lazybones! Come and see.'

Marie knew there would be no peace until she did. Besides, sleep had now deserted her. She turned back the bedclothes, shivering when cold air greeted her. She swung out of bed, grateful that Veronica was holding her dressing-gown ready for her. Marie pulled it round her and tied the cord.

'Look, it's beautiful,' enthused Veronica, heading for the window.

Wide awake now, Marie slipped her feet into her slippers and, glancing at the clock on the table beside her bed, saw it was six o'clock. She heaved an inaudible sigh; there'd be no more sleep for her, she was wide awake now. She joined her friend at the window.

'Isn't it beautiful?' said Veronica in a whisper, as if anything louder would tarnish the beauty of the scene.

Marie did not answer but Veronica instinctively knew her friend felt the same way as she did. They stood silently together, fearing to break the magical spell of the gently falling snow laying another carpet of white over that already stretching towards and beyond the frozen river.

After five minutes, Veronica broke the silence. 'Let's go out.'

Marie had just been thinking she would like to feel the snow and breathe the pure frosty air. She nodded and started to dress.

They shrugged themselves into warm outdoor coats and donned fur-lined boots. They pulled on caps and gloves and went downstairs quietly. In the hall, Marie turned the big iron key to the front door. Veronica lifted the latch and blessed the fact that it was kept well oiled. A blast of cold air met them but, ignoring it, they stepped outside and eased the door to.

They stood for a few moments, absorbing the wintery beauty which was further enhanced when the clouds thinned a little, allowing the pale light from the waning moon to silver the enchanting scene.

'It's beautiful,' whispered Marie. 'I will always carry this picture in my heart.'

Veronica nodded but did not speak. She felt there was something special in this scene, born from this particular moment, filled with a sense of peace that would come to mean so much to them in the future.

Though snow lay on the ground and still decorated the trees, it was not sufficient to prevent them from leaving for the Christmas holiday at home, nor to hinder their return during the third week of January in the New Year of 1914.

The day was cold, turning warm breath into thin clouds, when the young ladies were deposited by parents and friends or returned after being met in Kelso by the academy vehicle. There was a spirit of camaraderie amidst the laughter as greetings were exchanged and questions exchanged about each other's holiday.

Marie and Veronica had spent the preceding two days together. Veronica and her father had met Marie from the train at York station. Jeremy had sought an excuse to accompany them but was disappointed by Marie's reticence on meeting him. He took heart as her coolness gradually thawed by evening, though he sensed something was worrying her. He held back from questioning her for fear of causing a permanent rift with this young woman who was beginning to have such a hold on his emotions, causing him to wish fervently that she lived nearer or that their meetings were more regular. Maybe that could be put right in time...

Marie had sensed Jeremy's feelings about her but she dared not reciprocate as she would have liked to do. Her father's words of warning still hung over her like a cloud. Besides Jacques had the pre-eminent place in her heart, she told herself. Their close relationship, which had begun in early childhood and matured over the years, could not be wiped out at a single stroke.

These thoughts slipped to the back of her mind in the maelstrom caused by all the young women returning to Mrs Latimer's Academy for Young Ladies after their Christmas break. Marie lost sight of Veronica so started for their room, expecting to find her there, but it was deserted. She had begun to unpack her own suitcase when the door burst open and Veronica flew in.

'Oh, there you are. Have you heard?' she asked, gasping to get her words out.

'Heard what?' queried Marie, mystified.

'There's a rumour that Janina and Dagmar are not coming back!'

'Why?' asked Marie, surprised by this unexpected news. 'They're in their last term.'

'Lizzie Caldwell said it came from a friend of her mother's.'

'Oh, you know Dizzy Lizzie ... just the one to get things wrong. Janina and Dagmar always arrive after everyone else.'

But when the staff and girls assembled in the refectory for the evening meal and Mrs Latimer announced that she wanted to see everyone in the assembly room twenty minutes after it had finished, there was a low murmur of speculation that Lizzie might be right. With her instruction given, Mrs Latimer said grace. Immediately that ended, the noise of chatter and clatter of crockery filled the room, until it was silenced by the grace of thanksgiving.

Twenty minutes later every young lady, seated comfortably in easy chairs or relaxing on settees in the assembly room, was speculating if Mrs Latimer's usual welcome back for another term might contain something different this time.

They rose when she entered the room but with a quick gesture of her hand she settled them again.

'I have a little more to say than my usual welcome back and hope that you will all have an enjoyable and successful term.' Speculation about what might be coming next ran through every mind then. 'You will no doubt have noticed that Janina and Dagmar, our two Germans, were not with us this evening. I know they are generally later than the rest of you, but I have to tell you now that they are not coming back.' A buzz ran round the room then died down as everyone hung on what might be coming next. 'It is no fault of their own that they are not rejoining us, but the wish of their parents. In their letters to me both families say that it is because of the worsening political situation.' Once again a buzz of speculation filled the air.

Mrs Latimer raised her hand to silence it and continued. 'As you know, twice a week I encourage discussion of the present-day political scene. Why am I reminding you of all this? Because the absence of Janina and Dagmar indicates to me that their parents believe war is coming, and they want their daughters safely at home with them.'

Once again words flowed as the young ladies speculated about this, until Mrs Latimer silenced them. 'Of course, I hope they are wrong. When I received their letters four days ago, I gave thought to my academy – how would it be influenced by war? After discussion with my staff, I concluded that it should remain open and continue as near normal as possible. So that is what I intend to do.' There was an audible sigh of relief in the room. 'I have told you all this because I know my young ladies are intelligent enough to have reached their own conclusions after the things they will have heard during the recent break. Should any other circumstance develop that requires me to write to your parents, I will do so. If your parents, in their letters to you, query the position here, you know how to explain it and reassure them.' She paused momentarily then added, 'That will be all.'

The head student sprang to her feet. 'Mrs Latimer,' she called, quieting the hum of conversation that had started up again, 'I believe I am speaking on behalf of all your students when I say thank you for being so forthright with us. It was natural that we should wonder how the academy would be affected. Thank you for reassuring us.'

'Thank you, Isobel,' the headmistress said with a smile. 'Let us all carry on as if everything is normal, at least until we know to the contrary.' She walked from the room.

As they got to their feet Veronica grabbed Marie's arm and said, 'Our room! Now!'

Marie nodded. 'I was just going to say the same thing.'

'I wanted us to be on our own,' said Veronica, closing the door to their room. 'First,' she went on quickly, 'what will your parents think about the situation? Your father must have formed an opinion because of his line of business.'

'He'd never discuss the possibility of war with me. He might tell me what I should do if it affects me.'

'Do you think they'll want you home now?'

'I hope not. I want to finish my full time here.'

'I hope you can too. It would be awful without you.'

'There's nothing we can do, though. No point in bringing it to their notice – it may never happen,' concluded Marie, and then added in a hesitant tone, 'Do you think Jeremy would go?'

'You mean, volunteer if there's a war?'

'Yes.'

'I have no idea, I've never thought about it. I suppose it's a possibility. I mean, Mother and Father wouldn't want him to go, but I don't think they'd object if he was determined. What about Jacques? Would he be exempt because of his work?'

'Like you, I don't know. We'll just have to wait and see.' Marie made her tone light to give the impression there was nothing more she could add. She did not want to be drawn into a discussion about the two young men who were causing such confusion in her mind; a conflict that was further heightened by her father's express wishes.

'A letter from Marie,' said Henri, when he'd

sorted the mail that had been brought to the breakfast table. He slit the envelope with the letter-opener, which was always placed with the new mail, and passed it to his wife. She slipped the sheet of paper out and read aloud to him while he glanced at his other mail.

Dear Mama and Papa,
I hope you are both well. Life here is good. I am well, and my academy work has earned me some praise.
The main purpose of this letter, now that we are halfway through the term, is to tell you that Veronica has invited me to spend some time with her, and accompany her and her mother to a cottage that Mr Attwood has recently purchased for family use on the coast near Whitby. I do hope you will say yes. I would propose that I spend the first half of the holiday with you and the second half with them.
I look forward to receiving your answer.
A special kiss to you both,
Your loving daughter

Margaret, wondering what was going round in his mind, watched her husband until she could no longer bear the thoughtful silence even though only a few seconds had passed. 'What do you think?' she asked.

'The maids will be coming to clear the table soon. Let us go to the small drawing room. We won't be disturbed there.'

He led her to the room and, when he had closed the door, answered her question with one of his own. 'Do you think this is a ploy so that Marie can spend more time with Jeremy Attwood?'

115

Margaret was taken aback. 'You told me that you had spoken to her before she returned to England. You said she understood the position and made no protest against it. Surely you trust her, Henri?'

'Of course I do, it's just...'

'You have doubts?' His wife's question came out as an accusation.

He hesitated, and then stepped over to her. His hands gripped her waist in a gesture from which she derived reassurance as he said, 'Marie has grown into a lovely young woman. I merely want her to do the right thing.'

Margaret met his eyes, saw his concern for her and for Marie. She said gently but firmly, 'She will. She will.'

'Sit with me. I need to talk to you.'

She looked at him, trying to fathom from his expression what lay behind this request. When they were seated and half turned to each other, he took her hands in his and held her gaze.

'You know the situation in Europe is not good. I fear it may grow worse. Germany seems bent on showing her teeth. The Kaiser and Bismarck seek more and more to show they are the masters of Europe.'

'You think there will be war?' Alarm made her voice falter.

'I hope not, but we have to be prepared for the worst.' Henri hesitated slightly and then went on, 'If war breaks out I fear that the German Army will invade France, trying to sweep her out of their way, recalling their victories in the nineteenth century. I would like you and Marie to be safe; to go over to England and seek shelter with the Attwoods. I will write to them and request their help. I'm sure they will oblige. It would be for the best. I couldn't bear to think of you in danger from the invading army. I...'

'Stop it, Henri, please stop.' The distress in Margaret's voice was matched by the look in her eyes. 'I will not leave you; it is a wife's duty to be beside her husband, in bad times as well as good.'

'But I don't want you to be...'

'NO! Henri, I will NOT leave you. I will be at your side whatever happens.'

He saw the look in her eyes and knew that attempting to persuade her further would be useless. He kissed her gently on the cheek. 'You are an angel ... my guardian angel.'

Margaret placed her hand gently on his cheek and held it there while her expression showed him that she felt no need of further words.

He raised his hand and closed it on hers. 'I love you,' he whispered, and took her in his arms, holding her tight as if to offer protection from any disaster that might come their way.

Finally, when she straightened up from his embrace, she said, 'Maybe we should ask the Attwoods if they will take just Marie if war breaks out. I think they would, and it would be good for her to be with Veronica.' She saw a flash of doubt in his eyes and knew immediately her husband was thinking of Jeremy. Margaret said quietly, 'Trust her, Henri,' and pressed his hand, encouraging him to do so.

He nodded, and then straightened up. 'I will and make the request now. You write to Marie.

Give her permission to stay with the Attwoods at Easter, and tell her what is in our minds; I think it best she be prepared for the worst.'

'Letters!' Both girls took them eagerly from the table in the hall of Teviot Manor, where they were laid out ready for collection when the students left the refectory after luncheon. They raced up the stairs to their room, eager to read them before the afternoon's activities. They threw themselves on their beds and slit the envelopes open. Quietly they devoured the words.

Veronica broke the silence. 'Mama says she has heard from your mother and that you may come to us during the Easter holidays!'

While still reading Marie said, 'Yes, my mama mentions it too, but there is more.' She started to read:

…so after careful consideration, your father is writing to Mr and Mrs Attwood to ask if you could go to them if the situation in Europe deteriorates. We hope it doesn't and that our rulers, whatever their persuasion, will see sense. However, we thought it wise to take this precautionary step now.

I've heard from Mrs Attwood about Easter and she is looking forward to having you.

Love,
Mama

They looked at each other in silence for a few moments. Marie's thoughts were confused. This was most unexpected. Considering his parting words to her, she could not see her father agreeing easily to what might be a long stay with the Attwoods. She knew her mother's persuasive powers, but Papa could be obstinate and commanding too. Maybe they were more aware of the seriousness of the situation in Europe than the staff and young ladies of Teviot Manor, beside the quiet waters of the Tweed. She wondered what was ahead of her and where her destiny lay.

'The Balkan States are in upheaval; there's no telling what might happen. I know there are members of our government who view the situation with heavy hearts and are very pessimistic about the situation being permanently resolved without military action. It only needs one spark to send Europe up in flames ... Marie, you are going to the Attwoods in two days. Your mother and I think you should pack more things, in case your stay has to be longer.'

'That means you will have more luggage than can be managed the usual way, so your father and I will take you by car,' said her mother.

So it was that on a blustery April day, Henri, Margaret and Marie watched their car hoisted on to the deck of the ship that would transport them to Dover. The crossing was somewhat rough but they survived it without being seasick and chose to motor thirty miles inland before seeking accommodation for the night.

The following day they were given a warm welcome on the threshold by Charles and Catherine, and by Jeremy too when he came in from the tree-felling he had been supervising. When he greeted Marie she was aware that the welcome in his eyes was only for her. Delight ran through her but she was very aware of her watchful father and tempered her greeting in reply.

'Marie, you'll have the room that you had when you stayed with us before. Make it your own for as long as you need it,' said Catherine.

'Thank you, Mrs Attwood. I hope I won't be any trouble,' replied Marie.

'Of course you won't. Think of this as your home.'

'It is most kind of you,' put in Margaret.

'Please, do not think of it. We are only too pleased you suggested this,' said Catherine.

'Do you think war is likely?' asked Charles, directing his question at Henri.

He shrugged his shoulders and said, 'Who knows? The situation is very volatile.'

'We are in the hands of the politicians,' sighed Charles.

'What do you think will happen to the suffragette cause if war breaks out?' Margaret asked. 'I've heard it is very strong in England at the moment.'

'It is,' replied Catherine. 'Demonstrations in London and some of the other big cities. Window breaking, clashes with the police, women arrested and subjected to foul conditions in jail, hunger strikes that have resulted in horrible force-feeding. I don't agree with the violent side of the protest, though I sympathise with the movement's aims. The government will have to take notice of us one day, so why not now? We in the countryside continually make our views known, but without big rallies and violence. I believe Mrs Pankhurst will call a halt for the duration if hostilities are declared. Sensible, because I believe women can contribute to the war effort if needed, and that could help win the day for universal suffrage in due course. It's a chance to be seized. We must prove that we deserve equality with men.'

Beneath the frantic diplomatic activity to hold the fragile peace together lay an underlying sense of futility. To those in the know it seemed that war was inevitable. Germany's ambitions for European expansion caused widespread concern and, with the German leaders covetously eyeing parts of the British Empire, there was a move towards retaliation, not just in the realms of the powerful but throughout the whole country. People went about their normal lives hoping they would not be interrupted, but prepared to accept war should it come.

Mrs Latimer thought it wise to keep her young ladies informed, to the best of her knowledge, without being unduly alarmist.

The men at Brunton Manor and Rushbrook Hall, knowing food production would be important if war should come, made preparations to increase the output from the estates. Though they didn't voice it to their wives and mothers, they discussed among themselves the possibility of serving their country in a military way. Such was the candour between fathers and sons that Charles and Clive knew Jeremy and Michael would not hesitate to volunteer. Both men knew they would not be able to dissuade their sons despite the dangers, and quietly admired them for their attitude. Knowing this, and that they could lose younger employees, Charles and Clive quietly recruited older men as replacements.

As goodbyes were said at the end of the Easter holiday, Jeremy wished he had had the opportunity to be more open about his feelings for Marie, but the opportunity had never arisen in the short time before she and Veronica returned to Teviot Manor. Watching his mother manoeuvre the car for her first long journey since learning to drive, he wondered if Marie, for some reason, had deliberately sought to avoid being alone with him. He consoled himself for the lost chances with the thought that she would be living as part of the family at the start of the summer holiday.

When those started there was a general feeling throughout the country that the conflagration which would set Europe on fire was fast closing in on them. Each day families nervously awaited news while trying to go about their lives as if everything were normal, while knowing it wasn't. They sensed normality slipping away from them.

The young ladies of Mrs Latimer's Academy realised that the slip was becoming an unstoppable slide when, on 28 June, their headmistress called a special assembly and announced that Archduke Franz Ferdinand and his wife had been assassinated in Sarajevo by a Serbian student.

Speculation about the repercussions was still rife when the academy broke-up for the summer.

'Whatever happens before you return, I and my staff hope to see all of you who are due to resume your studies in September. Six new young ladies should be joining us then. To those of you who are leaving us, I hope you will always remember us and look back at your time at Teviot Manor with affection and pleasure. You will be taking your places in a world that is changing rapidly. I wish you well; be a credit to yourselves and your families, and always do what is right. May God walk with every one of you.'

Goodbyes were made, hugs given, promises to write exchanged, and tears shed.

Catherine, who had stayed in Kelso the night, arrived at ten o'clock to drive the girls to Brunton.

Once they had set off, she gave them the news from home, saying that things were little altered by the expectation of war except that the men on the estate were anxiously waiting and there was much speculation as to whether they should volunteer now, as appeared to be the case in London and other cities.

'Have Papa and Jeremy decided what...'

'No,' cut in Catherine, not wanting to contemplate the worst, 'nor have Mr Eakins and Michael. They are waiting to see what happens, though I must say that your father and Mr Eakins have started hiring older men to work on the land. Marie, I have heard from your mother; she tells me that she and your father are well. They believe if war comes it will be a short one. The Germans will soon see sense, hopefully before a shot is fired, when they realise they will have war on two fronts – with Britain and France on the west and Russia on the east. Now, let us enjoy the ride home. We'll have lunch in Alnwick.'

Once they reached Brunton Manor they settled in before dinner. As much as Veronica wanted to see Michael, she knew that would have to wait until morning. Marie, sensing Jeremy's deepening feelings for her, knew she would have to do something about this ... but that meant making a decision and she did not truly know what she wanted. Jeremy was prepared to wait but he did raise the question of the future with his sister.

'Veronica, do you think Marie has any feelings for me? Do you think...'

'Hold on, brother. I don't want to get involved in your affairs of the heart. Ask her yourself.'

'But what do you think of my chances?'

'Ask her,' Veronica replied with a finality that prevented him from raising the matter with her again.

Several times he was on the point of doing so, but something always prevented him. He did not realize that this resulted from Marie's wishing to avoid making a decision. Then events in Europe escalated.

Marie received a letter from her father, in which he said:

...and I fear that the situation is coming to a head and war is inevitable. I personally believe it may be prolonged and not as soon over as many people believe. I hope I am wrong. I am pleased you are in safe hands with Mr and Mrs Attwood. May I remind you of what I said about Jacques?
Take care.
We miss you,
Love,
Papa

This reminder made Marie wonder about Jacques. He had not been a regular correspondent since she came to England, but he was open about his respect and admiration for her. He admitted that he knew of her father's expectations, and that his own father felt the same. She knew that by marrying him she would want for nothing, she would have his devotion, but wondered if this went as far as love and if she should accept marriage on such terms? If she didn't, her life, and those of others, could be blighted. Was she prepared to be the cause of that? Weren't daughters expected to follow the lives mapped out for them by their parents? If they were, she could not deny that this could be a good marriage for her.

And then, on 4 August 1914, Britain declared war on Germany after their troops moved into Belgium following a declaration of war on France the previous day.

10

Catherine, sitting at her dressing table, heard the bedroom door open. Without turning round she knew it was her husband. Nevertheless she glanced in the mirror. A chill swept over her; she felt as if all the life was being drained out of her.

She knew the uncertainty that had hung over them for so long was over.

'It's happened, my love,' Charles said gently as he came to her.

'War?' The question came out automatically even though she knew the answer from the gravity of his expression.

'I'm afraid so.' He pressed his hands down upon her shoulders and kissed her neck.

She placed one hand on his. 'Oh, Charles, what will happen?' Tears sprang to her eyes as she thought of the upheaval that was about to erupt. Their lives might never be the same again. She turned to him for comfort. As he sank down beside her on the stool, he took her in his arms and said, 'You must be brave, Catherine.'

'I know,' she whispered.

'As I know you can be,' he continued. 'You have always been a pillar of strength to this family and I know you will remain so now and in the future, no matter how this war affects us.'

'Will you have to go, Charles?'

'We'll have to wait and see; they'll call on the younger men first.'

'Jeremy?' A lump came into her throat.

'Probably.'

'Oh, no.'

'Be strong for him.'

There was a sharp knock on the door.

'Come,' called Charles, guessing who it would be.

Jeremy poked his head round the door. Excitement filled his voice, 'I'm off to see Michael.'

'Jeremy, wait. I...'

Charles pressed his wife's hand tightly. 'He's twenty; he has to make his own decisions. Let him go,' he said, quietly but firmly, letting her know that it was the best thing to do. 'Give him

126

your blessing and he'll love you all the more.'

'I'm going too,' Veronica called from behind her brother.

'To see Michael?'

'Yes,' she shouted, and was gone.

'You have a lovesick eighteen-year-old daughter, Mrs Attwood.' There was a catch in Charles's voice. 'Our children are rushing to confront the world. Pray that it is kind to them.'

Jeremy's horse was ready first. He did not wait for his sister who was cajoling the stable-boy to hurry. Once she was in the saddle she sent the horse after her brother but he was not easing his speed one bit. With Rushbrook in sight, Jeremy saw a rider emerge from the stable-yard and turn his mount away from the buildings. Michael! He raised one hand and received a wave in reply. Earth beat beneath the pounding hoofs of the horses racing towards each other. Their riders brought them to a swirling halt.

'It's happened!' shouted Michael, barely keeping his mount under control.

'It has,' agreed Jeremy. 'Are we away to war?'

'Yes, as planned.' Michael grinned.

'Too right,' laughed Jeremy.

Veronica caught the last few words as she brought her panting horse to a halt beside them.

'You're not going?' she asked, her face wreathed in love and fear.

'Got to, Smudge. They'll need us to finish it!' laughed Michael.

'The sooner we go, the sooner it will be over.' Jeremy grinned.

Veronica scowled. 'Don't joke about it. Men will be killed.'

Jeremy ignored his sister. 'When are we going to volunteer?' he said.

'Tomorrow,' was Michael's instant reply.

'No!' screamed Veronica. 'You can't!' Her faced paled as desperation came into her voice. 'Do your parents know?'

'I'm off back to see ours now,' said Jeremy.

'You can't! You'll break their hearts!'

He ignored the plea behind her words and started to turn his horse, catching Michael's eye as he did so. 'I'll leave my sister to you.'

Jeremy knew how Veronica and Michael felt about each other, that in the future they expected to marry. Now it would have to wait until after the war.

As her brother rode away, Veronica turned to Michael. 'You can't be serious? Tell me you're not going away?' Even as she put the question she knew it was futile.

Michael did not answer but instead slipped from the saddle and took the few strides that brought him beside her. He reached up to her. She could not mistake the love in his eyes; she had seen it there before, but it had never held the intensity it did now. Her tremulous smile tried to dispel the tears in her eyes. She slid from the saddle and felt his strong hands slide around her waist. He lowered her gently to the ground and held her close, looking into her eyes. 'Smudge, I've got to volunteer. Thousands already have in expectation of what would happen. Now that it has, thousands more will do so. I've got to do my bit, for my country and for you.'

'But there's no need. I don't...' she started.

He placed a finger on her lips, silencing her.

'I've got to,' he said firmly. 'I could not live with myself if I didn't. Besides, I could not bear all the indignation if I did not. Fingers would be pointed, insults thrown. You wouldn't like me to receive a white feather, would you?'

She bit her lip and said nothing; she knew he was right.

'You've got to let me go. Please do that, with your blessing.'

She could not deny the pleading in his eyes, could not deny the request of a man bound for war. She nodded reluctantly, but her eyes told him she understood.

He kissed her lightly on her lips, sending a tremor through her. 'I love you, Smudge. I think I have since childhood, but I know I do now.'

She smiled through her tears. 'It's been the same for me ... and still is.' She struggled to laugh. 'You promised there'd be no more Smudge. We left that behind.'

He nodded. 'So we did. Goodbye, Smudge.' He gave a regretful smile, then kissed her with unexpected passion

She took his hand. 'Let's walk a little.' After a few yards she asked, 'What are we going to do, Michael?'

'I've got to go to war. You have another year at the academy; you must finish that. We can think no further ahead, but I will make you one pledge. When this is all over I'll marry you, if you'll have me?'

'Have you? That would make all my childhood dreams come true.'

Their lips sealed the promise.

'Let us keep this to ourselves, at least until I've finished at the academy,' she suggested.

'As you wish,' he agreed.

'You and Jeremy planned on volunteering as soon as war broke out?'

'We did when we saw it coming, but unlike many decided to wait until the actual declaration.'

'So tomorrow will be the day when my dearest goes to war, with all my love and blessing. May God keep you safe.'

Jeremy rode slowly back towards the house. Regret stabbed him and he cursed the war that would take him away from the home and the land he loved. A figure in the landscape caught his eye, interrupting his thoughts. Marie! She was coming in his direction, causing his mind to switch tack and dwell on her instead. A few moments later he saw her wave and quicken her pace. In response he put his horse into a trot.

'Hello, Marie,' he called as he slowed the animal to a halt. He dropped from the saddle. 'Sorry we rushed off.'

'I suppose you had things to do and Michael to see.'

'You suppose right. With the news of war, I had to see him. I think Veronica guessed what we were up to and felt she had to see him too.'

'You are both going to volunteer?'

'Yes.' He paused for a moment then asked, 'May I walk with you?'

'Of course. It would please me.'

Leading his horse he fell into step beside her, matching her pace. Silence stretched between them until she asked, 'Do your mother and father know?'

'Not yet. I'll tell them when we get back.'

'What would you do if they said no ... if they refused to give their consent?' asked Marie, relating his position to her own with her father's expectations for her and Jacques.

Jeremy's hesitation was only momentary. 'I would still go.'

'You'd defy their wishes ... their plans for your future?'

'Yes. I hope it won't come to that, though. I don't think it will. My parents are tolerant and understanding. I see my future here on this estate. I love this life; they've always known that. Once this is over, life will go on for me where it left off.'

'But it won't be the same for the people who lose loved ones.'

'I know; I accept that. That is one reason why I want to volunteer now, at the beginning, to help get it over with as quickly as possible, so fewer people will suffer.'

She stopped walking and placed a hand on his arm. 'You are a thoughtful and brave man, Jeremy.'

'No more so than many others.'

'I think you are.'

'Your thoughts will sustain me when I am away.'

'You will always have them.'

'And treasure them. It will be a comfort to me, knowing you are safe at Brunton.'

'For me, being there will bring you close.' She

131

slipped a delicate silver chain, on which hung a small matching cross, from around her neck and handed it to him. 'Wear that for me, and I pray that God will always keep you from harm.'

'I ... I ...' Words refused to come.

'Don't say you can't. You can take it. I want you to be safe.'

He kissed her and held the embrace a moment longer.

'Don't say anything, Jeremy, please.' Tears welled in Marie's eyes

'But I...'

'No, please. There is a war and that could change things. Please respect my wishes, and never forget that you will always have my deepest friendship.'

He kissed her on the cheek this time.

They walked home, holding hands, saying little, each lost in their own thoughts.

Jeremy wished he had poured out his heart to her, but felt he had to respect her wishes. Afterwards he was haunted by the thought that there might be more to her relationship with the family friend than had appeared to be the case when he had visited France. He would not press her, though. As she had said, the war could change things.

Marie was torn. She had felt a growing love for Jeremy, but her father's words were hanging over her like a pall. Jeremy had said he would defy his parents' wishes if they tried to stop him volunteering. Should she do the same? Jacques was part of her life, but now war had forced a wedge between them and drawn Jeremy further into her heart. Some time in the future a decision would have to be made, a decision that would hurt someone.

Though both sets of parents did not want their sons to walk off to war, they respected their wishes and gave them their love and prayers. They knew that by doing so they would take one anxiety from their son's mind.

Veronica and Marie went back to the academy where they found little changed; the war seemed far away, but Mrs Latimer kept her young ladies up-to-date with the news as far as she knew it. It was never better than second-hand, though, and often expressed in terms calculated to boost public morale rather than the literal truth.

Jeremy and Michael, along with other young men, who had affinity with horses and volunteered for the Yorkshire Hussars, were plunged into drill and fitness exercises and weapon and combat training. Speculation ran rife about their ultimate destination but Jeremy and Michael were surprised when the Sergeant in charge called them at the end of a training session.

'Attwood!'

'Sarge!

'Eakins!'

'Sarge!'

'Fall out. Report to the Commanding Officer immediately.'

'Sarge!'

Jeremy and Michael, curious about this order coming on their last day of training, marched from the parade ground to the office-block.

'What's this about?' queried Jeremy, knowing his friend could have no idea.

'Why us?' was Michael's reply. 'Unless we're getting torn off a strip for challenging Sergeant O' Hara's order last week.'

'Thought he'd dealt with that himself by putting us on jankers.'

'We'll soon know.'

Within a few minutes the Orderly Corporal was marching them into the Commanding Officer's office. They came smartly to attention, eyes fixed straight ahead, and saluted. The Commanding Officer nodded to the Corporal who left the room. The officer eyed the two men then said, 'Stand easy.'

Michael and Jeremy relaxed in the knowledge that, from his last order, their CO was not about to mete out extra punishment for their offence.

He leaned back in his chair. 'So, it's the end of your training course. The reports from all your instructors are good apart from that one blip, but Sergeant O'Hara chose to make light of it. He punished you himself and asked me to take no more account of it. I have done so and made a note on your report to that effect. I have linked my own observation of you here with what I know of your backgrounds, and note that your families are neighbours and you have been close friends all your lives. Because of the recruiting situation at the moment, I am empowered to grant commissions at the end of each course; therefore I am offering you the chance to move on to an Officers' Training Unit in Cambridge.'

For a moment it didn't sink in, then their new status hit them and they both smiled broadly and said simultaneously, 'Thank you, sir.'

The CO nodded and gave a little wave of his hand to dismiss their thanks.

'I'm afraid this means you get no leave now. Your posting to OTU is immediate. My Orderly Corporal will direct you to the Sergeant in charge of the arrangements for postings. He will no doubt have all your documents ready; you will be leaving tomorrow.' The CO pushed himself out of his chair and came out from behind his desk.

'Good luck, Eakins.' He held out his hand to Michael.

'Thank you, sir.'

'Good luck to you too, Attwood.' The handshake was firm.

'Thank you, sir.'

They both sprang to attention, saluted, did a smart turn and marched out. The Corporal jumped to his feet when they appeared.

'Sirs, I'm to take you to the Sergeant who has all the documents for your posting.'

'Carry on, Corporal,' said Jeremy, with a touch of newfound authority, and a wink at Michael as the Corporal turned for the door.

'The third door on the left,' he said when they reached the ground floor of the building taken over for Army purposes.

'Thank you, Corporal.'

'Sir.' He looked embarrassed, not knowing whether he should salute them or not. He knew they had both been commissioned but they were not wearing officers' uniforms. Instead, he spluttered, 'Best of luck, sirs,' and hurried away.

As soon as the Corporal had rounded the corner they both grinned broadly and playfully punched each other. They collected the documents connected with their posting along with travel warrants to get them to Cambridge.

Back in their billet, in the knowledge that transport would be arriving in one hour to take them to the station, they packed quickly and snatched a few minutes to write home

Jeremy wrote:

Dear Mother, Father, and Veronica,
We had good news today. Both of us have been granted a commission and tomorrow will be going to OTU (Officers' Training Unit). We don't know how long the course is until we get to the depot, nor do we know what will happen after that. We hope we will be able to stay together in our next posting.

Hope everyone is well. Keep us and all our troops in your prayers.

Will write again as soon as I am settled.
Love,
Jeremy

Michael wrote a similar letter to his parents then took a few minutes more to write of his love to Veronica while Jeremy penned a quick note to Marie, both of them hoping they might all meet again at Christmas.

11

'No Christmas leave!' Jeremy announced when he walked into the billet he shared with eight other volunteers; hastily erected to house officers under training at the outbreak of war it was spartan, with an iron stove standing in the centre, a bed each, some shared chests of drawers.

'What?' The gasp from those huddled round the red glow from the stove, or seeking warmth under the blankets on their beds, was followed by expletives that turned the air blue on the back of shattered hopes.

'Who told you?'

'An announcement has just gone up on the noticeboard in the Mess.'

'Why?'

'Heavy casualties. I asked the Orderly Officer who'd just put the notice up. He told me they were heavier than had been expected in the first months of the war, and heaviest of all among officers.'

'Aye, lead from the front,' someone derided. 'Like bloody pigs to the slaughter.'

'We're standing by for postings.'

No leave brought disappointment for their families at home and dampened their own enthusiasm for Christmas. Catherine Attwood and Elspeth Eakins tried to emulate the usual tradition of bringing all the employees of the two estates and their families together for a joint Christmas dinner, but with so many of the younger men missing the atmosphere lacked its usual sparkle.

They drifted into the New Year.

'No postings! We might just as well have had leave,' everyone grumbled.

Veronica and Marie returned to the academy in mid-January, still with no news of postings for Michael and Jeremy.

With the start of a new term, Mrs Latimer announced that she was introducing new subjects to the syllabus. 'While we will continue with all the usual instruction in etiquette, deportment, languages, and the other attributes to enable you to step out into the wider world, they will be curtailed somewhat. I believe that under present conditions we should look at some of the things that will fit you to play your own part in the war. We can all knit for the troops in our spare time, but I am also introducing instruction in nursing and first aid. Our local doctor has agreed to help. I have a nurse from the local hospital and a retired nursing sister to help too.

'I know that some men may look on certain occupations as being beyond women's capabilities, but I disagree. I think we can play a wider role in helping the war effort so I have engaged the help of two men to teach some of you to drive, with an eye to the possibility of eventually driving ambulances. Many younger men have left farming to go into military service; this is causing the government much concern about food production. I have therefore enlisted the help of my husband to introduce you to the ways in which I believe women could play a part in working on the land; we are not all weaklings as men would have us believe.'

Mrs Latimer smiled when this statement raised a cheer. 'Good, I can see you all agree. Other ideas about what we can do will be forthcoming. So, as you can see, our curriculum will be slightly different from now on but we will not neglect the basics on which I established the academy.'

When they left assembly, the young ladies buzzed with excitement; the new curriculum gave them a chance to help the war effort and the soldiers serving at the front. Inevitably there were one or two girls who were not in favour of Mrs Latimer's plans but they soon fell into line when they realised their attitude would only lead to their being ostracised by the rest of their fellow students; they didn't want to lose friends.

Veronica and Marie wrote letters home full of enthusiasm for the changes, and received the approval of their parents and of Michael and Jeremy.

Daily visits to the letter table brought the same query to Veronica's and Marie's lips: 'Did you get one?' They received letters regularly from their parents, though the arrival of Marie's from France was less predictable. News came from Michael and Jeremy, but when letters abruptly stopped the girls knew they must have moved, and that there was every possibility that they would be in France where they would face the horrors of war. They feared for their men's safety but kept their emotions locked in their hearts. They wrote cheerful letters, keeping their misgivings from the paper, not knowing when their letters would reach the men, wherever they may be.

Returning to their Regiment from their Officer's Course in Cambridge, Jeremy and Michael were assigned to different Cavalry Squadrons, Jeremy to B Squadron and Michael to C Squadron. The uneasiness about their destination that hung over them was finally broken when, one day in February, Jeremy told his friend 'B Squadron has been attached to the 46th Division, ordered to be ready to leave tomorrow and is likely to become Infantry, it seems that horses are not as practical in the front line now. Have you heard anything about C Squadron?'

'No word yet,' replied Michael. 'Looks like we're splitting up,' he added with regret, and held out his hand.

Jeremy shook it.

'We'll meet up again somewhere. Take care, my friend. Look after yourself,' said Michael. 'Must go. Lots to see to.'

'I will. You too,' said Jeremy, and slapped his friend on the shoulder.

As he watched him walk away Michael regretted that they would not be together. He shook off the despondency and hoped that a new posting for his Squadron, attached to the 49th Division, would soon mean he followed Jeremy into action.

It came in April and a new spirit surged through his Squadron when they heard they were on their way to France, despite realising they would be marching headlong into danger.

When he reached France Michael's first objective, once he'd seen his men settled into camp, was to make enquiries about the whereabouts of Jeremy's outfit, but all that he could learn was that it was at the front. He prayed his friend was safe.

One evening two weeks later, as evening darkened over the battle area, the usual time for changeover, his division moved out of camp to take over from one at the front. They moved forward 'at ease'. Their CO knew what awaited his men and reckoned this was no time to impose strict discipline. The men, knowing the score and what was expected of them, appreciated his relaxation of the usual regulations and did not take advantage of it.

'They're coming.' Word swept back along the line and the men, realising what it meant, were curious to meet and exchange words in passing with others who had seen action.

Michael anxiously made enquiries of the first man as to which division he belonged to.

'Forty-sixth,' the man muttered, and staggered on.

Jeremy's!

In the gloom, Michael searched the faces as they moved past. His own men, expecting military banter, were shocked to hear so little of it. What they saw instead were weary men, mud-stained, eyes once bright, now dulled by the horrors of what they had seen. Some were barely able to drag one foot in front of the other, walking wounded helped by their pals, the whole outfit straggling in a long line.

Shocked by what he was seeing, Michael's

anxiety heightened when there was still no sight of Jeremy. The line of men was thinning. Michael grabbed one of the soldiers by the arm. 'Second Lieutenant Attwood?' he gasped.

The soldier looked at him without any spark of interest and made a gesture with his thumb towards the rear of the line. With no comment offered, Michael's fear rose. His footsteps dragged. Then he saw a familiar figure. 'Jeremy!' He grabbed his friend by the shoulders in joy and relief.

Jeremy looked up blankly. 'Michael!' he croaked wearily. He gazed hard at his friend, with eyes burned out by what he had seen. 'You don't want to go there.'

Michael sought for words. Patting Jeremy on the shoulder and knowing he must move on, he said, 'Take care, my friend.'

Jeremy gave him a weak smile. 'Not me. You. Be lucky, you'll need to be. Got to go. Have to look after this lot.'

Michael nodded and watched his friend stumble, almost fall. Automatically he moved towards him.

Jeremy did not turn but he must have instinctively known of Michael's desire to help, and waved him away. Michael nodded to himself. He realised Jeremy's attitude was, 'Among my command there are more in need of help than I.'

Michael walked on; the same thing that had brought these men to this state would soon face him. He felt chilled by fear of what might be.

They reached their positions: a maze of trenches still a little way back from the actual front. From here they would be in the immediate support position but within range of enemy bombardment. Michael saw his men into their new homes. Homes? He laughed at the thought and tried to deal with the men's grumbling about the state in which their dugouts had been left. There was nothing to be done but order them to do their best to clear up.

Earth squelched between the duckboards. Clay bore down upon retaining timbers. Props shoring up the roof were used as corner posts for make-shift beds. Troops trying to make the best of bad conditions cursed the rats that scurried around freely attempting to find whatever they could to feed on.

Michael found the officers' dugout little better, not that he'd expected it to be; what else could be done, and who cared enough to do it? Tomorrow he might be past caring.

'Head down! Head!' Michael believed he would call out these warnings in his sleep for ever, if he were lucky enough to survive. It had started the first day they took over the forward position, when enemy snipers did not miss two men curious to see what 'No Man's Land' was like. The warning had been on his lips constantly ever since. The expected pitched battles and hand-to-hand combat had not materialised to the extent he had expected, though there had been sniping, some prolonged firing, and shelling on some days. By the sounds coming from the central section of the line the brunt of the fighting was taking place there and he assumed that was where the Germans were attempting to break through. Thankful that they were not involved, he was nevertheless aware that the low level of activity in their section created the tense expectation that they were next in the firing line.

On the evening of 25 June they were ordered to move to the central section. The men reckoned casualties must have been heavy and they were being assigned to plug the gap. Morale dipped; troops and officers felt fear intensify, though no one admitted it.

Packing his belongings, Michael found himself muttering the date to himself. 'The twenty-fifth of June? The twenty-fifth of June? What's the significance of the twenty-fifth of June?' Irritated, he tightened his lips. He picked up letters from home and started to stuff them into his bag. He paused. That was it! Veronica, in her last letter to him, had mentioned that today was her last day at the academy. He looked at his watch. She would be home now. Michael cursed. But for this damned war they would have been together, celebrating.

12

Catherine and Charles were prepared for what would be a different homecoming for Veronica and Marie, especially Marie who would normally have been on her way to France and her family. But they knew her to be resilient, and that her friendship with Veronica was of a depth that would help ease her exile from France until peace could take her home again.

'Mr and Mrs Attwood,' said Marie, when they had settled down on the first evening back at Brunton Manor, 'from the last news we received at the academy about the progress of the war, I think I may be with you for quite a while. I cannot sit around idly waiting for it to end. Can you find me something useful to do?'

Catherine smiled. 'You have beaten me to it. Mr Attwood and I have been discussing what you and Veronica might do. We deduced from your letters that you both wish to be active in some way that will help the war effort. So we have a suggestion.' Charles was sitting filling his pipe, but his wife's glance invited him to take over.

He nodded, cleared his throat and said, 'Well, I've lost men to the war, and my efforts to find replacements bore fruit at first, but now, what with one thing and another, I'm short again. I'm reduced to a couple of older men who are willing but limited in what they can do.'

'So you'd like us to help?' asked Veronica hopefully. Marie added her agreement.

'You told us in your letters that Mrs Latimer introduced certain additions to the curriculum. You enthused about one in particular.'

'Helping her husband on the estate,' said Veronica, quickly taking up the tack her father was on.

'Exactly. You mentioned milking...'

'That was fun,' laughed Marie.

'I'm glad you think so.' Charles smiled. 'I never

saw it so. Oh, yes, I learned to milk a cow, my father insisted, but as soon as I was left the estate and farm, I employed men to do it.' He glanced at his wife. 'If Marie likes milking, we might have found ourselves a gem.'

'Mr Latimer taught me to drive a tractor,' put in Veronica.

'What sort?' her father asked.

'A four-wheeled Saunderson model, just like yours.'

'He's up-to-date then. What else did you do?'

'Digging ... brashing.'

'Well, you can certainly help out,' he said.

'And when it becomes known what you are doing, it will help our cause,' said Catherine.

'Your cause?' queried Veronica.

'War work for women is the general cause, but more specifically for women to work on the land.'

'But I thought they were already doing that?'

'There are some, but it's not really organised at any official level. Various societies do something locally, or farmers, if so inclined, will hire women for farm work, but there are still many who don't regard us as capable. There are steps afoot to get something done on a countrywide basis and attempts are being made to get the Minister of Agriculture to organise at national level,' explained her mother.

'In the meantime we do things ourselves,' said Charles. 'Let me see in the next week what you can do, and if I'm satisfied I'll employ you.'

'You mean, you'll put us on your payroll?' asked Marie doubtfully.

'Of course. I don't employ anyone for nothing.'

Marie and Veronica looked at each other, expressions delighted.

'You'll not regret it, Papa,' Veronica told him.

Letters from Michael and Jeremy were infrequent and, because of censorship, little was learned of the progress of the fighting, but reading between the lines they deduced both men had been on the front line.

'I wish we knew where they are, especially with Christmas drawing near,' said Veronica regret-fully one evening.

'We'll send a Christmas parcel to each of them. Mrs Eakins is doing the same,' said Catherine. 'If you have anything special to put in, let me have it next week.'

'Where will we send them?' Marie asked.

'We can only use the forwarding address we have been given. The Army will sort them out for their final destinations,' said Charles. 'Troops are moved around according to the situation at the front.'

At that moment both Michael's and Jeremy's units were receiving orders to move up the front line where they would be a joint force under one command.

They saw this as an opportunity to meet up again and each man had decided to try to make contact as soon as they saw their troops settled in conditions that had gone from bad to worse after the rains at the end of November. Duckboards tried to combat the pools of water and mud which were everywhere; vermin were a constant menace, creating unhygienic conditions that further depleted their troops. But before either of them could make contact the CO called a meeting of all officers.

'I was going to look for you,' said Michael, grasping Jeremy's hand in a firm grip when they met in the large dugout which served as field headquarters.

'And I you,' said Jeremy. 'Good to see you. How are you bearing up?'

Michael shrugged. 'Things could be better.'

Jeremy grinned. 'That's the understatement of the year!'

'And snow's forecast.'

'That's all I want to know. Heard from home lately?'

'Veronica, two weeks ago. All was well then. She and Marie are helping on the farm,' said Michael.

'Good grief, what state will it be in when we get back?' said Jeremy jokingly.

'What's this all about?' asked Michael, his glance taking in the officers who were still gathering.

'I haven't heard anything official. Rumours, as there always are, say that we're in for a big push before Christmas. But we'll soon know.' He nodded towards the entrance to the dugout.

Michael turned to see the CO stride in. He was a dapper man who exuded authority and always managed to look neat and tidy even in the worst conditions. 'Keeps morale up,' he would say. The officers sprang to attention and silence spread over the gathering; expectancy charged the atmosphere.

'Stand easy.' His officers relaxed. 'I know you are hoping I can tell you something concrete,' he said firmly, his voice carrying seemingly with little effort. 'I'm afraid I have no news at this moment. I called this meeting to tell you just that, so you can quell rumours of an imminent big push. Such rumours inevitably spread among the troops when units are brought together. I assure you, no word of that is coming from headquarters. So, scotch speculation. I will let you have anything further as soon as I have it. Most of you have served under me before and you know that I believe in keeping everyone, and I mean everyone, under my command informed of the situation – it makes for general confidence in me and you can feel confident in each other. So, gentlemen,' he left a small pause and allowed a little twitch of amusement to show on his lips when he said, 'enjoy your stay in the trenches.'

A buzz of conversation broke out once he had left the dugout.

'I'm fortunate ... I have a good batman, Angus McFergus. He'll have made a brew. Come and have one,' Michael suggested. 'He's a good soldier too, an old lag, one of my best shots.'

So it was that Michael and Jeremy drew comfort from their meetings with each other in the dreary winter days that dragged past until Christmas. There was little activity along the front but for the usual morning patrols, trying to get information on enemy positions and movements. If patrols on either side were aware of the enemy they avoided getting into hand-to-hand combat; their priority was information gathering. Shelling went on but it was never of an intensity to be the precursor of a major attack. 'Keep your heads down!' 'Snipers!' Troops on both sides had to be constantly on their guard against them. It was an uneasy peace amongst trenches, barbed-wire defences and No Man's Land.

Michael and Jeremy met, as planned, outside Michael's dugout late on Christmas Eve. More snow had fallen during the early-evening but now the clouds were thinning and drifting away, leaving a bright moon to add sparkle to the scene.

'Reminds me of those magic nights at home when our families used to meet for Midnight Mass and then drinks at one or other of the houses,' said Michael wistfully.

'It does,' agreed Jeremy. 'I wonder if they are keeping up the tradition.'

'It will be hard not to and yet hard to do, but one thing I'm certain of ... they'll be thinking of us.'

They lapsed into silence, each with their own special memories. A few minutes later Jeremy asked, 'What time is it?'

Michael fished a watch out of his pocket and turned it to catch the pale moonlight. 'A couple of minutes to midnight.'

Silence fell between them, and though they were aware of Angus standing behind them at the top of the steps to the dugout no one spoke.

Then: 'What's that?' asked Jeremy quietly, as if speaking louder would have been sacrilege.

'Singing,' whispered Michael. 'Coming from over there,' he added in surprise pointing towards No Man's Land.

'*Silent Night*. In German.'

They listened as the singing swelled. It brought other men from their dugouts to listen in hushed wonder. Then someone along the English trench joined in; a rich voice that started ripples in the frozen air. The carol spread and spread until the air seemed tranquil and at peace. Men who only a short time ago were trying to kill each other, and would try again before long, were singing together in unison.

As that died away an eerie peace hung over the battlefield.

'What the hell?' snarled Jeremy. 'They don't want to fight us; we don't want to fight them. It's the bloody politicians, the bloody rulers ... all power maniacs!'

'True,' agreed Michael. 'And we can't do anything about it. We're cannon fodder for their ends.'

'Why can't they preach love instead of warmongering?' snapped Jeremy.

'That goes for our Church men too and, I suspect, all religious leaders. None of them, no matter what their faith, preach often enough about love for each other.'

'If they did, men would take notice and the world would be a better place.'

'Too right, sirs,' Angus broke in behind them, 'but it'll take a hell of a long time before they do.'

'It doesn't matter how long, if it makes a better world and we have no more hell-holes like these trenches.'

'Sirs, we can't do anything about it. Here, have a dram.' Angus had three tin mugs hooked on the fingers of one hand and a bottle in the other.

The two officers looked at him in amazement as he started to pour.

'Whisky! Where did you get that?' asked Michael.

'Sir, ask no questions, get no lies.' The batman raised his mug.

'Thanks, Angus,' said Michael. They acknowledged his gesture in return. 'This will be a Christmas Eve we'll always remember.'

13

Marie, her mind in confusion, looked at the two letters she had placed side by side on her dressing table. It was ironic that they had both arrived that morning – both from France.

30 June 1916

My dear Marie,
I hope you are well. There is little news that I am able to tell you. As I have indicated before, we are kept busy with regular respite away from the front. The men are in good heart in spite of the conditions and the constant weariness that besets us all. We are in a good spell of weather at the moment and we try to take advantage of it to get dried out. It is good having Michael close. Talking about past times gives us both a touch of home. After all this, life can never be the same; the world will be changed. Whatever it becomes,

I hope you and I can share it together.

You are always in my thoughts. Please think of me and do keep writing. Your letters mean so much. Can't write more now. I have to go.

My love
Jeremy xxx

Marie wondered why this letter had not been the usual length. Why had he had to go? She pushed the worst scenario from her mind and took in the words 'share it together'. A veiled proposal? Her eyes dampened. When this war was over and Jeremy spoke those words to her, what would her answer be? Would that answer be influenced by the other letter that had also arrived from France?

28 September 1916

My dearest Marie,
I am sorry my letters have not been as frequent as they should have been but I think you will understand how occupied I am in keeping the supplies of military equipment moving, for the betterment of our glorious and gallant Army.

I am well but extremely busy. My father and mother are in good health and send their regards.

I regret that your mother and father took the decision to send you to safety in England. I understand their thinking but it showed no confidence in our glorious Army which repelled the Germans, halting their advance so that they have never threatened Paris since.

Your last letter said you are working on the land. I don't like to think of you doing that – I make my displeasure known because of my high regard for you and because it is no preparation for the life we will lead when you come home.

Claude was well the last time we heard, but of course we do not know where he is; the Navy is ever on the move.

I look forward to your return. There will be a fine home for you and a business so well established by this war that you will want for nothing.

Your Jacques

Marie tightened her lips. Words so different; sentiments so different; attitudes so different. As she looked at the letters, lying side by side, she knew the choice she would make. She took a sheet of paper from the drawer and picked up a pen. She wrote the date: 8 November 1916, then stopped, the pen poised above the paper. Her father's words returned to her mind. She put the pen down, stared at it for a moment, unsure, then started for the door. With her hand on the knob, she stopped and turned back. A strange certainty filled her. If I open this door part of my life will be lost for ever. She looked back at the table... 'My God, Jeremy! When did you get here?' She rushed towards him but pulled up sharp, staring in disbelief. There was no one there! Her gaze swept the room. She was alone. Her imagination must have been playing tricks.

She grabbed the pen and unhesitatingly wrote, *YES! YES! YES!* She folded the paper, pushed it into an envelope, sealed it and wrote on the front 'Lieutenant J. Attwood', and added the last forwarding address she had for him. She held the envelope in both hands for a moment, looked at it with a smile then kissed it.

The eastern sky began to lighten. Silence hung above the battle zone. Time stretched, reluctant to summon another day. Soldiers stirred. Got ready for...

Noise ripped the sky asunder. German shells arced over No Man's Land, pounded the earth, tore barbed-wire defences apart, hurtled into dugouts, burying men dead or alive. Soldiers cursed, orders were yelled, machine-guns sent bullets rattling in retaliation. Screams of sudden pain resounded along the trenches; blood flowed, saturating clothes, staining the ground. Officers tried to bring some stability to chaos, even as they struggled to staunch their own wounds. Some sort of order had to be brought because they knew they could suffer this the whole day through or until their own artillery responded and found the right range to battle their counter-parts into silence.

An hour later the guns were still. An eerie quiet embraced the battlefield. Soldiers emerged slowly from their dugouts, dazed, trembling, fear in the eyes of some, disbelief in others, some with determination on their faces to 'get their own back' one day, but all anxious for the fate of their comrades.

Michael counted himself very lucky when he emerged unscathed. The ground was churned into stark upheaval; bodies lay in lifeless attitudes and, though shocked by the carnage, troops started to bring order to the scene.

Michael caught a remark: 'Eastern section bore the brunt.'

Jeremy's section! Jeremy...

Though there was plenty to do here, Michael had to know. He hurried through the maze of trenches, winding his way past the dead and wounded with not a thought.

Reaching the Eastern section, he grabbed the first soldier by the arm. 'Lieutenant Attwood?' he asked, concern and urgency in his voice.

The man tightened his lips. 'I wouldn't go there, sir. His dugout took a direct hit.'

Michael had gone cold. 'I've got to,' he said, and moved on.

What he saw shocked him to the core. No one could possibly have survived that direct hit or, if they had, they would have been buried with no chance of escape. He turned away, retched and was sick.

In a daze he made his way back to his own section. Shocked though he was, numbed by the loss of his closest friend, he still had responsibilities and a job to do. As horrific as the scene had been, he had to try and erase it from his mind. 'Easier said than done,' he muttered to himself, but made an effort to cope and combat the shock by telling himself to forget 1916. But how did he write home with such news? He chose what he later called to himself 'the coward's way out' – he would leave it to official channels. He himself would write later.

Catherine, Veronica and Marie were sitting down to luncheon when the mail arrived. Catherine flicked through the dozen letters. 'Two for me,' she said, putting the others aside for her husband to read.

Veronica and Marie started helping themselves to some cold meat while Catherine opened her letters. 'A bill,' she said dismissively. She slipped a sheet of paper from the other envelope and scanned it quickly.

'Oh, my goodness,' she gasped.

'What is it, Mother?' asked Veronica.

'You know I have been corresponding with Lady Brentwood about recruiting women to work on the land? This letter is from her.'

Catherine read:

Dear Mrs Attwood,
I am pleased to tell you that I have it on good authority that we will get our way and women's work on the land will soon be officially recognised. It may still take some time but I think that we, as a body, should be looking at the core of our organization, which will be called the Women's Land Army.

We will need to divide the country into sections, each with its own authority to run that area according to what the land has to offer. Since the inception of the WLA I have kept my eyes and mind open to who might be likely people to run these sections.

You have always been a strong advocate of women aiding the war effort by working on the land and have been forthright with your ideas. Therefore I would ask you to be in charge of a section in the Vale of Pickering, with your estate being at the hub.

I would be grateful if you would give this proposition some thought and hope your decision will be in favour of taking on this role.

'You'll do it, Mother, won't you?' asked Veronica with undisguised excitement.

'You must, Mrs Attwood, you must!' urged Marie.

Catherine laughed at their excitement. 'Of course. It will strike a blow for suffrage as well as the war effort. And you will be my first two recruits.'

The two friends let out a whoop of delight.

'What's going on?' asked Charles, entering the room at that moment.

Everyone spoke at once, wanting to tell him the good news.

'Splendid,' he enthused. He went to his wife, kissed her and said, 'You'll do a splendid job.'

She smiled her thanks and patted his hand.

'Who else are you going to recruit?' asked Veronica.

Catherine smiled. 'Don't rush things. We aren't fully recognised yet – that may take time, as it says in the letter, Meanwhile we carry on as we are until headquarters lets us know more.'

Life settled into a fixed routine on the Brunton and Rushbrook Estates. No news came from the Western Front but everyone knew, from official bulletins, that heavy fighting was taking place at the Somme. As November advanced the year towards 1917, some relief came with the news that the Somme offensive had been halted by heavy falls of snow.

One morning, shortly after that news had come

through, Veronica woke to find the landscape outside covered in white.

She shivered as she slid out of bed, pulled a dressing gown around her and went to see if Marie was awake. 'Up you get, sleepy-head. Snow may stop the fighting but it won't stop cows wanting milking.'

When they'd finished and were heading back to the house for breakfast, Marie remarked hopefully, 'If there's a lull in the fighting we might get letters.'

Two days later one addressed to Mr Attwood lay on the table when they came into breakfast.

Charles picked it up. It looked official. Catherine felt his tension and sensed a reluctance to open it.

Veronica and Marie, busy exchanging comments about the cows, came in together. The atmosphere in the room froze. They stared at Charles and Catherine. Veronica saw the envelope in her father's hand.

'What is it, Papa?' she asked, her voice scarcely above a whisper.

At the question Charles slit the envelope open and withdrew a piece of paper. He stared at the notice, his usually florid face draining of colour. He looked at his wife but could not speak. She stepped over to him and took the letter. The words blurred in front of her eyes.

'Oh, no!'

'Mother!' called Veronica in alarm, and took the letter from her. 'No, no!' she wailed and turned to Marie.

Her friend had no need to read the letter; she knew by the reactions of the family what it said.

A chill gripped her but she felt no sensation; numbness had taken over. She did not speak; she did not cry. Her world was shattered; she could do nothing about it, but she knew life would never be the same for her. She walked slowly from the room. No one stopped her. Grief had to be suffered individually, no one else could eliminate it. She stepped into the hall and closed the door without a sound.

She walked slowly across the hall. The words YES, YES, YES were blazing in her mind. Had Jeremy read those words and died happy? She would never know.

She stepped outside into the silence of the snow and knew Jeremy would live for ever in her heart, a love untold.

14

Marie stood immobile, snowflakes settling on her. She sensed Veronica come and stand beside her and slip a hand into hers, seeking to give consolation and find comfort for herself. They stood locked in that moment together then turned and flung their arms round each other. The contact opened the flood-gates of sorrow until neither of them could weep any longer.

'Oh, Veronica, I'm so so sorry.' Marie's words caught in her throat. 'I know how close you were. He was always kind to me.' She bit her lip to stop herself from expressing her real feelings for

Jeremy. Keeping them to herself created a sensation of closeness not to be shared, and all the more precious for that.

'I was always grateful that you and he got on so well,' Veronica went on. 'He will always be part of our lives.'

Marie smiled weakly and they both turned back into the house, letting the snow cast a white shroud behind them.

When the Eakins heard, they too were devastated. A letter from Michael arrived. He tried to explain what he knew of Jeremy's death during the Battle of the Ancre. There was little consolation in knowing, especially as it was likely that Jeremy's burial place would remain the dugout he had shared with his troops, and where they had died together far from home.

Elspeth Eakins looked out of the window. The clouds were clearing and the brightening afternoon sky kindled some hope on this first day of spring 1917. Maybe it augured well, not only for better weather after the dreary winter, but for the outcome of the war that seemed to be dragging on endlessly. She watched her husband striding purposefully down the drive. Word had come that some cattle had got out. They must be brought back. She sighed. Oh, for the days when staff were plentiful and reliable.

She was turning from the window when she saw Clive stop. She followed his gaze towards the entrance gates that gave on to the main road to the village. A car was turning in. Unusual. They weren't expecting anyone. Somebody must have got some petrol from somewhere.

The car stopped beside Clive. She saw him bend down to say something to the driver. Then he straightened up and rushed round the other side. The passenger door opened. Someone was struggling to get out. Clive was reaching forward to help. Elspeth's eyes widened in disbelief. Michael! She ran from the room and out of the front door, taking the shortest route to reach him. Her mind couldn't assimilate what she was seeing, but her son was here!

She flung herself into his embrace, barely hearing his greeting. She leaned back in his arms to look at him, and with tears of relief and joy streaming from her eyes, could only muster, 'You're home!'

He laughed. 'Yes, I'm home, Mother.'

She turned to her husband. 'Clive, can this be true?'

'As true as Michael is standing there. He's home for good.'

'For good? But what...?' She cut her question short when she saw that Michael was holding up a walking stick.

'Invalided out,' he said.

The horror of what that might mean gripped her. 'Michael! What...? Are...? Come on, let's help you. Clive, help him.'

'Mother, calm down. I'm all right. I'm about to throw this stick away.'

'You can't be if you've been invalided out! Why are you? What happened?'

'Let me thank Mr Severs first. He kindly gave me a lift from the village, using his precious petrol. Then we'll walk up to the house together.'

Michael explained that he had been injured in a blast, taking a lot of shrapnel in his legs and right side. 'I was saved by a couple of medical orderlies, and then I was taken back to the base hospital and operated on straight away. The doc got most of it out but there are a few pieces still inside me.' He saw the look of concern and horror come over his mother's face. 'It's all right, Mother, don't worry. Think of it as saving me from going back to the front. Not like poor Jeremy.' The words choked in his throat. With concern he asked quietly, 'How are they all?'

'Devastated, but putting on a brave face.'

'I must go and see them when I've dumped my few things.'

'And you've had a rest and a good meal,' said his mother firmly. 'You look as if you need building up.'

'I won't say no to both of those, Mother, but I don't want you fussing. Everything is going to be all right.' He turned to his father. 'May I take the car to go to Brunton?'

'I don't think you ought to be driving, and horseback is out of the question as yet. Don't be foolhardy about this, Michael. A full recovery is the most important thing at the moment.'

Seeing her son about to protest, Elspeth spoke up quickly. 'Your father's right, Michael. Forget about going over to Brunton. I'll send word to Veronica. I know she'll come.'

While waiting impatiently for Veronica's arrival Michael relished some good food, in marked contrast to what he had been receiving in the trenches.

'That was lovely, Mother. I wish...' The sound of a galloping horse broke into his words.

Elspeth was quickly on her feet and hurrying from the room. Michael started for the door but was pulled up short by the stab of pain in his side. A moment later it was gone, but he waited. He heard the horse coming to a halt and then footsteps to the front door. 'In there,' he heard his mother say.

The door burst open. Veronica, excitement in her eyes, hair dishevelled and cheeks glowing after the fast ride, rushed in.

'Michael!' Ready for this exuberance he had steadied himself to grasp her tight when she flung herself into his open arms.

Without a word he let his lips speak for him. Veronica accepted them, knowing what they truly said.

'Michael! Michael! Michael!' she gasped between kisses.

With the last kiss he smoothed back her hair and held her face between his hands. Looking deep into her eyes, he said, 'I love you so very, very much.'

She smiled. 'And I love you.'

Now he felt he was truly home and she felt he was truly here and that the future for them at least was secure.

They had so much to plan but they agreed to wait. As much as Veronica wanted to know why he had been invalided out and to learn something of Jeremy's death, the time was not right.

164

Michael would have to choose his own moment to talk about the things that must be seared on his mind.

Ten minutes later Marie quietly walked in. 'Hello, Michael,' she said. He stood up. She crossed the room and accepted a kiss on the cheek. 'I hope I'm not intruding, but I had to come and say welcome home. It's good to have you back.'

'Thank you, Marie. That's most kind of you.'

There were a few seconds of unease but he broke them with a question. 'I hear you are both working on the land?'

'And liking it,' said Veronica.

'So many men left to join the Army, we women had to do something,' said Marie.

'Mother has really taken to it. In anticipation of a woman's organisation being recognised, she is recruiting women from all around here. Farmers are not taking readily to the idea, but she is trying to soften them up.'

'Tell her that anything I can do to help she should just ask.'

Catherine was not slow to take up that offer. Michael explained to local farmers that knowing what their womenfolk were doing to help the war effort boosted the morale of men serving at the front. Farmers began to change their minds after that. When the Women's Land Army was officially recognised and organised on a national basis, Catherine was asked to take charge of the section she had previously been privately organising. As promised, her first two recruits were

165

Veronica and Marie, who were followed by many more eager to make their own contribution.

One evening, after a talk by a district official, organised by Catherine and held in the nearby village hall, Veronica and Marie came out to find Michael waiting.

Surprised, Veronica asked, 'What are you doing here?'

'Look,' he spread his arms, 'no stick. I've thrown it away.'

'But you...'

'I saw the doctor earlier today when you were out on the land. I didn't tell you in case his examination didn't bring good news. But it did and he saw no reason for me not to get rid of the stick. In fact, he thought it a good idea so that I didn't get too dependent on it. So here I am, ready to walk you home.'

'That's truly wonderful news.' Veronica hugged him to her.

'I'm so glad,' said Marie. She glanced round. Young women were still coming out of the hall. 'Oh, there's Betty, I'm working with her tomorrow ... I want a word. See you back at Brunton.' She hurried off.

Michael smiled and winked at Veronica. They both knew Marie had left so that they could walk home alone. Their hands met, fingers twined. A single touch conveyed their feelings. The silence was charged with love. There was no need for words. But Michael knew they had to be said.

Reaching Brunton Manor, he guided Veronica in the direction of the summer house which was hidden from the main house yet on one side overlooked a section of the lawn.

'Warm enough?' he asked as they sat down.

'Yes,' she nodded.

He leaned close and kissed her, holding the kiss for as long as he could.

'Veronica,' he said, when their lips parted, 'I once hinted at marriage.'

'Yes, and I agreed. Now we'll make it official...'

'Say no more,' he broke in quickly as he put one finger to her lips.

'Why? What is it?' she asked, concern darkening her expression.

'There's something I must tell you. It may lead you to change your mind about us. It might be advisable for you to do so.'

'Michael, what are you saying?' Alarm rang in her tone.

'You know my body took a lot of shrapnel; there are still pieces inside me that the surgeons couldn't remove or else thought it advisable not to try. They are seventy per cent sure it's all right, but there is a thirty per cent chance that a piece might move.' He paused.

'And if it does?'

'It might kill me.'

'Or it might not.'

'Yes.'

'So what's the problem?' asked Veronica calmly, though her heart was racing at the thought that Michael carried within him a shard of metal that might kill him at any moment.

'I wanted you to know, and to know that I won't hold you to marrying me.'

She held his gaze and said, 'Michael Eakins, do

you want to marry me? A one word answer. NOW!'

'Yes,' he replied quietly.

'Then there is no more to be said.' She kissed him with all the intoxicating fervour that she could.

'But, Veronica, I could be...'

'Don't say it!' she stopped him. 'I know what might happen but my love for you overrides everything else.' She stood up, held out her hand. 'Come on, you can ask Father's permission. NOW!'

'Be serious.'

'I am serious. Get up. I want to many you.'

He got up, pulled her close and met her lips with a passion that showed he wanted her too.

They headed for the house.

'What if he says no?' asked Michael with a teasing twinkle in his eyes.

'He wouldn't dare,' Veronica replied indignantly. 'He'd know I'd persuade you to elope.'

On hearing someone hurrying up behind them, they turned and saw Marie. Veronica told her the news.

'I'm delighted for you both,' she said in all sincerity. 'I hope you'll be extremely happy.'

'We intend to be,' said Veronica, 'and you can complete our happiness by saying you will be my bridesmaid.'

'Oh, yes! It will please me very much,' replied Marie. She kissed them both on the cheek.

They hurried to the house, confronted Charles, and within ten minutes everyone was raising their glasses in a toast.

15

Catherine looked up from her porridge when Veronica walked into the dining room.

'Good morning, my dear.' Catherine was pleased to see her daughter looking radiant, especially so early in the day. Her happiness warmed the room.

'Good morning, Mother.' Veronica went to her and kissed her on the cheek. 'Good morning, Father.' She repeated the gesture at the other end of the table.

He smiled with pride. 'Be happy,' he whispered as she kissed him.

'Oh, I am.' She pirouetted on her way back to her chair.

'You won't have thought of dates. No doubt you'll be waiting until...'

'No, Mother,' Veronica interrupted. 'We decided, when Michael was leaving yesterday evening, not to wait. We don't expect a big wedding under the present conditions. We'll be happy with a small one. We want to grasp our happiness while we can, just in case ... but we hope it will be with us for years and years.'

Catherine glanced questioningly at her husband and received an indication not to protest.

'You won't have decided on a date?' he asked.

'Not an actual date, but as soon as possible. If we could give a little thought to that now it would help. I'm going over to see Michael's parents after breakfast.'

Catherine rose from her chair. 'I'll get my diary,' she said, knowing it was better to go along with her daughter's wishes; that way she would not risk losing her love.

When Veronica was leaving Catherine told her to invite the Eakins over that evening to discuss possible dates.

Two months later Veronica and Michael were married in the Catholic church in the local market town. Veronica looked glowing in a day dress of pale blue, and was attended by Marie in a pink dress that complemented the bride's.

It had been a busy two months. Not only had Catherine wedding arrangements to see to in her capacity as mother of the bride, but two days after the engagement word had come through that the Women's Land Army had at last received official confirmation and status, throwing extra work on her as a section leader. The enthusiasm of her recruits enabled things to go smoothly, and those recruits sprang a surprise; when bride and groom emerged from the church they found a guard of honour formed by some of the new girls in their new Land Army uniforms.

Michael closed the door of what had once been the gatehouse of the Rushbrook Estate. Pausing in the small vestibule, he took Veronica in his arms. 'I love you, Mrs Eakins. Thank you for marrying me and for the wonderful week's honeymoon. Scarborough was not what I would have planned but it will always hold a special place in my heart now.'

'It will for me too,' she said. 'And I love you, Mr Eakins.'

'Welcome home,' he said.

Michael and his father had mustered builders and helpers to prepare the gatehouse. They had worked wonders with the materials they had at hand. Furniture had been gathered from here and there. Veronica had been banned from going near the house and the whole enterprise had been kept a secret from her.

'Show me,' she asked.

He pushed open the door from the vestibule, took her hand and stepped into the sitting room.

'This is wonderful,' she said, admiring the transformation. A fire, radiating welcoming warmth, burned brightly in the grate. A settee was drawn up in front of the warmth. The red carpet which covered most of the flagged floor glowed in the firelight. A table and two chairs stood to one side of the fireplace.

'I'm sorry it's not palatial,' apologised Michael, 'but one day...'

'This is palatial enough. You make it so.' Veronica kissed him. 'And there?' she asked, indicating a door.

He led her into a room carpeted in light blue and furnished with a double bed, dressing table and wardrobe.

'This is nice,' she said. 'That bed looks so comfortable.'

'It is. It used to be mine.'

'Oh. Are you sure you don't mind sharing it?' she teased.

'As soon as possible,' he whispered in her ear. 'But it will have to wait. Mother has invited us to dine this evening.'

She nodded. 'That's kind. Now what else have you to show me?'

He took her back into the main room and over to another door. As he opened it he said teasingly, 'Your workplace.'

'Oh! I see. A big black range, a stone sink, a table and dresser. Well, I'll warn you, I'm no cook.'

'You'll learn, and you'll find all the utensils you need in the drawers and cupboards.'

'Oh, thank you very much,' she muttered sarcastically.

'I'll bring our things in,' he said, and headed out to the car which his father had loaned them for their honeymoon.

An hour later when they arrived at the main house on the Rushbrook Estate they found Charles, Catherine and Marie already there, each with their own special 'Welcome back!'

Life settled down for the Attwoods and the Eakins, though it could never again be the same. War still raged on the Western Front and in the other campaigns, but they were played down in conversation between the two families as a safeguard against heartache from personal experiences and loss.

Marie, still suffering from her unspoken love for Jeremy, also felt the previous closeness of her relationship with Veronica had been breached by Michael's return, but she bore him no animosity. He was kindness itself towards her and she saw

Veronica most days, keeping her inner feelings locked away in her heart and mind. She found solace in her Land Army work and shared a new joy with both families when Veronica announced she was pregnant.

Michael immediately fussed and suggested his wife resign from the Women's Land Army, but she would hear none of it. 'I will know when I should do that,' she told him firmly. The moment came sooner than she'd thought, however, when, after a check-up, the doctor told her to take more rest. 'If you don't you will be in danger of losing the baby.'

On hearing this warning, her mother and father and the Eakins worried even more.

Though she was against any suffragette action while war was being waged, Catherine still penned letters in support of the movement. Being kept informed of political developments, she was delighted to learn that their persistent lobbying had brought about the raising of new proposals in Parliament by Lloyd George in 1917.

'You've done it!' shouted Charles one day, bursting into the study where he knew his wife was working on Land Army correspondence.

Startled, she looked round to see him striding towards her, waving a newspaper in the air. His face was wreathed in smiles as he grabbed her from her chair and took her in a little jig across the floor.

'Done what?' Catherine cried, laughing at his exuberance.

He pulled up short and thrust the paper at her. 'That!'

She read quickly that the Representation of the People Act had been passed, and from February 1918 women over the age of thirty had the right to vote, provided they were registered to do so or married to someone who'd registered.

'That's good,' she enthused, 'but it should have gone further. It's given all males over twenty-one the right to vote, so why not all women?'

'It will come, Catherine. This is a step in the right direction.'

'Yes, I suppose so; and it brings a warm light to this cold 1918 February day, and opens the door to a new future for women.'

The brightness grew stronger and brought fresh hope as the year progressed, with the news that the Allied Armies were gaining more and more ground, raising the possibility of an end to the war.

Joy came to the two families when Sylvia was born in May. Though the Attwoods felt a little regret that she was not a boy to replace Jeremy, they only spoke of it between themselves and their disappointment was vanquished by the gurgling smiles Sylvia gave them, whenever they were near.

Marie was one of the first to visit Veronica and the newborn. 'She's lovely,' she said, 'charming.' Then hid the tears that threatened with the thought that she and Jeremy could have experienced this same joy.

'Marie,' Veronica reached out and took her friend's hand, 'I want you to be Sylvia's godmother.'

'Oh, Veronica.' Marie fought back the lump in

her throat. 'I'd love that. Thank you so much for asking me.'

The only stain on their happiness came two weeks later when the doctor visited Veronica and Michael in their cottage and warned them, 'I have something to say, though I know you won't want to hear it. I must tell you, it would be most inadvisable for you to have another baby after your last very difficult pregnancy.'

The shock was palpable. Each could sense it in the other. Their hands met and held on tight.

Michael paled. Veronica was stunned. This could not be. After a stricken moment, Michael said with heart-rending resignation, 'Ah, well, what will be, will be.'

'I know how much you looked forward to having a playmate for Sylvia, even before she was born, but please heed my advice,' urged the doctor.

Veronica nodded with silent tears running down her cheeks.

'We will,' said Michael.

'At some time in the future, you might think of adopting.'

'I suppose it's a thought,' said Michael, not really taking in this suggestion.

'Oh, and one other thing ... be particularly vigilant at the moment. Spanish 'flu, as it is being called, is still taking its toll. It has not run its course yet.'

They saw the doctor out and fell into each other's arms.

'Oh, Michael, I'm so sorry, so sorry,' sobbed Veronica.

He held her tight for a moment and then eased her away to look into her tear-filled eyes. 'Don't be. You are the one who matters. Always remember that I love you. We will have a good life with Sylvia.'

She nodded, brushed away the tears and said, 'You are so wonderful.'

During the following days they found solace in each other's arms until their minds were settled to accepting the news and they were prepared to break it to their families.

After they had told Catherine and Charles, Veronica said to her mother, 'I want to take up my Land Army work again.'

'There's no need,' Catherine started to point out

'There is – I want to.'

'What about Sylvia?' asked Catherine. 'In my official capacity, I can't give you the necessary time off to look after her. The same thing applies to Michael's mother who is helping us now.'

'I'm not asking for time off. I've seen Mrs Harrison about her daughter Lucy.'

'You mean, to look after Sylvia?' Catherine could not disguise her shock. 'She's far too young.'

'She's older than her years and very capable, after helping her mother with her younger siblings. Mrs Harrison was in agreement and the extra money will help her too. I have it all arranged. The only thing that stands in my way is your power, as the person in charge of this section, to refuse to sign me back on as a member of the Women's Land Army. I beg you, please don't turn me down.'

Catherine looked doubtful. Veronica knew that behind that look all sorts of considerations were being weighed in her mother's mind.

After what seemed a long time but was only a matter of minutes, she said, 'I see you are determined. What I will allow is for you to work part-time alongside the others.'

'Do you think that will work?' Veronica queried.

'I see no reason why not. They're a good, tolerant and understanding bunch. Besides you will be working on our estate, so in effect I am employing you privately. Officially you will not be a member of the WLA but you'll be doing the same work, which I think is what you have in mind.'

'That suits me. Thank you so much.' Veronica gave her mother a hug. Catherine knew from the light in her daughter's eyes that she had done the right thing and recognised it as part of the road to a full recovery from Veronica's difficult pregnancy and the trials of first motherhood.

'You must promise me that if you find the arrangement detrimental to Sylvia's welfare, you will give up work to look after her yourself?'

'Of course I will,' replied Veronica, with undisguised delight.

On hearing Veronica's two pieces of news, Marie expressed her sympathy that there would be no playmate for Sylvia, and her joy that Veronica would be rejoining her alongside the other members of their WLA section.

On her first day back Veronica received an exceptionally warm welcome from them all. The atmosphere among them had changed. The little cliques that had formed initially had disappeared and the young women mixed more freely. 'We're all doing the same dirty jobs, no matter what our background,' was the prevailing mood. Camaraderie was much more evident as lives were drawn closer by the dictates of war.

Veronica and Michael adjusted their way of living according to their change of circumstances and thrust aside thoughts of what might have been. Adoption slipped from their thoughts as they became more and more interested in the land after deciding that their future lay there

Catherine and Elspeth were particularly pleased about this because it meant Veronica and Michael would be staying close to home. The Women's Land Army was growing in strength and showing that, along with other occupations, women could be seen as capable of doing many of the jobs which had been regarded as fit for men only. With this came a newfound freedom, especially for young women ready to cut their ties with home, but Veronica and Michael were settling back to the life they knew.

Marie stopped mid-stride as she made her way back to the tractor she'd had to abandon when it spluttered to a stop. On this murky November day she was meant to start turning the soil before it lay fallow for the winter. She knew what the trouble was and found the spanner she wanted in the tool box then inclined her head to listen hard. No, she wasn't mistaken. Church bells! Their sound, not heard for four years, now seemed to ring all the more sweetly.

'It's over!' she whispered to herself. 'It's over!' she yelled out loud, and again as she jigged around the forlorn tractor. With a couple of turns on the offending nuts she had the petrol flowing again. The field was forgotten as she gunned the engine and directed the tractor towards the place where she knew most of the young women were catching up on maintenance work, clearing the ditches. She saw them laughing, hugging and dancing with joy. It was then that she realised that she would be going home to France and would miss all these people who had helped her to settle and adapt to life here. She felt that a curtain was being drawn across this part of her life, closing off the past and with it the memory of Jeremy. She pushed away the melancholy feeling, jumped off the tractor and ran towards the excited welcome they gave her.

They heard a car and saw Veronica's father, waving one arm out of the window, driving fast along the lane beside the field. He pulled to a halt at the entrance to it and jumped out. He was laughing and shouting the news, confirming that the war had ended.

'Back to the house! Mrs Attwood's getting a celebratory drink ready and then work is finished for the day.'

The women all cheered and set off for the house, wondering if other land girls were being similarly well treated.

As they began to disperse after their drinks, Catherine told them they should all continue to report for their various assignments until she had word from headquarters as to what would be happening in the future.

After they had seen them off and Veronica was about to head back to Rushbrook, Marie said, 'Can I walk with you?'

'Of course,' she replied.

They linked arms and set off.

'You are looking serious,' Veronica observed.

Marie gave a smile and apologised. 'Sorry. This means I'll be going home.'

'Do I detect a note of regret?'

'Well, we've been together a long time.'

'Yes. And we've become close.'

'I'll miss you,' said Marie

'Me too,' agreed Veronica. She squeezed her friend's arm. 'But we'll still be friends and see each other as often as we can.'

'I know that, but it feels as if I'll be leaving something of myself behind.'

'You mean because of Jeremy?' asked Veronica sympathetically.

Marie stopped and looked questioningly at her friend. 'You knew?'

'I had been friends with you long enough to guess how you felt.'

'Did he say anything?'

Veronica detected a hopeful note in Marie's voice. 'Not in so many words, but I knew my brother better than anyone and I know that one day he would have asked you to marry him. Alas, that was not to be.'

Tears started to roll down Marie's cheeks. Her lips tightened and she cried out, 'Damn the war, damn it! Why did it have to take him from me?' Then she fell against Veronica and sobbed.

Veronica let her cry until her immediate heartache had been washed away, but she knew Marie would always feel regret. As she pressed her friend to walk further, she said, 'You must push thoughts of Jeremy aside; not altogether because you will always remember him, but you must let him fade in your memory. Remember, he would not want you to be miserable. He would want you to get on with life.'

'With Jacques, I suppose, to please Father.'

16

'Goodbye, Marie. You know you will always be welcome at Brunton,' said Catherine as she took the young woman into her arms on the platform at York station.

'Thank you, Mrs Attwood. You have been extremely kind to me ever since I went to the convent – that seems so long ago; a lifetime really.'

'You have been a good friend to Veronica and I'm grateful for that.'

'So am I,' said Charles, stepping forward to embrace Marie. 'Don't forget us.'

'As if I could.' She kissed him on the cheek, holding back the tears that had risen in her eyes.

But she released them as she watched the two older people walk away to leave Veronica and Marie to themselves.

They stood in silence, looking at each other for a moment with no words to express what lay deep in their hearts. Then they flung their arms around each other.

'Oh, I'll miss you so much,' said Veronica.

'And I'll miss you too. You have been a pillar of strength to me,' said Marie appreciatively.

Veronica knew she was referring to the months after Jeremy was lost to her, and knew Marie was still not truly reconciled to the idea of marrying Jacques. 'I'll always be here for you. If you need a shoulder ... no, I hope there will be no tears. All I want for you is happiness.'

A rumble heralded the approaching train. Both felt a deep pang at parting, not knowing when they might see each other again. They hugged. Silent tears flowed. The train fussed to a hissing, clanging stop. Doors opened, passengers emerged to hurry towards the exit, oblivious to the heart-rending parting taking place close by. One last hug. Marie picked up her travelling bag and turned to the open carriage door. Once on board she closed it, let the window down, leaned out and held out her hand to Veronica, who took it in a tight, loving grip. No words were spoken.

Doors left open were slammed shut by porters striding along the platform. A whistle blew, a green flag was waved. The engine hissed and clattered into motion. Still holding Marie's hand, Veronica walked alongside until finally the train's gathering speed forced a separation. Fingers slid apart. A few more paces then Veronica stopped. Eyes held until even that contact was no more. Veronica watched until the train was lost to sight.

Marie leaned back in her seat. Two other occupants, a man and a woman, gave her cursory glances and settled back to their books which she assumed they had been reading since boarding the train at a more northerly station. She was thankful for that; she wanted to be left to reflect, and endeavour to come to grips with her emotions.

She tried to anticipate the world to which she was returning – returning? No! That world had gone for ever. War had torn it apart. Her life too. It had let her glimpse true love and then ripped it from her. She would never regret that short-lived glimpse, but she would lament never expressing her feelings freely to the man she had loved.

She would have to see Jacques again. She had a great respect for him, but love? Maybe the passage of time and marriage to him could bring love. She knew from the letters she had received since leaving home that he loved her, and the two families would be happy when the long-anticipated wedding took place.

The train ran on, metal against metal, with a clickety-clack, clickety-clack, that became wedding-day, wedding-day.

'No! Not yet! Not yet!' Marie woke with a start to find the other passengers staring at her.

The lady smiled sympathetically; the man was nonplussed. 'Dreaming, my dear?' the woman asked.

Marie's face reddened with embarrassment. 'Sorry.'

The man was already reading his book again.

The woman nodded and returned to hers, leaving Marie to ponder on the thoughts that had brought the protest to her lips. By the time she reached Calais the next day that 'Not yet!' had become a constant refrain, her resolve for the future.

'Marie!' Margaret Gabin held out her arms to her daughter.

'Mama!' Marie dropped her bag and ran to her mother.

They hugged, joyful to be back together again. Henri, proud of the two women in his life, looked on patiently while passengers from the ship streamed past them. Then Marie turned to him. 'Papa!' She kissed him on both cheeks. Still holding her hands, he stepped back to see her better.

'It's been so long. Just look at you. A beautiful young lady. Isn't she, Margaret?'

'I'm envious,' her mother replied with a smile.

'Come, the car awaits you,' said Henri.

'I'll take your luggage, mam'selle.'

Marie turned to see Alain.

'Alain! It's good to see you.'

'And to see you too, mam'selle. Welcome home.'

As they all started for the car, Marie thought, This is typical. Papa using his influence to park a car where no one else, apart from port officials, can!

Within a few minutes they were heading for Paris.

'How are Roland and Claude?' she asked.

184

'They are both in good health. Claude has fully recovered and is back supervising the vineyards,' said her mother.

'Roland's contribution to the war effort was magnificent,' put in Henri with undisguised pride. 'He was commended by the Government.'

'Where did he serve?' Marie asked.

'No, no, he didn't join the Army. I got him exemption on the grounds that he was vital to the production of war materials in our factory.'

'You never mentioned that in any of the letters that reached me.'

'I thought it best not to. Such information might not have sat well with the Attwoods while their son was serving.'

'Not only serving, Papa, but being killed!' snapped Marie.

'I know, that was tragic. But in a war...'

Margaret, sensing that her daughter was about to argue, laid a gentle hand on her arm. Marie bit back her words. She knew her mother's touch signalled that she should not let her emotion surface in front of her father.

'We are going to have a welcome-home party for you with just the Martineaus and a few friends,' Henri announced. 'They are eager to see you, especially Jacques, but I explained, and they understand, that after so long away, you will need time to adjust.'

'Thank you, Papa. That is considerate of you. I'd like to get used to France again.'

The rest of the way home was spent in the exchange of news and chatter about friends.

When they stepped out of the car, Henri smiled

185

at Marie. 'Welcome back to your home. We managed to preserve it just as it was. You will think you have never been away.'

Marie did not reply to that observation, thinking, But I have been away, seen a different life, lived through a war; I have been scarred by a lost love, I have grown up; I'm a young woman with her own thoughts, her own desires. One day they may fall in with your ideas for me, but first...

Her thoughts were interrupted when her brothers appeared and another joyful reunion took place, with the two men surprised that they were now facing an attractive young woman with an aura of self-assurance in place of the shy schoolgirl they had last seen.

A servant had appeared from the house when they arrived. Now he took Marie's case, saying, 'Welcome home, mam'selle. Your main luggage arrived yesterday and has been put in your room.'

'Thank you,' replied Marie.

When they reached the house Margaret said to her, 'Off you go, freshen up after your journey. I'll be with you in a few minutes. We'll all have refreshments together in half an hour and dinner will be at the usual time.'

Margaret found her daughter sitting in front of her dressing-table when she joined her.

She took her mother's hand as Margaret sat down beside her, both of them savouring being together again. 'I had a quick look round when I came upstairs. Nothing's changed,' Marie commented.

'We were lucky. Left unmolested. Buildings don't change, though those who occupy them do.'

186

'You mean Papa?'

Margaret hesitated. 'Yes. It's no use pretending otherwise. I think there were moments in the car when you sensed it.'

Marie gave a little nod. 'There was a certain sharpness in his voice now and again, and at times he seemed irritated and agitated – not with us but when expressing his opinion about the people and things we talked about.'

'You are quite right. You'll have to remember that the war has changed him. There are times when you won't think so; you'll see the loving side still there, but more often than not it has been swallowed up by ambition and his desire to continue along the path the war took him on.'

Marie frowned as she asked, 'How do you mean?'

'He took advantage of the conflict to make money, expand the business. All legitimate, of course, but he did use his influence at the expense of others. He was shrewd enough to cultivate the right people in politics and industry to help him. Oh, he did well without any wrongdoing, I can't deny that.'

'But he prospered amidst other people's sufferings?'

'You shouldn't look at it that way. He prospered while helping to defeat our enemies.' Margaret left a little pause. 'But it changed him in many ways. It made him more ruthless ... but always with his beloved business in mind. There were those who realised its potential, especially in time of war and in the rebuilding that must come to protect ourselves in the future; they wanted to

187

take it over, seize it for themselves, but your father beat them off. I admire him for that but do not admire some of the actions he took to do it. I suppose the factory was, and is, dear to him, and of course he had the welfare of his family in mind too. I can tell you, the way he has put the business on a solid foundation, our whole family will want for nothing, especially if there is a partnership with the Gabin family.'

She looked hard at her daughter. 'I must say this, Marie. I don't think he has come to terms yet with the fact that you are no longer the young girl who left us, even though outwardly he sees a fine young woman. He'll come round. He'll see you for what you are. But remember, he also sees you as the key to his ambitions.'

'You mean, by making an alliance between Jacques and me?'

'Yes. And because of the changes in him, he might be adamant and dictatorial about the way your life should go.' Margaret dampened her lips. 'But, my darling, don't be bowed by his attitude. It is your happiness that is important and I will do all I can to preserve it.'

'Thank you, Mama, for telling me this. I think it will make things easier for me. I don't want to rush into my new life, at least not yet.'

Margaret deemed it wise to leave Marie on her own for most of the day, to get used to being back in the house after so long away. Marie appreciated the thoughtfulness and found the experience comforting.

As she got ready for the evening her mind

wandered back to Brunton Manor, Rushbrook Hall and Jeremy. It was only two days ago that she had left Brunton Manor and yet it seemed so long ago – a different life. What would it have been like for her had Jeremy lived?

She sat down slowly on her bed, her mind still dwelling uselessly on what might have been, lost in time, until she heard a gong and knew she should be going down.

She stood up slowly, looked at herself in the cheval glass, primped her hair and smoothed her pale green dress with its slightly high waist, the line curving over her hips to a calf-length hemline. She liked its easy fit and now, as she looked at herself, knew she had been fortunate that Mrs Attwood had been skilful enough to alter a dress she had worn only once, to match the new fashion that had evolved in Paris in the last two years of the war. Marie thought she might surprise everyone when she went downstairs. It felt good.

Reaching the door, she paused and looked back into the room. 'I'll miss you, Jeremy.' She stepped out on to the landing, a movement that marked the beginning of a new life for her.

17

The following morning Marie's first thought when she came out of a deep sleep was Where am I? She felt so comfortable; the bed was so soft. She snuggled down sleepily.

Light flooded into the room. Marie started, came awake, and shielded her eyes against the brightness.

'Good morning, *ma chérie*.' The voice was soft, the tone apologetic. It drove sleep from her mind. Mother!

She pushed herself up in bed. 'Mama.'

Margaret Gabin chuckled as she sat on the mattress. 'I thought you wouldn't want to sleep all day.'

'What time is it?'

'Midday.'

'What?' Marie was shocked. 'Oh, dear. I must be up.'

'There's no need to rush,' her mother said.

'Oh, but...' She let the words drift away and sank back against the pillows. Her mother was right.

'Travelling must have tired you. I nearly let you sleep longer but I thought you'd like some luncheon.'

'Oh, yes, I suppose so.'

'Right, in an hour then.' Margaret stood up. 'Papa sends his love. He'll see us this evening, as will your brothers; they're about their various occupations.'

'Is all well with them?'

'Oh, yes. They are pleased to have you home. I suggest you and I just spend the rest of the day here relaxing. Tomorrow I think we'll go into Paris and get you fitted with some new clothes: dresses, shoes and evening outfits, the best of the ready-made, and then fittings for haute couture – whatever you desire. I'm not criticising the dress

190

you wore yesterday evening, Mrs Attwood had done a splendid job with it, but you will need a completely new wardrobe. So we'll have fun tomorrow.'

That was exactly what they did. Marie was surprised by how quickly many of the shops had returned to near normal after the war, making best use of the materials they had managed to obtain. 'As soon as signs of victory were showing, they prepared for the moment when they could display their new creations,' explained her mother. 'Even with the signs of conflict still evident, people wanted to throw off austerity as soon as possible.'

Though Paris seemed quickly to have taken on the mantle of peacetime, there were signs of the recent conflict that could not be ignored; men still in uniform seeking pleasures they had missed for so long, or merely absorbing once more the atmosphere of the city that was so close to their hearts. Some were in civilian clothes, with arms in slings or patches over their eyes; others in rickety wheel-chairs, holding out begging bowls. But along the crowded boulevards, healthy men and women bustled to reinstate the world they once knew. Soon, for the uninjured at least, the war would be a distant memory.

Over lunch in Paris, Margaret broached the subject of meeting the Martineaus. 'They are our closest friends and I know they are anxious to see you and get back to how we were.'

'We can never do that, Mama. There's been a war. I've been away nearly six years. Things have changed.'

Margaret caught the tremor in her daughter's voice. She reached across the table and took Marie's hand in hers. 'Did you have feelings for Jeremy?'

Marie hesitated, on the point of denying it. Then, almost overwhelmed by the situation and needing to share her feelings with her mother, she nodded. 'Yes.'

'Oh, my dear, your father sensed it when the Attwoods visited, but I thought he was exaggerating.'

'I know he suspected my feelings when he made a veiled reference to what he saw as my obligations to him and to the family.'

Margaret seemed taken aback by this. 'I didn't know that he had spoken to you about what he sees as your duty. I wish you had told me.'

'I thought you would know.'

'No. Your father never mentioned he had spoken to you about that side of your future.' Annoyance showed in the tightening of her lips. Then she relaxed, an expression of sympathy on her face. 'I'm so sorry about what happened to Veronica's brother.'

'There's nothing we can do about it. Don't fret, Mama. Jeremy will remain alive in my memory, but that won't affect the rest of my life. I'm glad you know how I felt but I must ask you to keep it to yourself. There is no need for anyone else to know. Life goes on. Please arrange for the Martineaus to visit. I'm sure when Jacques and I meet it will be as it was before except that now we are both a little older and with more experience. That should help to bring us closer.'

Margaret pressed her hand with deep affection.

'You do not have to take up where you left off just to please your father.'

'I know what he has his heart set on and his dreams would be shattered if I didn't marry Jacques.'

'You don't have to do that just to satisfy your father. Your happiness means a lot to me. If you have any doubt at all about you and Jacques, please tell me.'

Marie gave a wan smile.

'Promise me, Marie, promise me?'

'Of course I will. I promise. But I think everything will be all right.'

'Remember, it's a long while since you've seen him. You will both have changed – that's inevitable given the momentous times we've lived through.'

'I'll remember, Mama.' She gripped her mother's hand in reassurance. 'Don't forget, your little girl has grown up.'

Margaret gave a jolly laugh. 'As if I could. Just look at you ... assured, sophisticated, beautiful. You'll be the centre of attention when the Martineaus and a few of our special friends come to welcome you home.'

Marie nodded approvingly at herself in the cheval glass. The evening dress she had chosen in Paris was of simple style, loose-fitting, with sleeves partially slit to give them an attractive see-through effect. The rich brown silk velvet was patterned in an intricate Renaissance motif, with a matching belt tied loosely at the waist. Marie picked up a string of pearls and fastened them in place to ease the severity of the dress's round neckline against her pale skin. She slipped her silk-stockinged feet into light brown high-heeled pointed shoes and moved her toes around to accommodate them.

One last pat of her hair and she headed for the door. She paused with it ajar and listened. Not a sound. She glanced at her tiny wrist watch. Almost time for the Martineaus to arrive. Then there was the sound of an approaching car. It slowed and came to a halt. Doors opened. Doors shut. Voices. Mama. Papa. Words of welcome. Footsteps coming into the hall. Marie could picture it all. Maids in attendance to take charge of outdoor apparel. Menservants to dispense warm welcoming punch. The war seemed a million miles away. How quickly her parents had managed to slip back into the old ways and yet even from here she could sense them looking forward too, adapting the old ways to the new. Even so soon after hostilities had ended a feeling of joie de vivre had crept back. Marie inclined her head. Conversation was flowing. Now was the moment.

She opened the door and stepped on to the landing. She paused at the head of the stairs, but only for a moment to take in the scene below. No one had as yet looked up. She started down slowly, with deliberate steps. The movement caught the attention of those below. Conversation was replaced by gasps of surprise, wonder and admiration. Then the silence was filled with a new magic that emanated from the beautiful young lady making her stately, eye-catching entrance.

194

Immediately she reached the bottom step everyone started to clap and in a few moments cries of admiration filled the hall.

Henri, the light of approval bright in his eyes, came forward quickly. He took her hand and proudly said, 'Everyone, please welcome home my lovely daughter. We have missed her.'

Clapping broke out again and then the guests made their own individual greetings.

Jacques held back but his eyes never left Marie until finally he had her to himself. He gave a smile of pleasure as he took her hand and raised it to his lips.

'You look wonderful,' he said. 'The girl I last knew has turned into a beautiful woman.'

Marie could not mistake the sincerity in his tone. 'I thank you for those words,' she said, 'and they come from someone who looks far from shabby himself.'

He was pleased she admired his perfectly fitting black dinner jacket and exquisitely tailored trousers, white waistcoat, white shirt and black bow tie. The cut of his clothes showed off his athletic figure, and the way he held himself seemed to lend him extra height. His eyes were lively but always directed steadily at the person to whom he was talking, giving them the feeling that they were, at that moment, the most important person in the world to him. Marie felt that too, and was flattered.

'Now the praises are over,' she said, 'hello Jacques, it's good to see you after all this time.'

He returned her smile. 'Hello to you too.'

'It seems we'll have to get to know each other

again,' she commented, holding his gaze.

'You left home a schoolgirl about to blossom, and have returned a very attractive young lady. It will be my pleasure to get to know that person. Maybe I could start tomorrow.'

She gave a little smile. 'You waste no time, Jacques Martineau.'

'It would be a sin to waste time where a beautiful young lady is involved.'

She accepted his compliment with a slight inclination of her head. 'Jacques, I am flattered. But I have to get used to being back home. I have to get to know France again and learn what the war has done to her, and that means to you and to everyone dear to me, so, please, don't rush me.'

'My dear Marie, your wish is my command.' He raised his glass to her.

'Now please excuse me, I should start circulating.'

He gave a little bow of acceptance. 'As long as we are not apart too long.'

She slipped away without comment.

As she passed from one group to another she experienced pleasure at what she saw as a new beginning for her, but reminded herself she owed much of her good fortune to her English friends. Friends? she asked herself. No, they were much more than that to her and always would be.

The evening passed with much gaiety, and the guests left still under the spell of Marie's charm.

As he was making his farewell, Jacques said, 'It has been a delight to be with you this evening. May I call on you soon?'

'Of course,' she replied. 'But please give me two weeks. I need to think about what I am going to do with myself.'

'Very well, Marie, but they will be barren days for me and I will hope only to be part of your new future.'

She made no comment to this but said, 'I'm sure you have more to your life than that.'

The next morning at breakfast, which was an informal meal, Marie was pleased to find only her brother Claude in the dining room.

'Are you going to the vineyard this morning?' she asked.

'Yes, Marie,' he replied. 'Why, do you want to come?'

'If you'll put up with me?'

'It will be my pleasure. Give us the chance to talk. We haven't managed very much of that since you came home.'

'That's what I thought too.'

'Right, let's make it straight after breakfast. I've looked outside. It's a nice morning but on the cold side. Wrap up well.'

An hour later she was getting into the front passenger seat of an old car, purchased by her brother when he'd left the Army at the end of the war.

'Always get Cook to pack me a lunch,' said Claude as he was depositing a picnic basket on the back seat. 'I asked her to make it special today.'

'It's a bit cold for a picnic.' Marie gave a little shiver to emphasise her comment.

'Remember the old building Papa turned into an office and workplace close to the vineyards? Well, it's more comfortable now, so you won't freeze.'

'Did the vineyards suffer much during the war?'

'Fortunately, very little. Father was lucky enough to find men too old for military service to take over when the younger employees left to join the Army. They managed quite well and some wanted to stay on after the war when the younger men who had survived returned.'

Half an hour's drive brought them to the vineyards.

'Have you much to do today?' she asked, as he helped her from the car.

'Not a lot. I have to keep my eye on pruning at this time of the year. I have nearly completed that, so I'll have time for you.'

She studied him while he examined some of his recent pruning and added to the impressions she had gained of him since coming home. Physically he was no different from the young man she had last seen before the war, but she saw the marks left by that terrible conflict in the lines of strain in his face.

'Was it bad, Claude?' she asked with tender concern.

There was no need for him to ask to what she was referring. 'Yes,' he replied quietly.

She saw his troubled expression. 'Want to talk about it? Would it help?'

'You don't want to hear about the horrors.'

'I don't mind. It might help me.'

He looked at her curiously for a moment, then,

198

seeing a distant look come to her eyes, said with surprise, 'You and someone...?' He left the question hanging.

'Well, there was a possibility with Jeremy. It hit me hard when I heard he had been killed,' she said quietly. 'I couldn't fathom my emotions, still have some difficulty doing so. Claude, please help me try and understand. You are the only one in my family who can.'

'Didn't the Attwoods...?'

'Of course they did. They'd lost a son, and Veronica a brother. But they're not my family. Mother tried to help me, but you have experienced the horror, so please...'

He took her hand. Oblivious to the cold they strolled through the vineyard, finally reaching the office where they settled to enjoy their picnic.

When he had finished relating his experiences she understood him better than she had done before. He had grown in stature in her eyes, showing a depth of consideration for those who had served and for those who had lost loved ones which was impressive.

'Claude, thank you for that; it has been a big help. I understand some things, particularly my own feelings, more clearly.'

'Marie, it is I who should thank you for listening. It has done me the world of good too. Now I won't dwell so much on what happened, knowing you at least have tried to grasp all its horrors and emotions.'

'But you and I should remind ourselves that the people we mourn for would not want us to be miserable. Let's remember them without mourning. Get on with our lives and keep young in heart and mind.'

'You are right, Marie, so right. I feel a weight has been lifted from my shoulders.'

'Then we have both benefited. Have you never talked to anyone else here about this? Father ... Roland?'

'To Mother. She was sympathetic and to a degree helpful, but she has no real idea of all the horrors and I did not want to heap mine on her. Roland?' He gave a little laugh of derision. 'He would never listen. He thinks only of the factory, as does Father. Roland jumped at the chance when Father said he could get him exempt from Army service. He wanted to do the same for me but I refused. I didn't work in the factory and I didn't want to be part of a lie. Father was furious when I went off and volunteered. He threatened to cut me off completely but Mother smoothed that over. She's a strong person, Marie. Always remember that if ever you are in trouble. I think she had something to do with what happened when I came out of the Army too.'

'What was that?'

'Well, it seemed Father had forgiven me for defying him ... maybe he was proud of my Army service, I don't know ... and signed the farm and vineyards over to me. At the same time he gave me to understand that I had no call on the armaments business; that is to be all Roland's.'

'That's wonderful,' said Marie with an exuberance that pleased him. 'I'm so glad for you. So you are completely independent?'

'Yes, and I think that's a very good thing to be.'

200

He paused and then said, 'Oh, listen to me preaching to you.'

'Don't stop, Claude. I appreciate what you are telling me. It will help me settle back into life here.'

He gave a little shrug. 'Ah, well, I suppose there's no harm in forewarning you: both Father and Roland are changed men. They've become obsessed with the factory and turning out new instruments for the Army. They profited greatly from the wartime business, and from what I have heard they have been shrewd enough to maintain their association with the military so that their future and that of the factory are safe. And Monsieur Martineau and Jacques are tied in with this too. They are all out to make the most of the military situation as it develops.'

'Are you talking about another war?' asked an astonished Marie.

'No. God forbid that there'll be another, but all governments have to have an Army and Navy, and now no doubt an Air Force too, so there are still ways to profit from armaments – and the Gabin-Matineau alliance is there, ready to do so.'

'And I am to be used as a pawn cementing this alliance,' said Marie wistfully.

'Is that how you see it?' queried Claude, somewhat surprised. 'From our childhood days, even I thought it would be Jacques you married.'

'So did I until I met Jeremy, and that made me question my own mind.'

'Isn't there still a spark of affection for Jacques?'

'Maybe ... I like him a lot. I have seen some changes in him since I got back, but I don't think

201

they would be an obstacle. And he wants to see more of me.'

'Then why not?'

Marie smiled. 'It would make Father happy, and keep the peace between him and Mother. If I refuse he may well cut me off without a penny. I don't think I'd be strong enough to live in poverty, with no real skills to lift me out of it. And if Mother dared to support me to the slightest degree, I shudder to think what would happen to her.'

'You'll have to reach a decision some time. Why don't you and I live it up a little by visiting some Paris night-life before you decide?' suggested Claude.

'You sound as though you've seen something of it already?'

'I have. I come and go as I please now. Paris has burst into a new era, with people wanting to make up for lost time and enjoy days and nights free from war. So let's live a little before you are tied down!'

18

'Where are you taking me?' Marie asked her brother as he manoeuvred his car through the outskirts of Paris.

'To a small club that was renovated very well, as soon as the war finished.'

'You've been here before?'

'Yes.'

When he gave her no more information she realised he wanted to spring a surprise on her so did not press him further. Instead she asked, 'Has Roland been here with you?'

He gave a little laugh. 'Roland won't let Paris night-life distract him; he's too staid. But Father keeps him that way too. Being so preoccupied with the factory and winning orders, he never got the chance to spread his wings during the war. I suppose with much of the work secret, he had to be careful who he mixed with. And now that caution is habitual with him.'

'I'll see if I can shake him out of himself,' proposed Marie.

'I wouldn't try,' returned Claude. Realising he had been a little brusque, he tempered his tone and added, 'I don't think Father would approve of where I'm taking you.'

'I'll say nothing then. You are making it all sound so mysterious!'

Claude said no more, concentrating on driving cautiously through the narrow streets until, after a final turn, he parked the car with two wheels on the pavement behind a similarly parked vehicle. The street was dimly lit by three lights which struggled against the darkness weighing down the four-storeyed buildings that loomed above them.

Claude was quickly out of the car and opening the door for Marie. She swivelled in her seat and stepped out gracefully into a pool of light from a lantern placed above an adjacent door. The stillness was broken only by the distant sound of music played at a quick tempo.

'Through here.' Claude led her along a narrow passage and, as they neared a door on the right, Marie picked up the notes of a ragtime rendering of 'The Oceans Roll'. When the doorbell was answered by a short man whose face lit up on recognizing Claude, Marie felt more comfortable.

'Good evening, Marcel,' Claude returned. 'This is my sister Marie.'

Marcel stepped to one side, held the door open, smiled, and greeted her. 'Good evening, mam'selle. Welcome to La Corinne.'

'Thank you.' Marie's smile widened as she reacted to the jaunty rhythm of the music floating towards them. 'Your usual table is free, Monsieur.'

'Thank you, Marcel.'

'Mam'selle,' said Marcel, indicating he would escort her.

She followed him along the corridor, pausing at a small desk where their outdoor clothes were whisked away into a cloakroom. When Marcel opened a blue-painted door at the end of the corridor, the music hit them full force. Marie found herself in a room painted in a multitude of bright colours and crammed with people sitting around café tables or dancing on a small raised floor.

Marcel led the way around the back of the tables surrounding the dance floor, to an unoccupied one discreetly placed in a corner, but with a view of the floor and the four-piece band.

Marcel held a chair for Marie. As she sat down he said quietly, 'Enjoy your first visit, mam'selle, I hope there will be many more.'

She inclined her head in acknowledgement. When he had left, Marie looked shrewdly at her brother. 'You were acknowledged by a number of people here. Marcel fussed ... a table kept for you. You must come here often?'

Claude smiled. 'I can't hide anything from my sister.'

She laughed. 'Not if you so blatantly parade it.'

'I wasn't parading it on purpose.'

'That sounds as if you had another reason for bringing me here?'

'We agreed we should enjoy ourselves before you tie yourself down, so this is a first step.'

'I believe there's more to it than that.'

'You will see.'

Any further interrogation by her was interrupted by a neatly dressed young waitress who arrived and said with a warm smile, 'Good evening, Monsieur Gabin, nice to see you again.' She placed two glasses of champagne on the table. 'With Monsieur Marcel's compliments for the lady's first visit.'

'Thank you, Claudie,' said Claude, 'and please thank Marcel.'

'Yet another sign that you are well known here,' commented Marie. 'Come on, tell me about this place.' She had been tapping her hand to the rhythm of the music. 'It's all so exciting.'

'Though he's older than me, Marcel and I served in the same unit in the Army. He had this night club before the war, and, recognising that people would want to immerse themselves in pleasures they had been denied for years, lost no time in reopening it once peace was declared.'

'But this seems to be a rundown area.' Marie's inference was obvious. As she spoke, she cast a glance around her at the elegantly dressed customers.

Claude smiled. 'You've been away from Paris too long. The approach is not the best, especially at night, but as a matter of fact we are in one of the most elegant parts of Paris. Marcel is very particular about his clientele and keeps an exclusive membership who can, of course, bring guests.' He nodded in the direction of a party of ten. 'Nine of them are here as guests of the imposing man with grey hair. I have no doubt some of them would dearly like to become members, but by restricting the numbers in this way Marcel is able to observe his would-be clients and maintain an exclusive atmosphere.'

'All very commendable,' commented Marie. 'And I'm sure from what you have told me it will always remain a success.'

'I'm sure of it too. And I know Marcel intends to bring his two sons into the business when they grow up.'

'How old are they now?'

'Eight and nine, Pierre and Laurent. Nice boys, can be a bit wild – the exuberance of youth – but their mother, Paulette, a real charmer, has their measure. They'll turn out all right.'

'You sound fond of them?'

'I am. The whole family.' Claude hesitated momentarily then, feeling he shouldn't keep secrets from his sister, said, just as the band struck up with the gentle strains of 'My Melancholy Baby', 'I owe Marcel my life.'

'What?' Marie gaped at him.

'Afterwards.' He moved his lips without speaking and put one finger to them.

Marie was aware of a hush falling around the room and sensed an air of expectancy. The lights dimmed. A spotlight came on, directed at a door to the right of the band. They had reached the end of the first verse and, as the pianist effortlessly restarted it, the sound of someone humming came from the doorway. Into the spotlight stepped a beautiful young woman with cropped hair, whose sheer fitted black dress, falling to her ankles, showed off an exquisite figure. The only sign of any ornament was a string of pearls wound once around her neck and falling to the neckline of the dress that curved above her firm breasts. She carried a pair of long-sleeved white gloves, dazzling against the black.

Struck by the riveting sight, Marie raised her hands to clap, but lowered them when everyone around her remained silent. She realised no one wanted to spoil the spectacle.

The vocalist stopped humming and began to sing. Her clear diction effortlessly reached every corner of the room. The audience was entranced by the beauty of her voice. Marie shot a glance at Claude and saw that his expression went beyond enchantment. He couldn't take his eyes off the beautiful woman in black. Now Marie herself fell under the spell of this magical beauty whose thrilling voice seemed directed at each individual person in the room.

The song ended. There was a moment when it seemed to hang in the air. Then it was gone and in

its place there was clapping and shouts of appreciation that rapidly changed to cries for more.

The singer smiled, graciously accepting the
applause. She held up her hands in a gesture for
silence. After a few moments it came.

'Thank you,' she said. 'There will be more in a
few minutes, after I have said hello to my friends.'

There were no protests and Marie marvelled at
the respect the audience gave this person. 'Who
is this?' she whispered to her brother.

'Corinne Boucher, Marcel's sister-in-law.'

'Paulette's sister?'

'Yes.'

As they were speaking Marie saw Corinne
heading for their table, pausing now and then to
have a word with an admirer.

'Corinne.' Claude was on his feet, reaching out
to take her hand. They came together and kissed
on both cheeks. Marie was struck by the light in
Corinne's deep blue eyes. She saw love and respect for Claude, which was reciprocated by him.

'Corinne, I want you to meet my sister Marie.'

They exchanged kisses.

'I've heard so much about you, Marie. Claude
is so proud of you and now here you are. This
meeting is a great joy to me.'

In return Marie decided to go for the truth. 'I'm
sorry to say he has never mentioned you to me.
You have been his well-kept secret.' She glanced
at Claude. 'That was wrong of you, Corinne de-
serves better.'

The newcomer smiled at the admonishment
and placed her hand on Marie's arm. 'Don't hold
it against him. He would have his reasons.' She

turned to Claude and teased, 'I hope you weren't ashamed of me?'

'You know I could never be that,' he said, blushing with embarrassment. He turned to Marie to explain, 'I wanted it to be a surprise for you.'

'It was certainly that, but what a wonderful surprise! Corinne, I hope you and I are going to get to know each other better.'

'Shall we start immediately I finish here? Come home with me and meet my sister and her two boys. You'll have met my brother-in-law when you arrived?'

Marie glanced at Claude and received his approval in an almost imperceptible nod.

'I'd love to,' she returned.

'Good. I must get back to the band. People will get restless if I keep them waiting too long.'

'Rightly so,' said Marie. 'You have a wonderful voice.'

Corinne smiled. 'Thank you, but I only make the best of what God gave me.' She pressed Marie's hand and slipped away as she said, 'See you later.'

As Claude sat down, Marie said, 'Now I know why you were treated as you were on our arrival. Marcel...' She looked at Claude, realising she did not know his friend's full name.

'Fontaine,' he said.

'Marcel Fontaine.' Marie savoured the names. 'They have a nice ring together and seem to fit him perfectly. I must thank him for what he did for you.'

'He won't tell you much. He'll only say it was what anyone would have done.'

'Ah, a modest man, but I'll winkle it out of him, or there'll be something missing from my knowledge of my brother.'

These exchanges had been made quietly because Corrine had started singing again. Quiet came over the room, leaving the accompaniment of soft piano and gentle clarinet intertwining with Corinne's smooth, caressing delivery of 'Moonlight Bay'. As it moved smoothly into its second playing, people left their tables to dance.

'Shall we?' asked Claude.

Marie rose from her chair, stepped into his arms and followed his slow movements.

After a few minutes he said, 'You dance so well. Like the smooth drift of a falling feather.'

Marie laughed, pleased with the compliment. 'That's a fanciful description of my poor ability.'

'Don't be modest, Marie. Where did you learn?'

'You forget, I went to finishing school. Dancing was one of the accomplishments we had to learn.'

'Then you were well taught.'

The music stopped, people clapped, then the band swung into a fast jazz rendition of the American hit 'Swanee'. The tempo of the evening was set and, though there were quieter interludes for the dancers to catch their breath, the room rocked until the early hours of the morning.

'What a gift,' Marie observed, referring to Corinne's ability to switch the mood of her singing through every fresh interpretation of the music.

From the tone of her praise, Claude could tell his sister was under Corinne's spell, and that pleased him.

Later on, they accompanied Corinne to Marcel's

home where Marie received a warm greeting from his wife. When she realised that Corinne lived here too, she sensed she was in a happy and loving family home, one in which she felt comfortable and accepted. She knew Claude had found a treasure in this talented and lovely woman.

She remarked as much on their way home.

'I'm pleased you think that. I know I'm lucky and often think if it hadn't been for a German sniper I might never have become close to Marcel and would not have met Corinne. It's strange how things work out.'

'A sniper?'

'Poor shot. I'm still here.'

'Don't joke about it. You said Marcel...'

'Dragged me to safety before a second shot. Now you have it, you won't have to winkle it out of him.'

'Have you told Mama and Papa about this, and about Corinne?'

He gave a little shake of his head. 'No. I think she and the Fontaines may not be of the right social standing in Father's eyes.'

'They are as successful in their world as he is in his. I think you should tell him sooner rather than later. He would have some respect for Marcel, for saving you, and after all, he has given you the farm and vineyards. Maybe your war record has made him look at relationships with different eyes. Well, yours anyway. I doubt it's true in my case. He still expects me to marry Jacques, but don't let's think of that now. You and I still have some living to do.'

19

'A letter, mam'selle,' the maid announced as she came into the breakfast room.

'Thank you,' said Marie, taking the envelope from the silver tray. She glanced at the writing. Veronica's! She quickly slit the envelope open.

Dear Marie,

I hope you are well and that you are settling into your new life, or rather your old one brought up to date after all that has happened since you came to England. The war must have changed many things, but knowing you as I do I am sure you will soon slip back into your French surroundings.

I am pleased you are taking time to adjust and seeing something of the new France, with Claude for escort. The news of Corinne intrigues me and I wait to hear more of what sounds to be a developing friendship. I think you are wise to stand back and consider Jacques through adult eyes before embarking on closer contact with him. Think carefully, dear friend, your whole future is at stake.

Here, daily life on the two estates goes on much as you saw it. Of course, we all miss Jeremy badly. His loss has brought Mother and Father closer together and they draw much support from each other. I am pleased to say Sylvia is a great joy to them. It would be so easy for them to spoil her but they are sensible in the way they lavish their affection on her.

Michael is well at the moment but I am sorry to say that there are times when the horror of the trenches reaches out to him still. On those days he needs all the love and support I can give him. It does not help that his father is not well – his breathing is not good at times. As you know, Clive is not a person to remain idle and so he does not take easily to the days when he feels 'under the weather', conscious of them adding more to Michael's burden. I do what I can to help, thankful that we did some agricultural work at finishing school and with the Land Army. It is surprising how useful these experiences have become.

I think of you often, dear friend. Write soon. I cherish your letters.

Love,
Veronica

Jacques, in a bright mood, drove his sporty two-seater American LaFrance special Speedster towards Senlis. The two weeks he had promised to leave Marie to her own devices were up. Now he was determined to see as much of her as he could.

He stopped in front of the house and climbed out of the car, eyeing it with pride before he stepped quickly to the front door and yanked the bell-pull. A few moments later the oak door was swung open by a manservant. Recognising Jacques, he said, 'Good morning, sir.'

'Is Mademoiselle Marie at home?' asked Jacques.

'I believe she is in the breakfast room, sir.' The servant, knowing of the close friendship between the Martineau and Gabin families, dispensed with the more formal attention he would have given other visitors. He stepped to one side, allowing Jacques to enter, and closed the door as he said, 'I'll inform Mademoiselle Marie you are here, sir.'

A few moments later he returned to say, 'Mademoiselle Marie says please go in.' In anticipation of being admitted Jacques had already taken off his overcoat, gloves and cap, which the servant took.

'Jacques.' Marie, alone in the room, greeted him with a warm smile and held out her hand to him while remaining seated.

He took it and bent to touch her fingers with his lips. As he straightened, he said teasingly, 'The two weeks are up, Marie.'

She laughed. 'I never expected you to forget.'

'I'm here to claim some of your time.'

'You shall have it. I'm looking forward to us getting to know each other again.'

'From the little I've seen of you since your return, I think ... no ... I know it is going to be a journey full of pleasure and exciting discoveries.'

She laughed and said, 'You flatter me with your high expectations. Do sit down and join me in a cup of coffee. Or breakfast if you like?'

'I'll have some coffee, thank you.'

Marie rose from her chair, went to the sideboard and poured him a cup of hot, dark coffee.

'What have you been doing this past fortnight?' he asked.

'Shopping in Paris; visiting Mother's friends who were eager to meet the long-absent daughter.'

'No doubt those who knew you before were surprised to find that the imp they remembered is now a sophisticated charmer. What else have you been doing?'

'Enjoying the estate. I'm so pleased Claude now has the farm and vineyards in his own right.'

'I think it was a good move on your father's part. His vision for the company means he'll have less time to devote to agriculture. The factory is nearer to his heart and to Roland's, so everything is turning out well. New developments in optical instruments are providing us with many fresh opportunities that we believe will be to the advantage of both firms. The close relationship forged during the war can be very profitably continued.'

As he was talking Marie heard a new enthusiasm enter his voice. He could easily be carried away on the topic of factories, weapons and instrument production, it seemed. Once again her mind cautioned her, be careful Jacques' ambitions don't thwart your expectations of a loving marriage. Almost immediately she chided herself for thinking this way. Marriage had not been mentioned yet, but she felt sure it would be possibly soon. There and then she swore she would not be rushed. She would make the coming months a time of assessment and consideration.

'And what else have you been doing?' he asked.

'Claude introduced me to some night-life.'

'Where did he take you?'

'A small club called La Corinne, owned by Marcel Fontaine and named after his sister-in-law who sings there.'

'Ah, yes. I have heard of it, but I have never been.'

Marie noted a faint hint of disdain in his tone. About to voice her own opinion, she held back; something was telling her to keep the place to herself and let the Fontaine family remain her own private escape route.

'I shall show you some first-class places of entertainment and dining,' Jacques added with an air of superiority. He had the aura of a man who was very sure of himself, however, and Marie liked that. 'Let me take you for a drive now,' he suggested.

'A good idea,' she agreed enthusiastically. She rose quickly from her chair and he followed suit. 'No, wait, you finish your coffee. I'll go and get ready.' She was on her way to the door. 'I won't be long,' she called over her shoulder.

'Wrap up well!'

Marie raised her hand in acknowledgement and was gone.

He finished his coffee and a few minutes later returned to the hall where he recovered his outdoor clothes, donned the overcoat and waited at the bottom of the stairs.

Marie appeared shortly afterwards. She knew he was studying her as she came towards him but could only guess what he was thinking. The beige gabardine loose-fitting top coat she wore was drawn tight at its belted waist. Triangular-shaped lapels ran into a large collar which she had turned up but left open enough to teasingly reveal a white tie-necked blouse. She carried a brown fur cap and a long yellow scarf. 'See, I did as I was

216

told,' she announced.

'That augurs well for the future!' he replied.

She gave an amused smile. 'That's as may be.' She did not wait for a reply but opened the door and stepped outside. She stopped in her tracks then and gasped, 'We're going in this?'

He grinned as he stepped out beside her. 'That's what I came in and there's not another car in sight.'

Marie caught her breath and said, 'It's beautiful. Where and when did you get it?'

'I came across it during the war. Kept it in view until the end of hostilities and made an offer for it, a little over the odds, to make sure I got it before you came home.'

Her eyes lit up even more. 'Oh, Jacques, that was so thoughtful of you.' Marie flung her arms round his neck and kissed him on the lips.

His arms came round her waist and he held her a little longer, letting his kiss express his feelings. 'I want my pleasures to be your pleasures too. So, my dear, your carriage awaits.' He made an exaggerated bow and swept out his arm as he opened the passenger door. He helped her into the car, saw she was comfortable and climbed into his own seat. In a matter of moments they were speeding into the countryside, Marie with laughter in her eyes, relishing what a future shared with Jacques Martineau might hold.

That evening she wrote to Veronica:

Dear Veronica,
The two weeks I told you about were up today.
Jacques did not forget. He was here early, arriving in

his latest purchase – a sporty two-seater American LaFrance special Speedster. Red! Off we went. Drove to the coast. I tell you, we made a few heads turn. He was so proud of the car and wanted to show it off to me. I wonder what else he plans now my two weeks embargo is over. But I am going to be cautious; I'm not going to let him commandeer all my time. Besides, he'll have work to do.

I enjoyed my two weeks with Claude for an escort and intend to take up some more of his time if he'll let me. Meeting Corinne was a pleasure. Such a fascinating person. I hope Claude makes the best of his chance because I believe she thinks a lot of him.

I am sorry that Michael's father is not in the best of health. I hope it doesn't place too much strain on you both. I know you will be every support to him and his father, and Mrs Eakins is always so capable and helpful too.

Give everyone at Brunton and Rushbrook my love, but most of it is for you.

Your friend for ever,
Marie

During the next six months Jacques paid court to Marie, escorting her to high-class night clubs, dining with her in exclusive restaurants, taking her on shopping expeditions, promenading along the banks of the Seine and around the Bois de Boulogne, and driving the LaFrance Speedster into the countryside as far as the Normandy coast. Whenever she queried the time he was lavishing on her, he casually dismissed her questions, until one day when they had returned to the car after walking on the beach she raised the point again with more concern.

'Jacques, I really think you shouldn't be spending as much time with me. You must be neglecting your work to do so.'

'I neglect nothing at work. The factory is running smoothly, the staff are content. I work twice as hard when I am there, in order to have time with you.'

She leaned close to kiss him and said, 'That is sweet of you, and I do appreciate the time you spend with me. I am thoroughly enjoying every minute. You and my family have really made me feel at home in France again.'

'That pleases me.' He drew her closer. She saw adoration in his eyes. Their lips met and she sensed a new desire in their touch, and that desire was also in the tone of his voice as he said, 'Marry me, Marie. Make a permanent home with me.'

After six weeks the expectation of a proposal had been in her mind, but somehow any serious consideration of her answer had been obliterated by the whirlwind of enjoyment she was having.

'Jacques, I am flattered.'

He reached out and took her hand, in his mind urging her to give him the answer he sought.

'But,' Marie went on, 'I don't want to commit myself just yet. I'm so enjoying the time we are spending together as the best of friends.'

'I thought it was more than that,' he protested.

'I think it is, but I want to be really sure. I want to give you the right answer. I don't want to make a mistake that would spoil both our lives.'

'But I am devoted to you! What else can I do to prove it to you?'

'Oh, I don't know, Jacques. Please, give me a little more time. It's a big step for me. After all, I haven't been back very long. France and the whole world are still changing – who knows what that will mean for us?'

'You can't view our lives together...' he started, but she stopped him.

'Please, Jacques, just a little more time.'

His lips tightened. She saw a dark cloud of displeasure tinged with anger flash across his face, but it was gone almost immediately. 'Time?' he said amiably. 'You can have it. I'm going away tomorrow for two months. I'd hoped for an answer before I left. I'll have to hope for one when I get back instead.'

Marie was taken aback by his news. 'Going away? On business?'

'Yes.'

She began to feel annoyed. He must have known this before. Why wait until the eve of his departure to make what she regarded as an important step in their lives, almost forcing her into making a decision at once? Well, she didn't like being cornered.

Before she responded he said, 'Please try and realise that the business I run must succeed in order to secure our future together. I must attend these meetings; if they are successful I will be able to give you all the things you desire.'

'Why didn't you tell me before?' she demanded. 'You must have known.'

'I guessed how you might feel and didn't want to spoil our time together before I was due to leave.'

'You shouldn't have presumed you knew how I

would react. You propose to me and in the next breath walk off! How do you think that makes me feel?'

'I've just said, it's for your sake that I'm going.'

'Me? Don't use me as an excuse! You damned well know it isn't for me. It's to further your own bloody ambitions.' Marie's temper was rising. 'And don't look so damned shocked at my language, we pick up all sorts in convents and finishing schools. You'd blanch if you knew it all.'

'Marie, I'm sorry if I've hurt you. I didn't mean to. Please understand...'

Understand? she thought. Yes, I understand only too well. You are going to walk away at an important stage in our lives, assuming I will fall in meekly with your plans. Well, you'll have to learn that I have a mind of my own and will not be told what to do, by you or anyone else. Thank God for that finishing school education! At least I know how to stand on my own two feet.

She did not voice her thoughts. Jacques looked so contrite, and after all she knew her love for him was developing to a point where it would not be denied.

He broke into her thoughts. 'Please, Marie, don't be angry. I understand I haven't handled this very well. Of course I'll give you more time. Please have an answer ready for me when I get back. I'm sorry I won't be here for a while, but do enjoy yourself while I'm away. Only ... be careful where you go and who you go with. You've met a lot of my friends these past weeks; they are always around to escort you.' He paused then added, 'I really don't like you going to La Corinne.'

Protests sprang to her lips but she held them back. 'Drive me home, please,' she said calmly.

'But I'd planned for us to dine on our way back this evening.'

'Home,' she commanded.

The drive to Senlis was amiable enough, conversation desultory and without sparkle. Jacques put it down to the fact that she was dreading the coming weeks without him, but Marie was secretly furious at his assumption that he could tell her what she should do and whose company she should keep.

When he pulled up outside the house Jacques got out quickly and opened the car door. He grasped Marie's hand and swung her towards him. His lips met hers with a passion he made sure she would not forget, saying, 'Remember me when I am gone.' He broke away then, climbed into the car which he had left running, and roared away.

Marie stood watching the dust rise behind him then strode quickly into the house.

She shut the door and leaned back against it. In the silence, she tried to forget her annoyance but found she could not. Though Jacques had finally condescended to her request for more time, had she glimpsed a side of him she had not suspected before: a need to dominate? With that prospect facing her, she really did need time to think about his proposal. But now there was another aspect to it for her to consider. Could she handle his tendency to expect his own way in everything? Would her love for him, which had grown over the last weeks, be strong enough? Even as these challenging aspects of their relationship began to occur to her, she was angry that she had to consider them at all. Tight-lipped, she hurried to her room, threw on a jacket, and went to find Claude.

By the time she had reached the vineyard she had made a decision. She found her brother and said, 'Take me to La Corinne tonight.'

Though he sensed something was wrong, he knew Marie did not want to talk about it. 'Call for you at seven?'

'Ideal.'

Knowing him to be a perfect time-keeper, she was coming down the stairs when he walked into the hall.

'You look good,' he complimented her, appreciating her casual dress cut straight almost to mid-calf. The frills round the hem line matched those on the short sleeves. The straight neckline was plain, relieved only by a string of wooden beads of a darker shade of green than the dress.

'Thank you,' said Marie, giving him a wan smile on which he passed no comment. Something was still upsetting her. 'Let's go.'

'No Jacques tonight?' The question came from someone descending the staircase after her. They both turned round to see their father coming down.

'No, Papa. He has other plans,' Marie said quickly. Rather too quickly for Claude's liking.

Her father gave a quick nod. 'Don't neglect him,' he said.

A quick retort sprang to her lips but Marie held it back. It was no good asking for trouble. 'No, Papa,' was all she said, and turned to the door.

Claude, sensing his sister wanted to be away before any further comment from their father, opened the door. Marie was quickly out. He followed, saw her into the car and drove away.

Turning out of the gateway, he said, 'Something troubling you?'

'No.'

Ignoring her denial, he asked, 'Concerning Jacques?'

'I should have known you would realise.'

'And don't worry about Father; he won't have noticed. He's never attentive enough for that.' When she did not respond, he said, 'If you want to talk about it, you know I'm a good listener.'

She gave a little smile. 'And a good adviser. You always were my best friend when we were young.' She placed her hand on his arm. 'Thanks, Claude. It's nothing I can't handle. It will resolve itself.'

'If you need me, don't forget I will help.'

'You are good to me.' She gave a little shiver. 'Now let's enjoy ourselves.'

On arrival at the night club, they found several cars parked in the street.

'It's busier than usual for this time,' commented Claude.

'All the better,' Marie approved.

'Good,' he said, reading into her tone the implication that she wanted an exciting time, to take her mind off whatever had transpired between her and Jacques.

Marcel greeted them enthusiastically as he escorted them to their table. 'Managed to keep it free,' he said, 'but it could have become difficult.'

'Thanks,' said Claude.

'You are busy,' commented Marie.

'Old friends from my pre-war days,' replied Marcel. They live in Rouen but come into Paris every two months, to live it up and enjoy themselves for a week. They're a lively lot. They always have some hangers-on who I'll probably never see again, but that's their concern not mine; the regulars always come back.'

Drinks came. The tempo of the music quickened and filled the whole room with its heightened rhythm. No sooner had one piece of music finished than the band swept into the next, keeping the tempo going. It only changed when Corinne appeared to enchant the audience with her sultry renditions.

She came to the table when her first session drew to a close. Claude rose from his chair to greet her with a clasp of her hands and kisses to both cheeks. Marie saw they were oblivious to their surroundings and to everyone else in the room. This was what it should have been like for her and Jacques. It had been, she knew that, until today when he had spoiled it by his high-handed attitude. Then Corinne spoke to her, diverting her from her anger. The three of them chatted amiably, enjoying being together in listening to the lively music which heightened their spirits.

Then, with no word spoken and no gesture made, Claude and Corinne rose as one, stepped away from the table, came into each other's arms and glided in unison to the music of the band. Marie felt a pang of jealousy of their mutual understanding, without a word being spoken. Suddenly she felt regret for what had happened today. Maybe she was at fault. Maybe she should have been more understanding. She could have been if only Jacques had not given the impression that he was always right and things should have been done his way, there and then. She had wanted just a little more time before answering his proposal, but he hadn't really been willing to give her that one concession. She had seen how piqued he had been to agree to it. He still believed that men should dominate, and that angered her. Times had changed, the war had already seen to that, and they would change even more. She had had glimpses of that in England, and knew the new attitudes promoted by women's suffrage would gather momentum. Her lips tightened. Jacques had better realise that. Maybe his absence would give him time to realise she was not going to be an old-fashioned wife, attentive to his every whim, but had a mind of her own and would use it in this changing world.

'You look forlorn. Would you do me the honour of this dance and allow me to banish the blues I can see hovering over you?'

Marie was startled by the sound of a man's voice close to her ear. She glanced up at the speaker and found herself looking into a pair of startlingly light blue eyes that were insisting the speaker would not take no for an answer. He smiled at her and said, as he held the back of the chair vacated by Claude, 'May I sit down and enjoy your charms while you make up your mind?'

Marie, about to refuse, asked herself, What harm is there? She gestured to the chair; he smiled his thanks and sat down.

'What makes you think you can cheer me up?' she asked cautiously, though she was curiously intrigued by his approach and the challenge she sensed behind his offer.

'I'm an expert,' he said, his eyes holding her attention. 'I'll ask no questions about why you feel as you do, that is your private concern.'

While considering his words, Marie found herself wanting to know more about this man. He was not particularly handsome, more attractive in a rugged sort of way, with his brown hair immaculately groomed, a perfectly fitting grey suit that enhanced his athletic appearance, and long delicate fingers that seemed to tempt her to touch them. There was one way to do so without making that desire obvious – dance with him.

'Do you dance as smoothly as you talk?' she asked.

'There's only one way to find out.' He stood and held out one hand to her.

They touched and she felt a tingle that immediately drove away the uneasiness she'd been feeling since her bruising encounter with Jacques. Then, when he drew her into the pattern of his steps in time with the slow waltz, all the tension brought about by the earlier disagreement van-ished.

'What do you think of my dancing?' he asked.

'It lives up to your promise.'

'Then I am delighted.'

'You are...?'

'Oh, call me Pierre,' he said in an offhand way.

Realising from his manner that Pierre was not his real name, she responded with, 'And you shall call me Cinderella.'

He raised one eyebrow and smiled at her. 'Is that because you have to be home by midnight?'

'Something like that.'

'The gentleman you came with...?'

'My brother,' put in Marie in haste, wanting to assure him there was no other attachment.

'And he will expect to see his sister safely home.'

Marie was thankful that she detected no mockery in his tone, rather an acceptance of the situation, but he did say, 'I'll slip away before he returns, then he can ask me no questions, but the rest of my evening will be bereft of your company.' The tone he used only added to his mystery and made Marie want to meet him again, something she knew he reciprocated when he said, 'Where can I meet you tomorrow?'

'Seven tomorrow evening, outside the Hôtel de Ville in Senlis,' she answered without any hesitation. 'Father's away; Mother's visiting friends. Both of them will be late home.'

The music stopped. Dancers clapped.

'See you tomorrow.' He pressed her hand and hurried from the floor.

20

Claude asked Corinne as the music faded, 'See the man leaving ... he was dancing with Marie. Do you know him?'

'No, he's a stranger here. Probably with the party from Rouen. Don't be concerned, Claude.

228

She'll know how to look after herself.' During this exchange the floor had cleared of dancers and Marie had returned to their table. 'The band is waiting for me, I'll have to go,' said Corinne. 'See you soon.' She pressed his arm and hurried over to join the musicians. By the time he reached his table the first notes of a blues number were drifting plaintively across the room.

Claude slid into his chair. 'Did you enjoy that?' he asked casually.

'Mmm, yes,' Marie answered.

Knowing her brother, she was expecting the next question. 'Who was he?'

'I don't know. We didn't exchange names. He must have been here earlier because we only had those two dances and then he had to go. A pity because he danced divinely, and chatted pleasantly.'

Claude nodded; there was nothing more he could say except, 'Can I compare?'

Amused by his reaction to the stranger's attentions, Marie said mischievously, 'Let's find out!'

Snuggled down into her soft bed after an enjoyable night at La Corinne, which had extended into a Fontaine family party, Marie's thoughts strayed to the stranger. She could still feel his hands sending new sensations down her spine as he held her gently but with sufficient strength to lead her. He was so light on his feet that, coupled with his natural skill, he had drawn her into a world where nothing else seemed to matter.

It was easy to fall into daydreams of him, but one face kept on intruding. Jacques.

She shuffled in her bed, uneasy at the thought of him. But Jacques was away. Who knew what he might be doing? She didn't. Why should she have a conscience about what *she* was doing? And hadn't Jacques told her to enjoy herself? There had been a few 'buts', which could easily be ignored. Why shouldn't they be? She was still her own woman.

Thankful that her mother had been driven by Alain to visit friends to the east of Paris and was likely to return late, Marie slipped quietly from the house by a little-used side door. She pulled her shawl closer to her face and hurried away without seeming to be in haste. The pleasantly warm August evening had brought a considerable number of people out in Senlis on their way to visit friends or for an evening's shopping, a rendezvous or a quiet drink at one of the small cafés, but thankfully Marie saw no one she knew, though she would never know if she had been recognised as the daughter of 'those at the château'.

Her eyes searched the area as she neared the Hôtel de Ville, but she saw no sign of the stranger. Maybe he wasn't coming? No, that couldn't be, she told herself. Maybe I'm early. She slowed her pace a little. Reaching the corner, her heart skipped a beat. He was standing beside a car parked down a side street. He saw her, gave a small wave and moved towards her.

'Hello,' he said, taking her hand.

She wanted to cry out at his touch but all she said quietly was a shy, 'Hello.'

'I know you said the front of the Hotel de Ville

but I thought it was maybe wiser to meet here.'

She nodded, accepting his explanation with a smile.

'Good. Now let's drive away,' he said romantically.

'Where are you taking me?'

'Ah, you must wait and see.' He said it in a way that intrigued her, but lightly enough that she felt in no danger at all.

He saw her settled comfortably in the car, which she found herself comparing with Jacques'. This one was not quite as sporty in its looks, but it had a sense of comforting solidity and she soon found out that did not detract from its speed, which matched the Speedster's.

'Have you had a good day?' he asked.

'Yes, looking forward to this meeting.'

'If that is so, we are going to have a perfect night.'

'Evening,' she corrected him. 'I must be back before my mother – but she won't be home until the early hours.'

He smiled. 'So you are going to act like Cinderella as well?'

'It might be a good idea.'

'Ah, but who knows what the future will bring?'

She made no immediate reply. It seemed as though he wanted to keep their meetings completely anonymous, yet now he was hinting at a future. Who was he? What did he really want?

'Last night I detected you like dancing?' he asked.

'Yes, I do.'

'You would like to dance this evening?'

'It would be a pleasure,' she replied, anticipating being held by him again.

'Good. I'll take you to a place I know.'

Silence settled naturally between them, bringing them close rather than producing any awkwardness.

Marie judged they were heading in the direction of Meaux. Reaching the suburbs, 'Pierre' turned off the main road and on to a track that was signed 'Maison Ducasse'.

'I thought we had come dancing?' she observed.

'So we have, as you will see.'

He drove on. A turn in the track brought the building into view.

'Surprised?' he asked.

'I am,' replied Marie.

The complex before her bore all the signs of being a farmhouse with its accompanying buildings, but now they had all been joined into one unit.

'What is this place?' she queried.

'The farm was owned by Monsieur Albert Ducasse. His two sons were not interested in farming so he sold the farm without the buildings – made a lot of money from the sale and backed his sons' ambitions with it. They were just plain crazy about music. They could have made their names in almost any branch of it but chose popular music in all its forms. They decided to open this place and they have never looked back. Maison Ducasse is very popular, though not as widely known as it should be. A lot of people think you've got to go to Paris for this sort of entertainment, but the Ducasse brothers saw an opportunity to open up here and have been proved right.' While he had been speaking, he had driven round to the back of the complex.

'Well, it seems to be paying off,' commented Marie, on seeing the number of parked cars.

'You'll realise why when we get inside.'

He escorted her to the door. When they stepped inside, an atmosphere of well-being struck Marie. The furnishings, decoration, the positioning of mirrors and lights, all conveyed an impression of opulence aimed at cosseting a particular clientele, who enjoyed entertainment in the midst of luxury.

'Good evening, Monsieur Pierre.' A dapper middle-aged man in immaculate evening dress was greeting them.

So his anonymity is kept up even here, thought Marie.

'Good evening, Gerard,' her escort said.

'Table for two, sir?'

'Please. And this is Mademoiselle Cinderella.'

'I understand, sir.'

He led them to a room where the dance floor was surrounded by two rows of tables. When Gerard had seen them seated, he asked, 'Usual wine, sir?'

'Please.'

'And a table in the restaurant, sir?'

'Yes. Thank you.'

'You seem well known here?' commented Marie.

'I am.' He gave a little smile. 'Don't ever think of trying to find out who I am from anyone here, because you won't.'

'So you have everyone sworn to secrecy?'

'No need to. They know a good customer when

233

they see one. Now shall we forget who we are and enjoy our time together?'

While they had been speaking the band had moved from a foxtrot into some slow jazz that called them to match its tempo on the dance floor. They left their table and immediately moved as one, drawn together by the rhythm.

It was the same throughout the whole evening. They shared laughter, gaiety, allowed conversation to flow or recognised when moments of silence between them were more eloquent. They both enjoyed the chef's expertise when they chose to dine in the restaurant.

Marie was so enchanted by the evening that she lost all sense of time until Pierre said, 'Well, Cinderella, I think your visit to the ball is over. I should take you home.'

'Oh.' Her disappointment showed. 'Must you?'

He smiled. 'I must. I have a journey to make after I take you to Senlis.'

'Where might your destination be?'

He smiled. 'You will never know.'

She pouted. 'That sounds as if we will not meet again?'

'Not if you wish to meet next week?'

She paused, not wanting to appear too eager. 'Will it be another night like this?' she asked cautiously.

'Whatever you want.'

'More dancing, more fine food?'

'The pleasure of accommodating your wishes will be all mine.'

'If that is so then it would be wrong of me to deny you that pleasure,' she said, her eyes sparkling with promise, buoyed by the thought of another evening with him.

'Very well. Same place, same time?'

'Yes,' she agreed.

When they reached Senlis, she asked him to drop her at the Hôtel de Ville.

'But I should see you safely home.'

'I will be perfectly all right,' she insisted. 'If everything about you is to remain a mystery, then I will be similarly discreet.'

When he'd stopped the car, he was quickly out to open the door for her. As she straightened up, he took her hand in his and drew her gently to him. She did not resist but met his lips willingly. Her whole body came alive with a deep yearning, which heightened as he prolonged the kiss.

When he allowed their lips to part, he said, 'It has been a wonderful night. Let's not wait a week, let's meet again tomorrow evening?'

Thrilled by his suggestion and with the warmth of his arms still around her, making her feel special, Marie succumbed to desire. 'Let's,' she agreed.

She wanted to know more about him. Why he had imposed a condition of anonymity? Had he something to hide? Was he married? To find out more about him was imperative. Could she breach his desire to keep his life a secret? Had she made a start by not pressing him this evening? Could he be lured into a position where he let something slip?

As she snuggled down in bed later she lost herself in pleasurable reveries, recalling every facet of the man she had been with. When thoughts of

Jacques arose she experienced no qualms, telling herself that he had not been truly passionate in his proposal. But, she reminded herself, a marriage between them was expected; she would have a settled stable life with Jacques, want for nothing. In the same position with Pierre, she imagined life could be adventurous. After all, wasn't it filled with mystery and challenge even now?

Was she making problems for herself? Was she taking a decision that would affect her whole future? Or should she go along with the anonymity and break the relationship with Pierre once Jacques returned? He need never know of her liaison with the stranger.

The next evening, after leaving a note for her mother saying she had gone to visit a friend from the past, Marie hurried to the rendezvous at the Hôtel de Ville. She had just arrived when Pierre pulled up. She was into the car before he had time to get out.

She leaned across and kissed him. 'Where to?' she asked, her eyes bright in anticipation of the time ahead.

'Maison Ducasse?'

'Lovely,' she said, and settled herself more comfortably.

The atmosphere at the night club was even more lively than the previous evening. More people gave it an extra buzz and, recognising an appreciative clientele, the band excelled themselves, especially when playing jazz in all its forms. Marie was carried away by the change of rhythm and, under the expert guidance of Pierre, danced as she had never danced before. The flow of wine continued during their delightful meal. Marie expected to dance again afterwards, but Pierre did not return her to their table. Instead he said, 'Get your cloak, I've something to show you.'

She made no enquiry but pulled her cloak close around her and got back in the car. She watched the headlights slicing into the darkness. She had no idea of the direction they were taking, but the distance display told her they had travelled thirty kilometres before they pulled up at a cottage about a quarter of a mile beyond a village they had just passed through.

'Where are we?' asked Marie as he helped her out of the car.

'It doesn't matter. Here, hold my arm – the path is a little uneven.'

She did as she was told and was thankful she had when she stumbled, uncertain whether the path was the cause or the night air combined with the wine.

Pierre unlocked the door and took her inside. She got some idea of the room by the light of the fire burning in the large grate. 'Stay there,' he ordered. 'We don't want you falling over anything.' He turned to a small table close to the door and in a matter of moments had lit an oil lamp. He moved quickly round the room, drawing the curtains and lighting three more lamps.

Each extra light revealed more of a comfortably furnished room, with two large settees drawn at angles to one another at either side of an open fireplace. A low chest was positioned between them. The walls had been left with the stonework unadorned yet did not detract from the room's charm.

'This is lovely. Yours?' she queried.

'It belongs to a friend. Let me take your cloak.' He stepped behind her. She allowed it to slip from her shoulders. He took it and threw it on to the nearest settee. His hands came firmly down on her bare shoulders. Marie inclined her head backwards, revealing her throat. He ran his lips over it. She revelled in the sensation for a few moments then turned slowly in his arms to face him and devour him with her kiss.

When their lips parted he asked, 'Want to see more?'

She nodded. 'Yes, please.' The simplicity of the two words was overlaid with a seductive promise.

He picked up a lamp, led her to a door and opened it. They stepped inside the bedroom. In one movement he put the lamp down and pulled her into his arms. His lips found hers in a kiss she could not refuse. She wanted it to go on for ever.

Her passion heightened with every movement of his fingers, which were undoing the buttons of her dress. She did not stop him.

21

Lulled by contentment, Marie lay deep in her feather bed. Nothing that had gone before this evening mattered; nothing that was to come could spoil the wonderful hours she had spent in

Pierre's arms. She lay happily anticipating the next time, which had been arranged for the day after tomorrow, before drifting into sleep.

She woke in a panic. The dream that had taken her and Pierre floating on a soothing sea, beneath a sky of diamond stars, was shattered.

Jacques!

She sat up in bed, gripped by anxiety. Her heart beat faster, driven by her conscience. What had she done? Gone to bed with a stranger! She did not know Pierre ... who he was, where he was from ... yet she had given herself to him. Angry with herself, she drew up her knees and hugged them, trying to find some solace and a reason for what she had done. If only Jacques hadn't proposed and then in the same breath told her he was going away. Had she done what she had out of sheer bloody-mindedness? Had she thought she was getting back at him for his insensitive proposal? Or had she genuinely felt drawn to Pierre? She had held back from Jacques' proposal. Had she had a premonition? Was she not destined to share her life with him after all? The day after tomorrow might give her the answers.

Marie hurried to the Hôtel de Ville. An invitation from Claude to accompany him to La Corinne had delayed her. She hoped her reason for refusing had sounded plausible. Any doubts were banished when she saw Pierre standing beside his car. A brief greeting passed between them and in a matter of moments they were heading out of Senlis.

'Should we forego the dancing?' he suggested.

She quickly shrugged aside her disappointment. 'If you wish.'

'I've brought a picnic and champagne.'

'You've put some thought into this,' she commented.

'It's basic but I hope you'll like it.'

'I'm sure I will, because I'll be sharing it with you. I presume we are going to the cottage?'

'Yes. You seemed to enjoy it there?'

'I did. It's so cosy. Maybe we'll get to know more about each other this time.'

He made no reply but drove on in silence.

On reaching the cottage, he heaved a large wicker basket from the back seat. 'Bring the bottles.'

On reaching into the car, Marie queried in surprise, 'Six?'

The note of alarm in her mind was instantly dismissed when he laughed. 'It doesn't mean we have to drink all of them! What we don't have, I'll leave here for next time.'

'I'm hungry. Should we eat now?' Marie asked, as they put everything on the kitchen table.

'Good idea. It will give us more energy.'

She smiled at the inference and set about arranging the food on the table. Within a few minutes they were each taking a glass of wine in one hand and a plate of food in the other, placing them on a low table in front of the sofa.

She took a slow sip of champagne, studying him for a moment while she did so. He was handsome, sure of himself, exuded the type of charisma that attracted her, but there was a certain mystery about him and she wanted to know more.

240

'This is a lovely cottage,' she said. 'Your friend must be very generous to let you use it, or do you rent it on a permanent basis?'

'We have an understanding,' he replied casually.

'Are you here often?'

'It depends where my business takes me.'

'And what is that?'

'I deal in commodities.'

'That is a wide term.'

'You wouldn't be interested.'

'Try me.'

He pursed his lips thoughtfully and then turned his head to look her in the eye 'Too many questions will spoil our night.'

Marie felt that the tables had been turned. To persist in her questions would be to sour the mood of the evening ahead.

Why was Pierre so evasive? She was getting nowhere with her questions. It was as if he did not want to impart any information at all about himself. Why? The strong suspicion arose in her that he was married, but after all why worry? They were both here, weren't they? What they did for the rest of the night was up to her. She felt a rising desire for this man to take her again. She put her plate on the table, took his glass from him and set it down.

'We'll come back to those later,' she said.

'I've had such a wonderful time.' Marie sighed with pleasure as the car neared Senlis.

He did not speak.

'I hope you have too?' she queried, a little hurt by his silence.

241

He drew the car to a halt and half-turned towards her. She was troubled by the expressionless look in his eyes. 'I have,' he said, with little apparent emotion.

'Pierre, what's the matter?' Alarm came over her as her eyes searched his cold face.

'Nothing,' he replied brusquely. 'It must be over between us. We will never meet again.'

'What? What do you mean?' she cried.

'Exactly that.'

'But...?' The question died in her throat.

'I can't see you again.'

'Why? Why?' Her mind was churning.

'I have to leave.'

'I don't understand...'

'The firm I work for requires me to go abroad and the posting will be permanent. It's best you forget me.' There was neither compassion, nor regret in his voice.

Marie sensed there was no 'abroad'. There wasn't a permanent posting either. Anger surged in her, not only at him but at herself. 'You're a liar! You aren't going abroad.'

'Believe what you like,' he said with a dismissive shrug of his shoulders. 'It makes no difference.'

'You duped me, played me for a gullible fool, to get me into bed. Now you cast me aside like so much rubbish! How many more girls have you fooled? I'll find you and...'

His mocking laughter stopped her. 'You'll never find me, Cinderella. You don't know who I am or where I live. The cottage, as I told you, belongs to a friend and you'll never track him down. The people at the night club don't know me. I'm a

242

stranger to them as I am to you, Cinderella. You'll never find me. Never!'

'You planned all this!' she screamed at him, eyes wild and flaming with hatred.

'From the moment I saw you, I was curious. Now my curiosity has been satisfied.'

'So all of this was done without any feeling whatsoever for me?' she demanded in disgust.

'Not all, but I sensed, even at this early stage, that you were having thoughts about the future. I was not going to be drawn into that. Goodbye, Cinderella.' With a quick movement that she realised could only have come from long practice he leaned across her and opened the door. 'Please get out. Now!' he ordered.

Marie hesitated for one brief moment, but the look in his eyes frightened her. He looked so different from the man she had believed she was falling in love with – something she would admit only to herself. It would be kept a secret, locked away in her mind, until the shameful memory could be erased completely. She swung her feet out of the car, stood up but did not close the door.

He reached across once more, but before he closed the door he said in a more gentle tone, 'Forget me, Cinderella. It will be best for both of us.' He closed the door, slammed the car into gear and roared away, leaving Marie staring after him blankly.

Marie walked home, cursing herself for being so gullible as to fall for the smooth-talking charms of... 'Pierre!' She spat the word with venom. She was so angry with herself she could not even cry.

'What good would that do?' she asked herself. 'None! None at all!' Shouting the words to the night sky helped to relieve some of their sting.

Then she thought of Jacques. If he had not left her none of this would have happened. Irritated by the thought of her coming confrontation with him, she stamped her foot and headed for home.

During the next two weeks she pushed the episode with Pierre further and further into the back of her mind. After another three weeks had passed, however, she realised that all was not well with her.

Thankful that her father and Roland were away with Jacques, she hid her anxiety from her mother and Claude, only entertaining it in the silence of her room or when walking alone.

Another month passed and still there were no signs of what she had hoped for.

Then her father, Roland and Jacques arrived home, having sent word ahead for the two families to meet at the house in Senlis to await their arrival. Because there was no explanation given, Marie feared Jacques was going to announce to everyone that they planned to marry. Her mind raced with thoughts of what she would do, but then she told herself surely he would not do that without making any reference to it to her first? But when he did, what could she tell him?

With greetings made, glasses charged, excitement was in the air. Silence fell when Victor Martineau stood up.

'I am as eager as the rest of you to know what news Henri, Roland and Jacques bring us. I was sorry I was not able to go with them but I knew that Martineau's interests were safe in the capable hands of my son, Jacques. I know it must be something important for them to have called this gathering on their arrival so now I ask – no, I plead with them to spare the rest of us the misery of speculating.'

As he sat down, Henri rose from his chair. He cleared his throat, took a sip of his wine and started to explain.

'This trip was very successful for both firms. Not only that, it made the idea of our amalgamation much more appealing. There are many aspects of our operations that would work better if we were more closely related.' As he spoke these last words he let his eyes drift towards Jacques and Marie. The meaning behind them was not lost on her and a shiver ran down her spine. 'We learned much from our visit and met many people from different parts of the world who are engaged in developing optical instruments for commercial and military interests. The outcome of one of our meetings is that we have been invited to visit four similar firms in America. I will not go into the details, but what it means is that Victor, Jacques, Roland and myself will be in America for the next year or eighteen months.'

A gasp went up from those who had just heard this news. Henri sipped his wine again, then held up his hand for silence.

'The rest of our families are invited to stay for three months. In their own expansive way, the Americans gave us a detailed proposal for our itinerary and worked out accommodation for us all. We gave them provisional numbers so they could go ahead with the arrangements. It only remains for us to confirm the details. It means a rush because we need to leave a week today.'

'Father,' Claude raised his hand, 'I am grateful for the opportunity to see America but I think, as I will be contributing nothing to the business side of the visit, I should refuse. Besides I have three wine growers' meetings to attend and I really shouldn't leave my vineyards for that length of time. So please accept my thanks, but regretfully I cannot go.'

'Very well, Claude, that is understandable,' his father agreed.

Marie's mind had been racing. She felt trapped by her own folly in agreeing to something she should never have let happen. Her whole world was falling in on her. Soon her behaviour and deceit would be exposed for everyone to know. If she did not act now she would soon have a very awkward confrontation with Jacques. She needed time – time to think, time to find a way out of the humiliation and the shame – but the prospect of leaving for America within a week did not allow her any, so she took the only course open to her at that moment. Refusal.

'I can't go. I've just made arrangements to visit Veronica,' she said, crossing her fingers behind her back.

'You didn't tell me,' said her mother.

'I'm sorry, Mama. I only heard yesterday that Michael is suffering again from his war wounds and his father is not at all well. Veronica is having a hard time so I said I would go to help and give her my support.'

'Can't you cancel it?' her mother asked. 'I'm sure Veronica would understand. After all, this is a wonderful chance for you to see something of America and it would be good for you to share the experience with Jacques.'

'I understand what you are saying, Mama, but as you know the Attwoods are a second family to me. I don't want to disappoint Veronica. Besides, I'm sure I will get another opportunity to see America.'

'But, Marie, you can't throw this tremendously kind offer back at the Americans,' her father insisted sternly.

'I'm not part of your business team,' she pointed out.

'No, but that doesn't come into it,' he said. 'The Americans like to meet the families of the people with whom they are dealing. It gives them insight into their background; they look for stability in families and in relationships, individuals' interest in their family firm, and their social standing.'

'I know that, Father, but I think with Mother by your side you won't miss me.'

'That's not true, Marie. A pretty girl is always an advantage.'

'Maybe, but I have promised Veronica, Papa. You've always taught us never to go back on our word. You've brought me up to be independent; please don't force this visit on me.'

As she was speaking her father shot a glance at Jacques, as much as to say, See what you can do.

Jacques was quick to take the hint. 'Marie, will you please step outside with me?' he said, rising from his chair.

She stood up. Her mind was awhirl as he escorted her from the room. She had berated him in July when he had announced he would be away on business; she could not adopt that attitude again. She had been invited to accompany him to America and that meant making a decision that could affect the lives of their two families.

He did not speak until they had stepped outside into the garden. 'Marie,' he said gently, 'I know we did not part on the most amiable of terms but you did promise me an answer when I got back.'

'Yes, I did. I had it ready ... and what do I find? You are proposing to go off again without any thought for me.'

'That is not true, Marie. As your father said, the American invitation extends to our families and that includes you. I thought we would be together. And I think it would be a wonderful idea for us to get married over there.'

Marie raised a hand to stop him. 'No, I won't have that. My answer was ready for you. It was yes, but I was supposing we would marry in Senlis, with all our old friends from here and the Attwoods and Eakins from England. None of them could come to America, so the answer is still no ... at least not yet. I will wait until you return, I promise you that, but I won't go to America.' He was about to protest but she stopped him. 'No, Jacques, no more trying to persuade me. Back me up now and I'll keep my promise to you. And I don't believe you would respect me either if I went back on my commitment to Veronica.'

She started for the door, but when she reached it she stopped and turned back to him. She slid her arms around him and gave him a passionate kiss which she hoped would be all the persuasion he needed to do as she asked. That way she would be free to go to England, though how she would arrange things there she had as yet no idea.

22

With Marie's decision backed by Jacques, their parents could do nothing but comply. The general disappointment was assuaged by the couple's announcement that they would marry on everyone's return from America.

The next seven days were hectic in the Gabin and Martineau households – confirming the visit with the Americans, packing, arranging to leave the two businesses in capable hands, organising skeleton staffs to look after the two houses, and the thousand and one other things related to the prolonged absence of the men.

Marie telegraphed Veronica and received the answer she'd expected from her dear friend. Making arrangements to travel between Senlis and the heart of Yorkshire, coupled with her frantic packing, helped her set aside the problem she still faced.

She did not think of it again until she was on the train, rattling north from London to York. In the flurry of meeting Veronica, her heart sank to hear her friend saying, 'I just can't believe this is happening – having you again for three months! It's just simply wonderful. Couldn't you have gone to America with the others?'

'Yes, but I didn't want to. I expect when Mama returns she'll want me back. But if it's possible, may I stay longer?'

'Of course it's possible,' replied Veronica. 'You know you are always welcome, for as long as you like. Now, you'll be staying in the cottage with me, Michael and Sylvia.'

'Lovely,' enthused Marie. 'How are they?'

'Very well. Sylvia is thriving and at the moment Michael is enjoying a spell of good health, though we never know when the effects of his wounds may cause more distress. Hopefully it won't happen while you are here.'

'His father and mother?'

'In reasonable health, but his father won't slow down. I suppose it's not in his nature.'

Marie smiled to herself at these reports which contrasted with the ones she had given her parents as an excuse for not going to America.

Veronica broke into her thoughts. 'We've made a few alterations to the cottage, to gain more space. I hope you'll like them.'

'I'm sure I will but the great thing is that we are together again.' The catch in Marie's voice caught Veronica's attention but, recalling her friend's sentimental streak, she made no comment. 'I hope I'm not imposing on you too much,' Marie continued.

'My dear Marie, this was and always will be

your second home. And I'm so glad you are to marry Jacques on his return. I thought you might have done it before now.'

It was on the tip of Marie's tongue to blurt out the full story, but she held back. This was not the moment. However, she knew it would have to come out before too long and evidence of her condition came to Veronica's attention.

She settled in with her friends quickly. Their parents, delighted to see her again, gave her a warm welcome, but that stirred Marie's conscience – she couldn't lay her problem at their door. She had to find a way out, and find it quickly. Then fate stepped in.

'Breakfast, sleepyhead!' Marie woke to the cheery call to find Veronica standing at her bedside with a tray on which there was a steaming bowl of porridge and a cup of tea.

Still bleary-eyed, she hauled herself up the bed. 'Oh, dear, I've slept in. I'm sorry.'

Veronica laughed as she put the tray on the bedside table. 'No need for that. I looked in twice before but you were sound asleep so I left you.'

'I'll be up as soon as I have had this.'

'Don't rush, but you might like to see...' As she was speaking she had crossed the room to the window; she pulled the curtains back '...this.'

Marie looked out of the window. 'Snow!' she gasped, and swung herself quickly out of bed, grabbing her dressing gown as she went to join her friend at the window.

'It's a bit early this year, we are hardly into November,' said Veronica. 'Maybe it won't last long, or else it's a portent of more to come. But whatever the reason, it feels much colder. Wrap up well.'

They stood in silence, watching the snowflakes drifting slowly down, settling their never-ending profusion of white across the trees and buildings.

'Mr Eakins! Mr Eakins!' A cry of alarm shattered the silence.

Veronica stiffened.

A young man, still shouting, came into view, racing towards the cottage.

'It's Luke ... something's wrong!' Veronica spun away from the window and ran from the room.

The distress in her friend's voice brought Marie hurrying after her.

They found Michael already at the door, stepping aside to let a snow-covered Luke in.

'An accident, sir, to your father!'

'What...? Where?'

'Cowslip field. He was bringing a load of fencing posts, the tractor skidded in the snow, threw your father off. It overturned and fell on him.'

'Oh, my God!' Michael grabbed a coat from a peg beside the door and ran from the house with Luke beside him. 'Why the devil didn't he leave it to us?'

'Dan and I told him we could manage, but you know your father, sir.'

'I do,' gasped Michael.

'He insisted on helping, said we had to beat the snow before it was too deep.'

Michael could hear the anxiety in Luke's voice. 'It was an accident. You can't be blamed,' he panted to reassure his employee even as they drove themselves harder.

The next few minutes seemed an eternity to both men. Michael's heart lurched when he saw the wrecked tractor, the broken trailer and posts strewn all around, but the sight that drove fear to his heart was that of Dan, with tears streaming down his face, kneeling beside an inert body. It spoke of only one thing.

'No!' Michael's scream tore at the heavens. 'No! No!' He dropped to his knees, reaching out to his father. There was no response to his touch. He gasped for breath. Sobs choked him and feelings of utter dejection and helplessness rendered him powerless. How long he stayed cradling his father, while snow fell around them, he never knew. He moved only when he felt a gentle touch on his shoulder. He looked up and saw Veronica, shedding silent tears, standing beside him.

'Come, Michael, we must get help,' she said quietly but firmly as she gripped his arm, forcing him to get up.

He nodded without speaking, released his hold on his father and stood up. He looked longingly at Veronica. She knew what he wanted because she wanted it too. They embraced and knew, in that moment, they would give each other the strength to face the future.

Aware of movement, they turned to see Marie running towards them. She had dressed quickly and thrown her outdoor clothes on as she ran from the house. Stricken by the sight before her, she knew the answer to the question without asking it. She went to Veronica and Michael and, putting her arms around them both, encircled them with her love.

Ten days later Clive Eakins' funeral took place in the Catholic church in the neighbouring village. The day after the accident the snow had ceased, but there was little change in the temperature. On the morning of the funeral snow started to fall again, gently, seeming to convey a message of comfort and peace to the mourning congregation. There was no wind to drive it away or to disturb the white covering that settled over the quiet countryside.

The Eakins were popular in the district after playing an active role in many village and countryside activities. It was a big funeral, the church packed to capacity, those who had to stand outside ignoring the falling snow. Elspeth Eakins and Michael were moved by the support they received from so many people, and in particular from their lifelong friends, Charles and Catherine Attwood.

As the last of the sympathisers left Rushbrook, Michael said to his mother, 'We'll stay here tonight or as long as you like.'

'There is no need,' said Elspeth firmly. 'I'll be all right.'

'I know that and I know how strong you are,' he replied.

'But I still think it best if we stay for a few nights.'

'I think we should too,' put in Veronica.

'But you'll have to bring Sylvia and upset her routine.'

'She'll get over that. You know how much she likes coming here.'

'Very well, but only for a short while. I've got to get on with my new life. It's no good moping around, your father wouldn't want me to do that. I'm not being disrespectful to his memory thinking like this so soon.'

Michael left his chair to embrace his mother and say, 'We know that, and so does he.'

'Then it is settled,' said Elspeth firmly. 'You come to me for a short while. Marie, that includes you too.'

'But I should not intrude on you at this time.'

'Nonsense. You won't be doing that. You've been part of our families since your convent days. I know Veronica would want you to be with her.'

'Marie, you must stay, please, for as long as it suits you,' Veronica implored.

'Thank you. I'm grateful to all of you for this,' she replied. Her words were genuine but her thoughts were elsewhere. What was she going to do about the shame and disgrace that loomed ever closer for her?

'I have something else to say,' said Elspeth. 'It may as well be said now. You will hear some of it tomorrow when the lawyer comes to read the will.' She saw a look of distaste cross her son's face at the mention of the will so soon. 'Don't looked shocked, Michael. These things have to be dealt with sooner or later. The sooner the better, say I, and then we can get on with our lives, changed as they will be. So please listen to what I have to say.' Marie, regarding this as a family matter, rose from her chair but was halted by Elspeth. 'You should hear this too and know my plans.' Marie sat down again.

'Michael, let us have a sherry,' his mother said, settling herself more comfortably in her chair.

With glasses charged and Michael seated again, she spoke carefully, weighing her words, not wanting there to be any misunderstanding. 'I know the main items in my husband's will. There are several smaller bequests to employees and special friends, and of course Clive has made ample provision for me. I could live a life of idleness but, as you know, that is not to my taste.'

'Mother, you know as much about the estate as I do. In spite of our very capable employees and advisers, your guidance will be most valuable. Besides, you keep your eye on the day-to-day accounts. They will still need doing.'

Elspeth read the inference correctly. 'We'll work something out. Now, as I say, I am provided for. The estate, some cash, buildings and land are all yours, Michael.'

He was stunned. 'I did not expect...' His voice faltered and tears came to his eyes.

Not wanting him to break down, his mother went on quickly, 'There is a proviso. I am allowed to spend the rest of my life here.'

'Mother, we would hear of nothing else,' he said firmly. 'Of course you must remain here. Rushbrook would not be the same without you.'

'That is kind. There is one other condition which I must divulge so that your tenure is safe. If I marry again, I forfeit all rights as stated in the will.' Silence hung over the room for a few moments until she said, 'Now I am going to have my say as to how we will arrange things between us. Michael, Veronica, you and Sylvia will move into this house and I will go into the Lodge.'

'No. You must stay...'

Elspeth interrupted him with a sharp, 'We don't live under the same roof now and will not do so in the future. This is your home, to live in and to run as you please. I will do the same in the Lodge. We will be near enough each other if needed, and far enough away stop us getting in each other's hair. I for one value my independence.'

'Very well, if that is the way you want it,' he agreed, knowing it was no use trying to persuade her otherwise.

Veronica rose and went to her mother-in-law. She knelt down beside her, kissed her and remained hugging her until Elspeth patted her hand in appreciation. As Veronica stood up, Elspeth said, 'No sense in wasting time, we'll start planning the moves tomorrow. Please don't think I am being insensitive. I feel my loss terribly but – well, you know my views.'

They did, but they also knew she would weep in the silence of her room that night and for many nights to come.

Elspeth added, 'I asked Cook to prepare a special meal for tonight, one of your father's favourites.'

As everyone left the dining room, after a meal worthy of Clive Eakins' memory, Marie, desiring some sharp winter air to clear her mind, found an excuse to go to her room for an outdoor coat. When she came down the stairs she was relieved to hear voices coming from the drawing room. She slipped quickly out of the front door on to the paved verandah and crossed to the snow-covered balustrade.

She snuggled into her woollen, calf-length coat, seeking comfort and warmth. The moonlight silvered the snow, bringing tranquillity to the scene but not to her mind. A tear trickled down her cheek. She brushed it away and sighed.

'If only.' Her lips tightened. She really shouldn't contemplate the meaning behind those two words. The past was the past, the future...

Filled with regrets, she stood staring out at the wintry landscape.

'Ah, there you are.' Veronica's gentle voice broke into her thoughts.

Marie gathered herself. 'Sorry, I should have told you I'd come out.' She stepped towards the doorway.

'No, Marie, stay there. I'll get a coat and join you. Sylvia is settled with the nursemaid.'

Marie watched her friend go. A few minutes later, clad in a Burberry trenchcoat, Veronica came out of the house and slipped her hand into Marie's.

'It's so beautiful,' said Marie, watching large white flakes drifting slowly down from a sky that still displayed the magic of its stars.

'It is,' agreed Veronica. 'On a night like this you can hear silence in the falling snow; there seems to be peace everywhere. I never thought when Michael and I married that I would be living at Rushbrook so soon. Why did this terrible accident have to happen just when he was getting over the horror of the trenches and his wounds were healing?'

'With your help I'm sure he'll cope. You'll be

happy here together for ever,' she commented quietly, as if to speak louder would disturb the wonder of the night. She felt an overwhelming urge to hold this moment in time, keep it close to her and never let it go.

'You're a true friend,' Veronica was saying.

'So are you.'

Marie turned, took hold of Veronica's hands and looked at her friend with an expression of sadness and regret. 'I've some news I wish I didn't have to break to you.'

Disturbed by the ominous note in Marie's voice, Veronica said, 'Then don't.'

Marie gave a little shake of her head. 'I must tell my best friend.' She paused a moment and then added, 'I'm pregnant.'

The words came quietly but nevertheless they made a shattering impact.

'What?' The shock in Veronica's voice was matched by the disbelief in her eyes. 'Are you sure?'

Marie gave a little laugh that had no joy in it. 'Oh, I'm sure.'

There was an infinitesimal pause before Veronica's next words poured out. 'You'll be rearranging the wedding then ... it will have to be brought forward. I suppose Jacques knows?'

'No.'

'You haven't told him?'

'I can't. He's not the father!'

'What?' Veronica reeled with the shock. 'I don't believe this!'

Marie tightened her lips as she fought the tears flooding her eyes. 'I let a charmer turn my head after being upset by Jacques' handling of the proposal.' She went on to give her friend the details of her reaction and the affair with Pierre.

'I understand why you took offence at Jacques' attitude but I think you were foolish to react so strongly. You could have got over it.'

'I know that now, but at the time I was upset and ... it just happened. I was flattered by a handsome stranger who turned my head.'

'Have you told him, whoever he is?'

'No.'

'You're going to have to.'

'I can't. I don't know where to find him. I only knew him as Pierre and he never talked much about himself.'

Veronica raised her eyebrows. 'That alone should have made you suspicious.'

'I know. I suspect that he was married.'

'So what are you going to do?'

Marie shrugged her shoulders, but there was desperation in her voice when she said, 'I don't know. I can't risk a scandal. You know what that would mean to our two families who are so set on this marriage. At this time, in a rapidly changing world, they see an alliance between Jacques and me as a way of strengthening both companies.'

'Your father is in favour of this then?'

'Oh, yes. He likes Jacques. Admires his business acumen, and the knowledge Jacques gained during the war about future arms development will be an asset to both companies. When they formally merge, which cannot be far into the future, I know Papa would expect Jacques to play an important part. So you see it would be a shattering blow to both families if I revealed what

I've done.'

'Do you love Jacques?' Veronica asked insistently.

'Yes,' replied Marie, but Veronica detected a note of hesitation in her friend's voice.

'You still have doubts?'

'Not really. And it's what has been expected of us since we were children.'

'That should not be your main criterion for marriage. So, do you love him?' Veronica asked again.

'He has an annoying way sometimes of letting business get in the way of how he handles personal relationships. He upset me by going away so soon after his proposal. It was a silly overreaction on my part, and look where it has led me, but at heart he is a kind, considerate man. He backed me when I said I didn't want to go to America, without trying to overrule me. Yes, I do love him and I ... but now?'

'Then, confide in him.'

'What? You expect him to say the child is his and...' Marie gave a little snort. 'That's not Jacques. He'd never agree, not even for the sake of his ambitions. Any child bearing the family name would have to be his. He could never tolerate another man's son, even passed off as his; not if it meant they'd inherit the family business and all that goes with it in the future.'

Veronica gave a little shake of her head. 'So what are you going to do?'

Marie tightened her lips in regret. She shrugged her shoulders and let the tears flow. 'I don't know. I've promised to marry Jacques when he returns from America in eighteen months' time. What can I do?' she asked miserably.

Veronica held out her arms and Marie sought comfort there.

In the silence of the snow, two friends faced a problem that was already shaping their futures.

After a few moments Veronica eased a sobbing Marie away but still held her. Marie was surprised by the change in her friend's expression. She felt hope rise within her.

'Marie, there is a solution but it will need careful consideration and planning so that only a few people know.'

'You are not suggesting an abortion?' queried Marie with alarm. 'I'd rather die than that.'

'Of course I'm not, and I'm not even suggesting you keep the baby.'

'Adoption? But how am I going to explain it, and who can I find to adopt my child?'

Veronica gave a little smile. 'You are looking at her.'

There was a moment's charged silence.

'You?' Marie gasped.

'Yes. Why not? You know I've always wanted another child, especially for Sylvia's sake.'

'You'd do this for me?'

'No. For both of us, and for Michael and me.'

'What can I say?'

'Say nothing more now. Think about it, and you and I will find an opportunity tomorrow to make further plans.' Veronica took her into her arms.

In the falling snow Marie felt the depth of a friend's love, strong enough to make her blighted life full of relief and thanks and hope again.

23

In the drab dark hours Marie's problems seemed insurmountable. With the new light she walked into the dining room where Veronica and Elspeth were already having breakfast.

'There's been only a little more snow during the night and it's a nice morning so, if Marie feels like me, we'll take Thor and Hector for a walk and get some fresh air,' Veronica announced.

'A good idea,' Elspeth approved. She rose from the table. 'I'll see you both at lunch.'

As the door closed behind her, Veronica gave a little smile. 'We can have our talk without being disturbed, but wrap up well; there was a heavy frost during the night.'

As soon as they collected Thor and Hector from the kennels the dogs raced into the snow, relishing the freedom. When she stepped outside Marie was glad she had heeded Veronica's warning. The sharp air took her breath away but she had the feeling that it was readying her mind for what was to come. The sun, though not strong, turned the hoar frost over the trees and grass into a glittering rime.

Snow crunched beneath their feet. After a while Veronica said, 'I've had a long night, trying to decide how we are going to go about solving your problem. First of all, tell me, will you be able to convince your mother to let you stay here until after the baby is born?'

'I think so, if you don't mind my using Michael's health as an excuse?'

Veronica looked thoughtful and Marie's doubts rose again. She was relieved when Veronica said, 'I have no objection, but it will mean that he has to know about your condition.'

Marie's lips tightened. 'If that is essential then so be it.'

'He won't be the only one. As I see it, his mother will have to know too as will my parents. I can envisage no other way.'

'Not even if I disappear as soon as possible?' asked Marie, shrinking from the prospect.

'Questions would be asked, and if your mother corresponded with mine I know the truth would come out. I strongly believe that we need to take them into our confidence. When they know that I plan, with Michael's approval of course, to adopt the child, they will comply.'

Marie nodded. 'You're right but I've got to get away soon or your servants will recognise the signs.'

Veronica heard the desperation coming into Marie's voice and quickly tried to reassure her. 'This is what I suggest. You need to be far from here, but you do need the company of someone who knows you.' Sensing protests coming, Veronica went on quickly, 'I propose we write to Mrs Latimer and seek her help.'

'What?' Marie was astounded. 'No, I can't! She would see it as a blight on the reputation of her school. She'd be disgusted with me. I couldn't.'

Veronica saw hysteria rising in her friend. She

grabbed Marie's arm and swung her round to face her. 'Marie!' she snapped. 'Think! Mrs Latimer is a very discreet person, as is her husband. They've got to be. You won't be the only one of their young ladies to have slipped up. I'm sure they will know somewhere where you could go and nothing said. The academy is far enough away; no word of it would reach this far. It will be easier for me to collect the baby there and arrive back with the child I have just adopted. That part of it will be no different from a child being taken in by an aunt or other close relative, as happens probably more than we know. There are no laws governing adoption, but the birth will have to be registered. Your name and the child's will have to appear; the father will be recorded as unknown. The birth certificate can be kept under lock and key.'

Veronica looked hard at her friend and saw that her plan had struck a favourable chord with her. 'So, what do you think?'

'This all sounds feasible. And if Mr and Mrs Latimer can and will help, we can put everything in motion straight away.' A catch came into her voice. 'Oh, you are so wonderful.' She hugged her friend. 'What would I have done without you?'

'This hasn't worked out yet; thank me when it does. There's a lot to do. The first thing is to put the plan to Michael, and if he agrees we'll tell the parents. Then I'll write to Mrs Latimer. Let's make our way back. I'll try to get hold of Michael and we'll get things underway. Mother said he had gone to see Crosby. In this weather it must be about some inside job so they'll be at the farm.' As they neared the farm buildings they

265

heard hammering. 'Must be repair jobs. You head for the house and I'll see you later.'

Left alone, Marie's spirits dipped until she forcibly reminded herself of what Veronica was doing for her. Reaching the house, she slipped in without anybody knowing and went to her room. She spent a lonely uneasy hour there until she heard a knock on the door. Before she got to it, it was opened and Veronica asked, 'May I come in?'

'Of course,' replied Marie and eyed her friend anxiously as Veronica stepped inside.

'First hurdle over,' she announced with an encouraging smile.

With a sigh of relief, Marie sat down on the edge of the bed.

'Naturally Michael was shocked by the news at first, but then, when I explained your dilemma and the chance of us achieving our dream by adopting the child, he realised the sense of my argument and agreed.'

With tears streaming down her face, Marie flung her arms round Veronica. 'I don't deserve a friend like you.'

'You'd have done the same for me,' she replied. 'And look what you are going to do – give your child to us. But it isn't over yet. Now for Mama.'

They found Elspeth finishing off her letters. In a few minutes she was in possession of the facts. She hid her initial shock, served out no reprimand and was understanding about why Marie had chosen to come here rather than go to America. 'I will agree to Veronica's plan,' she concluded, 'and, because you must write to Mrs Latimer immediately, we had better ask Veronica's mother and father to dine with us this evening. I'll get word to them right away.'

Marie's spirits had been lifted and she got ready for the evening in a lighter frame of mind. She had expected Michael and his mother to be harder to convince than Mrs Attwood who had been like a second mother to her during the war. She had expected Catherine to be sympathetic, so was shocked when her immediate reaction was one of horror and opposition to Veronica's plan to adopt, even though the plan had Michael's backing.

Dismayed by her mother's attitude, Veronica said, 'Mother, you knew we planned to adopt at some time. Here is an opportunity to do so while helping my best friend out of an impossible situation.'

'But you know nothing about the father except that he's a philanderer. You'd be better knowing something about both parents...'

'We know a lot about one of them,' Veronica pointed out, 'more than we would know about the mother if we went through the usual channels. The way we give this child our love and the way we bring it up will counteract any traits it may have inherited from its father.'

Catherine glanced at her husband, seeking his support. He gave a slight shake of his head that only she would notice. She knew he disapproved of her objections.

'If any one of us does not support Veronica's plan we will ruin more than one life,' he pointed out. 'Consider Jacques and his family. Marie has explained that situation to us. Consider each and every one of us here, but more than that ... consider the unborn child. Veronica and Michael can give it a good home and a good life. It will never replace Jeremy but, Catherine, you and I can give it the love we would have given him.' He saw his wife bite her lip in an effort to hold back the tears. He knew his own passionate plea and the mention of Jeremy had carried the day.

She nodded. 'Very well. I'm sorry for my initial reaction but it was such a shock to me.' She looked at Marie. 'Come here,' she said gently, and held out her arms. 'You were a second daughter to me and I'll always love you for that. Now you'll bring us another child and I thank you for that.'

The next day Veronica wrote the all-important letter to Mrs Latimer, received Marie's approval and posted it.

An anxious week passed before the letter of reply arrived addressed to Veronica. She found Marie in her room and held up the envelope. Marie's heart missed a beat. All their planning could be for nothing if the contents of this envelope were not as they hoped. Veronica withdrew the letter and read:

Dear Veronica,
Of course I remember you and Marie; two of my star pupils.
I am sorry to hear of her problem. Let me say at the outset, to ease both your minds – yes, I believe I can help you. I have faced this situation before infrequently I must say, but this is not the first time and

I don't suppose it will be the last.

Tell Marie I fully understand why she did not write in the first place. You were both very close and I know, Veronica, that under the circumstances, you wanted to save her the embarrassment. Your wish to adopt the child presents no problem. From what you tell me, it solves your own desire to have another child. No doubt you and Marie will remain friends, so she will still have contact with the child. This seems to be a wonderful solution and will save her from much of the grief that often comes when a child has to be taken away from its natural mother.

Now, these are my connections in a case like this. There is a congregation of twenty nuns living on a small estate about forty miles from here. They are chiefly a contemplative group but they do certain works of mercy, and that includes intervening in such situations as Marie's. Their facilities are good – nothing luxurious but the nuns are kind and Marie will be well looked after and no questions asked. I will go there tomorrow to make arrangements. If there are any problems, I will let you know immediately.

I am glad you have been so forthright about the whole situation and dates. I think it best if Marie comes here as soon as possible. May we say a week today? I look forward to meeting you both, if you accompany her on that day.

With my good wishes.

Yours,

Rachel Latimer

Veronica looked at Marie. 'Well, there it is.'

'Oh, Veronica, that's marvellous. I can't thank you enough.'

'Don't try. Just bring Michael and me a healthy baby.'

'I will, I promise you that.'

Preparations were quickly made, one of the most important being Marie's letter to await her mother's arrival home in Senlis in January.

Dear Mama,

Please forgive me for not being at home on your arrival from America. I have had to prolong my stay with Veronica because Michael has suffered a relapse triggered by his sufferings in the trenches and the loss of his father.

I will be home as soon as is possible. Please understand.

I hope Father, Monsieur Martineau and Jacques are meeting with success and were in good health when you left, and that your voyage home was a smooth one.

Your loving daughter,
Marie

Veronica approved it and agreed to post the letter four days before Marie's mother was due in Senlis. 'I also will write to her,' she added. 'It will add credence to your request if I point out how much I am relying on you under the present circumstances.'

Five months later the birth of a baby girl was entered in the records of a church in a quiet part of the Tweed Valley on the Scottish side of the border as the daughter of Marie Gabin. A surname was omitted and the father's name entered as 'Unknown'.

A week later Veronica and Michael took rooms in Kelso. The following day they kept an appointment with Mrs Latimer who took them to a tiny convent forty miles away. They were shown into a small room which, though sparsely furnished, exuded an atmosphere more important than comfort – of peace and spirituality. Each of them felt it and no one wanted to disturb it. Five minutes later the door opened, admitting a nun whose age was difficult to tell thanks to the serenity that suffused her face. She smiled broadly at Marie and Veronica, as if asking, 'To whom should I hand the baby I am holding?'

Marie smiled and indicated Veronica.

The nun stepped over to her and held out the baby, sleeping peacefully in the folds of a white crocheted shawl. Veronica, expecting Marie to take her child, hesitated momentarily but then gently took the bundle. 'Hello, Elise,' she said quietly. As if she knew her, the baby opened her eyes, looked straight at Veronica and smiled the most gorgeous smile Marie had ever seen. A silent tear trickled down her cheek but, knowing that what was happening was the best thing for everyone, she hugged her friend and daughter with love and relief.

Four days later, dressed for her journey, Marie looked round her room in Rushbrook Hall, full of confused emotions. Elise was no longer hers to bring up, that privilege was now Veronica's. Have I done what is best for my daughter and me? she asked herself. As filled with regret as she was at leaving Elise, cold reasoning told her it had to be.

Even though Veronica had assured her she would be able to visit and spend time with them all, she knew it would not be the same hearing her child call her 'Aunty Marie' rather than 'Mama'. She shivered, grabbed her handbag and strode from the room.

Reaching the top of the stairs, she stopped. She saw people in the hall waiting to say goodbye, among them Veronica holding Elise. For one moment she was tempted ... but reason prevailed.

She descended the stairs quickly and made her goodbyes, leaving Veronica and Elise until last. Her embrace was full of love for them both. She took hold of Elise's tiny hand and, when her daughter looked straight at her and smiled with bright shining eyes, Marie's heart nearly broke. She held out her arms, in a gesture that embraced everyone in a final goodbye, turned and walked away, heading for France, home and Jacques.

24

Standing at the rail of the ferry from Dover, Marie, searched the quay hopefully. The melancholy mood which had descended upon her during the Channel crossing had given her time to reflect on her life. Sadness vanished with the sight of her mother. Marie waved frantically and a moment later received Margaret's joyous wave in return.

She was relieved that the name of Gabin still had influence in the port when she received preferential treatment and was escorted quickly through Customs.

Mother and daughter, with obvious delight at being together again, embraced in a loving welcome. Margaret linked arms with her daughter and hurried her quickly to the waiting car as the first drops of rain began to fall.

'Welcome home, mam'selle,' smiled Alain, as he held the door open for his passengers.

'Thank you, Alain. It is good to be back.'

'For a long while,' commented her mother as they made themselves comfortable. 'Has everything settled down with Veronica and the Eakins?'

'Yes. Michael suffered greatly after the tragic accident that killed his father and it led to a big upheaval; Veronica begged me to stay and I felt I should. Now things have settled down they are thinking of adopting a playmate for Sylvia.'

'A good idea under the circumstances.'

'Now, Mother, tell me how Father and Roland are – and Jacques,' said Marie, wanting to divert the course their conversation was taking.

'When I left them they were well, as I told you in my letter. Jacques has been very busy, more so because he wanted to cut down his time in America. He reckoned that they didn't need eighteen months there. But,' she added with a knowing look, 'I think he was missing you.'

'Is he well?'

'Oh, yes. He seems to thrive on hard work, but as I say I think he really wants to be here now you are back.'

Marie felt flattered. How she wished she had not taken offence at his attitude in the past, but hopefully her indiscretion was buried now. There was no reason for it ever to be resurrected.

Marie settled down quickly to life back in Senlis, visiting Jacques' family and friends, and shopping in Paris with her mother.

Claude proudly showed her how his vineyard was developing and the expansions he proposed to make at the farm. One day as they were walking home from the farm, he asked, 'Marie, would you come with me to La Corinne tomorrow evening? You seemed to enjoy your visits there, and we should celebrate your return.'

The thought of reviving memories of Pierre disturbed her, but to refuse would upset her brother and cause him to question her.

When they walked into the club the next night she received a rapturous welcome from the Fontaines and Bouchers, in particular Corinne whose singing seemed to be exceptional that evening. The club was packed and whenever she finished a song the audience clamoured for more. Marie was not short of partners on the dance floor but showed them no other encouragement than her enjoyment of the dance and the music. She threw herself wholeheartedly into the pleasures of the evening and found that doing so finally purged her recollections of Pierre. She felt this marked a turning point in her life.

Corinne finished one of her songs amidst a storm of applause. When she announced she was taking a break there were groans all round, but they changed to cheers when she proclaimed, 'I'll be back.' She sought out Claude and Marie at the discreet corner table Marcel had kept for them. Marie noticed Claude and Corinne make eye contact, and then he rose from his seat and kissed her. After that Corinne turned a dazzling smile of welcome on Marie. 'It's so nice to see you again, Marie, it's been too long. I kept hearing snippets of news from Claude. I hope all your friends in England were in good health when you left?'

'They were, thank you. It was a longer stay than I'd originally intended but when tragedy struck...'

'Of course.' Corinne looked at Claude. 'Are you going to tell her?'

He hesitated which made Marie ask, 'Tell me what?'

'I've asked Corinne to marry me.'

'And I've said yes,' she said, reaching for his hand.

Marie's eyes lit up with delight. She had liked Corinne from the first moment they had met, and now she was going to be Marie's favourite brother's wife. What could be better? She let out a whoop of delight, jumped to her feet, hugged and kissed them both and rushed across the empty dance floor where she spoke quickly to the leader of the band. When he saw that Marie had regained her seat he signalled to the drummer whose roll on the drums brought silence to the room. The band leader announced, 'I have just been informed that our lovely singer Corinne has recently become engaged.' At that precise moment the band struck up her favourite song, 'Look for the silver lining'. Clapping broke out and resounded round the room. After a few moments the clapping faded, leaving the tune to tell its story. Everyone looked in the direction of Corinne and Claude. He stood up and held out his hand to her. She rose and took it. As they left the table they turned to a smiling, approving Marie and quietly said a heartfelt, 'Thank you.' As they danced as one, everybody knew they were watching two people very much in love.

Marie hoped that when Jacques returned she would experience the same feeling when he took her on to the dance floor, wherever it may be.

With the end of the waltz clapping broke out again and well-wishers came to talk to them from all around the room. When Corinne joined the band it was the start of an evening full of joviality that stretched into the early hours of the morning.

'Do Mother and Father know about you and Corinne?' Marie asked when they got out of the car at home.

'No. I will tell Mama at breakfast in the morning.' Claude added the plea, 'You'll be there, won't you?'

'Of course, if you want me there?'

'I do. She might not approve of a nightclub singer for a daughter-in-law.'

'I think Mama will be more considerate than that; she'll judge Corinne as a person, so the sooner you bring her home the better. You might need Mama's support when you tell Father. Will you write him?'

'No. I want to tell him face to face. But even if he disapproves, I'll not give up Corinne.'

'And he can't do anything. After all, he gave you your independence when he signed the vineyard and farm over to you.'

'I know, but I would be happier with his approval.'

'I'm sure it will be all right. Jacques turned his nose up a little when I told him about La Corinne, that bit of snobbery in him, but I'll change that.'

'Maybe you won't have to. Corinne will probably change it for him. She's auditioning at one of the big nightclubs in Paris, the Blue Lagoon.'

'That would make him change his mind. He took me there once and was full of praise for it, telling me all the top singers performed there.'

'It would be four spots a week for Corinne. She wouldn't take more because she won't desert those who put her on the map. She'll always sing at the club named after her.'

The following morning, Margaret's first question when her two children came into the dining room was, 'Did you two have a pleasant evening?'

'Yes, Mama. We did,' replied Marie enthusiastically.

'La Corinne, was it?'

Claude and Marie exchanged looks of surprise.

Margaret chuckled. 'Oh, your mama isn't so straightlaced. And don't think I've been spying on you. I haven't and wouldn't. No, a friend had seen Claude going in there a couple of times and happened to tell me. He went on to describe La Corinne in fulsome terms. So you enjoyed yourselves?'

'And I have something to tell you,' said Claude,

'something for which I would very much like your approval. Last night I asked Corinne to marry me.'

'She being the person after whom the night club is named?'

'Yes, Mama.'

'She's a lovely person,' broke in Marie enthusiastically. 'And a wonderful singer.'

'Well. This is news,' said Margaret sitting back in her chair. 'What can I say? You'll need to tell your father.'

'I want to do it face to face.'

'Good. I'm glad you said that. So I think I'd better meet this young lady. She can leave her singing for one night and dine with us, I'm sure. It is no good wasting time. Arrange it for two days from now.'

'Thank you, Mama,' said Claude, relieved that what he'd thought might be an ordeal had passed off so well.

By the time they finished breakfast, Claude's and Marie's praises for Corinne and the Fontaines left their mother with a vivid picture of them as a kind and close-knit family.

After the initial sizing up, Margaret and Corinne found that their mutual respect quickly developed into a much closer relationship. Barriers that might have been raised were never allowed to appear; the friendly candour of question and answer, always subtly put and answered, saw to that. The friendship between them deepened when Margaret asked Corinne to sing her favourite song, 'My Melancholy Baby', and Corinne obliged without a second thought.

When the song ended no one spoke, allowing Margaret to dwell where her thoughts had taken her. Then she said quietly, 'Sing that for my husband with such feeling and you'll have no trouble gaining his approval.'

Corinne accepted the advice with a gracious inclination of her head and said, 'I look forward to doing so.'

It came sooner than anyone expected; four weeks later a cable arrived from Henri. Margaret was able to read out, 'Done all we can here. Sailing next Tuesday on the *France*. Dock Le Havre Thursday following week.'

She contacted Josette Martineau who informed her that she too had had a similar cable from her husband Victor, and they decided that two cars would be needed to meet the arrivals from America

'Pleased, Mama?' Marie asked.

Margaret beamed. 'There's only one answer to that. Of course I'm pleased! And I'd like us to get settled back into life in Senlis as a family.'

'Times change, Mama, life moves on. We can't take up as if things were still the same,' Claude pointed out.

'Ah, ever the wise one,' said his mother. 'You are right. You are hoping your father will approve of Corinne and the change in your life?'

'You know I am.'

The Gabins and Martineaus motored to Le Havre the day before the *France* was due to dock, and were in a good position to witness her arrival.

'What a ship!' commented Claude on seeing the four-funnelled vessel approaching, and he continued to marvel at the skill of the captain and crew manoeuvring the huge vessel to its berth. No time was lost in running out gangways for the disembarking passengers.

The Martineaus and Gabins were among the first to reach the quay and, while effusive greetings were exchanged, the luggage was handed over to the chauffeurs. Marie's eyes were on Jacques as he hurried away from the towering ship. The handsome young man came striding towards her, full of confidence. He swept Marie into his arms and she experienced the strength of his love for her as he held her tight and kissed her fiercely. In those moments she realised how much she had missed him and that their young friendship had truly blossomed into deep love.

'It's good to be back, Marie. I've missed you.'

'And I you,' she whispered with intense feeling.

'Everyone, listen.' Josette caught their attention. 'We'll be parting now, so all have a safe journey home. I have arranged with Margaret for us to dine together tomorrow evening – a celebration to mark our men's return from what I understand has been a very successful time with the Americans. Until tomorrow evening, farewell.'

Jacques escorted Marie to her car and, as he helped her into it, whispered, 'Until then you'll be in my thoughts.'

As she waved and returned his smile, she sensed that his sharp edges and occasional brusqueness had been smoothed away, maybe as a result of his visit to America or maybe because of her stance before he had left. Marie hoped it was the case; she did not want the love she felt for him now to be marred by his gracelessness or by her own indiscretion – that must always remain a secret.

The following evening the mood was celebratory. After their successful tour of America, Henri and Victor visualised a business partnership that would bring increased power and profit to them both.

Jacques managed to slip away with Marie on to the terrace that ran around three sides of the house. With laughter on his lips, he hurried her around the first corner. He stopped suddenly and spun her into his arms.

'I love you, Marie. Marry me soon?'

Though she had anticipated what was coming, the words still swept over her sweetly.

'Yes, Jacques. Of course I will.'

Their lips met, sealing their desire to be together always and to embrace their new life with passion and a love that would never die.

When their lips parted, Marie said, 'Are we going to announce it now or are you going to ask Papa first?'

Jacques gave a little laugh. 'I suppose I should consult him, but I'm going to forget that. Our marriage is expected after all.'

'We could give them all a shock and tell them I said no.' Marie laughed at the thought of the reaction that would provoke.

Jacques chuckled too and that pleased her; formerly it wouldn't have amused him at all. America must have lightened his attitude to life.

The impression was strengthened when he added as they reached the door, 'Solemn now ... give nothing away.'

Conversation flowed, *joie de vivre* filled the room, and everyone enjoyed a scrumptious meal which won wide praise for the Martineaus' cook. Finally, after making sure that all glasses had been recharged, Victor stood up and picked up his own. 'As you all know, the visit to America was highly successful. I will not bore you with the details but our spirits are high and we can see a period of expansion ahead for both firms. Now ... I ask you to raise your glasses to a successful future.'

Everyone stood and picked up their glasses.

Victor said, 'To success!'

That was repeated by everyone. They all sat down, but Jacques remained standing. 'I have something to say.' All eyes turned to him. 'A few moments ago I asked Marie to marry me as soon as it can be arranged. Maybe I should have asked her father's assent first but I thought I would dispense with that. I am proud to say that she has agreed!'

Congratulations flew as everyone stood up again. Victor raised his glass and said, 'To Marie and Jacques, may their future together be full of joy and happiness!'

With the toast completed, delight was expressed by everyone. Victor called for champagne and the excited throng flocked to the drawing room where the butler supervised its distribution.

Naturally talk for the rest of the evening centred on the forthcoming wedding and it was decided it would take place in three months' time in Senlis Cathedral and the reception be held at the Gabin residence.

The next day, the first thing Marie did was to write to Veronica.

My dear friend,
Apart from family you have to be the first to know that Jacques and I are to be married in three months' time. You must be my Matron of Honour. Please say yes! The day would not be complete without you there.
Michael, of course, is invited but formal invitations will be going out to all guests soon.
Please, please accept.
Love,
Marie

'We will go,' said Michael when Marie's letter arrived. 'You must be her Matron of Honour.'

'Of course. We mean so much to each other.' Veronica paused thoughtfully, 'I wonder if she will want Elise to be there?'

Michael looked surprised. 'I wouldn't think Marie would want reminding of the past on her wedding day.'

'Maybe not, but would she look back in the future and regret that her daughter wasn't there?'

'I don't think so. Besides, if we take Elise, questions may be asked.'

'But that's not likely. As far as the other guests are concerned, Elise is ours.'

25

Senlis was buzzing; the pretty and popular daughter of Monsieur and Madame Gabin was to marry the handsome son of Monsieur and Madame Martineau in the cathedral today.

Guests from far and wide had flocked into the town and neighbouring villages, to take every available room. Members of the government and the military, people from the business world, the wine trade, farming community and clergy as well as those of the younger set with whom Marie had developed friendships, were among the guests seeking their places in the cathedral.

Veronica had made two visits to France for dress fittings and to rehearse the wedding ceremony. On each occasion Marie had sought out a suitable chance to learn all about Elise, and only last night had pressed her friend for more stories about the child who would never know her real mother's identity. Veronica had found it heart-rending to see how much Marie longed for her child but was prepared to sacrifice her own feelings rather than destroy the future of two families and the love she now felt for Jacques.

But, knowing the depth of Marie's feeling, Veronica feared she might still publicly claim her. It was only as the bridal procession made its way down the aisle and she saw Marie moving towards her new life that Veronica knew all was well and

Elise's life lay with her and not her natural mother.

As the day moved on and her responsibilities as Matron of Honour were fulfilled, Veronica found her energy had been drained away by the tension of the subterfuge. Michael noticed and was solicitous towards his wife. He hovered close by for the emotional farewells when Marie and Jacques left on their honeymoon.

Suppressed tears filled their eyes when Veronica and Marie embraced, expressing their love and gratitude for such a deep friendship.

'Take care of Elise,' Marie whispered close to Veronica's ear.

'You know I will,' she replied. 'Visit us whenever you wish.'

A kiss and then, among the cries of the wellwishers, Marie was helped into the car and driven away by Jacques.

When they retired for the night, Veronica sank on to the bed, looked at Michael and said, 'Let's go home.'

'Forget the holiday we planned?' he asked in surprise as he sat down beside her and put an arm round her shoulders.

'Yes.'

'Sleep on it. You've had a long day; you'll feel more like the holiday in the morning.'

'I won't. I want to be back in Yorkshire with my children.'

Michael knew his wife well enough to realise there would be no change of mind tomorrow.

Two days later they walked into Rushbrook to

be greeted by their staff and the nurse, with an energetic Sylvia and a sleeping Elise. When they reached the privacy of their room Veronica put her arms round her husband. 'I'm sorry if I spoiled your holiday.'

He met the apology in her eyes with a reassuring smile. 'You did no such thing. As a matter of fact I was glad you suggested we come home to our two beautiful daughters.'

Life settled down for them again, its rhythm dictated by the changing seasons and the demands of running the estate. Veronica's father was always there with advice, but carefully avoided giving it unless it was asked for. Keeping the estates running as viable propositions occupied much of their time and energy.

'You have something on your mind, Michael,' observed Veronica one evening when they had settled in the drawing room. 'You have been wearing a worried, thoughtful expression for a few days now. I've been waiting for you to tell me why.'

He hesitated for a moment then said with a regretful smile, 'Obvious, was it? I'm sorry. It's a question of policy regarding the estate. I was trying to make up my mind so I didn't have to saddle you with the problem.'

'Michael,' she said indignantly, 'you know I share your interest in the estate. After all, we were both brought up loving the land.'

'Yes, but you have other responsibilities now.'

'Well, a trouble shared is a trouble halved, so out with it.'

'Times are not easy; not as we expected them to be after the war. I can see farming and country life changing all the more over the coming years. Trying to see where it is going, and therefore what policies to pursue for the best, has been occupying my mind.'

'Have you drawn any conclusions?'

'Nothing definite.'

'Well, let's talk about it.'

'The mass unemployment of the last couple of years is coming to an end; 1924 will see a different picture emerge and I'm afraid some of the younger men will be away to Teesside, seeking better wages and what they see as a more attractive life in towns.'

'But the Government is looking to fix a minimum wage of twenty-five shillings for a fifty-hour week.'

'I know, and there is talk of it going higher.'

'Are you saying we are going to have to lay men off?'

'No, God forbid I ever have to do that. As I say, there will be men wanting to leave, but I believe we will always have a core of loyal employees who want to live in this area. What I need is the income to keep these men and their families happy with us and that might mean changing our policies, especially as food imports, especially of grain, will be increased.'

'You mean, after all the farmers' hard work in growing increased crops during the war, the government will more or less disregard that?'

'Well … we'll still be able to sell our corn, but it will have to be at a reduced price to compete with the imports.'

'So are you thinking we should stop growing it?'

'Not altogether. We'll still do so as a defence against any instability that may arise in farming. But I was thinking of turning more land over to grazing.'

'Cattle.' Veronica pondered the thought.

'And a dairy herd. And maybe increase our poultry.'

Veronica was silent for a moment then said, 'Why not?'

'There is one other thing. You know we have a considerable acreage along the edge of the moors that is of little use for farming. What would you think of selling it off to the Forestry Commission, which is buying land to redress the shortage of timber after the war?'

'Are you sure you want to do that?'

'It makes sense to me and will give us a bit more capital. I want to have everything in a good sound order for you and the girls.'

'Michael! Don't talk like that. It sounds as if – well, it sounds horrible!'

He was out of his chair and beside her in a flash, his expression troubled as he folded her in his arms. 'I'm sorry, I didn't mean it like that. I'm only thinking of the future. The three of you are important to me.' He kissed her gently.

Veronica leaned back and gave him a look that he recognised as telling him it would be no good refusing what she was about to ask him. 'Sell the moorland if you want to, but please keep sufficient to provide yourself with a shoot.'

He smiled. 'That was my plan. Then, at some time in the future, we could consider renting it out to rich individuals, companies, maybe foreign visitors. That could make for a nice little supplementary income.'

'A good idea,' she said with enthusiasm. 'We'll work to make all your plans come to fruition.' She was delighted at the interest he was showing in developing the estate. For a while she had been worried that he was stagnating, still affected by his wartime experiences. She had held back from making suggestions herself, hoping ideas would come from him and more powerfully counteract the depression she could sometimes detect in him. 'It's all so exciting,' she said encouragingly.

'Do you mind if I tell my mother?'

'Of course not. She was very much part of all this together with your father. I know she is still interested, even though she does not say much. I believe she's afraid of us thinking she's interfering.'

'Well, these plans will help to reassure her and focus her interest again,' replied Michael.

At that very moment Charles Attwood was escorting his wife Catherine and Elspeth Eakins from the dining room to the drawing room of Brunton Hall.

'I so enjoyed that meal,' said Elspeth. 'Thank you for asking me to visit.'

'Our pleasure,' said Catherine. 'There was an ulterior motive this time.'

'I know what's coming, Elspeth,' said Charles with a secretive smile, 'so if you'll excuse me, I'll leave you two ladies to it.'

'This sounds mysterious or serious, but whatever it is, Charles, of course I'll excuse you.' She glanced enquiringly at her hostess.

Catherine gave a little laugh. 'Oh, I'll let him go now, but another day he'll have to stay.'

'This sounds even more mysterious,' said Elspeth, settling herself comfortably in her chair, but at that point a maid arrived with the coffee so she had to wait until the door had closed again before she learned what this was about.

'Well, Elspeth, as you know, people are looking to enjoy themselves more these days, and this doesn't merely apply to those living in the towns where amenities are close at hand. Now country people are looking for those amenities in their villages too. Charles and I have talked about this and think we might provide the village with a hall which can be used for a variety of functions: dances, whist-drives, concerts, talks, and so on. It could be used for meetings of various bodies like the cricket club, football club, darts club, billiards club and so on.'

'But some of these don't exist locally,' Elspeth pointed out.

'True, but there is no reason why they shouldn't. People would be encouraged to form them if there was a village hall to use. I think we would be more likely to establish a branch of the Women's Institute, a Young Farmers' Club, as well as various other new interests. With this expansion on their doorstep, I think more of our young folk would be encouraged to remain in the country rather than move to the towns. If they want town facilities now and again, we have motorised transport available in the nearby market town where charabancs can be hired for outings; such excursions would be organised from our own village hall. And a new hall would provide better facilities for holding functions than we presently have at the school.'

The fervour of Catherine's voice was causing Elspeth to become enthusiastic too. 'We could organise a library, have a billiard room ... but I shouldn't be jumping to conclusions about what you had in mind.'

Catherine smiled. Secretly she was pleased by her friend's enthusiasm. 'Well, at the moment our plans are rather elementary, but if we are to go ahead we believe we should get on with it as soon as possible. We have been life-long friends so Charles and I thought we would seek your opinion. It came to us that we would like to do something that was a lasting memorial to Jeremy. Then we thought that, as there were others in the village and neighbourhood who had made the ultimate sacrifice too, we shouldn't single him out. So, with the village's approval, we would call it the Memorial Hall, with a plaque naming all those who were killed in the war.'

'I think it is a wonderful thing to do and it will be much appreciated by the local people. If you are to go through with this, I will do all I can to help and contribute in some way.'

'I hoped you would say that. You've always been an organiser so maybe you could pull all the strings together on this one and keep us on the right path?'

'That's a very generous opinion of me. But certainly I'll do what I can, provided you and I can work closely together. But as it is your baby, so to speak, you have the last word. Other people will have to run the various organisations but we will see that they understand your opinion counts on the use of the hall.'

'Very well, but I will not be dictatorial.'

'I know. It's not in your nature. So, tell me what you have it in mind to provide? I am not talking about money but the building itself.'

'Basically one big room suitable for dances, with a stage at one end, cloakrooms at the other. Also the possibility of some kitchen facilities.'

'I think those are essential and will greatly widen the use of the hall, which is really what we want; it is no use having it standing idle.'

Catherine nodded. The scheme was already assuming grander proportions than she and Charles had thought of; it was good to have another voice's contribution and someone who had a wider vision. 'We'll see what can be done when we instruct an architect, but I suppose the first thing will be finding a site.'

'I have been thinking about that as we were talking. None of your land comes near enough to the village, but Michael has some land which is right on the side of the road running through it.'

'The field with a stable in one corner?'

'Yes. His father bought it years ago, for no particular purpose at the time. I think the then owner needed cash. Michael has occasionally stabled a horse there but it's not in permanent use. I'll ask him about it.'

They talked on, enthusiasm rising all the time even though they spoke in general terms. They concluded that, as enthusiastic as they were, they needed the support and input of ideas from the whole village.

Catherine, delighted by Elspeth's acceptance of the idea, called Charles from his study and he too expressed his elation that what could be the start of an upturn in the life of Rushbrook village had been decided.

26

'Ma'am, Mrs Eakins is here and would like to see you.'

Catherine stopped buttering her breakfast toast and looked surprised at this announcement from her maid. 'Show her in, Rachel, show her in; don't leave her waiting.'

The maid turned from the dining room.

'Here so early ... it must be something important,' observed Catherine.

'Doesn't surprise me,' returned Charles laconically. 'The way she was bubbling over our proposal last night. Elspeth's not one to let the grass grow.'

As if on cue the door opened and Elspeth swept in. 'Come on, you two, we've a lot to do to get this project going.'

'Hold on,' said Catherine. 'There's time enough.'

'Not if we want this to succeed. We've got to show enthusiasm or else ... well, you know how lackadaisical some folk are. They need a push, and it will be up to us to give it.'

'A word, Elspeth, if you don't mind,' put in Charles gently. 'You can lead a horse to water but you can't make it drink. Don't try to lead the villagers. Let them have their say and feel part of the whole scheme. We must call a meeting and put the whole idea to them.'

'I know, Charles.' She struck her own breast in a gesture of contrition. 'You know me, always keen to get things underway if we are going to do something. I entirely agree, we should have a meeting of the village, but I do think the first thing to do is to see if Michael is willing to part with that piece of land. We can go and visit him now. If we announce at a village meeting that we have the land, folk are more likely to agree with what we are trying to do.'

'You are right,' Charles agreed.

While this exchange had been taking place, Catherine had poured a cup of coffee. She passed it to her friend. 'Have that, then we'll go to see Michael.'

Half an hour later they were stepping out of the car at Rushbrook Hall and quickly located Michael, who was surprised to see the three of them but sensed an air of excitement about their demeanour. His curiosity was heightened when they asked him to find Veronica.

'Come into the house,' he offered.

'No,' said Elspeth. 'We want to see something and we want Veronica to be with us.'

Knowing he would get no more out of his mother, he hurried off and returned a few minutes later with his wife, who was equally puzzled by their request. They all piled into the car and Charles drove off.

Little was said until they pulled up at the field in question. 'All out,' said Elspeth breezily

When they were all assembled, Michael said, 'What are we doing here?'

'You don't want that field, do you?' his mother asked, so unexpectedly that he looked dazed.

'Maybe Catherine had better explain,' Charles suggested. 'It was her idea in the first place. Well, not the field ... that was your mother's suggestion after she had heard what Catherine had in mind.'

'This gets more and more curious,' put in Michael when Charles paused. 'What's it all about?'

'Catherine,' said Elspeth, indicating the stage was hers.

She told Michael the whole idea, explaining how this piece of land came to be in the equation.

'This is a surprise,' he said. 'Though I think the idea of stimulating more activity and interest in village life is splendid. I see that if you want the backing of the village, having a place already in mind for the hall would be a great boost to people's confidence.' He paused thoughtfully. 'So, I am the first stumbling block.'

'And we don't want a bad fall right at the beginning,' said his mother pointedly.

'True, Mother, but Veronica and I have talked about this field which has a stable, such as it is, as a suitable place for our daughters to learn to ride.'

The three older people all felt a little deflated by this information, and for a few moments there was disappointment in the air.

Then Veronica spoke up. She had been looking at the position of the field in relation to the village. 'This is an ideal place for a village hall, Michael. A good area of flat land, near the village, with easy access from this road which is an extension of the main street. It couldn't be better.' She stepped nearer and slipped her hand into his. 'We don't really need this field for the girls. There are some nearer the Hall that we could use.'

'There are,' Michael agreed. He looked pensive and the others knew it was best to let him work this out for himself. Consideration duly made, Michael resumed: 'You can call a village meeting as soon as possible, and at that meeting you can announce that the field and the hall will be a memorial to all the local men who fell in the war. I want nothing for the field. I will get documents drawn up assigning it to a village trust, or whatever it has to be. I'll leave that to my solicitors.'

After dropping Veronica and Michael back at Rushbrook Hall, Charles drove Catherine and Elspeth to Brunton Manor where they had, at his insistence, a celebratory drink.

'Well, we're on our way.' He raised his glass.

'We can start immediately,' said Elspeth with an enthusiasm that was catching. 'I'll book the school for a meeting and we'll get some leaflets and posters done, announcing a meeting to discuss the future of the village. We'll keep to general terms to raise curiosity; that may tempt people to come and find out what it's all about. I'll let Michael and Veronica know that's how we are approaching things.'

Rushbrook was buzzing after the leaflets were delivered to every household in the parish and posters were prominently displayed. Questions were asked about the reason for the meeting, but no one had an answer.

The conspirators were thankful that the evening of the meeting was mild and bright, and relished the sight of people heading for the school as the appointed time approached. The response was overwhelming and people willingly put up with the crush that was generated in the school's main classroom.

Speculation rose again when Mr and Mrs Attwood, accompanied by Mrs Elspeth Eakins, appeared from a door at the rear of the room, and sat down. After a word with his wife, Charles stood up which brought an expectant hush to the room.

'Ladies and gentlemen, we have called this meeting out of concern for the future of our village. After a short explanation, we would like suggestions from you about how you would like to see our village developing and what we might do about it.

'I have to say that we think the first step must be a village hall that can be used for many purposes, helping to bring us all closer in ways which should benefit the whole community. If this is agreed we propose that it be named the Memorial Hall in memory of all those who fell in the war. We realised that before we could proceed with building a village hall, we needed a site; it would be no good pursuing this project if we could not find one.' He paused, allowing a murmur of acceptance of this point to filter through the room, then he said, 'Mrs Eakins, my wife and I, went to look at a possible site with the owner and I can tell you here and now that the owner, Mr Michael Eakins, has given us the field at the east end of the village.'

There was silence as if the gathering could not believe what they were hearing. Then someone at the back of the room shouted, 'Did you say, given?'

'I did,' said Charles, loudly enough that no one could be mistaken. 'If you accept this gift, documents will be drawn up and the field will become the property of the village.'

Someone towards the back of the room shouted, 'I'd say we'd be fools to put anything in the way of this generous offer.' Shouts of agreement rang around the room to be followed, as the noise began to fade, by, 'Three cheers for young Mr Eakins!' The noise rose to a crescendo at the third cheer.

Charles silenced the room again. 'I think that should be all for this evening. Go away, think about your village and what you would like to see here. A football team? Cricket team? WI? Concerts? Bring your ideas here a week tonight. We'll discuss them and form some plans. Rushbrook is on its way, let's be proud of what we do.'

The cheers that rang out died away, to leave groups of people talking excitedly among themselves as they left the school.

Regular meetings kept interest in the new village hall high, and once committees and teams were formed life in Rushbrook became a great deal more pleasant for all. Youngsters grew up, babies were born, people grew older, others died. It took the country as a whole time to recover from the horrors of war and come to grips with what it had cost in human lives. The Attwoods knew this only too well, and wondered if they would ever get over the loss of Jeremy, so they were thankful that they not only had the estate to occupy them but also the new life that had come to the village. They derived much happiness from Sylvia and Elise too. Watching them grow up was a great pleasure.

The family was wary when Veronica suggested she should invite Marie to Rushbrook Hall but they bowed to her wishes. 'She has been a dear friend to me since schooldays and I trust her implicitly; she'll handle her contact with Elise so that there are no repercussions, I'm sure.' Veronica's opinion proved to be sound and Sylvia and Elise took immediately to 'Aunty' Marie. It paved the way for future visits which Marie always carefully arranged when she knew Jacques would not be able to accompany her due to pressure of work.

During her visit a year before the girls started school, when she and Veronica were alone, she said, 'I am going to put a suggestion to you about Elise's education. I am not interfering; this is the only suggestion I will make. I do so in the belief that you will be sending the girls to the convent where you and I were educated?'

'That time is a little way off but it will come all too quickly,' replied Veronica. 'Yes, it was our intention to send them there at the appropriate time. Prior to that, we will send them to a small private school run by a Mrs Martinglake in the neighbouring village of Ditchfield. She is highly thought of. If all remains the same there we will send them both to the convent when Sylvia leaves Mrs Martinglake's.'

'That sounds an admirable plan,' commented Marie.

'And your suggestion?' asked Veronica.

'That whenever I am here, I should improve their French.'

'Why not?' Veronica agreed. 'It will make them much more competent at their school studies.'

On a visit six months after Sylvia and Elise had started at Mrs Martinglake's, they thought it good fun when their 'Aunty' Marie suggested she should help them to speak French 'like a native'.

'It will help when you go to the convent where your mother and I met,' she promised. So it proved; they were quick learners and readily took to speaking French. With that and an excellent French teacher at school, able to build on the natural ability fostered so well by Marie and kept up by Veronica between visits, they became adept at fooling people into thinking they were of French origin.

The twenties were good to Veronica and Michael, but they played their part too by hard work and shrewd handling of the estate. They survived setbacks in farming policies and were appreciative of the loyalty of their employees. In 1928 they were pleased to celebrate with Veronica's mother the granting of the vote to all women over the age of twenty-one. Amidst all the work Veronica and Michael were not slow to take advantage of any possible source of enjoyment. Local dances and Hunt Balls would always see them dancing the night away to the latest tunes and they were particularly adept at adapting to the jazz craze. Plays in York at the Theatre Royal attracted them and they motored to York and Scarborough to see the latest films. Their social life revolved around their parents and local friends, who would always round off visits to Agricultural Shows with a 'get-together' that would extend their day into a night of dining and fun.

The economic troubles the country faced – unemployment resulting in protest marches, the attempt by governments to ease the lot of hard-hit communities, and the worsening relationships between countries, especially those in Europe – were not lost on them, but these things merely impinged briefly on their lives as they did those of the 'bright young things' in London, on whom some of the wilder elements of the county set modelled themselves.

Attitudes of rejoicing, cultivated in the aftermath of the Great War were revived, but with a different slogan – enjoy ourselves while we can.

When the time came Sylvia and Elise settled easily into convent life, but always enjoyed holidays at home with their parents.

The girls had only just returned to the convent after their Christmas break when, on 20 January 1936, the King died and his son became Edward VIII. To most of the girls he was a handsome heart-throb, his photograph pinned up on the inside of locker-doors alongside pictures of film stars like Clark Gable, Tyrone Power and Gary Cooper, but girlish dreams of him were shattered when he abdicated in December 1936 for the love of an American divorcee. Film stars remained the only adornment after that. Even those pictures came down from Sylvia's and Elise's lockers during the following July when their time at the convent was drawing to a close.

But before that tragedy struck.

27

As they walked out of the dining room Marie's eyes sparkled with amusement at something her husband had suggested. It was rare for Jacques to be home for lunch; maybe today she should take advantage of it. She raised her eyebrows in response but was prevented from taking a step towards the stairs by the appearance of Chantal, one of their housemaids.

'Ma'am, this has just been delivered.' Suspicious of what a cable might mean, she tentatively held out the envelope to Marie.

'Thank you, Chantal.' Marie ran her finger under the flap and unfolded the sheet of paper that she had taken from the envelope. Colour drained rapidly from her face as she stared in disbelief at the brief message it contained. 'Oh, my God!' she gasped.

Alarmed by her sudden distress, Jacques reached out to take her weight as she swayed. There was concern on his face as he lowered her gently on to a straight-backed chair that stood near the dining-room door. 'A glass of water quickly, Chantal,' he ordered.

Marie's arm had flopped weakly by her side but she still held the sheet of paper. Jacques took it from her fingers and read: *'Michael died. Heart attack. Veronica.'*

He placed a comforting hand on her shoulder and then took the glass of water from Chantal and gave it to his wife.

Marie, shocked by the news, was in a daze as she took a sip. Tears filled her eyes. 'I must go to her.'

'Of course,' Jacques agreed. 'Chantal,' he called to the maid, who had hovered in case she was needed again. 'Tell Madame's personal maid to pack some things for her, sufficient for two weeks' stay in England.'

'*Oui, Monsieur.*'

'And tell Simone to do the same for me.'

Marie reached out to take hold of his arm. 'No,' she said. 'There is no need for you to come. You have important meetings this next week.'

'But you cannot go alone.'

Marie gave a weak smile. 'I've done it many times before; I'll be all right. You've told me how vital these meeting are for you.'

'I can leave them to Father.'

'I know, but he likes you by his side and wants you to be involved in everything. He loves his company and wants it to survive long into the future. Anything that upsets that dream would devastate him.'

'I didn't know you realised this,' said Jacques, somewhat surprised that his wife had read his father and himself so well. 'Claude or Roland could accompany you instead.'

'No,' she replied firmly, knowing she had to take a grip on the situation. 'They've their own work. I don't want to tie them to me. Roland is part of the company; Claude can't be away for long, and he has Corinne to consider. Besides I don't know the true situation with Veronica. I might stay a little while to help her through this.'

'Very well, if that's the way you want it. Stay as long as you want.' He helped her to her feet. Chantal had disappeared but Jacques knew she would have taken in hand the orders for Marie's packing. 'I'll get Simone to send a cable saying you are on your way.'

'Thank you, Jacques.' Marie kissed him on his cheek, 'I don't deserve you.'

The journey was a nightmare for Marie. Though it went well, with everything running to its appointed time, her mind continually urged the train and ship to go faster. She wanted to be with those she loved in Yorkshire, wanted to be a solid rock of support – and to none more so than her own daughter. At an age where a girl was most vulnerable to the loss of a father, Elise must be suffering. Believing Michael to be her father, her sorrow would be deep and she would be thinking her heart would never mend. Marie needed to be there for her.

Reaching York station, she could not waste any more time, but commandeered a taxi to take her to Rushbrook Hall. The driver's well-meant pleasantries were irksome to her. She made no complaint, but when she explained that she was on a sad mission he judged that she wanted to be left to her own thoughts.

As she was getting out of the car the front door of Rushbrook Hall burst open and Sylvia and Elise raced out, shouting, 'Aunt Marie! Aunt Marie!' and flung themselves into her outstretched arms.

As he was taking the luggage from the car, the driver said, 'That was a lovely welcome, ma'am.'

'We knew you'd come!' said Elise.

'We really did!' shouted Sylvia.

Veronica, starkly dressed in a plain well-cut black dress, had appeared in the doorway. Marie, her arms round the two girls, walked towards her. When they came close the women held out their arms to each other and then hugged as if they would never let go. Silent tears flowed; their throats were too choked to speak.

When they judged each other was ready, they turned and walked into the house, holding hands.

Three days later a packed church overflowing with mourners paid its last respects to 'Young Mr Eakins', as he would always be known, on an autumn day when the trees took on their mantle of brown and yellow to mingle with the green, as if bowing to Michael's love of this time of year.

The sun was sinking towards the west when the last of the sympathisers left Rushbrook Hall, and Veronica flopped on to the large sofa in the drawing room.

'Tired, my dear?' asked her mother. 'It's been a hard day.'

'What I expected,' she said, as her daughters gave her a reassuring hug.

'Best if we get out of your hair,' suggested her father. 'We'll expect you for one o'clock lunch tomorrow. You too, Elspeth.'

She smiled weakly. 'Thank you, I appreciate the invitation.'

Catherine, who had marvelled at Elspeth's composure after the loss of her only child, recognised heartfelt pain in her expression. 'As always you are most welcome.'

'I am deeply grateful for your help and support. Another void has been left in my life, but I mean to try to fill it as best I can. How thankful I am now for the part you gave me in the regeneration of the village.' She turned to Veronica. 'You have many decisions to make now that the estate is yours, but you know that if there is anything I can do in any way, you only have to ask.'

Veronica came to her. 'Thank you,' she said, and hugged her; two women sharing a devastating loss.

When Veronica returned after seeing her parents out, Elspeth said, 'I think I had better go.' She looked at Sylvia and Elise. 'What would these two young ladies say to spending tonight with their grandma? I'd welcome the company.'

At any normal time they would have responded to the suggestion with wild enthusiasm, but this evening they were subdued. They glanced at their mother for guidance.

'I'll be all right if that's what you are thinking. I'll have Aunt Marie with me. Gran would appreciate your being with her. It's up to you what you do,' said Veronica.

They glanced at each other and saw in each other's expression what the decision should be. Sylvia spoke for them both. 'We don't like leaving you on this night, Mum, but Granny will be the only one on her own if we don't go.'

'Then that settles it,' said Veronica. 'Off you go and pack what you need to take.'

They hurried away and when the door closed behind them, Elspeth said, 'Thanks, Veronica. I know I'm used to being on my own by now but tonight would have been different.'

The girls were soon back and, rather than prolong the leave-taking, Elspeth made her good nights to Marie and Veronica. 'You two can have a catch-up. It will do Veronica good to have you here, Marie.'

As the two women were returning to the drawing room a maid appeared.

'Excuse me, ma'am,' she said, 'but Cook would like to know about this evening's meal.'

'Tell her there will only be the two of us so something simple that can be served in the drawing room and eaten on our knees.' She looked at Marie. 'Is that all right for you?'

'Of course. It will be nice to relax that way.'

'How do you think Elise looks?' asked Veronica, taking the opportunity, now they were alone together for the first time since Marie's arrival, to pose what had become a familiar question whenever they met.

'Remarkably well,' replied Marie. 'They both do. I did not know what to expect; sixteen is such a vulnerable age.'

'They have coped well and have been a great support to me, but no matter how good and supportive people are, and there have been many kindnesses shown, they cannot ever know how the loss feels in here.' She laid a hand above her heart. 'There's an enormous void; you think you'll never cope, but you know that somehow you've got to.'

'It's early days but do you know what you will do now?'

'In detail, no, I don't. But overall I do. Michael loved Rushbrook Hall, it had been in his family for many, many years, and he always said he would never desert it. I am determined that that will remain so. I know what he'd planned for its future; he used to confer with me, knowing you and I had learned about estate management at finishing school and in the Land Army. I will try to implement his plans and keep the estate alive.'

Marie recognised the passion in Veronica's voice. 'You'll do it,' she said firmly. 'I know you will. You have good people around you and a group of loyal workers.'

'I'm fortunate,' Veronica agreed. 'Father's experience is valuable too and he is so careful never to push his ideas.' She smiled. 'I know he dropped them in when talking to Michael in the days following Mr Eakins' death, but he did so in such a subtle way he made them seem like Michael's own. It was so sweet of him. I'm sure he'll help me, as will Michael's mother. Elspeth's experience of farming was a great support to her son. Not only that, her sterling work in the village brings its reward in loyalty from the villagers. As for my own staff, they are all so willing and I have two gems in the farm manager and the foreman.'

'It is good to hear you sound so positive,' said Marie. 'And I'm pleased you will go on living here. I think it is the right thing for you. And you know you only have to call and I'll be here.'

'Thanks, Marie. Who would have predicted how close our lives would become when we met that first day at St Mary's? But what about you? Is all well in your world?'

'Mother is still suffering a little from her fall in the Alps when she and Papa were skiing, but I have no worries about her. Papa is fine, still as active as ever; still devoted to the factory. It is the be-all-and-end-all to him. Thank goodness he has Roland, who is just as committed. I believe Papa indoctrinated him so the factory would go on and on. Roland had better find someone to provide Father with a grandson.'

'Not Claude and Corinne?'

'They've two girls who are sweeties and have won their grandfather's heart, but they're not heirs. Besides Claude is not interested in the factory, and if a son did come along he'd probably inherit his father's love of the land or his mother's love of music.'

'Isn't it possible that you...' Veronica was interrupted by Marie's little laugh of dismissal.

'You know from what I have told you and from our correspondence that that is now most unlikely. My latest test confirmed the previous ones.'

'Adoption?'

Marie threw up her hands in horror. 'What? Father would be outraged at the thought of outside blood coming into the family.'

'What does Jacques think? I know he is as involved in the factory as his father and yours since the amalgamation.'

'Even more so, I would say. But he's just got to accept that it will be up to Roland to provide a male successor.'

'Has he any prospects for marriage?'

'He gets around. Father encourages him to bring his latest girlfriends home. I think he wants to look them over; doesn't want Roland marrying a gold-digger.'

'It sounds as though business is good.'

'Booming.'

'I suppose that is on the back of rumours of war?'

'I believe it is.'

'Do you think it will come?'

'I hope not, but the mood in France is not good. On the surface people tend to ignore the facts and pass off Hitler's rantings and ravings as those of a madman, but even madmen can cause havoc and he seems to be getting the German people behind him. Father and Jacques are gearing up as if war were inevitable. I hope that it is a mistaken belief.'

'If the worst happens, Marie, you will be in more danger than we are; at least we have water between us and the Continent. So if war comes, don't forget you can make your home here for as long as is needed.'

'That is most kind, and it is a great consolation

to me to know that Elise will be safe here.'

'She and Sylvia are due to leave the convent in 1937, so, if we don't see you before, we'll see you then.'

'I wouldn't miss their graduation for all the world. Have they any idea what they want to do beyond that?'

'Not really. They keep chopping and changing their minds. I don't want to push them into making decisions. It's better they reach them naturally.' Marie looked a little doubtful so Veronica quickly added, 'Don't worry, it will all work out. I don't think finishing school is for them; it's a different life now and they show no inclinations in that direction. Sylvia is very much of the land and would be a great asset in a practical way around the estate. She loves horses and has two of her own. I can see her developing a riding school or a bloodstock business.'

'Elise?' Marie put the query tentatively.

'As you know, she and Sylvia are very close but I don't think she would want to have anything to do with horses. Oh, she rides but she enjoys other aspects of the estate more. She has a sharp mind, is good with figures and has a natural talent for organising. She would be a great asset working alongside me. If she asks me, I will suggest she does a secretarial course in York, stays the week there and comes home at weekends. Even if she doesn't direct her talents to the estate, secretarial qualifications, along with her talent for languages, could open many worlds to her, particularly as she speaks French like a native. Beyond that, who knows? They'll meet someone, fall in love, marry...'

'And whoever that is might not be interested in the estate,' cut in Marie.

Veronica gave a little shrug of her shoulders. 'True, but we can't plan for that. Such things have to be dealt with as they arise, but one thing is certain – the estate will be a valuable asset to them both.' She left a thoughtful pause. 'And when the time comes, I will have no one to share Brunton with so I will add it to Rushbrook; our daughters will be well provided for.'

Marie noted that Veronica had said 'our daughters' and was grateful for that, but she made no comment. Instead she said, 'Let us hope these dreams and plans can be fulfilled in a peaceful future.'

28

'If we leave here at nine in the morning we'll have time to call in at the convent on our way to York, for you to say goodbye to Elise and Sylvia,' Veronica informed Marie as they were finishing their evening meal.

'Thank you. I'd like that.'

The visit to the convent, brief though it was, brought excitement, pleasure and regret along with a promise from Marie: 'I will be back for your Speech Day.'

Recalling that, as she and Marie walked into York station, Veronica said with a touch of regret in her voice, 'It will be their last one.' If possible she would have halted their final steps towards adulthood. Marie leaned out of the carriage window to hold her friend's hand.

The train hissed and clattered. Officials shouted, flags were waved and wheels began to turn. Fingers lingered and then slipped apart, leaving a widening gap that permitted only a last wave before the train passed from sight.

Veronica walked slowly from the station, wondering what lay ahead for them all.

Marie was there to watch proudly when Elise won the top awards for French, Mathematics and English, the latter being shared with Sylvia.

In a celebration of their achievements and their first steps into a new life, Veronica took them on a motoring tour of the west of Scotland. Marie took little persuading to join them for the month. Veronica hoped that by the time of their return Sylvia and Elise would have made a final decision about their futures. At the end of the holiday Sylvia declared she wanted nothing more than to work on the estate and, while learning all the intricacies of running an enterprise such as Rushbrook, she would also develop an equestrian business; Elise saw her future as helping to run the estate by dealing with the financial and administrative sides of it. For a start she would attend a secretarial course in York, and Sylvia would serve time with an equestrian establishment near Malton.

Accordingly, when they returned to Yorkshire after a wonderful Scottish holiday that included much walking among the dramatic and spectacular mountain scenery and beside the gentle, inviting lochs, they promised they would share their weekends at home walking the North York Moors and entrancing Yorkshire coast, seeing that, apart from the pleasure, the exercise would stand them in good stead for work on the estate.

Having enjoyed her time with them, and pleased that her daughter was settled on what promised to be a rewarding career, Marie returned to France in a contented frame of mind. However, on arrival she was disturbed by the uneasy atmosphere there engendered by the unsettled political parties which seemed unable to counteract what was being seen as the threat from Hitler's Germany.

During a meal to welcome her home, she brought up her concern about this state of affairs with her husband and father. 'How do you see the European situation, Father?'

'Unstable at the moment, but you've nothing to fear. I know things regarding our rearmament that are not generally known, so anything I say here must be strictly between us. I know you can all be trusted so I can tell you that the factory is working to almost full capacity, and some of the things we are working on are top secret. I cannot divulge them even to you. I will only say that we are in a strong position. When you were in England, Marie, you probably heard that the British Prime Minister has authorised rearmament in his country. Between us we present a formidable force, if we present it correctly, along with the defences we have installed, Hitler should think again about making any further demands.'

Henri's optimistic words reassured them on that occasion, but he did not reveal his doubts about Hitler's sincerity. These proved to be well grounded when the German leader annexed Austria and the Nazis stepped up their attacks on Jews within their borders. Realising that war was looking more certain, especially as Hitler was now eyeing Czechoslovakia, Henri called an immediate meeting with Victor and Jacques Martineau, and his own son Roland.

'In spite of all that has been done in the cause of peace, I think Hitler will keep pressing his demands. I believe he wishes to dominate the world and is not going to hold back. We should do all we can to increase production above what we regard as current capacity. This gives us a unique opportunity to generate huge profits from our patriotic endeavours. Our factory is vital to the war effort and must be protected at all times. You and I, Victor, must woo the politicians as well as the military. We can talk from a position of strength as we are one of only two factories in France producing these particular vital instruments.'

Henri's strategy proved sound and he gained the go-ahead from the government and the military to increase production.

Like so many other people, he carefully monitored the meeting in Munich when Chamberlain and Daladier met Hitler. And like many, he thought the agreement to cede land in Czechoslovakia, which Hitler considered rightfully belonged to Germany, was only a postponement of war.

'Look closely at those photographs of Daladier

... there's despondency and the admission of the inevitable in his eyes,' he pointed out to Roland.

'But the British Prime Minister, waving that piece of paper with Hitler's signature on it and declaring, "I believe it is peace for our time", seems hopeful.'

'True, and that is what he intended to convey, but I think he has seen through Hitler and regards this agreement as merely giving Britain and France more time to rearm. Maybe he has gained a respite that will be significant to us both. Our company should take advantage of it.'

'Congratulations, love,' Veronica whispered when Elise returned to her seat, proudly holding her diplomas at the end-of-term ceremony at the secretarial college in York where she had taken not only office studies but also elementary accountancy, which she could pursue in greater depth at a later date if she thought the Rushbrook work merited it.

Sylvia whispered her congratulations too. It was a happy trio who returned to Rushbrook Hall.

But that evening Veronica felt she had to raise the subject of their future. 'I'm sure you are aware that there is every possibility of war. I believe it to be inevitable. Recruiting is already taking place and I'm sure women will become more and more involved in every aspect of the conflict. I think it might be wise to consider what you will both do in wartime. Have you thought about it at all?'

'Not really, Mother,' said Elise. 'I've been too busy getting my diplomas.'

'Of course.'

'I thought I would wait and see too,' said Sylvia.

'Not always a good idea,' replied Veronica. 'But I'll leave you both to think further about it.' She let the subject drop, knowing that one day they would bring it up themselves.

The following morning, Elise suggested to Sylvia that they take a walk into Rushbrook. 'We'll see what entertainment is on offer in the hall this week.'

It was a pleasant summer's day and the sisters enjoyed a leisurely walk into the village with the retrievers which had replaced Thor and Hector. The 'young ladies from the Hall' were greeted with pleasantries. They heard exchanges between the villagers that made Elise observe, 'My course has prevented me from spending much time in the village over the last two years, but do I perceive a more friendly and genial atmosphere here?'

'I hadn't really thought about it, not being away like you, but now you mention it, I think you are right.' Sylvia agreed. 'Must be the possibility of war that has drawn people closer.' They had reached the Memorial Hall by then and stopped to read the notices protected from the weather by a glass-fronted cabinet fixed to the wall.

'Cricket match here on Saturday,' Elise pointed out. 'So life goes on.'

'A whist drive and dance on Friday,' said Sylvia. 'That might be fun.'

'This could be more amusing,' Elise said jokingly, tapping at the glass, and then read aloud, 'Meeting in the Memorial Hall, Tuesday 7.30 p.m.

317

Philatelic Club. Election of Officers.'

'Life certainly does still go on,' agreed Sylvia. 'Good luck to them. I think my school-days stamps are in the attic.'

'I gave mine away the day I left, to that podgy girl in the third form.'

Sylvia frowned and said, 'Read this one.'

'Sounds serious?'

'The Women's Land Army is seeking recruits. So things must be getting grim.'

'Right. Does that settle it then?' said Elise, with a decisive tone to her voice.

'It does!'

'Then look out, Mr Hitler, here we come!'

With laughter on their lips and the light of resolution in their eyes they linked arms, fell into step and walked briskly down the street.

29

On reaching Rushbrook Hall they hurried to their mother's study and burst in, declaring: 'We've decided. We're going to join the Land Army!'

Veronica, taken aback by the sudden decision, sat back in her chair. 'This is a serious undertaking,' she warned. 'Have you thought it through carefully?'

Sylvia and Elise glanced at each other with expressions that said, What is Mother getting at now?

'We will be doing something we know about

and we'll be able to remain here.'

Veronica gave a little smile. 'So you don't really know anything about it at all! First, you don't know everything about farming, so you will have to do a training course, and then you'll be allocated to a farmer, either on your own or with other girls, depending on the need. When you sign on, you will be agreeing to work anywhere in the country.'

'But we have a farm here – we thought we'd be able to work on that,' protested Elise.

'You might be able to. You can put that point to the authorities, if you still decide to sign on. I'm sure we will lose some of our workers to the Armed Forces so that would be a point in favour of your request, but it can't be taken as a foregone conclusion. Without a doubt, you would have to move if ordered to.'

'Anywhere in the country?' asked Sylvia.

'Yes, but as you are established here it would be more likely to be within this area, depending which division we come under. The North Riding, I would think.'

'What about my horses?'

'You'd have to make alternative arrangement for them if you had to work elsewhere. You might have to move into a hostel or be billeted with a farmer and his family. It's not going to be easy, but there is one thing to bear in mind. You won't be under a strict regime, as you would be in military service, so you'd have more freedom. It all depends what you want.' Veronica saw doubt creeping in. 'Go away and think about it some more. It's up to you. I will not hold you back if you want to volunteer for something else.'

At lunch Sylvia spoke up for them both. 'We have definitely decided on the Land Army.'

'Good, I'm pleased,' said Veronica with a smile of pleasure. 'And I've decided to see if I'd be any use to them again. My experiences in the last war and knowledge of this estate might prove useful. We'll drive to Malton after lunch and see where we can offer our services.'

Their enquiries soon led to their being interviewed by the District Representative, Mrs Gatenbie, who welcomed the two girls with open arms.

Once introductions had been made, she said, 'Mrs Eakins, are you thinking of rejoining the Land Army too?'

'I might be, but it would have to fit in with the running of my own estate.'

Mrs Gatenbie nodded. 'Those kind of details would need to be worked out with the County Office. When I was looking at some early records I came across a mention of Veronica Attwood. Would that be you?'

Veronica smiled. 'It certainly would.'

'I am delighted to hear it. With your previous experience of the Land Army, you are more than welcome. Heaven-sent, in fact. I am looking after a larger area than I should be. The County Office is looking to split it. After some training to refresh your knowledge, I think you would be the ideal person for that role.'

'It is very kind of you to think so.'

'Not at all. Now for your daughters ... have you

told them both all that becoming a Land Girl entails?'

'Yes, I have, and told them to think about it carefully. They did and here they both are.'

'We already have some experience through helping on the estate,' said Sylvia.

'And while we are willing to go anywhere, we are hoping that our work will enable us to stay on the estate or at least in this area,' said Elise, in a questioning tone.

'That would depend on circumstances, the needs of your area, and finally the decision of your District Representative.'

'Supposing she was our mother?'

Mrs Gatenbie laughed. 'Then I hope she would be impartial.'

Veronica put on a mock stern expression and wagged a finger at them. 'You will do as you are told.'

Documents were signed and the three of them left, awaiting official approval for their becoming full members of the Land Army.

It came through quickly, Mrs Gatenbie's report saw to that, and within the following week Veronica accompanied her to the County Offices where it was arranged she would report for a four-day training session, at the end of which she would take over part of the division run by Mrs Gatenbie with Rushbrook Hall as its headquarters.

When they were finally called up, Sylvia and Elise were each kitted out with a uniform mackintosh, an overall coat, corduroy breeches, a pair of dungarees, a green pullover, a pair of heavy brown shoes, a brown felt hat and two shirts. Rubber gumboots were in short supply and would be issued later. Two days later they were sent on a two-week training course on a farm five miles south of York.

On returning to Rushbrook Hall they found their mother had twenty recruits under her jurisdiction and they had been housed five miles away in a roadside pub, The Heifer, which had been empty for a year. Mrs Gatenbie and Veronica had recommended that headquarters should commandeer it as a hostel for Land Army girls. 'I think it would be a good idea if you lived in The Heifer with the others,' Veronica suggested to Sylvia and Elise. 'It will make for better relationships between you. The newcomers won't have any reason then to think you are getting special privileges because of me.'

Sylvia, seeing Elise about to object, stopped her with a slight grimace and said, 'If you think so, Mother.'

'You'll be near home and can still help out here until I get schedules organised.'

'What are these girls like?' Elise asked cautiously.

'A real mixture; four from London, three from Liverpool, two from the Lake District, four from Hull, three from Scarborough and four from Leeds. Some joined up to escape home and get some freedom, others to see what country life is like; some preferred the Land Army to military service, and so on.'

So a new pattern of life was forged. Because of Veronica's position of authority and the fact that they came from 'the big house', as the other girls named Rushbrook Hall, Sylvia and Elise were regarded with some suspicion at first, but when it was seen that they did not shirk any job, no matter how rough or menial, they were accepted and new friendships blossomed. In their free time they made forays into Malton and were always ready to make the most of dances in Rushbrook Memorial Hall. The girls from the towns complained amongst themselves about the reluctance of most of the village boys to come forward and dance, but once that barrier had been broken the Saturday night dances became lively affairs, with the younger generation ignoring the disturbing news coming out of Europe, not thinking of what might be lying ahead. Everyone was hoping that Prime Minister Chamberlain's 1938 negotiations, completed in September in Munich, were not a false dawn.

That hope was dented one day in November when Sylvia and Elise were working on the Rushbrook Estate. Veronica called them into her office in the 'big house'. She told them, 'Last week I had visits from government officials, and today it has been confirmed in writing that some of our land and adjoining fields belonging to Brunton Manor will be taken over for the construction of an aerodrome, to be built to the standard required by bombers.'

'Mother, can they do this? It's your land,' protested Elise.

'It seems so. We'll receive some sort of compensation, I suppose, and the land will be returned to us after the crisis is over.'

'But it's going to mean a big upheaval.'

'It certainly will,' put in Sylvia, 'but we'll have to comply and manage the best we can. Once we know something more definite, we can make plans accordingly.' A sparkle came into her eyes. 'It could be rather interesting with glamour-boy flyers stationed here!'

'We'll be spoiled for choice!' agreed Elise.

'Don't you two get any big ideas. It won't all be glamour,' warned Veronica, remembering her own youth and how girls of her time had felt when war brought them a newfound freedom. When men and women met in new and unusual circumstances, it could lead to the sentiment 'live for today and make hay while the sun shines'.

'The other girls will love to hear this news,' said Elise, 'and be glad they joined the Land Army and were posted to Rushbrook.'

Two weeks later Veronica sent a message to The Heifer, saying that she wanted Sylvia and Elise to report to her at nine the following morning. Believing they might be facing a move, they were surprised to be told, 'The two gentlemen I am expecting today will be making the final decision about the site of the proposed airfield. I would like you both to be with me to hear what they say.'

'Can we comment?' asked Sylvia.

'Of course. You know what is happening; you know that your grandfather and I are in favour of helping all we can at this time. If it means turning over some of our land then so be it. Grandfather has a meeting in Malton so he has given me permission to speak for him. You will have your own opinions and there is no reason why you shouldn't voice them.'

'Will they want any figures?' asked Elise.

'I don't suppose so. It's the land and its suitability that they'll be interested in. I suggest you have the maps of the estate ready.'

'Yes, Mama. We need a big table to spread them out. May I suggest we use the dining room? The table there will give us ample room.'

'That's a good idea. I'll warn Mrs Cole to leave the table free but have everything ready for lunch. I've ordered a cold one so that fits in nicely with your suggestion. It can be easily set once we have finished. Oh, and I have told the managers of both estate's to stand by in case we need them.'

'What time are they due?' asked Sylvia.

'Ten o'clock.'

Sylvia glanced at her watch. 'We have an hour then.'

'About right,' said Elise, rising from her chair. 'I'll go and get the maps.'

'And I'll see the table gets cleared for you. Have you any jobs on the land to do?'

'The milking has all been done before breakfast, as usual,' said Sylvia.

'Did you have any trouble with Bonnie this morning?'

'No. I let Elise deal with her. She must have a gentler touch than I have.'

'You don't handle her right,' said Elise. 'You should go up to Mr Jackson's; he'll teach you a thing or two about milking – tips we didn't get on our training course. I'm glad I was sent there to help out for a couple of days.'

'You can keep your cows, give me horses any

day; much more intelligent.'

'You can't milk horses,' called Elise over her shoulder just as she reached the door on her way to get the maps.

Veronica smiled at the rapport between them. 'If this airfield materialises you might have to consider stabling elsewhere.'

'That has crossed my mind,' Sylvia said. 'I've only two horses; expansion is going to have to wait. I think I could stable these two with Mr Mangrove in the village.'

'That would be a good place. I know he likes horses but hasn't any at the moment.'

Ten o'clock approached. Veronica and her two daughters, calmly resigned to whatever the outcome might be, shared the moments in silence. So absorbed had they become in their thoughts that they were startled by the sound of a car approaching the house. The crunching of the tyres on the gravel surface ceased, the engine was silenced, car doors opened and shut, the faint sound of a bell reached the drawing room.

'Three gentlemen to see you, ma'am,' announced the maid.

'Show them in, please, Lily.'

Veronica rose from her chair and Sylvia and Elise came to stand beside her. Three men walked in. Two of them, in their early-fifties, wore civilian grey suits; the third was in RAF uniform.

'Good day, Mrs Eakins.' One of the suited men stepped forward. 'It is a pleasure to meet you again.'

'Good day to you, Mr Evans.'

They shook hands and he said, 'May I introduce Mr Smurthwaite, my assistant, and Squadron Leader Hawkesley.'

'Good day, gentlemen.' Veronica shook hands and added, 'My daughters, Sylvia and Elise.' She noted the wings on the breast of the Squadron Leader's uniform, and thought they must have been awarded during the First World War. She liked his kindly, fatherly face. As greetings were being exchanged, the door opened and two maids came in carrying trays.

'I anticipated you might like coffee,' said Veronica.

'That's most kind of you,' replied Mr Evans.

The maids left and Sylvia and Elise took over the pouring out and serving of the coffee.

'I have brought Mr Smurthwaite because he has made himself familiar with the area and looked at the topographical possibilities for an airfield. Squadron Leader Hawkesley is looking at its suitability from the RAF point of view,' Mr Evans explained.

As they settled down, Veronica said, 'My father apologises for not being here, but I have the authority to make any decision regarding Brunton Manor as well as my own home, Rushbrook Hall.'

'That makes things easier,' said Mr Evans, a note of relief in his voice.

Discussions continued, Mr Smurthwaite assuring them that there were many points in favour of placing an airfield locally, in particular one for bombers.

'So are you saying there won't be much interruption to village life?' asked Sylvia.

'Oh, there will be interruption,' replied Mr Smurthwaite. 'An influx of maybe two thousand personnel is bound to have an effect in different ways, according to the way the villagers accept these strangers and the way the RAF people take to finding themselves in a world that will be completely alien to most of them. Looking around, I noticed a well-established village hall running many varied events and clubs; this can be a big advantage to integration, as can the two sports fields I noted.'

With a knowing smile the Squadron Leader put in, 'And two village pubs ... what could be better to help our fliers settle down? There'll be boisterous nights but very rarely do they get completely out of hand; the village people should know that these men follow an unusual way of life – normality for a while then all hell breaking out. And, if they survive that, back to normality ... or as near as is possible.'

'Is it certain that you will take land from our two estates?' asked Elise.

'That is what we are here to decide,' replied Mr Evans with a questioning glance at his two companions.

Mr Smurthwaite gave a little nod. The Squadron Leader said, 'I'd like to take another look.'

Not a word was spoken as they all trooped outside, where they watched the RAF man study distant aspects in every direction, sometimes through binoculars. Finally he said, 'I was a little worried about positioning an airfield on the higher land of the North York Moors, but if we could move it about two hundred yards south all will be well. This would make an excellent site.'

'Let us go and study the maps,' said Veronica. 'Elise has made them available on our dining-room table.'

'Excellent,' said Mr Evans.

'A pity this peaceful countryside will soon be shattered by the roar of aero-engines,' commented Sylvia to Squadron Leader Hawkesley.

'It is,' he agreed. 'I have a daughter who would have said the same thing. My usual answer is a question: Wouldn't you rather put up with that for a while than to be permanently under the German jackboot?'

They studied the map for some time, charting the repositioning of the various necessary sites and the reorientation of access roads.

Then Sylvia enquired, 'How many acres will we lose?'

'From both estates combined, it will be about six hundred and fifty in total,' replied Mr Evans, 'roughly half and half. That may alter slightly because of the new orientation.'

'After your earlier visit, I thought Mother said it was less than that?'

'That is so, but since this site was first mooted instructions have come that we should keep in mind a new type of bomber that is already on the production line. I would ask you to say nothing of this to anyone, of course.'

'We won't,' Sylvia promised on behalf of every-one.

'Thank you, all of you, for your understanding and for accepting the report on the suitability of your land and that of Mr Attwood.'

'When can we expect work to start?' Veronica asked.

'I can't give you a date. It will depend on a number of factors, such as the availability of lorries, the organising of a workforce, etc, and of course the weather. This is not a good time to start building airfields, but we must make plans well ahead. I don't expect construction will start before March 1939, when we would anticipate better weather. It might even be later, because there are certain things we must be sure of concerning the runways.'

It was not until May that Veronica received word that work would start on the first of June. She thought it wisest to inform the Land Army girls of what was about to happen on their doorstep. The news was greeted by 'Oohs' and 'Ahs' and promises of what would happen to the husky navvies who would be moving in. Then the girls directed their attention to the fliers.

Veronica deflated their ambitions. 'We aren't at war yet. It may never happen.' Though in her heart of hearts she thought it couldn't be avoided.

30

Paying close attention to the developing situation, Henri came to the conclusion that, because of the number of defence and alliance treaties being signed across Europe, the international powers were lining up for war. Even ordinary people were feeling the tension and, though they tried to retain hope that efforts to maintain peace would succeed, deep in their hearts they all believed that war was inevitable.

This general acceptance was compounded when they saw sandbags being filled and lining the Paris boulevards, to protect those buildings dear to their hearts and essential to the running of their country. It was the same in London, and what happened in the capitals soon spread to other parts of their country.

Rushbrook inhabitants felt drawn into the war preparations when gas masks were brought to their village hall to be distributed. Elspeth immediately rushed to see Veronica and requested that some of her Land Army girls help with the distribution, to which Veronica readily agreed. They made light of it and even brought smiles to the faces of the more jittery villagers when they demonstrated how the masks should and should not be worn.

When work started on the airfield, some of the older village men immediately inaugurated a Rushbrook ARP (Air Raid Precautions) unit, anticipating that the airfield would be attacked and inevitably bombs would fall on the village. They began to dig holes in their gardens ready for the Anderson air-raid shelters, and flowerbeds were adapted for vegetables. As far as Rushbrook village was concerned Hitler was not going to catch them unprepared.

People without wireless sets were invited by neighbours to listen to theirs at news time. A new sense of camaraderie was in the air. People who hardly ever spoke to each other, or else merely passed the time of day, would now stop and exchange views on the behaviour of the children from Hull who had been evacuated and billeted with some of the villagers. Worlds had been turned upside down.

The Eakins and Attwoods watched their beloved land torn up by a whole army of machines.

'How badly do you think all this will affect our farming?' asked Veronica one day when she and her father were watching lorry-loads of material being tipped for the foundations of the three runways.

'We'll still be able to use the land that isn't taken over, and we'll have to get on as best we can with the disruptions. We've got to; after all, as much land as possible will have to produce food one way or another. Imports by sea are going to be more difficult. I think we should consider running what's left of our estates as one. We'll both lose men through those volunteering for armed service and the call up of others without exemption. Think it over, Veronica, then if you approve we'll get together with our managers and foremen.'

'It needs no thinking over, Papa. It's certainly best to pool resources at this uncertain time.'

'Good, then we'll have a meeting with our managers, two o'clock tomorrow.'

Work on the airfield was not finished before the flames of war were finally ignited. Hitler, with his eyes fixed on Danzig, ordered the German invasion of Poland on 1 September 1939.

People around the world still clung to the forlorn hope that a last-minute solution might be found and they would step back from the brink of disaster. But it was not to be.

On Sunday 3 September like so many people in Britain, the Eakins and Attwoods gathered together to hear the Prime Minister's broadcast.

At 11.15 a.m., with anguish in his voice, Neville Chamberlain made the announcement: 'This morning, the British Ambassador in Berlin handed the German government a final note, stating that unless we heard from them – by 11 o'clock – that they were prepared at once to withdraw their troops from Poland, a state of war would exist between us. I have to tell you now that no such undertaking has been received and that, consequently, this country is at war with Germany.'

Without moving from her chair, Veronica did what she thought was the right thing to do; she reached out and switched the wireless off. In the sudden silence everyone was left to face the bewildering question, What happens now?

Nobody seemed to want to speak; each of them needed to be left with their own thoughts, to try and comprehend what this might mean to them. Although they knew their lives would be turned upside down, here, in the quiet of Rushbrook Hall, on this fine Sunday morning, outwardly everything seemed normal. Maybe for the time being that was how life would remain. No one wanted at this stage to predict what changes would come.

After a few minutes, Veronica stood up and said quietly, 'I'll order some tea.' She started for the door and, as if she had to explain why she wasn't going to the bell-pull, said over her shoulder, 'I'll see how the staff are first. They were all going to gather in the kitchen to hear the Prime Minister.'

She returned a short while later followed by the maids carrying tea trays. Once they had left, Veronica said, 'There were a few tears in the kitchen, but Cook had anticipated we would probably appreciate a cup of tea and made sure the kettles were boiling in readiness.'

As she sat down after helping to hand out the cups of tea, Elise said, 'I wonder how Aunt Marie and her family are reacting to this?'

'There's been no announcement from the French government yet, but I don't see how they can hold out. After all, they made promises to Poland along with us.'

Thoughts about the future of their factory and the important role it would play were already occupying the minds of the Gabin and Martineau families even before the French Premier, Edouard Daladier, announced at 8.30 that same evening that France was at war with Germany. He blamed Hitler, saying, 'The destiny of peace was in Hitler's hands. He wanted war.'

La Corinne was packed every night, and Corinne found the Blue Lagoon was the same during her performances there four nights a week. It seemed that the prospect of war was encouraging people to make the most of the time they had.

Minds were sharpened as to the real cost of war by the sinking of the British liner SS Athenia with 1,400 passengers aboard, mistaken for an armed merchant cruiser by the captain of a U-boat. Apart from news of German victories in Poland and other minor incidents, the conflict seemed to be at a stalemate. The air attacks that Britain expected did not come; sirens sounded but most were false alarms.

Elspeth likened it to a game of chess where the opponents were fearful of making a wrong move. But the Germans' successful invasion of Norway proved it was more than that; the first major offensive in the West had been mounted. Then on 9 May 1940 Hitler set in motion a major campaign that would sweep aside Belgium and Holland, outflank the Maginot Line, and humiliate the French.

The mounting noise of approaching vehicles brought Henri from his office chair to the window, which gave him a good view of the entrance to the factory. The sight of a line of German military vehicles sent a chill down his spine. So rumours of the swiftness of the German advance were true. There was no sign of any Allied resistance; he could only conclude that it had been swept aside or eliminated. He turned from the window and strode out of his office, deep in thought.

He flung open the doors of the three adjacent offices in turn and said, 'My office, now! The Germans are here!'

In a matter of moments Victor, Jacques and Roland were beside him at the window, staring in dismay at the length of the German convoy of vehicles, grinding on with nothing to stop them. Louder and louder grew the din of engines, seemingly heralding their nation's defeat.

'We must preserve the factory, no matter what that entails.' Henri's words were cold with resignation.

'But we can't just give in,' groaned Victor.

'Look at that force! What do you propose we do to stop it?' Henri snapped.

The two younger men glanced at each other and both of them realised the hopelessness of their situation. They would follow Henri's wishes.

They saw the moment of truth was close as two armoured cars turned in at the factory gates, followed by two troop-carrying vehicles. The rest of the convoy ground irresistibly forward.

As soon as the German cars had come to a halt, two officers got out and strode to the factory entrance. Soldiers overseen by an officer jumped from their vehicles and ran to strategic points, in what was clearly a pre-planned occupation of the premises.

'Where's the person in charge?' demanded the leading officer, his dark eyes piercing beneath the shining peak of his cap. He struck an imposing figure in his well-fitting greatcoat and shining black boots.

'First floor,' spluttered the man behind the reception desk. 'First door on the left.'

The two officers strode quickly up the stairs and flung open the door to which they had been directed.

'Monsieur Henri Gabin?' demanded the German.

Henri stepped forward.

'Ah.' The officer smiled. 'You seem surprised that I know who is in charge here. That is the first lesson for you – we Germans are thorough.' He glanced at Victor. 'You must be Monsieur Martineau, and these, I take it, are your respective sons?'

Henri stepped forward and introduced Roland and Jacques.

'Well, gentlemen, I am Major Schulz and this is Hauptmann Adler. We are here to secure the factory and your instrument business for the use of the Fatherland. You have two alternatives: cooperate with us, and you can go on running the factory as formerly, under our surveillance; refuse to cooperate and we take over completely, with no compensation on offer. It is your choice, gentlemen.' His words were curt and delivered with an air of authority that left the Gabin and Martineau men no choice.

'That is perfectly clear,' said Henri, trying to strike a businesslike pose. 'Once war was declared we foresaw what the outcome would be and prepared our business to fall in line with your requirements. Major, you need have no doubt that we will fully cooperate with your directives.'

'I am pleased to hear that. Hauptmann Adler will be visiting you fairly frequently to see that all is well. I will visit occasionally. When our subjugation of France is complete, it is more than likely we two will be moved on and you will meet fresh faces, so make sure all is in order when they take our places.'

'Very well. You can rest assured that all will be

in order here, Major.' Henri glanced at the other three men who gave their own agreement.

'I am pleased to hear it,' said Major Schulz, and strode quickly from the room followed by Hauptmann Alder.

Henri, with the others beside him, watched from the window as the Germans drove away. 'It was the wisest thing to do,' he said. 'This way the factory is still ours and can be under our sole control when this war is over, if we cooperate now.' He felt he had gained a victory and was determined he would remain in charge of his beloved business.

He felt sure his policy of cooperation with the Germans was right when, by early June, the British Expeditionary Force had been driven on to the beaches of Dunkirk and only a miraculous evacuation saved it. He took little notice of the rallying call, made by Prime Minister Churchill to the British people, who were expecting to be invaded: 'We shall fight on the beaches, we shall fight on the landing grounds, we shall fight in the fields and in the streets, we shall fight in the hills; we shall never surrender.'

Even the remotest village and its inhabitants felt drawn into the war effort, part of the same crusade for survival. The people of Rushbrook experienced it more than most – the expanding airfield on their doorstep was a constant reminder of the additional part they would have to play on its completion. Everyone was on tenterhooks, wondering how the invasion would come: by sea, of course, but would that be supported by parachute landings elsewhere in the country? People watched and waited nervously.

31

So did Hitler until he decided the destruction of the RAF was necessary before he could order the invasion of Britain. After spasmodic attacks, his campaign started in earnest on 13 August 1940. Three days later was a day that Rushbrook villagers would remember when news broke that twenty-one-year-old Len Westland had been killed after shooting down two Dornier bombers earlier in the day. The village mourned the likeable young man and rallied round his parents and sister in their loss. It brought them closer to the fierce fighting over south-east England, though being near industrial Teesside they did not completely escape air activity themselves.

Hitler, expecting his superior numbers of bombers and fighters to prevail, had miscalculated the bravery and tenacity of British fighter pilots like Len Westland, who threw themselves fearlessly into the fray. Seeing his attempt failing, he turned his bomber force on London, expecting to bombard it and the whole country into submission.

Veronica needed to see her father about an alteration to a parcel of land required for the airfield. She went to Brunton the morning she received the request.

With no evidence of Charles anywhere outside, Veronica glanced at her watch. Ten o'clock. Of course! Coffee time. No matter what else they were doing, her father and mother always had coffee together. She knew she would find them in the drawing room taking a twenty-minute break.

'Ring for another cup,' said her mother, as greetings were exchanged.

'Haven't time,' said Veronica, and added with a teasing twinkle in her eye, 'not like some people I know.'

'Have you forgotten we'll soon be on our way to London?'

Veronica tightened her lips in annoyance. 'Of course. Your wedding anniversary. You always celebrate it at the Alexandra Hotel.' She frowned and asked with concern, 'Do you think you ought to be going to London at a time like this?'

'Why not?' asked her father.

'The bombing.'

'London's a big place.'

'I know, but...'

'There are a lot of people living there; they and many visitors aren't submitting to Hitler's attempts to scare them. Why should we?'

'We can't change the date we were married,' her mother put in.

'And we never miss our usual celebration in the hotel where we spent our wedding night,' added Charles. 'It's all arranged, all booked.'

'But...'

'No buts, love, please,' her mother appealed.

'Your mother and I have talked it over and we are going. We are not breaking with tradition. We've never missed a year yet.'

Veronica saw their determination. She knew

that when her parents had their minds set, nothing would put them off. She shrugged and said with resignation, 'Very well. Do you want me to run you to York station tomorrow?'

'No, of course not,' said her mother, a little indignantly. 'You've plenty to see to here without running us to York. Josh can do that, and be there to pick us up in four days' time.'

'If that's the way you want it, enjoy your anniversary.' Veronica gave them both a kiss and hurried away.

'Would you rather not go?' Charles asked Catherine as they walked into York station the next day.

'Of course not,' she replied firmly. 'We are not going to miss our usual anniversary.' The suggestive twinkle in her eyes brought a satisfied smile to his lips and the accompanying smile acknowledged how pleased he was with her agreement.

Their journey went well and the train was only five minutes late into King's Cross. They were soon sitting in a taxi, struck dumb by the evidence of destruction around which people were conducting their everyday lives. Rubble lay in mountainous piles; the sides of houses were torn down, leaving whole rooms exposed to view; shop windows, shattered by blast, were scattered on the pavements in thousands of pieces; blocked roads forced endless detours.

'Look.' Catherine pointed to a bath hanging by a couple of pipes from the second storey of a shattered building. The sign on the front of it read only 'Hotel', the rest of its name shorn away. They saw smoke rising from the building and being treated as serious by fire fighters and police, who were directing people away from the area.

'Those poor folk,' commented Catherine, shocked by the sight of three women with tattered bundles under their arms, scrambling away from a row of ruined houses.

'That must be all they have left,' said Charles. 'What on earth can life be like here?'

'Terrible,' said his wife, visibly shaken by what they were seeing.

Charles reached out to take her hand. They both lapsed into silence.

By the time they arrived at the Alexandra Hotel in Knightsbridge they were sensing and marvelling at the resilience of the Londoners who were attempting to go about their lives with some sort of normality, beneath which lay a fierce determination never to bow to Hitler's will.

They were greeted warmly once inside and made to feel at home, particularly by the friendly bell-boy who took them to their room.

'The city looked so awful,' commented Catherine. 'I had no idea it would be as bad as that.'

'Nor did I. You have to see it for yourself, don't you?' Charles agreed. He took one step towards his wife, put his arms round her waist and pulled her to him. He looked earnestly into her eyes. 'Amidst all the devastation we have just seen, I sensed a determination to get on with life. That is what we must do too. We are here to celebrate our wedding day and the wonderful life we have shared. Thank you for so much happiness, Catherine. I love you more than ever.'

Tears dampened her eyes. 'Charles.' The emotion in that one word matched his sentiments.

Their lips met in a long kiss, just as they had done on their wedding day.

As she did every morning, Veronica switched on the wireless to get the early-morning news. She froze in the process of filling the kettle, something she had taken to doing herself since losing several staff to the war effort. The announcer said that London had suffered one of the heaviest bombing attacks of the war. Destruction had been widespread and there were many casualties and dead. Though the voice droned on she heard no more. Even the sound of running water made no impression on her until the kettle overflowed and the splashes chilled her fingers.

A terrible premonition gripped her. Silently she said, They shouldn't have gone!

How long she stood there, leaning against the sink, her mind numb, drained of any desire to move, she did not know. Then the door opened and Sylvia and Elise, who had had permission to sleep at the Hall that night in order to be ready for early work on the estate, burst in.

'Oh, you're up. We were going to bring you a cup of tea in bed...' Sylvia's voice faded away. She shot a quick glance of concern at Elise. Then, moving quickly to her mother's side, she grasped her by the shoulders and asked, 'What is it, Mother?'

'London was heavily bombed last night.'

'Oh, no! What about Granny and Granddad?' Elise's voice faltered.

'Have we the hotel telephone number?' asked Sylvia.

'On the pad,' replied her mother.

As Sylvia hurried from the kitchen, Elise said to Veronica, 'Sit down, I'll finish making the tea.'

It had brewed and Elise was pouring the first cup when Sylvia returned. Veronica feared the worst when she saw her daughter's serious expression.

'The line to the hotel is dead. I tried to get the police and then the civil authorities, but all lines are engaged.'

Veronica merely nodded. There was nothing she could say; nothing any of them could do but wait and try again later.

'We'll stay with you, Mother, if that's all right?' said Sylvia.

'Thank you,' replied Veronica quietly. 'The work you were going to do can wait for another day. The rest of the girls know what they have to do, but I'll send word to The Heifer telling Gerty Sullivan she's in charge today.'

The rest of the day dragged by at Rushbrook Hall. Whatever the three of them tried to do, they could not concentrate. Phone calls brought no result and they realised why when they heard on the news the scale of the raid: whole areas devastated, buildings pounded into mounds of rubble. The ambulance services had been stretched to the limit, and the search still went on for the survivors and the dead.

After hearing the news, knowing that Mrs Eakins' parents had gone to London, Mrs Cole had come on duty even though it was her day off.

She tried to tempt them to eat something special from the meagre rations available to her. Though they appreciated her effort, no one could do it justice.

It was a long night too for mother and daughters left in limbo; anxiety meant they could not sleep.

At ten o'clock the next morning that changed when a maid answered the doorbell and came to announce, 'Constable Waldron is here, ma'am.'

Veronica's heart missed a beat and her mouth went dry as she said, 'Show him in.' The silence was filled with foreboding.

The Constable, helmet in hand, came in wearing an expression that clearly read: I wish I hadn't to do this.

'Morning, ma'am.' He nodded a greeting to the girls. 'I am afraid I have some bad news.' He cleared his throat. 'Information has been received that Mr and Mrs Charles Attwood were killed when the Alexandra Hotel in Knightsbridge was hit during last night's bombing. They were identified by documents on their persons, and by one of the staff who survived the bombing. I am so sorry, ma'am.'

Veronica's face had lost every vestige of colour. Her knuckles gleamed as she gripped the arms of her chair in an effort to keep herself under control. 'Thank you, Constable,' she said quietly.

'Ma'am, I took it upon myself...' His voice faltered in the face of her grief but he drew back his shoulders and forced his tone to be as normal as possible. 'I believed that you would want Mr and Mrs Attwood to be brought back for burial. I will be informed of the date in a few days' time.'

'Thank you,' was all she could say, as tears started to fill her eyes.

'Good day, ma'am.'

Sylvia sprang to her feet and saw him out, offering her thanks for the delicacy with which he had conducted his difficult task. Elise went to her mother, knelt down, and they wept in each other's arms.

'I wish Aunt Marie could have been here for you,' Elise said between sobs.

Veronica hugged her tighter and said, 'So do I.'

'She was always good for you when she came. She helped so much when Papa died.'

'And she was there for you too,' said Veronica.

'But primarily for you.'

'Maybe,' she replied, struck by the sudden feeling that she wanted to tell Elise about Marie. She had made a promise of secrecy long ago but in the stricken present, when violent tragedy had hit so near to home, she wondered if it was right for Elise not to know the truth. But there was no way she could seek Marie's opinion now so she put aside the thought.

When Elspeth Eakins arrived half an hour later she was lost for words to express her feelings at the loss of her friends. Veronica understood and accepted the sympathy in the power of Elspeth's silent tears.

The moments passed until she took a grip on herself. 'I must not burden you with my grief, you have enough of your own. Constable Waldron told me. I came at once. Now, if there's anything I can do, or anything you want you must let me know. I

346

am here if you need me.'

'We are grateful,' said Veronica. 'It is good that you are near.'

Two weeks later the joint service took place in the local Catholic church. It was packed to over-flowing as the last of those bearing the Attwood name were laid to rest. As much as she was suff-ering at the loss of her parents, Veronica kept her deep mourning to herself, finding support in the love of her two daughters. At the same time she threw herself into running the Land Army section in her charge as well as the two estates, always careful that the two interests did not impinge on each other. She was thankful that she had a good and loyal farm manager in Jim Barbour, too old for military service, whom she could trust to run things to her liking.

But changes would have to be made.

One evening a week after the funeral Veronica called a meeting of Jim and her two daughters, timing it for when they were all off duty.

After they were seated in the drawing room and glasses had been charged with wine, one of the last bottles Michael had put down before he died, Veronica raised hers and said, 'To parents and grandparents, wherever they may be.'

She went on, 'I invited the three of you here in order to tell you that yesterday I visited my soli-citor about the Brunton Manor Estate. First of all, though, let me mention Rushbrook. As you know, after Michael's death, I inherited every-thing. Elspeth had been taken care of financially before his father died. I was fortunate in having her support, and that of my mother and father, as well as yours, Jim. You were most supportive and considerate and I could not have kept the estate running without you.'

He gave a little shake of his hand as if dismissing her praise. 'The Eakins were always good to me and were a pleasure to work for, just as you are, Mrs Eakins.'

'As I said, I saw my solicitor yesterday about the Brunton Manor Estate. I thought my mother and father were going to alter their wills to include you two, Sylvia and Marie, but the solicitor told me they had not as yet done so. It does not make any difference now. As Jeremy was killed in the First World War, I am the only remaining child and as such have inherited Brunton. In the light of that, I thought it wise to ask the solicitor to draw up a new will for me. He will have it ready in a day or so.'

She paused to take a sip of wine and let the implications of what she had said sink in.

'First, I will deal with the running of the two estates. It had been my father's plan and mine to run the two together once the airfield opened, but we never got around to implementing it. Maybe it was just as well, the way things turned out.' She raised her glass to her lips again and then continued, 'Jim, how would you like to run the two estates as one?'

He looked taken aback. 'Me, ma'am? What about Bert Simpson? He's a good man ... done well with the Brunton Estate?'

'He has,' agreed Veronica. 'My father thought

highly of him. I would have asked you both to work together, but yesterday he handed in his resignation. As a single man still of serving age, he feels he should volunteer. I accepted that view. I told him there would be a job for him here when he comes back, but that I couldn't say now what it would be. He accepted that. So, Jim, would you manage both estates for me?'

'Mrs Eakins, most of my life has been bound up with those estates, one way or another. I will be proud to manage them for you.'

'I would want you to hire and fire as necessary.'

'Fair enough, ma'am. I will be happy to do so as long as I can consult you on policy and any major changes.'

'Of course.' Veronica smiled. She felt a burden lifted from her shoulders. 'I suggest that we meet tomorrow morning, ten o'clock in the farm office, to iron out any necessary details.' She stood up.

'Very good, ma'am.' He drained his glass and shook the hand she offered him.

'Here's to a successful future, Jim.' Veronica went to the front door with him and watched him go down the steps and stride away with a light step.

She returned to the girls in the drawing room. 'I'm sorry if I've delayed you from what you wanted to do.'

'Not at all,' said Elise. 'It was just a Land Girls' sewing night.' She pulled a face.

Veronica smiled. 'I wanted you to hear what I had in mind for Jim, just as I will want you to know about everything affecting the two estates. Well, one now. You should have a say about what concerns it. Now, I'd like your thoughts on this. I am going to continue living at Rushbrook Hall; after all it was the home I shared with your father. Brunton Manor is empty, and it is not good for it to remain that way. With your approval, I would like to offer it on loan terms to the RAF, as an Officers' Mess for those who will be stationed on our doorstep.'

There was a moment's silence, and then...

'A fine idea, Mother!' said Elise.

'It is!' agreed Sylvia. 'Gorgeous officers nearby – and fliers at that!'

'Get it organised before they get somewhere else,' Elise urged.

Veronica laughed out loud. 'Steady on! There'll be no shenanigans for you, or fraternising with the RAF will be prohibited.'

'You wouldn't, Mother, would you?' asked Sylvia in some alarm.

'Don't try my patience then.' Veronica grinned and added, 'Not a word to the other girls yet. It may not happen. I don't know what the procedure is, but I'll get in touch with Squadron Leader Hawkesley tomorrow.'

They sat chatting for another twenty minutes before Sylvia said, 'We should be getting back. Early-morning start tomorrow.'

'Of course, you're going with Farmer Jackson to York cattle market. He's hoping to replace the two cows he lost. Well, have a good day.'

'We will.' Sylvia grinned as she stood up.

Knowing why she was grinning, Elise explained amidst much laughter, 'He's a grumpy old...' She pulled herself up short. 'Blames the politicians for everything, even the weather when it's doing good by raining on his crops.'

'Can't see a joke,' put in Sylvia as they went into the hall.

'Remember the day he turned up in the potato field, a little the worse for a morning session in the pub, and started flirting with Rosie?' said Elise,

'And his wife saw his antics and cheered Rosie when she tripped him up so that he sat down in a great pool of muddy water!'

They were still chuckling when they said good-bye to their mother at the front door.

'Get that Officers' Mess set up,' was Elise's parting instruction.

Veronica watched them stride away into the gathering dusk. Oh, to be young, she thought. Hang on, she added, scolding herself. You're not so old. Forty-four. Parties in the Mess? Better see if your dresses are in good order...

32

'Mrs Eakins, this is a fantastic offer you are making. Saying thank you doesn't seem enough.'

'Then say it and leave it at that, Squadron Leader,' said Veronica with an understanding smile.

He smiled back at her. 'Thank you.'

She gave a nod of acceptance. 'It is settled.'

'Not exactly,' said Squadron Leader Hawkesley. 'Documents must be drawn up giving the RAF, and only the RAF as you stipulated, permission to use the Manor, making any alterations and additions necessary to house the officers serving here.'

'I agree to that, of course.'

'This is a large house but, we may have to build an annexe and also an extension to the kitchen.'

'I thought that might be so when I first had the idea,' she replied.

'Full compensation will be written into the agreement. I will bring the necessary papers for signature next week.'

'There is the question of furniture,' she reminded him. 'There are several items that I will have removed to one of our barns. Also loose valuables will be packed and stored. But, for the most part, you will take over the house as it stands.'

'You are most kind and generous, Mrs Eakins. I am sure the officers who serve on this airfield will appreciate the comfort of your home – it will be a marked contrast to the usual cramped quarters of a bomber.'

'Have you any idea when a squadron will be moving in?'

'I haven't any set date. There have been a few problems about the sites for the bomb-dump and the storage of petrol, but they are just about sorted out. Some access roads will have to be altered; that is not a real problem, but it all takes time ... especially when suppliers don't meet their delivery dates. However, I can say confidentially that we are all anxious to get this new plane into action as soon as possible. We think it may have a marked influence on the war.'

Veronica watched the house where she had been brought up made more usable as an Officers' Mess, but was a little disappointed when the first planes to land were Wellington bombers, not the new ones Squadron Leader Hawkesley had mentioned. But at least the airfield was in use now. The squadron stayed there six months, leaving its mark on Rushbrook Village and its people. Though they were not involved directly with the airfield they felt its presence and impact in different ways, and were never more strongly involved than when they saw bombers returning damaged, holes in their wings and fuselage or limping home on one engine. Land Army girls who had counted the bombers leaving also counted their return. They all lived on a knife edge until each knew the flier who had wanted her company in particular was safely home. They let their hair down when their boyfriends were not flying and none more so than Sylvia and Elise, though they were careful not to become too strongly attached to anyone. It was a case of have a good time together while we can – let tomorrow take care of itself.

When the Wellington squadron was relocated to another station it left behind a sense of expectancy, which was not answered until one day in 1942.

The station was going about its regular duties when the drone of distant aero-engines began to grow louder and louder. By the time the thunderous sound of those engines shattered the sky above the airfield everyone had stopped what they were doing. They became captivated by a sound that was different from any they had previously heard. This was very distinctive and everyone knew that in future they would associate it with this new four-engine bomber. They were mesmerised by its pugnacious, determined lines, graceful in flight, that seemed to say: I'm here, I'll do the job, but I'll show you too how wonderful it is to fly with me.

Veronica had left her desk where she had been working out which five girls she could allocate to a week's work requested by Grimston Farm. She was thrilled by the arrival, not only by the skill of the pilots but by the appearance of this aircraft; somehow it seemed to strike a special chord with her; it seemed to be showing off and saying, You've never seen anything like me before.

One by one each bomber circled the airfield and landed, to taxi round the perimeter track to its allotted hard-standing. Silence spread across the airfield as the engines were switched off. But the lone bomber still circling, its engines purring smoothly with that distinctive sound, held Veronica's attention.

The pilot took it beyond the airfield, banked, lined it up on the main runway then took it down until it was only a few feet above the ground.

'Undercarriage!' Veronica screamed, but her instinctive attempt to warn the pilot was lost in the roar of the engines. Relief poured over her when she realised he was flying this low on purpose. She was mesmerised by the sight. At the end of the runway the pilot put his plane into a climbing turn, circled, dropped the nose and zoomed past the control tower. Veronica was fascinated but wished he would land before a misjudgement caused tragedy. He took the bomber up again, brought it round and then headed straight towards her house, faster and faster. The air was filled with a thunderous roar as the aircraft sped past the front of the house where she was standing. As it flew away to climb higher and come in to land, she realised she had not flinched once, even when the roaring around her became relentless. She knew then she had fallen in love with this aeroplane.

33

'Ma'm, there's an officer here asking to see you,' Veronica's maid announced with a little tremor of excitement in her voice.

'Very well, show him in, Gwen.'

'Here, ma'am?' asked Gwen, surprised that she would be bringing him into the dining room where her mistress was still having breakfast.

'Yes, and when you have shown him in, bring another cup and another pot of coffee,' said Veronica, thinking it must be Squadron Leader Hawkesley, whom she knew had arrived at the airfield two days ago. She guessed he was here because of the arrival of the new bombers.

So she was surprised when a stranger walked in. His blue battle-dress fitted him to perfection, the stripes on the shoulder epaulettes denoting he was a Wing Commander. Below the wings sewn at his left breast, which showed he was a pilot, was the DFC ribbon. He held himself erect in a relaxed way, with the air of authority that befitted his rank. But Veronica was captivated by the light in his steel-blue eyes. Their alertness was overlaid by an air of kindness, which she was sure could disappear fast if the situation warranted it. This was a man who naturally drew attention to himself, not in any way that would alienate people but rather that would generate deep trust; someone who could be relied upon even in extreme circumstances. She found herself thinking that his crew must worship him; in fact, maybe the whole squadron, aircrew and ground personnel alike, did. She felt Rushbrook airfield would be a happy and efficient place under this man's command.

'Mrs Eakins, I am Wing Commander Vine. I seem to have come at an inappropriate time ... I'm sorry to interrupt your breakfast.'

'Not at all, Wing Commander.' She had risen from her chair as he was speaking and now extended her hand to him. 'You are most welcome. You have interrupted nothing. As you see, I wear the Land Army uniform; I was merely contemplating the day ahead whilst I had my coffee. I hope you will join me.' She indicated a chair at the table.

'Thank you. That is most kind.'

As if on cue Gwen appeared with a tray on which there was a cup and saucer and a fresh pot of coffee. She placed it on the table and blushed when the Wing Commander thanked her.

'Mrs Eakins, I owe you an apology,' he

356

resumed, turning his gaze on to Veronica once more.

She was struck by the softness of his voice. 'For what?' She had only just met him, so what lay behind this statement?

'Were you standing at the front of this house when I buzzed the airfield yesterday?'

'Yes. So you were that pilot?'

He nodded. 'Mrs Eakins, I am so sorry if I alarmed you.'

She raised one hand, dismissing his apology. 'You did nothing of the sort. In fact, I want to thank you for bringing that beautiful 'plane to say hello to me.'

He chuckled and his eyes sparkled with delight and admiration. 'You sound as though you fell in love with her?'

'Oh. I certainly did. It...'

He held up a finger to stop her. 'Not "it".' He gave a little shake of his head. 'She.'

'Oh.'

'The Lancaster is never "it". She can be as temperamental as a woman, but, like a woman, handled properly ... caressed, treated gently ... she can return a love never experienced before.'

'And she was like that yesterday?'

'Oh, yes.' Veronica had no need to ask for further enlightenment, the feeling in those two words told her all. 'It delights me that you say you fell in love with her. I will be pleased to share her with you. That is, if your husband doesn't mind?'

'Even if he were alive, I'm sure he wouldn't mind my having a friendship with her.' Veronica

357

pursed her lips thoughtfully then said firmly, 'In fact, I'm certain he would approve of my new love.'

'Good. Then we'll share her. But I must still make my sincere apologies. I am very sorry for flying so close to your house. When I did see you standing there, it would have been too dangerous for me to pull out of the manoeuvre. I must scold my Bomb Aimer. He was directing me, but was supposed to be taking me over the Officers' Mess.'

'Oh, that's Brunton Manor, my home before I was married – three miles to the east of here.'

'I'm sorry for his mistake; he's normally spot on.'

'Please don't reprimand him,' pleaded Veronica. 'If he had got it right, you wouldn't be sitting here now.' The words were out before she realised how they could be taken, but she wasn't sorry they had slipped out.

'And I too am pleased he got it wrong. Mrs Eakins, though thankfully you demand no apology, I still feel I should make some recompense. Would you let me do so by agreeing to dine with me the evening after tomorrow?'

'That would be lovely, but there is no need.'

'There is every need, Look, this area's new to me; you'll know better than I where there is a good pub nearby that can manage some decent food in wartime. Out in the country most places seem to have secret sources.'

She smiled. 'I don't suppose you want it to be on the airfield's doorstep?'

He grinned like a schoolboy caught out in the

middle of his first kiss. His pilot's assurance had crumbled momentarily and she liked that in him. 'It might be wiser to go further afield,' he agreed. 'Aircrew are notorious gossips, especially about their CO and the company he keeps.'

'I know the very place. Friends of mine run it: The Broken Lock, ten miles away. And they have the sources you hinted at.'

'Splendid. I'll pick you up at six.'

'That sounds as if you have the means?'

He leaned forward, put a finger to his lips again and said, 'Ask no questions, hear no lies.' He stood up. 'Six then, two days' time.'

Veronica rose from her chair and accompanied him to the front door.

'It has been a pleasure meeting you, Wing Commander.'

'Terry, please.'

She acknowledged this with a nod of her head. 'Veronica.'

'Nice name. Until we meet again.' He put on his hat, adjusted it to the angle he liked, saluted her and walked briskly away.

She watched him go admiringly. He paused once to look back and raised his hand in farewell. She was pleased he had done so. It made her feel special.

Veronica turned back into the house, closed the door and leaned back against it with a contented sigh. A little smile curved her lips as she walked quickly to the stairs. In her bedroom, after closing the door, she spun around once in the middle of the room. A dinner date!

She pulled herself up sharply, conscience

pricking her for her own eagerness. She glanced at her bedside table, went to it and picked up the hinged photograph frame, left open to show two pictures of Michael: one looking handsome in his Army uniform, the other casual in outdoor clothes, collar turned up, cap at a jaunty angle, a broad smile on his face. She stood lost in memory for a while, and then with eyes fixed on him, whispered, 'You don't mind, darling, do you?' After a moment the atmosphere in the room changed. Afterwards she would always say, 'In those moments I am certain I heard him say, "Of course I don't. I want you to be happy."' Her lips moved in a silent, Thank you. You'll always be in my heart.

She slipped quickly into her overall coat and brown felt hat and hurried from the house. She was already behind time for her meeting at The Heifer, but it had been a pleasurable delay. Now she must make a call on the way. She drove quickly to the Lodge where she waited impatiently for someone to answer the bell.

'Hello, Veronica.' Elspeth greeted her daughter-in-law brightly. 'An early-morning visit, but no less welcome.'

'I haven't much time, but I have something I need to tell you before you hear any gossip that may give you the wrong impression.'

Elspeth had been ushering her into the cosy drawing room. 'This sounds intriguing.'

'You would have seen the bombers arriving yesterday?'

'Yes. I thought that last one was going to crash into your house. Silly man! Scared me to death.

Were you at home?'

'Yes, I was,' replied Veronica. 'I was thrilled by that display of flying.'

'You weren't scared?'

'No.'

'Oh, what it is to be young,' sighed Elspeth, realising had she been in her forties she too might have been thrilled.

'The pilot came to see me this morning, to apologise.'

Elspeth raised her eyebrows. 'Well, that was something.'

'He thought Rushbrook Hall was the Officers' Mess.'

'Easily done, I suppose, when flying at that speed.'

'As an apology, he has asked me to dine with him.'

'Quite right too!'

Veronica was a little taken aback by her mother-in-law's instant approval. 'I came 'specially to tell you. I didn't want you to hear it second-hand, and probably in the wrong context.'

Elspeth smiled. 'That was kind and gracious of you. I expect you thought I might disapprove.' She paused, came close to Veronica and placed her hands on her daughter-in-law's shoulders. Looking her straight in the eye, she continued with all the sincerity she could muster, 'We only live once and should make the most of it. But if you can bring some sort of comfort to a man thrust into deadly encounters, from which he may not return, then do so. Never, ever feel you are betraying Michael.'

Tears were coming to Veronica's eyes. She hugged her mother-in-law. 'Thank you,' she said in a choked voice. 'I can't linger. Speak later.' She hurried away.

'Terry, this has been a lovely evening,' Veronica said as he stopped the car at the front of Rushbrook Hall.

'I enjoyed it too,' he said, turning towards her in his seat. 'Thank you for accepting my invitation. You took my mind off my responsibilities.'

'Thank you for asking me.' After a slight pause, she added shyly. 'Would you care to come in for a nightcap?'

'That sounds very appealing but I think it might be wiser for us to avoid prying eyes. May I save it for another time if you will ask me again?'

She smiled. 'That goes without saying. Prying eyes?' she added thoughtfully. 'Then let's make next time a formal invitation. Dinner here at six-thirty on Wednesday? I'd like you to meet my two daughters and they'll be free that evening.'

'The pair of Land Girls you mentioned earlier?'

'That's right.'

'I look forward to meeting them. You made them sound very interesting.'

'I did rather hog the evening. I'm sorry. You can tell me all about yourself on Wednesday.' She swung quickly out of the car before he had time to move. 'Good night, Terry.' She closed the car door, stepped back and raised her hand in a wave. He returned the gesture and drove off.

He drove away feeling buoyed up by the evening he had just spent. Veronica had been more than just good company. He guessed with two daughters in their twenties she could be ten years older than he was, though she did not seem it. Did it matter anyway? An age was just a number whereas Veronica was a warm, caring, flesh-and-blood woman.

She watched the car disappear then walked slowly into the house. This evening she had felt young again.

Was she being foolish? She must be ten years older than him. But did age pose any barrier if you were young in heart and young in mind? And should past happiness be any barrier to a new friendship? Michael's mother had not thought so.

She paused at the doorstep and looked back across the darkened landscape. Out there was a silent airfield where bombers stood awaiting the day or night when men, some barely more than boys, would take them into a hostile sky, not knowing if they would return to the women who awaited them.

'I wonder what this is all about?' said Sylvia as she and Elise pedalled up the drive to Rushbrook Hall.

'Mysterious,' commented Elise. 'Mother was so insistent we must dine with her this evening, and that we should be here by six. She must have something up her sleeve.'

Sylvia glanced at her watch. 'Right on time!' she said, a note of satisfaction in her voice.

They propped their bicycles against the wall and hurried inside. They saw the door to the drawing room ajar and guessed their mother was

listening for their arrival. Sure enough, she appeared before they had time to reach the room.

'Ah, good, you are here,' she said. 'Run upstairs
and change into something nice.'

'What's going on?' asked Sylvia.

'You'll see. Off you go. Be down by half-past.'

Knowing they would get no more out of her,
the sisters hurried up the stairs.

'She's excited about something,' said Elise
when they reached the landing. 'She thinks she's
hiding it.'

'And why does she want us to smarten ourselves up?'

'There's only one way to find out.'

Ten minutes later, when they walked into the
drawing room together, they shot glances at each
other: Mother's keyed up – full of nervous excitement. They knew they both thought the same.
They looked questioningly at Veronica but all
they got was, 'You look nice.'

Sylvia had chosen a pale blue, calf-length skirt
and cream blouse with a high neck buttoned at
the throat. Elise had opted to wear red, her skirt
of a similar cut but the blouse had an open neck.
She wore a silk scarf tied loosely at her neck with
the ends hanging down her back. They both
noted their mother's tone of approval and that
made them wonder all the more what this evening was about.

A clock chimed six-thirty. They heard the
sound of a car drawing to a halt. Veronica jumped
to her feet, made as if to go to the door but
stopped. Instead she smoothed her dress.

There was a knock at the door and Gwen came

in. 'Your guest, ma'am. Wing Commander Vine.'

Sylvia and Elise goggled at each other. Mother entertaining a Wing Commander? They tried to control their startled reactions when a handsome man, wings and DFC ribbon on his best uniform, walked in.

'Veronica.'

She held out her hand to him. 'Terry. Welcome.'

Elise and Sylvia exchanged a quick glance which they both read as, Oh-oh, first-name terms!

'Terry, meet my daughters, Sylvia and Elise.'

He noted the pride in Veronica's voice and drew them in with his smile as he said, 'This is a great pleasure for me. I am delighted to meet you both.' His pleasure and approval showed in his eyes.

The sisters' thoughts were racing. How had their mother found this handsome man so soon – the squadron had only just arrived?

They sensed her relax a little. The first moments of this meeting had gone well, but they both wondered if she felt any guilt – a sense of betrayal towards their father? And was she thinking that they would not approve of her becoming involved with another man? They knew they would have to be cautious but did not want their mother to spend the evening wondering if they objected.

Sherry was served. Terry Vine raised his glass. 'To you all – and may life bring you whatever you wish for.'

They acknowledged his toast.

'You two young ladies are serving in the Land Army, I'm told,' he said pleasantly. 'Does your mother boss you about?'

'Oh, yes. Sends us on the most horrible jobs,'

replied Elise with a teasing grimace.

'You have the pleasure and comfort of being billeted at home,' he replied.

'That's what you think!' countered Sylvia. 'Mother insisted that we were billeted with the other girls at The Heifer.'

'And I don't suppose you objected to the chance of escaping from home?'

'Well, we didn't view it like that. Mother thought it best if we mixed with the other girls, no privileges and all that.'

'Quite right.' He gave a little nod, approving Veronica's decision. He knew these young women had been loved but never spoiled. And from their demeanour and ease with their mother, he also realised that all three of them had always been close. He liked that.

'And we were used to being away from home. You see, we both went to boarding school near York,' explained Sylvia.

'I never had the privilege ... well, the experience of completing my education at a minor public school. I still had two years to do there when Father lost a fortune. His business partner cheated him. We went to Canada. Father hoped to make a new life there but the upset and anxiety had taken its toll and he suffered a heart attack. Mother had a breakdown so I lost her too. I came back to England and got a job in an engineering firm. I was doing quite well, but when war appeared imminent I volunteered for aircrew. And here I am now.'

'You've done well in spite of early setbacks, and that is to be admired,' said Veronica.

He smiled his thanks. 'A lot of luck too,' he said, 'especially in this job.' Wanting to direct the conversation away from himself, he asked, 'You were all born and bred here?'

'Yes,' replied Veronica.

'And you are likely to live the rest of your lives here?'

'Possibly. We all love the land, but I would not hold my daughters back if they ever wanted to spread their wings.'

Before any more could be said there was a knock on the door. Gwen came in. 'Cook says everything is ready, ma'am.'

'Thank you, Gwen. We'll be there in a moment.'

When the door closed behind her, Terry said, 'You have managed to keep some staff?'

Veronica smiled. 'Only Gwen and Cook. Gwen arrived when everyone else left to do war work. She's a good girl but not altogether with it. We lost three indoor servants here and the same number at what is now your Officers' Mess. I lost my full-time cook so was lucky to find a villager who comes in when I want her.'

'So you own both properties?'

'Yes, and the combined estates. Some of the men left to join up. Several were exempt. I was lucky to have two managers at first, but one thought it best to join up so I combined the two jobs.' She stood up. 'But enough of that. Let us go and see what Cook has managed for this special occasion.'

'Special?' Terry queried.

'Of course it is,' said Elise brightly. 'We've never

had a Wing Commander to dine before, and one with the DFC at that.'

He laughed. 'So who should I escort to the dining room? Remember, I have only two arms and am not going to see one of you unescorted.'

'Then you must escort your hostess,' said Sylvia.

The smile he gave their mother was not lost on the two young women, nor was the gracious acknowledgement Veronica gave him. Sylvia and Elise winked at each other as they fell in behind; a wink of approval and agreement.

The meal passed off most pleasantly and they all remarked on the wonders Cook had created with the limited ingredients available.

'I wish Aunt Marie could have been with us,' said Elise as she laid her spoon on her plate after finishing her apple pie.

'Aunt Marie? You never mentioned you had a sister, Veronica?'

'I haven't. She is a very dear friend of mine from schooldays. We both started on the same day, at the same school my daughters later went to. You know how it is – children get to call such friends "Aunt". Marie is French. We get on so well.' Veronica went on to explain how her friend had come to live with them during the First World War. 'Her French rubbed off on me, I can speak it pretty well and so can Sylvia, but Elise speaks it so like "Aunt" Marie she's well, like a native.'

'Interesting,' he mused. 'And you've never thought of using that talent to benefit the war effort?'

'I wouldn't know how,' said Elise.

'If you are interested, I might be able to put you in touch with someone who could use your talent.'

'Should we make ourselves more comfortable in the drawing room?' Veronica suggested, bringing to an end that line of conversation.

Nearly an hour later, after giving her sister a little nod of the head and receiving her acknowledgement, Sylvia said, 'I think we had better get back to The Heifer.' She started to rise from her chair. 'We'll just change into our working clothes.'

A few minutes later they arrived back in the drawing room. Terry sprang to his feet. 'You look just as pretty in your new outfits,' he said graciously.

'Pull the other one,' said Sylvia with a laugh. 'Good night, Wing Commander.'

He bade 'Good night' to them both, adding to Elise, 'If ever you consider using your French, as I suggested, contact me. I hope we'll all meet again soon. I have no doubt my aircrew will soon seek out you and your fellow workers.'

'I believe you are not quite up-to-date with some of your crews,' said Elise with a wide smile. She turned to Veronica. 'Good night, Mother. Don't bother to come out.'

'No, don't leave our guest.' Sylvia kissed her.

'We'll both see them off,' said Terry, guessing Veronica would like to.

'They are delightful young women,' he said as they watched Sylvia and Elise pedal away into a countryside that was bathed in pale moonlight. 'Be sure of it, my aircrews will try to charm them when they meet up.'

Veronica smiled. 'Do your crews take lessons from you?' she teased.

'Is that what I've done with you?' he asked. As he put the question he slid his hand into hers. She did not pull away.

'I enjoy your company, Terry. Let's keep it that way for the present,' she answered quietly, and kissed him on the cheek.

He touched the place where she had kissed him. 'I'll feel that whenever I fly.'

Four nights later the sound of engines starting up, one by one, spread across the airfield. They brought Veronica on to the steps before the front door. She watched the dark shapes of sixteen Lancasters roar one by one down the runway and take majestically to the sky.

'God bring you safely home,' she whispered.

34

'Let us leave the gentlemen to get on with their weekly meeting, Marie,' her mother said, rising from the dining-room table.

Henri, Jacques and Roland rose to their feet. Margaret came over to her husband. 'Will it be a long one?' she asked.

'More than likely; don't wait up for me,' he replied, and kissed her on the cheek.

Marie kissed Jacques, knowing that her love for her husband, which had been through the fire of betrayal and regret without his knowledge, had strengthened with the passing of time. Now it was being tested again because of his close association with the Germans, intent on striding across Europe and crushing it beneath the heels of their jackboots.

'I'm sorry your father could not be with us,' Henri said, as he poured himself another glass of wine, while a servant cleared the table.

'He regrets it too,' replied Jacques, 'but he'll miss nothing. I will report to him tomorrow. He'll be at the factory for a time.'

'Good,' Henri approved. Once the servant had finished and the door was closed he went on, 'As I have said before, every one of us must be up-to-date at all times. Germans admire efficiency so it is essential that we meet their expectations; our dealings with them must be fully understood by us all. So far they see us as an asset to their war effort; so long as we remain that we will be in a strong position. We must also keep our employees happy under these unusual conditions.'

'I believe they know they are comfortably off under the circumstances,' replied Roland. 'I have heard no word of dissent for a considerable time. Though there were times when I sensed hostility towards the Germans, unrest seems to have died out within the factory. I believe resistance movements are growing in various parts of the country, but they don't appear to be affecting Paris in any worrying way. Though you never know what can be hatching below the surface. Obviously, any espionage activities have to be extremely discreet;

people know the consequences if they are found out by the Nazis – deportation or death.'

Henri frowned. 'We don't want any subversive activity among our employees; it would mean an end to the factory so far as we are concerned. The Germans would move in to manage it and it would be lost to us; all that our two families have built up would be gone for ever. We must stamp on anything that might jeopardise our business. Should you become aware of anything out of line, put a stop to it – but do so without the Germans knowing.'

As he was speaking a gradual dull droning had grown in intensity but remained far away.

'Bomber's moon,' said Roland.

'They are out again tonight,' commented Jacques.

'They won't touch Paris,' said Henri. 'So we should escape. Apart from that, bombing alone can never win a war; you've got to have troops on the ground, and that's impossible for the Allies. The German Army is far too strong. Allied invasion would be a disaster. I believe everything will settle down into a stalemate and then political agreements will be reached. I think we will be under German rule for a very long time to come. If we accept that, we will prosper. And if we go along with the Germans now, our factory will continue to flourish.'

Margaret saw Marie's face tense as she inclined her head, listening.

'Bombers,' she said, her voice scarcely above a whisper.

Her mother nodded.

'How do you feel, Mama? It must be strange to hear them when you are English?' Marie looked searchingly at her mother.

'Every time I do I pray that they will all get back safely.' Seeing the confusion in her daughter's eyes, she added, 'I know France is my home, but I can't help it. I've never been consulted, nor dare I pass an opinion, but I don't agree with your father's current policy of cooperating with the Germans.'

'Jacques says that it is the only way for us to survive.'

Margaret gave a shrug of her shoulders. 'If that is what he believes, then so be it. You look puzzled, Marie?'

'I don't know where I stand. I'm French by birth but have an English mother, and a great deal of my life has been spent in England where my most precious friends live. Where should my loyalties lie?'

'Marie, I can't answer that. You can only follow your own conscience when the time arrives for a decision to be made. All I can say at the present moment is, be careful who you trust and how you talk to them. At times like these you can never really know who your real friends are.'

'I'm going to check the animals,' said Claude, as he crossed the kitchen to where his wife was slicing apples. 'I won't be long, and then I'll take you to La Corinne for your performance this evening.' He came up behind her and slid his hands round her waist. She let the knife slip from her fingers, turned and smiled at him. 'Your eyes always dazzle me,' he whispered huskily, and let his lips meet hers with a passion that was always there whenever they touched. It had never left them in twenty-three years of marriage, during which time they had seen their two daughters make good marriages too.

'I'll be devastated by your absence,' she said. 'Time will drag until you return ... but I'll live.'

He kissed her again then hurried from the house. He strode quickly in the direction of the cattle sheds, turning at a bend in the track after waving to her – a ritual whenever he left by this way. He glanced in the direction of his vineyards, thankful that they and his farm had so far escaped any destruction, and that he was left to carry on farming as long as his produce was channelled towards the occupying Germans. He wished he still had the two men he had employed regularly but they had left to fight at the outbreak of war and both been killed. Keeping his establishment going had not been easy, but he had managed with casual help whenever he could get it.

He checked the first shed and found that all was well; the cattle had sufficient food until next feeding time. They looked contented, having recently been moved indoors ready for the coming winter. Here they would fatten until the Spring, and then go to slaughter to fill German bellies. At that thought, Claude's lips tightened and he kicked viciously at a clod of earth as he left the shed. He went to the next one and picked up a pitchfork as he entered, knowing he would have to give extra fodder to two of the cattle who had better appetites than the others. As he went to load a barrow the pile of fodder moved and a voice said weakly, 'Don't, please.' Startled, he held the pitchfork up, but kept it poised to use if necessary. Straw scattered as a bedraggled figure staggered to its feet. 'Please, help me.'

'English?'

The man nodded and there was relief in his expression that he had been understood. 'Yes.'

Claude had noted that the dishevelled and stained clothes he wore bore wings at the breast. 'Air Force?' he asked.

'Yes. Baled out some days ago,' the man gasped, 'near the Rhine.'

'Where were you headed?' Claude asked, lowering his fork.

The man shrugged his shoulders. 'Thought I might get to the coast, find a boat. All I ask is a little food and I'll move on. I know it will be bad for you if the Germans catch me.'

Claude hesitated. 'Wait here.' He felt the uncertainty emanating from the airman. 'It's all right, I'll not betray you. I hate the Germans as much as you do, but in my position it is better if I cooperate with them.' He saw the other man stiffen. 'No, I am not going to hand you over,' he added in reassurance. 'Just wait here... I'll get you some food. I'm Claude Gabin, and old enough to be your father no doubt.' He held out his hand.

The airman took it and felt encouragement in its strong grip. 'Martin Lincoln. I'm nineteen, sir.'

'All right, Martin. Wait here.'

Corinne looked up when the kitchen door opened. 'You're soon back.' Her voice faded; she had known immediately by Claude's serious expression that something troubled him. 'What is it?'

He came and stood beside her. He knew there was no need to beat about the bush with Corinne. 'There's an RAF flier in one of the sheds.'

She was dumb with shock for a moment before asking, 'Is he wounded?'

'No, but he's exhausted ... all in. Says if we can give him food he'll move on, head for the coast and be no trouble to us, but I think we should try to help him.'

Corinne looked hesitant.

'You don't think we should?' he queried, showing surprise.

'No, I don't think that,' she replied quickly.

'Then there is something else?'

She turned to him and rested her hands on his shoulders, looking hard into his eyes. 'Claude, we have never kept any secrets from each other.'

He nodded.

'But I have kept something from you for the last eighteen months. I'm sorry, but I had my reasons.'

'This will have to wait, there's a flier in one of our sheds,' he said, his voice revealing shock and annoyance.

'It concerns him,' she replied.

'How can it?' he rapped in disbelief.

'Hear me out, please.' He could not withstand the pleading in her eyes and nodded, granting her request.

'Eighteen months ago, Paulette and Marcel became involved with the Resistance movement.'

'Working underground against the Germans?'

'Yes. They sought my help. The Germans had allowed many night clubs to remain open, as places of entertainment for their soldiers and airmen, among them La Corinne and the Blue Lagoon, so I was in a good position to gain information.' She saw his face cloud over and added quickly, 'It involved nothing more than chatting on a friendly basis with them. Oh, some of them expected more but they soon realised it was not on offer and they would have to go elsewhere. They respected that and continued to enjoy my company. I believe it made them all the more eager to impress me with their talk, and inebriated tongues let things slip.'

'It was nothing more than that?'

'Nothing.'

'Why didn't you tell me? You could have trusted me.'

'I'm sorry; maybe I should have done, but if ever anything went wrong, I wanted you to be able to show you were not involved.'

'Well, now I am ... with that young man in the shed.' She saw he looked bemused, as if he did not know what the next move should be.

'This is all new to you, Claude. Marcel has helped several airmen already as well as being involved in more serious business, so when you take me to La Corinne later today we'll make everything known to him. He'll help. Now let's take that young man some food and tell him what we are proposing to do.'

Within a few minutes Corinne was being introduced to Martin who was surprised to learn he was to be helped by this attractive vivacious lady who was a night-club singer.

'We have brought you food and blankets. We want you to remain here until we return tomorrow morning. We will have to lock you in otherwise any prowlers might find you. If you hear any movement, do not do anything but remain still,' ordered Corinne.

'That window's too high for anyone to see in unless they have a ladder. They won't find one; ours is in here with you,' said Claude.

'There'll be enough light from it for a while, so I've brought you an English novel if you are inclined to read,' said Corinne. 'After dark, there is nothing we can do; we daren't risk a light here. Please, just be patient. There is much to arrange. The person we will be dealing with has had several airmen pass through his hands, but it may take a while to arrange onward travel for you. Is there anything you want to know?'

He gave a shake of his head. 'No. I'm just relieved I have found sympathetic people who can help me. Thank you.'

Corinne came to him and kissed him on the cheek. 'You should be safe here. Be patient.'

Two hours later Marcel Fontaine and his wife were in possession of all the facts about the young airman hidden on the Gabin farm.

'You have done exactly the right thing,' Marcel told his friend. 'Keep him there until I can make arrangements to move him on. I am sorry that you have become involved, Claude. It puts you in an awkward position when it appears your father, brother and brother-in-law are collaborating with the Germans by keeping the factory running.'

'I'm sure it's not done willingly,' he said.

Marcel made no comment. He was not so certain.

35

'Elise, Elise!' Sylvia leaned over her sister, shaking her by the shoulder. 'I need your help.'

Elise groaned and pulled the sheet tighter around her shoulders. Sylvia raised an eyebrow; her younger sister was always bad at getting up in the early morning. There was only one thing for it. She grabbed the bedclothes and yanked them off.

Elise let out a curse and sat bolt upright.

'Quiet, you'll wake the rest of them. Lizzie's sick, she can't do the milking so you'll have to help me. If we're late we'll get a taste of Farmer Carson's wrath and that won't be pleasant.'

'Silly old b ... doesn't know when he's well off, having us to do his milking,' muttered Elise, swinging sleepily out of bed. 'Brr... And it's cold!'

'Well, move, and then you won't feel it,' urged Sylvia.

Fifteen minutes later they were pedalling away from The Heifer and Sylvia was agreeing with her sister that it was indeed chilly.

'Not only that,' Elise added, 'it's still b ... dark. There must be a better way of helping the war effort than this.'

'We jumped at the chance of serving in the Land Army to keep us near home and the land we love.'

'Sure, but loving the land and enjoying it as we did was very different from anything we encountered after joining up,' Elise objected.

'I know, but moaning about it doesn't help,' said Sylvia. 'Let's just get on with it.'

Elise shrugged her shoulders. 'I suppose so.' She pedalled with noticeably less enthusiasm.

They reached the farm and turned into the cobbled yard. Everything looked dreary and uninspiring. They were propping their bikes against the wall when Farmer Carson hobbled out of the house. He plucked his watch from his waistcoat and peered at its face. 'Umph, just on time,' he said, as if he had hoped to catch them out being late. 'Well, don't just stand there ... get on with it. The cows need you.' He turned back into the house, calling over his shoulder, 'My arthritis is bad today.'

Elise grunted and put out her tongue as the door closed behind him. They went into the cowshed.

'He's lit a lantern,' Sylvia said with surprise.

'That's big of him, but he certainly doesn't do any cleaning up,' said Elise, wrinkling her nose in disgust. 'I'm due for a change. Wing Commander Vine's suggestion might just offer us a chance. I'm all for giving it a shot. What about you?'

Sylvia was cautious. 'I'm not so sure. We're

lucky to be here, doing a worthwhile war job that enables us to make our own estate more productive.' Then she added lightly, 'Besides, I couldn't take my horses and dogs.'

That evening Elise told her mother what she had been thinking.

'After what Terry said to you, I am not surprised. What about you, Sylvia?'

'I'm not so sure. I love Rushbrook and Brunton. The Land Army has given me a chance to stay here.'

'But you could be moved anywhere in the country at any time,' Elise pointed out.

'I know, but I'm willing to take that chance.'

'Mother, you said you wouldn't stand in our way if we wanted to spread our wings,' said Elise.

Veronica gave a wan smile. 'I did, didn't I? Would you want to do that without Sylvia?'

'If she wants to stay here then I would have to move on alone. She wouldn't have to come. We are both adults with our own lives to lead.'

'I know, my dear, but you will always be my children.' Veronica sighed and then said, 'To be honest, I don't want you to go. This land is your land; it belongs to you both, is your heritage. It will all be yours one day.'

'I'll be back, Mama,' said Elise, sure that she would.

Veronica said wistfully, 'Who knows what will happen and how you will change if you leave?' She gave a little shrug of her shoulders. 'If this is what you want, Elise, I'll not stand in your way, but please find out more from Terry. If you are set on this, I will be seeing him tomorrow

381

afternoon if he isn't flying. Would you like me to mention that you'd like to talk to him?'

'Would you? Oh, please do.' Elise sprang over to her mother and kissed her on the cheek. 'Thank you so much.'

The following evening, when Elise and Sylvia arrived at Rushbrook Hall from The Heifer, they saw Terry's car parked outside the front door.

'He's still here,' commented Elise.

They hurried into the house, threw their outdoor garb on to two chairs and rushed into the drawing room.

'Terry came this afternoon as planned,' Veronica explained. 'When I told him of your interest, Elise, he left me to go and see what he could find out. Since his return he has not told me anything. So, what news have you, Terry?'

'I was able to contact someone I know. I can't tell you what he does nor which part of the Services he works for; all I know is that he once asked me to let him know if ever I came across anyone who is good at languages. I told him about you. He was very interested and would like to meet you. He is based in London but the day after tomorrow will be on his way to a meeting in Edinburgh. He has suggested that he breaks his journey in York. He will leave on the 8.30 train from King's Cross and see you at the Station Hotel. He suggests lunch at 12.30, if that is agreeable to you?'

'That's wonderful,' gasped Elise. 'Well, it will be if my Land Army boss will let me have the time off?'

'I'm not sure she will,' teased Veronica, knowing from the excitement in Elise's eyes that she would not obey if told she could not have the time off.

'Splendid,' said Terry. 'I will take you into York. If there's any flying scheduled, my second-in-command will be in charge.'

'There's no need, if it's awkward for you. I can take her in,' said Veronica.

'I would like to see this friend of mine,' he said, 'so I'll do it. Better still, why don't you and Sylvia come too?'

'Do, Mother,' enthused Elise. 'The break will do you good. You'll have tomorrow to make any alterations to the duty rotas and free yourself.'

'All right,' she conceded.

The two girls whooped. 'And Farmer Carson can milk his own cows!' said Elise.

'I think you can manage that before we go,' grinned Veronica.

'You must be joking!' laughed Sylvia.

'Ah, there he is,' said Terry, as they entered the elegant foyer of the Station Hotel in York.

The man he indicated pushed himself from a chair positioned to give him a discreet vantage point before the entrance. He came briskly towards them. Veronica judged him to be in his forties, smart in an Army uniform which showed him to be a Captain who had won the DSO. His heavily lined face indicated he had been through experiences he would not wish to talk about, but Veronica saw there were still laughter lines around his eyes which were sharp and alert. He seemed interested in everything and everyone around him. Even now, Veronica recognised, he was making a rapid assessment of Sylvia and Elise.

'Terry, it's good to see you,' he said.

'And you, Leo.'

Veronica heard in the tone of their short exchange, and saw in their eye contact, a deep-seated friendship and a long-lasting respect for each other,

'May I introduce Mrs Veronica Eakins,' said Terry.

'I am pleased to meet you, Mrs Eakins.' He made a slight bow as he took her proffered hand.

'And I you, Captain...'

'Franklin.'

She acknowledged the name with a gracious smile.

'And these are your two daughters?'

Veronica introduced them.

He greeted them warmly. 'Elise, you are the one whose capabilities at French were especially lauded by Wing Commander Vine. What about you, Sylvia?'

'I am proficient but not so good as my sister. Besides, I'm happy in the Land Army.'

Captain Franklin nodded. 'It is good when you know where your talent lies and I am sure you are doing valuable work. The Land Army's job is vital to the war effort. Now, let us find a seat and relax over coffee which I've ordered to be brought to us. We will just chat generally, after which we will take lunch in the restaurant. Then I would like to talk to Elise by herself. For that I have reserved a small room – that one over there.' He indicated the door to the right at the foot of the staircase.

The coffee arrived and Veronica offered to pour.

'That would be kind, Mrs Eakins. I would only do something stupid and spill it all over the place.'

'I'm sure you wouldn't, Captain Franklin.'

'Leo, please. We are not standing on ceremony today.'

'Veronica,' she returned.

'I don't think I know any other Veronicas,' he said. 'A nice name.'

'That's what I told her when we met,' put in Terry.

'Rightly so. And are your family well? Is your wife fully recovered?' In the charged silence that followed, Leo felt the impact that one word had made. He realised he had made a horrible mistake. Terry had not told any of them he was married. Now he needed a quick exit from his faux pas, but how?

It was found for him. 'Not a serious illness, I hope, Terry?' Veronica asked, outwardly calm but with emotion churning inside her. She knew her daughters had picked up on the revelation too but she was not going to make anything of it now; this was Elise's day and there should be no distractions before her interview. 'You should have told me. I would have sent her my good wishes for a speedy recovery.'

'That would have been very nice,' he responded to the hidden barb. 'But there would have been quite a delay in passing on such a message. You see, she's in hospital in Calgary, a very long way away.'

Veronica raised an eyebrow. 'Such a distance between you. It must be a worry.'

'He's handled it very well, especially on top of his RAF duties,' put in Leo. 'And I know a friendship with you, Veronica, will help him get through.'

'I'll see that it does,' she replied. 'He's a good man; his wife is a lucky person.'

Leo, thankful that a situation which could have been explosive had been ably handled by Veronica, shot her an appreciative glance. He hoped the girl he was soon to interview was as resourceful.

'I will meet you in the room I pointed out to you in five minutes, if you would like to freshen up first,' said Leo as they walked out of the dining room.

Sylvia and Elise hurried to the Ladies' Room, Leo to the interview room, leaving Veronica and Terry to find seats in the lounge.

'I should have told you,' he apologised.

'Yes, you should.'

'Would it have made a difference?'

'Terry, I don't want to go into this now so let us leave it at that for the time being.'

After interviewing Elise for an hour, Captain Franklin told her, 'You must not – and I repeat *not* – divulge anything about this to anyone. I have told you what you can talk freely about with your mother, sister and Wing Commander Vine. As you know, I am going on to Edinburgh. I will be there two days then I'll return to London. In the following two days, I will be making my report on you and it will be considered in relation to the coming needs of the department. You will be informed of the result. In the meantime, carry on with your normal life.'

On the way home Veronica sensed her daughters were anxious to know how she was going to deal with her relationship with Wing Commander Vine. Knowing the question could not be asked in front of him, she eased the situation by concentrating on Elise's interview with Captain Franklin.

'There are some aspects of it and subjects I can't discuss,' her daughter pointed out.

This raised a surprised reaction from her mother. 'As secret as that?'

'Yes.'

'What are you getting into?'

'I don't even know myself except that Captain Franklin was particularly interested in my language skills. He conducted a lot of the interview in French. At times I thought he was testing the speed of my reactions to what he said.'

'I wonder why that could be... Terry, you are quiet, have you any idea?' Veronica asked.

'Please, don't press me. You know Leo wants nothing said about today, and what we say to each other has to be strictly limited. I think Elise will have exhausted what she is able to tell us.'

Veronica tightened her lips in annoyance. Elise saw this and said quickly, 'Mama, let us leave it at that. We will hear more when Captain Franklin is back in London.'

The rest of the ride was spent in silence, each of them lost in their own thoughts.

As Terry was bringing the car to a halt in front of Rushbrook Hall, Veronica said, 'You two girls had better become Land Girls again and get off back to The Heifer.' She sensed protests coming so added sternly, 'That's an order! And don't forget, not a word about today. You're with a lot of gossipy girls. One slip and it will be all over the countryside.' She turned to Terry and said coolly, 'You'll come in for a drink?' which he took as an order that could not be refused.

Veronica poured two glasses of whisky, and when they were settled looked askance at him.

'I offer you my sincere apologies,' he said immediately.

'And I accepted them back in York. I didn't invite you in for you to apologise again.'

'Invite?' His lips twitched with amusement. 'Order, you mean.'

Veronica faltered. Those blue eyes ... they stopped her from giving vent to the anger within her. She said, 'Did it really sound like that?'

'Sort of.'

'I didn't mean it to. Perhaps it was because I'd just ordered the girls back to The Heifer.'

'Then we are still friends?' She detected the hope in his voice.

'I said so in the Station Hotel, but I would like to discuss why I have only just learned you are married.'

He met her penetrating gaze, took a sip of his

whisky and said, 'What I told you about my mother and father and Canada was all perfectly true; my only sin was one of omission.'

'You can put that right now,' she said.

'Between my mother dying and my coming to England, I was married. My wife, Rita, was excited by the prospect of coming to England, but the reality was that she could not settle here. I agreed to her returning to Canada and said that I would rejoin her when my contract with the English firm I was working for ran out. War overtook all that and I volunteered for flying duties. I received word of my wife's illness two weeks before coming to Rushbrook. I met you and you offered a friendship that I realised I needed. I was going to tell you the whole story, but was frightened you would walk away from me. I didn't want that. You are an anchor for me, Veronica.'

As she listened she found herself feeling sympathetic towards him, but she was uncertain whether she felt anything more. She could not condemn him for feeling lonely. In a man's world, full of danger, he had needed the stability and reassurance a woman's interest could bring. She could not destroy that.

'Terry, answer me one question.' Her voice and eyes were serious. 'When this is all over, will you return to Canada?'

He did not hesitate. 'Yes, if Rita's circumstances remain the same.'

'Thank you for being honest, Terry. I wouldn't have competed with a sick wife.'

He met her gaze with the same intensity. 'Can we still see each other; still be friends?'

'If you feel the need of my friendship?'

'I do.'

'Then we shall continue with it. Who knows what tomorrow will bring?'

36

Ten days later the morning mail was brought to Veronica whilst she was having breakfast. She started to flick through the half dozen letters, but paused at one addressed to Elise. Her heart fluttered. Did it hold the message her daughter was eager to receive? A message that might take her from home? The typed address gave nothing away, but the postmark indicated it had been posted in London. Veronica turned the envelope over; there was nothing to indicate who it was from, but she believed she knew. She drained her coffee and went to her study.

She quickly perused the distribution of work she had organised for this week according to local farmers' requirements. Sylvia was at Dropwood Farm and Elise at Blackthorn Farm. She knew Elise would want her sister to be there when the letter was opened. Thankfully they were neighbouring farms so she would not need to meander all over the countryside.

Ten minutes after leaving Rushbrook Hall Veronica was at Dropwood Farm, explaining apologetically that she needed to take Sylvia away for a short while. When Veronica held up a letter, Sylvia

390

realized why she had come.

At Blackthorn Farm the farmer accepted Veronica's explanation and sent for Elise, who was busy cleaning out the pig-sties. She was soon out of her gum boots and overall and running to the car. The farmer left them together.

'What is it?' Elise panted, her expression a mixture of alarm and curiosity at this unexpected visit.

'There's a letter for you,' said Veronica. 'I thought you'd like Sylvia to be here when you opened it.'

Elise tore the envelope open and pulled out its contents. She scanned them quickly. 'I am to report to Adastral House in Kingsway, London, at three o'clock a week today,' she said, not knowing whether to be excited or not.

'So soon?' gasped Veronica. Her stomach churned; realisation that life would never be the same again struck her hard. Her face drained of colour, and she had to steady herself against the car.

'Mother, are you all right?' asked Sylvia, concerned by her reaction.

Veronica bit her lips and nodded. 'Even though I expected it, it's still a shock when the time comes.'

Elise put her arm round her mother's shoulders. 'Everything will be okay, Mother. Don't worry about me.'

'I can't help it. You and Sylvia are all I've got.' Veronica gulped back the threatening tears.

Elise hugged her. 'I'll visit you as often as I can, but maybe Captain Franklin will change his mind when he's seen me again. Let's go home and study the rest of these papers.'

'Apart from the formal letter telling me where to report, there's a train pass, first class, a sealed envelope for me to present when I arrive, and a list of clothing I should bring; they're erring on the warmer side. I know winter is coming but I wouldn't have thought they needed to remind me. I wonder if it signifies anything.'

'I can't imagine,' put in Veronica. 'You'll just have to wait and see.'

'Oh, here's a letter from Captain Franklin,' said Elise. She scanned it quickly. 'He's looking forward to meeting me again and says if there is any problem when I arrive, I am to ask for him personally.'

'And that's it?' Veronica asked

'Yes.'

She knew she had to be strong, give Elise her love and let her go. She wondered how Marie would feel about this decision.

'We'll have a little party tomorrow evening, just we three and Granny. Sylvia, you'd better get back to Dropwood, but could you call on Granny on your way there and invite her? Then go to The Heifer and inform Grace that Elise has resigned from the Land Army to join the WAAFs as from today. She'll call in to see the other girls in a couple of days.'

'Mother, shouldn't we invite the Wing Commander?' Elise asked. 'After all, it was through him making the suggestion that I...'

'I wish he hadn't,' said Veronica quietly, with

regret but no bitterness. Then: 'Of course,' she agreed. 'I'll ring Terry.'

The next few days were hectic for the Eakins family; Elise was kept busy packing, saying goodbye to the farmers she had worked for and the village folk who had always held the 'big house' girls in high esteem. There was a party for the Land Army girls in the village pub. Time sped by until the day Veronica and Sylvia took Elise to York station.

During the ten minutes before the train was due the uneasy silence was broken only by trivial words or repeated questions.

'I'll be all right, mother. Look after her, Sylvia.' 'Write.' 'Of course!' 'Don't forget us.' 'How could I?' Then came the clatter that announced the train was approaching the long curving platform to pick up the scores of passengers, most of them in uniform. 'It's here.' There were hugs that no one seemed to want to break. Tears they had all sworn not to shed refused to be held back. A hiss of steam. The train stopped. 'First class?' 'Two coaches forward.' Hurried steps along the platform. Into the train. Doors slammed. Elise pulled down the window, reached out with both arms; one hand for Sylvia and one for Mother. They held on. A whistle, blown from the back of the train, was accompanied by the waving of a green flag. The train started to move. Hands were held for as long as possible. Then they separated. 'Take care, love,' cried Veronica. Too full of emotion to answer, Elise nodded. 'Be good,' Sylvia called, trying to make light of the parting despite her damp eyes. Mother and daughter stood on the platform, arms raised, until they could no longer see Elise's waving hand.

Taking the simplest way out, Elise got a taxi from King's Cross. Producing her letter at the door of Adastral House, she was directed to the reception desk. After showing the letter again, she was instructed to take a seat. Nervously sitting on the edge of it she was mesmerised by the sight of RAF and WAAF personnel briskly moving about, as if what they were doing was vital to the moment. A few minutes later she was aware of a trim WAAF officer approaching her. She was of average height, her well-cut uniform emphasising her slim waist. Short light brown hair held a low attractive wave and was neatly rolled at the back of her neck.

'Miss Elise Eakins?'

Elise scrambled to her feet, saying, 'Yes.'

'I'm Flight Officer Felicity Norman.' She held out her hand, and Elise was relieved to find friendliness in her grip and reassurance in the smile that seemed to draw others to her. 'Welcome to Adastral House and the Air Force.' She made it all seem so casual, but Elise guessed this greeting had Captain Franklin's mark on it, or at least his approval. 'I'm pleased to meet you. I hope you had a good journey.'

'Yes, I did, thank you.'

'Just one more thing ... purely a precaution. May I see the information you were sent?'

Elise handed over the envelope she had received. The Flight Officer examined its contents, replaced them in the envelope and handed it all back to

Elise. 'Fine,' she said. 'Captain Franklin instructed me to take you to him immediately on arrival, so come this way.'

'Captain? I thought this was Air Force?' said Elise as they reached the stairs.

Felicity smiled. 'It is Air Force. Captain Franklin is seconded to us because the nature of the work necessitates an RAF liaison with the Army.'

When they reached the first floor, Felicity took her into an office where she spoke to the WAAF who was typing at a desk.

'Go right in,' she said. 'He's expecting you.'

Captain Franklin greeted Elise warmly, with an ease of manner that made her feel comfortable and eliminated any apprehension she was still harbouring. He glanced at Felicity, saying, 'You'll stay too, Flight Officer.'

As they sat down he glanced at the papers laid out on his desk. 'My report was received favourably by the senior members of my department. After studying that, along with the dossiers Flight Officer Norman and I compiled, they decided that you should be asked to join our section, engaged in special secret work. At this point I can say no more than that. On those flimsy terms, would you like to join our organisation?'

Elise, knowing Captain Franklin was watching her closely, hid any reaction she was experiencing. He noted that and was pleased she could control her feelings in such circumstances. 'It must be something worthwhile if you are unable to tell me more than that and yet bring me all the way to London, Captain Franklin. While I would like to know more, I will accept your offer.'

He smiled and relaxed in his chair. 'Splendid! Splendid. Don't you think so, Flight Officer?'

'I do indeed,' she replied, and he knew her quick summing up of Elise, in the few minutes of their initial contact, had been favourable.

'Now, Miss Eakins, I can tell you a little more. You will be immediately enrolled in the WAAFs. You will be issued with uniform, and tonight you will be billeted in a hotel that we use. Tomorrow you will be taken to a small unit on the outskirts of London where you will be put through a shortened version of the course that all WAAFs go through when they join up. It's a special crash course to familiarise you with what being a WAAF means and to give you some general training, but it will also include some special elements which will enable us to assess what role you are most suitable for in the future. There will be a few other girls on the course receiving the same basic training. That does not mean you will all be going on to the same sort of work afterwards. You must not discuss why you are there or how you were recruited. The course will last two weeks. You will probably wonder where it is taking you; just accept it, things will become clearer later. Have you any questions?'

'I got the impression when you interviewed me in York that it was my ability to speak French fluently that most impressed you and that it was something that would be useful in the job you had in mind. Is that still the case?' Elise asked.

'It is, but there are other attributes we want to check and link with your command of French. Just be patient about what we do with you and accept that it will be in the best interests of your country. Anything else?'

'I don't think so,' said Elise thoughtfully.

'Right. Flight Officer Norman will be with you from now until you finish your initial training, and maybe beyond. She will return with you to London, by which time we will have all the reports from her and your other instructors, and will be able to assess where you will be employed. One last word – keep silent about all aspects of your service from now on.

'You know the procedure,' said the Captain to Felicity. 'Miss Eakins is in your hands now.' He turned back to Elise. 'I wish you good luck in what lies ahead. I may not see you again, or not at least for some time. I move around a lot. But in extreme circumstances, and they would have to be extreme, you can always get a message to me through Flight Officer Norman. She will explain how. Good luck to you.'

Taking that as their dismissal, they left.

'Everything is in place,' said the Flight Officer. She glanced at her watch. 'We have an hour before I take you to get kitted out, so let's go to the canteen and get to know each other over a cup of tea.'

She chatted in friendly fashion as she led the way along the corridors before turning into a dining room that was functional but comfortable. Occupants at three of the tables cast them only casual glances as they came in. One young RAF officer acknowledged Felicity; the others were a mixture of RAF and Army commissioned ranks.

Though mystery still surrounded what was to

happen to her, Elise had a feeling that it was already mapped out, but it would ultimately be revealed according to her accomplishments on the courses ahead. She felt completely at ease with the situation thanks to Felicity's open and gracious manner while they enjoyed tea and scones.

She was then taken to get her uniform and on to the small hotel where they would both stay for the night. It had been taken over by the military for the duration of the war, but showed no sign of its true purpose.

'I suggest you ring your mother from here, but be careful what you tell her. Be informative but vague,' said her escort. 'We get an early evening meal here and then we'll go to see the show at the London Palladium.'

'To stop me dwelling on what might lie ahead of me?'

Felicity laughed. 'I can't afford to let you mope – bad for morale. Life is what you make of it, and give to it. So let's enjoy our evening together. Besides, when the tickets are provided, why waste them?'

When Elise lay down in bed a wave of homesickness came over her. During the day everything had felt new and exciting but now, in the quiet of her room, she felt lonely. She was missing Sylvia, felt bereft of life as she had known it. She wallowed in self-pity for a few minutes then shook herself; she had chosen this path and had to follow it or step away from it now. Giving way so easily was not her temperament; she would face the future with confidence and reach out to grasp any excitement it might bring. Excitement? She gave a little snort. She didn't even know what the future held, but whatever it was it must be more exciting than clearing out pig-sties or milking Farmer Carson's cows!

She felt steadier as she got ready the next morning, and approved her uniformed new look in the mirror. She tripped quickly down the stairs and into the dining room where she found Felicity just starting to eat.

After they'd exchanged greetings, Elise chose her own breakfast. 'Am I right, do I sit with you?' she asked.

Felicity laughed. 'Oh, ranks... Elise, in this organisation rank counts for little except on formal occasions, so relax and enjoy your breakfast.'

Felicity turned the conversation to Yorkshire. 'I believe your mother inherited two extensive estates?' She saw the surprise in Elise's expression and added, 'We had to do some research into your background.'

She accepted the explanation and said, 'Yes, she did.'

'Does that suit her?'

'Oh, yes. She is very competent about estate matters and farming, though of course we have the advantage of having a very efficient farm manager on whom she can rely.'

'Her heart must be in it?'

'It certainly is. Mother loves the country, loves those two estates. It hurt when she saw some of the land being torn up to make an airfield, but she understood and accepted it, knowing that one day it will all revert to her again. She made the best of the situation. She has become friendly with the Air Force people, and is respected by them. That gives her hope for the future of the land she loves.'

'And you ... will you return there?'

'Who knows what the future will bring, especially in time of war? I will wait and see what happens. My sister Sylvia is the one most likely to follow in Mother's footsteps. She too is a woman of the land. I hope she finds a young man who is as keen on it as she is.'

'Have you a young man in the offing?'

'No, not really. With an airfield so near none of the girls in the neighbourhood have been short of partners; Sylvia and I have had our moments, but no regular romance. Maybe with death riding the wings of those Lancasters we've been wary of getting too involved.'

'Wise,' agreed Felicity. 'I experienced it myself. I was on the point of getting engaged to a pilot when his plane crashed landing at base after a mission.' Her lips tightened at the memory. 'Having escaped the German fighters and anti-aircraft guns, to be killed so near safety was devastating. I saw it from the control tower. I nearly went under. The CO was brilliant; he saw I would be better away from an operational station and pulled a few strings to get me this job. It was the saving of me.' She sat up straight. 'That's enough of me and the past; never look back unless it's pleasant. I hope you are looking forward to your course?'

'I am, and eager to know what it entails. Cap-

400

tain Franklin gave me the impression that you would be with me throughout.'

Felicity smiled. 'I'll be around but you won't be tied to my apron strings all the time. I'll not be breathing down your neck. I have more work to do than that. My presence will be unobtrusive. However, there will be a comprehensive report on you forwarded to our seniors at the end of the course. That will stay the same throughout your training, whatever it might be and wherever it might take us. If at any stage you want out, you must contact me first. I repeat must.'

As she packed to leave, Elise pondered on Felicity's words. Nothing concrete about her future, but the air of mystery about what was planned for her made it all the more exciting. Then she reminded herself she could be reading more into her situation than there really was, and she might be destined for some humdrum job – but it must be better than mucking out those cows. So she set out in cheery mood, determined to field all that life was preparing to throw at her.

There were nine other girls on the course but none knew their likely destination afterwards. Six had been brought from various RAF stations, four of those had been serving on Bomber Command airfields; two had come from Army units, and the remaining girl straight from civilian life. Elise found them an interesting lot, all eager to get on together and make the most of the situation they were in, oblivious to what the future held.

The course was hard work with so much crammed into it. As well as the basic drill and lectures on aspects of life and work in the WAAFs, Elise was detailed, along with Laura Dundas, to concentrate on mastering Morse code. By the end of the course they were enjoying the camaraderie of life in the WAAFs and congratulations flew between them when it was announced they had all passed with high grades.

Felicity contemplated postings for Elise and Laura. She was pleased that her contributions to their assessments and recommendations as to their future employment had brought them together; they would be good for each other in what lay ahead ... if they survived the next part of their training. Laura, short and stocky but strong, with an effervescent cheery personality, was rarely without a smile and willing to have a go at anything. She would add a touch of audacity to any operation, while Elise could have a calming effect on what, at times, was Laura's impetuosity.

The day after the course finished, they were called to the office used by Felicity.

'You have both done exceedingly well on this course, especially in those aspects designed to give us an insight into your character; you would not realise which they were. The result is that you have both been granted commissions. I am pleased. You both deserve it.'

Their eyes widened in surprise. Not really knowing what to do, they spluttered their surprise. Then Flight Officer Norman said, 'Relax, let yourselves enjoy the moment.' They grinned at each other, whooped and hugged. Felicity came out from behind her desk to congratulate them. 'We'll have a little celebration this evening. You will be leaving

402

here in a week's time, so go into town for your new uniform. We have arrangements with Ross Brothers. Just present them with the authorisation I will give you. One more thing: your next posting will be to a small military establishment about fifteen miles from Fort William.'

'Fort William? Where's that?' asked Laura.

Felicity turned back to her desk. 'I thought you might want to check it out. There's a map and there's Fort William. Fifteen miles from there is where you'll be.' She pointed to a mark on the map.

'Bloody h...' gasped Laura. 'There's nothing there. Wilderness, just wilderness. What the hell are we going to do there?'

'You'll find out when we get there,' smiled Felicity, and continued to refuse to enlighten them, though she did issue an order. 'You can tell no one where you are going, and I mean *no one*. Any letters you want to write will have to be handed to me first; they will be sent to a posting point with no connection to where you are. Any letters for you will continue to go to your present address and will be sent to you under special Army delivery.'

Elise wrote:

Dear Mama and Sylvia,

The course has ended and I have great news – I have been granted a commission! Now you will have to address me as Acting Section Officer! What do you think of that?

We will be leaving here soon. I don't know where we're going. You can continue to write to me at this address and letters will be forwarded to me. The course has been interesting and they have been a good bunch to be with. I am sorry we are being split up, but there are many different jobs to be done. I am remaining with Laura Dundas – you remember I told you in a previous letter she and I were getting on well? I'm pleased we will go on the next part of our training together. She is good fun.

I hope all is well at home, and that the Wing Commander still visits. Tell him I am enjoying my new life and will strive to do my best to prove that his recommendation to Captain Franklin was justified.

Both of you, take care.

Love,

Elise

P.S. Sylvia, I hope you are pulling gallons of milk!!!

After a long, tedious journey north, Felicity, Elise and Laura were met at Fort William by a burly Army Sergeant who, from the way he put his question to Felicity, had obviously met her before. 'Better journey this time, Flight Officer?'

'Yes, thank you, Sergeant Crozier. Meet Acting Section Officers Elise Eakins and Laura Dundas.'

'Welcome to the wilds of Scotland,' he said as he cast a critical eye over them. 'Think these two will survive, Flight Officer?' he added with a mischievous twinkle in his eyes as the newcomers scrambled into his jeep

'We don't know why we're here, Sergeant, but we'll survive,' rapped Laura sharply.

The Sergeant laughed. 'We shall see.'

About five miles short of their destination they

left the tarmac road for a rough track that wound its way across wild country. Elise and Laura were quiet; they really were beginning to wonder what they had got into. Then the track steepened, the Sergeant coaxed the vehicle up the hill and stopped at the top.

'There you are ... your home for the next month!'

The two girls gasped. Below them was a valley completely surrounded by hills, while ahead and to their right rose a menacing mountainous landscape.

'Still think you'll survive?' asked Sergeant Crozier with a little chuckle.

'Yes, and anything you can throw at us in this Godforsaken place,' Laura cracked back at him. 'Where are we camping?'

The Sergeant did not reply but put the jeep into gear and took it down the slope to a fork in the track; he took the right side which rounded the spur of a hill with the valley to the left. Once again he stopped. 'There you are. Your rooms await you.'

The Flight Officer and Sergeant allowed a surprised silence to fill the jeep; they had been in this situation before.

'There?' gasped Elise, nodding towards the large house snuggling into the hillside. There was a sense of solidity about the three-storeyed stone building, with its corners dominated by circular turrets.

'What's this?' asked Laura.

'Steadfast hunting lodge,' replied Crozier.

'Some hunting lodge,' commented Elise.

'Built in late-Victorian times. It had to be as stout as that to exist out here, but no doubt it saw good stalking, good shooting, and good living.'

'But everything would have to be transported in by what ... pack horse?'

'And wagon,' said the Sergeant. 'They were tough folk. You'll be as tough by the time you leave here.' He put the jeep into gear and drove the rest of the way to the front of the house. By the time he'd switched the engine off, a young Army Captain had arrived.

'Good to see you again, Flight Officer Norman. All go well on the journey?'

'It did, thank you. These are Acting Section Officers Eakins and Dundas.'

His smile was warm as he said, 'I'm Captain Magson, but you'll probably call me many other things behind my back before you leave here. However, welcome to Steadfast.'

'Thank you, sir,' they responded, noting that he wore the ribbons of the MM and DSO.

He turned to Felicity. 'Usual procedure for new arrivals. Get things sorted out then bring them to me.'

A few minutes later Felicity took them up a broad oak staircase to the second floor and into a large square room with two single beds, a large wardrobe, two dressing tables with mirrors, and two chests of drawers.

'Surprised?' said Felicity.

To put it mildly,' said Elise. 'A place like this in the wilds of nowhere!'

'Built by a Scotsman who made his money in shipping and incorporated new ideas from around the world.' She nodded towards a door. 'You'll find a bathroom and lavatory in there – one of the earliest installations in the country, I'm told. All the other rooms have the same facilities. He wanted his shooting parties to have comfort too – it can be pretty bleak out here. After his death his eldest son kept it going, but beyond that no one was interested. The military heard of it. Its position suited their requirements so they bought it without anyone knowing the identity of the buyers.'

'The mystery of our involvement persists. When are we going to know why we're here?' queried Laura. 'I don't like being kept in the dark.'

'Okay. To all outward appearances you will be members of the RAF, but to you and me and those connected with your training, you will be members of the Special Operations Executive.'

Elise's heart and mind jolted. This was not at all what she had expected when she'd mooted the possibility of leaving the Land Army. She glanced at Laura and saw she had paled a little. A heavy silence filled the room.

'You mean the organisation we have only heard rumours about ... the one that sends agents into Europe?' asked Elise in awe.

'That is only part of its work. Whatever your role, whatever you do, the need for secrecy is of the highest level. You must not talk about what you do here, not to anyone – not your family and certainly not your boyfriends. You will be here for twelve weeks. Your training will be extremely tough. You will learn things you will never have contemplated, and after all that you may still have to face dangers you'll never have imagined. It may not come to that because there are other branches of our organisation to which you may be more suited. That will be decided while you are here. I'll leave you now to get settled in. You'll soon find your way around the Lodge. There's a notice-board in the Common Room. Always keep your eye on that. Schedules are posted there. The evening meal starts at six and goes on until nine-thirty. Your training will begin immediately after breakfast tomorrow morning.' Felicity had reached the door while she had been speaking.

As soon as it closed behind her both girls flopped on to their beds and said, 'What have we done?' The way they uttered the words, as one, brought smiles to their faces that immediately turned into laughter.

'Little did I think...' Laura began, but let the words trail away.

'Nor did I,' said Elise. 'It's a far cry from the Land Army.'

37

'It's your turn first for the bath,' said Elise as she and Laura walked wearily into Steadfast.

'That's been the hardest day since we came here a month ago,' commented Laura, thinking back to the long time they'd spent in one of the wildest parts of the hills searching for clues, set by Sergeant Crozier and his team, that would lead them back to the Lodge. 'That b ... Crozier's trying to break us.'

'It's what he's here for,' Elise reminded her. 'We'll be no good if we can't stick it out.'

'I know. I'm going to enjoy that bath.' Laura started for the stairs.

'I'll glance at the papers,' Elise called after her, 'and then I'll be up.'

Laura raised her hand in acknowledgement without turning round. Elise went to the table where newspapers were laid out. She cast a quick eye over two of them, gaining the latest reports on the war. She noted that at the Casablanca Conference there had been agreement that the US Air Force should deploy their aircraft on daylight raids while the RAF continued to use Bomber Command at night. Elise wondered to what extent Wing Commander Vine was involved, and hoped he was safe. As she was folding a final newspaper a small item caught her eye. It was an unconfirmed report that carried no by-line, but told of recent sabotage at the Michelin works in Clermont-Ferrand. That took her thoughts to Aunt Marie. Were she and her family safe? Had the Gabins' factory been destroyed, or had the Germans moved swiftly to take it over? That brought a horrible thought – had Aunt Marie and her family been shipped to a prison camp, and all the deprivations that entailed?

She walked thoughtfully to the stairs and climbed them slowly, trying to cast such questions from her mind.

Hearing the sound of approaching vehicles,

Henri Gabin rose from his chair and walked to the window that gave him a view across the large compound before the factory entrance. He saw the German guards spring to attention and hold their pose while two cars swept by. They pulled up outside the main door of the office block. The soldier occupying the front passenger seat in each car was out almost before the car had stopped and opening the door for the passengers occupying the rear seat.

Henri stepped back so that he would not be seen but was still able to observe the officers. He was thankful that they all looked to be in a good mood, exchanging words amicably with each other. He saw Jacques and his father hurry out of the front door to exchange pleasantries and shake hands with the German officers. Henri knew them; dealings with the Germans since the day they had first swept in to commandeer the factory had always been cordial. He had managed to maintain his position in charge, albeit closely supervised, but that satisfied him. His beloved factory was preserved. He hoped today's visit would cement his relationship with recently appointed Oberst Eisberg. Their previous three meetings had been cordial enough. He turned away from the window and went down to make his own greetings.

'Ah, Henri, my dear friend,' the immaculately turned out officer smiled. He slipped a black leather glove off his right hand and took Henri's hand, already held out in greeting.

'Welcome, Oberst Eisberg. It is a pleasure to greet you again. I hope you are settling into your new assignment. Three visits in as many weeks ... I trust this is merely a social call?'

'Was it ever anything else?' said Colonel Eisberg, spreading his hands.

Henri knew that behind that innocent statement lay an ardent Nazi who, unlike some German officers, was an unwavering supporter of Hitler. He was also a ruthless man. Henri knew that from what had happened to some of his friends who'd chosen to defy Oberst Eisberg. At their first meeting Henri had realised any lack of cooperation with him could mean the loss of his beloved factory, and maybe even death. Cooperate he would, and be damned to what people thought of him. As far as he was concerned they were blind to a future that was obviously going to be spent under German rule. There might be setbacks but Henri saw ultimate victory as lying with the Germans. They had Europe and they weren't going to relinquish it; his future, that of his factory and of all his family, must lie with the likes of Oberst Eisberg.

'This is just a courtesy call, keeping in touch with a loyal friend,' Eisberg went on smoothly. 'How is production?'

On the surface this appeared to be a friendly visit with the Oberst and his attendants, Major Huber and Hauptmann Kaufman, in a jovial mood, but Henri was wary.

'It is stable, is that not so, Jacques?'

'Yes, there are no concerns – production can easily be maintained at this level.'

'Splendid,' said the Colonel. 'May we go inside and talk?'

'Of course.'

Eisberg turned to Kaufman. 'You have never been here before. Take a look around, you'll find it interesting.'

'Sir.' Kaufman saluted smartly and left the party.

Henri knew this was a subtle way of ordering him to make a check on the factory; it was presented as a spur-of-the-moment decision, whereas it had probably been arranged previously between the visiting party. Henri suspected they were suspicious of something but he did not know what. Maybe he was being paranoid about these frequent visits. He must see that this one went as normal. He was pleased to see Jacques and Victor exchanging banter with Major Huber.

Reaching a small conference room, they were soon comfortably seated around the central table, each with a glass of wine and the decanters placed handily.

Oberst Eisberg asked to see the latest production figures and Jacques produced them. Eisberg studied them then sat back in his chair. After a few moments' thought, which no one dare break into, he said, 'We need to up production by one per cent.' He saw doubt appear on Victor's face and immediately opposed it. 'It can be done. Look at machines one and six. Not now,' he snapped as Victor reached for a sheet of paper. 'When I am gone. You'll see it can be done or I will want to know why.'

Henri, Jacques and Victor saw that as a threat, but they knew it was unwise to challenge him.

'Very well, Colonel. It will be done.'

Eisberg gave a cold smile. 'I know it will.' He

took another sip of his wine. 'This is a fine wine, very fine.' He looked at the liquid remaining in his glass. 'It charms the eye.' He sipped again. 'And teases the palate. Your son Claude's production, I would guess?'

'It is indeed.'

'Does his father still have a say in the vineyard?'

'No. I signed it all over to him before the war.'

'A very thoughtful and generous parent. I would like to meet this lucky young man, and of course his wife too. I am told Corinne is a charming and accomplished singer who can win any soldier's heart. Ah, don't look so surprised, Henri. We Germans know everything; we make sure we do.'

Henri didn't know whether there was a warning behind his words or not, but he was sure there was a hint being made for an invitation, so he made it. 'If you have not met either of them, I think it is time you did. I will arrange it for a week this evening at my home, if that is convenient to you?'

'Splendid. I thank you.'

'With your permission, I extend the invitation to Major Huber and Hauptmann Kaufman.'

'Of course,' agreed Oberst Eisberg with an expansive gesture and a smile of satisfaction that he had engineered what he had come here for. 'We look forward to that.' He reached out for the decanter and poured himself another glass. 'One for the road as the English say, do they not?'

When Claude and Corinne received the invitation to dine with Henri and meet Oberst Eisberg,

413

they were not thrilled at the prospect but knew it would be fatal in more ways than one to refuse. They realised also that they must be on their guard. One accidental slip of the tongue could undo the use made of La Corinne in helping RAF aircrew to escape the clutches of the Germans, especially the Gestapo.

Oberst Eisberg was charm itself. He played on this and used his lower ranking officers as sounding-boards in his attempts to learn more about Henri and his family, but he learned nothing more than he already knew. It still did not completely allay the suspicions that dwelt in the back of his mind. He had no evidence to hold them ... as yet. But if he could ever prove something against them it would earn him instant promotion.

'That was a most pleasant evening,' Henri commented as he and Margaret prepared for bed.

'Yes.' There was no enthusiasm in her reply.

'I knew it would not be easy for you, an English lady, sitting down at a table with Germans, but I thank you for being so charming to our guests. For me to keep possession of our factory it is vital that we keep on the right side of men like Oberst Eisberg.'

'And Jacques and Victor see it that way too?'

'Of course. It is the only means to our security in the future.'

'And what of Claude and Corinne? They have no interest in the factory.'

Henri smiled. He came to his wife, placed his hands on her shoulders and looked at her reflection in the mirror. 'I told them that Germans like Eisberg appreciate good wine and know it takes skill to produce it.' He bent and kissed her on the top of the head. 'Stop worrying and come to bed.'

'That man sent shivers through me,' commented Corinne on the way home.

'Not a man to cross,' agreed Claude. 'We'll have to tread carefully. You do know that he has already checked on the whole family, especially Mother and Marie because of their English connections? He was very subtle in his conversation this evening, probing for information as if he suspected something.'

'He can't have anything on our group, but I'll grant you he was probing.'

'He was fulsome in his praise of your singing,' said Claude.

'Only because he was after two things, information and ... well, he'll get neither from me; it makes me shudder to think of the second. We'd better put Paulette and Marcel on their guard. I don't think your mother enjoyed the evening, though she hid her true feelings with expertise as did Marie. It must be difficult for them both. I've no doubt Eisberg already has dossiers on them. If it comes to it, which I hope it doesn't, Marcel will get them both out.'

'And you? Are you prepared to flee if necessary?'

She took his hand. 'As long as you are with me.'

'Reports from Sergeant Crozier and his team

about you two are excellent,' reported Felicity when the three of them had settled down for an evening chat. 'You have stood up well to all they have thrown at you in the way of survival training, pushing you beyond what we would normally expect. You have shown ingenuity in the way you have dealt with the tasks you have been set, many of them based on real-life incidents. You've handled explosives with care and efficiency, your handling of the weapons you're likely to meet and your marksmanship are outstanding. Your French is impeccable.'

'That is thanks to Elise as well as the instructors,' said Laura, casting an appreciative glance at her friend.

'I thought being with her would help you, but you have helped her in other parts of the course. You have developed into a highly efficient team. I am going to recommend that you stay together.'

'That would be wonderful,' they both approved.

'It can't be guaranteed but that is the suggestion I will put on my final report in a week's time.'

'What will happen when we leave here?' asked Elise.

'You will go on a short intensive course at an airfield near Manchester where you will learn all about parachuting.'

There was a moment of stunned silence.

'So that means enemy-occupied territory,' said Laura quietly.

'Not necessarily,' replied Felicity. 'There might never be a situation suitable to your special talents. The people who run SOE will be aware of

416

them, and if need arises they'll use you. In the meantime you might find yourself at the base that is constantly listening to our agents, receiving messages and passing out instructions. Take whatever posting comes along and, no matter what the task, do it to the best of your ability.

'When you leave here I will accompany you until the end of your parachute course. I should say that it is unusual for one person to follow a recruit throughout their complete training. That signifies approval of you was strong early on and it was considered beneficial I should remain. I hope it has been. I have enjoyed it anyway. I will make my final report and recommendations after your last parachute jump. After that you will be under direct orders from headquarters. I know you are both already highly thought of there; your achievements at the parachute course will be, what you might call, the icing on the cake. From then on, be prepared for anything – and whatever it is, apply your knowledge to the best of your ability and you will be a credit to yourselves and to me. Now, let's relax and enjoy the rest of the evening.'

38

Flight Officer Felicity Norman shivered in the bleak wind blowing in from the Lancashire coast. She watched the Wellington bomber circle the airfield, its days of active service long over. In its fuselage, Acting Section Officers Eakins and Dundas were ready to make their last jump. The aircraft made a long turn before levelling out at 3,000 feet to approach the dropping zone. Felicity trained her binoculars on it, saw the front hatch was open, then a figure dropped, followed by another. They plummeted downward. Felicity had never liked these moments; she was tense, her breath held in. Then two white canopies floated up against the grey sky. Relief surged within her, tension draining away.

She watched her protégées float down as she hurried towards the two circles marked in the grass where four young leading-aircraftsmen awaited, ready to relieve the WAAF officers of their parachutes and harness. Felicity felt a great sense of relief when both landed in their designated circles.

'A fitting end to your training, hitting your targets,' she called, with a delighted smile. She was proud of them; they had proved to be among the best pupils she had ever had. She would be sorry to lose them. They were certainly the most pleasant girls she had worked with and she admired their acceptance of whatever life would bring.

The banter was jocular as the car that had awaited them whisked them around the airfield to their quarters.

'My office when you've changed,' said Felicity as they scrambled out.

Half an hour later they were sitting down opposite Felicity. She smiled. 'It has been a great pleasure working with you two. It will delight me to learn of your achievements, wherever you are.

The first of those, it gives me pleasure to tell you, is that you are both promoted to Section Officer.'

Elise and Laura grinned at each other and gave the thumbs up, then made their excited thanks to Felicity.

'Don't thank me,' she smiled. 'You've earned it.'

'What happens now?' Elise asked.

'The next two days will be occupied with final interviews with people you have never met before. Then you will have ten days' leave at the end of which you will report to our abode in Mortimer Street, London. From then on your fate is out of my hands. I will always be pleased to see you if ever you are in London.'

'It will be our pleasure too,' said Laura.

'And I thank you for all you have done for us,' said Elise.

'All part of the service,' replied Felicity. 'Oh, just one more thing. You already know this but I have to repeat it. Not one word about what you have been doing or what might lie ahead. As far as anyone else is concerned, you are still at the address you have been using for mail all the time. It will be obvious from your uniform that you have been promoted. Tell anyone who asks you have been kept on at the same base, as instructors, so will continue to use that address. You can pick up your travel passes from the orderly room any time.'

'We'll get our hands on those straight away,' Laura promised.

Three days later, having wangled a ride on an RAF vehicle going into Manchester, they caught the train to York. Veronica and Sylvia were on the platform eagerly awaiting their reunion with Elise and meeting Laura of whom they had heard so much in Elise's letters.

The train gradually came to a grumbling, hissing stop to disgorge passengers hurrying to enquire about onward travel or to join the exodus across the footbridge to the exit.

'There they are!' called Sylvia, straining to catch sight of the two WAAF officers.

In a matter of moments, with other travellers streaming around them, they were exchanging hugs and kisses and meeting Laura for the first time.

'And promoted too,' said Sylvia, noting the broader stripes on their greatcoats' epaulettes. 'Congratulations.'

Laura's onward train to Durham was due in an hour so they celebrated with a cup of tea in the busy station tea room and verified the times of trains from Stanhope, where she lived, to Durham and then back to York, where she and Elise would meet to journey back to London after their leave.

'She seems a nice person,' commented Veronica, as they watched Laura's train leave.

'She is,' Elise agreed. 'It's good that we are staying together.'

'And, according to your letter, back where you have done your training, so no upheaval for you,' commented Sylvia.

'Yes. Two officers were being posted and their positions as instructors had to be filled so we were chosen from our course. It also meant promotion.'

'Will you be happy instructing?' asked Sylvia.

'It will be different but I think it will work out all right, especially having Laura with me.' They had reached the car and Elise asked with a teasing smile, 'Land Army business in York, Mother?'

'Of course,' replied Veronica with a solemn expression, 'so there'll be no diversion from the shortest route back.'

The journey home was full of chatter. Elise had to be guarded in her replies when questions about her course came up. She put plenty of her own about life at Rushbrook, and how the airfield was affecting local people. She seemed to have been away a long time, and as she listened to the answers she realised how much she had missed this countryside. Although she had no regrets about the life she had chosen she found herself envying Sylvia, but consoled herself with the thought that Rushbrook would still welcome her after the war. For the next ten days she was free to enjoy the country life she had experienced in pre-Land Army days.

'It's good to be home,' she said as she stretched after getting out of the car and pausing to admire the front of Rushbrook Hall.

'And it's good to have you here,' said Veronica, putting her arm around Elise's shoulders. 'Sylvia's taken some leave, so you two can have a splendid time together.'

'We will,' Sylvia promised. 'You settle in while I go and fetch Granny Elspeth for the special meal Cook has prepared for your homecoming.'

'I'll come with you,' said Elise. 'Let Gran see

me in my uniform. All right, Mother?'

'Of course, but don't be too long or Cook will want to know the reason why.'

Enjoying being in civilian clothes again, Sylvia and Elise roamed the North York Moors and one day took a bus to Scarborough, revelling in the scent of the sea air. Elise visited the other girls at The Heifer and saw them again for a 'get-together' in the pub in Rushbrook, though she laughingly declined their invitation to help with the milking. The only time that Elise donned her uniform was when Wing Commander Vine invited her to an official dinner held in the Mess in honour of the visiting Group Captain, on a tour of the squadrons under his command.

In the moment alone with her that he was able to seize, the Wing Commander asked Elise how the change in career suited her.

'Very well,' she replied. 'I am grateful to you for starting it off. As you know I can tell you no more, except that the big test lies ahead – but where and how I do not yet know.' He nodded his understanding and she changed the subject. 'You and Mother...?'

She got no further for he raised his finger to stop her as he replied, 'I think a great deal of your mother. Veronica is a charming and wonderful lady. She will always have my admiration. She accepts my position, and I believe that has deepened our friendship.'

'And after the war?'

'If I survive, I will return to Canada with wonderful memories of her and the place she loves.'

The conversation changed course when it was announced that dinner was served. The Wing Commander signalled to one of his junior officers who came over to be introduced to Elise as Flying Officer Philip Pearson.

He gave a wide smile that gleamed with delight at meeting such a beautiful girl. Uniform did nothing but add to her attraction, as did the soft voice in which she expressed her pleasure at meeting him.

Elise was pleased that the Wing Commander had delegated as her escort a young man who oozed confidence without being overpowering. His fair hair was carefully groomed and worn brushed back from his high forehead, but it was his eyes that held her interest. They were observant without being bold; above all they were gentle. She knew there had to be an inner core of steel to him, judging by the DFC ribbon sewn beneath his Bomb Aimer wings. She was curious to know what he had done to earn the DFC, but that was something you did not ask the recipient; she would find out one day, she vowed.

As they walked to the dining room she asked, 'You fly with Wing Commander Vine?'

'Yes, I have always been with him.'

'Before he came here?'

'Yes. I applied to stay with him after our first tour.'

'You must have had great faith in him.'

'Had and still have.'

They had reached their places by then and stood behind their chairs waiting for the Padre to say grace. After the final word, Philip held her

423

chair for Elise while she sat down. After he had taken his, he said quietly, 'There was one point, just before coming here, when I thought he might be cracking up. He isn't one to talk about himself, though, and very soon after coming to Rushbrook he had thrown it off. We put that down to his friendship with the lady at the Hall.'

'My mother.'

Philip gasped, his face reddening with embarrassment.

Elise smiled. 'Don't look like that, Philip. I know about their friendship. It was good for my mother too. Let's leave it at that and enjoy our evening together.'

They did, and when the Group Captain left a party atmosphere took over in the manner known only to flyers on the edge of death. Even before it had started, Philip put his request to Elise, 'Can I walk you back to the Hall when this is over?'

'Of course.' Elise could see the pleasure her reply had given him. 'Philip,' she said seriously, 'I had better warn you ... I can't get involved at the moment.' She saw the flash of disappointment in his clear eyes. 'It has nothing to do with you,' she added quickly. 'I am enjoying your company, but it can't be more than friendship between us. Please don't ask me why.'

He hesitated, but seeing the pleading light in her eyes, said, 'Okay, if that's the way you want it.'

'It is.'

He gave a wry grimace. 'Just when I was beginning to...' He stopped and gave a little smile. 'It's a pity there isn't another one at home like you.'

424

'Oh, but there is,' she replied with a twinkle in her eyes, which changed to laughter as she said, 'You should see your face!'

'You're pulling my leg?'

She shook her head. 'No. I have a sister, Sylvia, a year older than me. I'm surprised you haven't noticed her. She's here in the Land Army but spends a lot of her time off with her horses.'

'Horses?' She noticed the way his eyes lit up. 'But where are they?'

'When the airfield was built, she had to move them to stables in the village. Are you familiar with horses? Silly question, I can see that you are. When you walk me home, come in and meet her. She generally lives with the other Land Army girls at The Heifer, but she'll be at home tonight.'

When the party spirit began to wane, Elise made her goodbyes to a lot of disappointed aircrew and left the Mess with Philip.

He paused when they stepped outside and glanced skywards. A crescent moon shone brightly, flooding the landscape with a magical light that would be obscured at intervals by the patchy black clouds approaching from the south-west.

'A beautiful night,' Elise commented.

'A bomber's moon,' said Philip. 'And they're going,' he added, picking up the steady drone of distant airborne heavy bombers.

He slipped his hand into hers as they started the walk to Rushbrook Hall. She accepted it. They walked in silence, just enjoying these moments with no thought for what tomorrow would bring.

'Do you wish you were with them?' Elise asked, breaking the silence.

'Yes and no. They're doing a job they have been trained to do, and those left behind feel they should be there to help; but at the same time you give thanks that you'll live for another day.'

She pressed his hand. 'Take care, Philip,' she said. 'Now come on, meet Sylvia and Mother – maybe even my grandmother if she has decided to stay the night, which I think she might.'

Making sure he was not gushing, Philip made a good impression when he was introduced to her family.

'He's anxious to meet you, Sylvia,' Elise announced, causing Philip to blush. 'He has more than a passing interest in horses.'

Formality was soon overcome and soon Sylvia and Philip were exchanging talk about their shared interest, though he was careful not to over-do it at the cost of neglecting the others.

After a pleasant twenty minutes he took his leave. Elise and Sylvia accompanied him to the door.

He made his thanks and then Sylvia said, 'Philip, I have the afternoon free on Sunday. If you aren't flying, would you like to meet my horses?'

'Love to,' he said, with noticeable enthusiasm. 'And it will be a delight to see you again.'

She gave him instructions on where the stables were, and concluded by saying, 'I look forward to seeing you too.'

He left with a light step, hoping there would be no flying for him on Sunday

'Nice,' commented Sylvia as the sisters turned

back into the house.

'I thought you'd like him,' said Elise.

'That was an enjoyable lunch,' said Elspeth the next day as they were about to leave the table. 'Oh, Veronica, you promised you would look out the citation that Michael received when he was invalided out of the Army. Remember, I mentioned it the other day when I was telling you about the WI meeting and was asked about my family by a newcomer to the village. I would like to see exactly what it said.'

'Of course, I had forgotten.' Veronica, busy stacking plates, said, 'Elise, run upstairs. The key to the central drawer in the secretaire in my bedroom is in the right-hand drawer of my dressing-table. The item Gran wants is in there. Be a dear and fetch it.'

Elise hurried away and Veronica proceeded to the kitchen where she sorted out the cutlery from the plates for washing.

Elise found the key without any trouble and quickly opened the drawer in the secretaire. There were several documents and she took them all from the drawer in order to find the one her grandmother wanted. She extracted that particular sheet. Then, as she was putting the rest back, she caught a glimpse of her own Christian name on a document. Curious, she unfolded it until it lay flat. A Birth Certificate. Her own Christian name, but who was Elise Gabin? And why was this certificate locked in her mother's secretaire? She read, 'Mother – Marie Gabin'. Her aunt? 'Father – Unknown'. What had she...?

427

The door burst open and her mother, speech-less, stood staring at Elise. Veronica cursed herself. Why had she forgotten that Elise's Birth Certificate shared the same drawer as the citation? She hadn't had any cause to look at them for so long she had forgotten how important the certificate was.

'What is this, Mother?' asked Elise in a low voice.

'Your Birth Certificate.'

'What?' Elise's voice shook with shock and disbelief.

'You weren't meant to see it,' replied Veronica regretfully.

'Why not?'

'You weren't supposed to know I adopted you and that your "Aunt" Marie is your real mother.'

Elise's eyes flared with anger. 'Why not?' she demanded. 'You should have told me!'

'Would it have made any difference?' sighed Veronica.

'How do I know? I never had the chance to find out. If I had known Aunt Marie was my mother...' She broke off as if searching for the words to express herself. Elise swallowed hard and her eyes dampened. 'Why didn't she want me?' The question almost choked her.

'That wasn't the case,' said Veronica gently.

'It looks as if it was,' Elise protested.

'Believe me, it wasn't. You'll understand when you have all the facts.'

'Then tell me!'

'I can't. I promised I wouldn't. I think you should hear them from your mother.'

'How can I when she's in France?'

'You'll have to wait until the war is over. Believe me, there were good reasons why Marie asked me to adopt you. Michael and I never regretted our decision to agree. You brought us tremendous happiness and that helped so much, especially when he died. I have always treated you as my daughter, a true sister to Sylvia.'

'Does she know I'm adopted?'

'No.'

'Good. I don't want her to know. I've got to sort things out and...'

'She won't hear it from anyone else but you. If ever and whenever you want her to know, that's up to you. But please wait until you know all the facts.'

Elise could not deny the love in Veronica's voice, nor the pleading in her eyes. She looked at the certificate again. 'Father unknown,' she read. Looking up, she asked, 'Is that true?'

'I believe so. I don't think Marie knows his real name.'

Veronica put her arm around Elise's shoulder. 'I'm sorry you found that certificate. I love you, Elise, and I don't want to lose you.'

'Let us leave things for now. I don't want to talk about it any more. We've had a nice family meal, let's enjoy the rest of the evening together. I have to go tomorrow.'

'Have you two found that citation?' Sylvia called from the bottom of the stairs. 'Gran is wanting to get home.'

'Coming,' Elise shouted back. 'Tell her to get her coat on. I'll take her back in the car and say my goodbyes for tomorrow. You can help Mum wash up.'

'There she is!' called out Elise as the train, coming into York from the north, slowed and finally clattered to a stop. Laura stepped on to the platform to let other passengers out of the carriage. In a moment Elise was hugging her friend. Hellos and goodbyes were being rolled into one but Elise took the opportunity, when Sylvia and Laura were together, to say to her mother, 'I'm sorry I was so angry last night. It was the shock.'

'I know, Elise. I don't blame you.'

'I need time to work things out.'

'I understand.'

'You have my love always. I'll miss you, Mother.'

Veronica cherished that final word as, through damp eyes, she watched the train until it was out of sight, believing her daughter was going to the safety of a job instructing new recruits.

39

'Good afternoon, ma'am.' One of the WAAFs behind the reception desk in the innocuous-looking building in Mortimer Street greeted Elise and Laura when they handed over their means of identification. 'Ah, Colonel Franklin is expecting you. I am to take you straight to him.'

Elise and Laura exchanged glances and Laura

430

silently mouthed, 'Promotion,' at the mention of his new rank.

When the WAAF announced them, they stepped into his office, came to attention and saluted. He acknowledged their gesture, got to his feet and came round the desk to shake hands and express his delight at seeing them again.

'You are both looking exceedingly well,' he commented, as he indicated for them to sit down.

'Who wouldn't, sir, after a relaxing time in the Highlands under Sergeant Crozier's supervision?' said Laura lightly.

The Colonel, resuming his seat behind his desk, laughed. 'He put you through it, no doubt? I've known really tough men fold under his regime, so it's good to see you two flourishing.' He turned to Elise. 'Did you see Wing Commander Vine when you were at home?'

'Yes, sir. He's well, and the station seems to be a happy place under his command.'

'Good. And your mother and sister?'

'Very well too ... both embroiled in the Land Army.'

'And doing a good job, no doubt. Now, you'll be wondering what is next for you. I've been studying your reports.' He tapped the two folders on his desk. 'They are excellent and come with strong recommendations to keep you two working together. That fits in well with something that might arise in the near future. It would be as well for us to have you on stand by. I can't go into details yet, I don't know how the situation will develop, but we are keeping a close eye on it. I would like you both to be ready at a moment's notice. In the meantime, brush up your Morse work; you won't have done any for a while and it is essential that it is back to your best speeds as soon as possible. Your accommodation has been arranged as before.'

As he was speaking he had pressed a bell. In a matter of moments the door opened and Squadron Officer Norman walked in. 'Once again you'll be looked after by Felicity.'

They smiled broadly as they greeted her. 'Couldn't be better, sir.'

'And another promotion, I see,' put in Elise, noting the changed bands on Felicity's sleeves. 'Congratulations to you both.'

'I'll leave you to it,' said the Colonel. 'I'm pleased with the way you have progressed, and I know, no matter what is put to you, you will fill the roles to the best of your ability.'

When they left his office, Felicity said, 'No doubt you'll be ready for coffee. I'll have some brought to my office.'

Once they were seated and pleasantries had been dispensed with, she said, 'My promotion means I have more direct responsibility for our agents in the field, so you won't be escaping me.'

'That suits us fine,' said Laura. 'Continuity of contact is always best.'

'Good. You will be housed in the same room as when you were here before. Colonel Franklin will have mentioned about sharpening up your Morse. That is vital to maintain communications between us. I want you to be on standby at all times from this moment on. We are concerned about a particular small cell operating in Paris. They have helped RAF aircrew to evade and escape. When they first came to our notice, they informed us they wanted nothing to do with the activities of the Resistance except where it concerned the onward passage of aircrew. We have not heard anything from them for over a month. We tried to contact an agent we'd placed in that area but have heard nothing from him either. The two things may not be connected but we are concerned. We may need you to go in, depending on what we learn about German activities in Paris. So keep fit, keep sharp, tone up your Morse and don't neglect your French.'

As she lay in bed that night, Elise recalled what Felicity had said. France! It seemed she and Laura were destined to go there. Would she have a chance of finding her real mother? Dare she exploit the possibility? As this thought became more and more prominent in her mind she had to take a steely grip on herself. What had she been trained for? To strike the enemy and not let anything sway her from that task. She must remain clear-headed. Even if she were going to France, she should not make even surreptitious enquiries about Marie. You've been trained to do a job, concentrate on that! she told herself.

'I hate this hanging about,' said Laura one night when they were getting ready for bed. 'I didn't put myself forward for this job to see no action.'

'Be patient, it will come,' said Elise.

'You're psychic,' Laura commented when they went in to breakfast the next morning and were

433

given verbal instructions by one of the WAAFs manning the reception desk to report to Squadron Officer Norman at ten o'clock.

Elise grinned. 'I told you. I wonder if this is it?'

'I hope so,' said Laura, feeling much perkier.

They walked into Squadron Officer Norman's office as the clock was striking ten.

'There is every possibility that you will be in action later this week in France,' she began. 'There was talk of postponing this mission until spring but contacts in France wanted action before the winter weather sets in. Our plans have been brought forward, though not finalised as yet. At this stage I cannot tell you more except that your final instructions will not be given until you are in situ. The day after tomorrow you will leave here at eleven in the morning and be taken to an airfield in Oxfordshire. You will wait until we have more details and plans for the drop are finalised. My only advice at this moment is to tell you to take good warm clothing with you. I will issue a note authorising you to draw anything you want from the store on the airfield. That is all for now. The next time I see you will be on the airfield.'

With that dismissal Elise and Laura returned to their billet, speculating as to what might lie ahead.

Two days later the car they were travelling in stopped at the barrier to a small remote airfield in Oxfordshire. A guard in RAF uniform stepped out of his hut and came over to them. Their driver had wound down his window and held out a pass. The guard examined it, nodded, handed it back, glanced at the passengers on the back seat, came snappily to attention and saluted before raising the barrier to allow the vehicle to pass through.

As it drove towards the domestic site, Elise and Laura noted the aircraft they could see parked along the tarmac as if awaiting instructions: Halifax, Liberator, Lysander, Oxford, Hudson, and three light aircraft.

'I wonder which of that motley crew is for us?' said Laura.

They came to a collection of Nissen huts and as the car stopped a WAAF sergeant and two leading aircraftswomen hurried from one of them. They saluted as Elise and Laura got out of the car.

'Your luggage, ma'ams?' asked the Sergeant.

In a matter of moments they were being shown into the hut which had been fitted out with six beds, all neatly made up. A glowing iron stove radiated warmth from the middle of the hut.

'You'll have this to yourselves, we've no one else in at the moment. The Officers' Mess is two huts along. There's tea available now and dinner is served at six-thirty. If there is anything at all you want, please contact one of us. I am Sergeant Miller and my two helpers are LAW Poole and LAW West. We are in hut four in the small site beyond the Admin. Block which is next to your Mess. When you are settled, the Adjutant would like to see you.' The Sergeant went on to offer an apology. 'The whole site leaves something to be desired, but we have tried to make it as comfortable as possible for people who are merely passing through. I hope you will be comfortable.'

As the door closed behind the WAAFs, Elise commented, 'And here we stay and twiddle our thumbs until Felicity turns up.'

'It looks a bit of a dreary place,' said Laura, 'and the wind that's getting up doesn't make it any better.'

'Thank goodness that stove is good and hot. We'd better make ourselves at home!'

A short while later they reported to the Adjutant, who held the rank of Flight Lieutenant, a fatherly man in his sixties; the wings on his tunic signified he must have flown in the First World War. After dispensing with formalities he took them to the Mess for a cup of tea. There they met a young pilot officer who had been drafted into Administration when, much to his disappointment, he had failed his medical for aircrew duties. They were also welcomed by Flight Officer Jean Pawson and her assistant, Section Officer Hazel Barton, there to see to the needs of any female agents passing through this airfield.

They settled in, trying not to think of what might lie ahead and when it might happen, both of them hoping they would not be kept waiting long.

The following morning Squadron Officer Norman arrived, took them into the room set aside for this purpose and told them, 'You'll be taking off at midnight.' Though neither of them commented, they felt an odd sensation in the pit of their stomachs. Knowing how they would react, Felicity immediately started the briefing.

'From now on, until you return to England, you Elise will be known as Mouse, and you Laura as Crow, these names to be used for identification purposes when communicating with us here in England and with the agents you will meet in France. For all other purposes you will use the names on the false documents I have here for you. They should be good enough to fool anyone asking you to identify yourselves. You will be parachuting in and will be met by members of the small cell that operates in Paris Their leader will identify himself as Leopard.'

'Does he already know the names Mouse and Crow?' asked Elise.

'Yes, he has been told,' replied Felicity. 'Above all, you must keep in contact with us every day at five in the afternoon. Leopard will arrange that. All I can say for now is, be alert to the developments you are notified of by us, and follow our instructions to the letter. We are monitoring this situation very carefully. Be prepared for anything.

'Now that is out of the way, we will prepare for your leaving. Let us go to your billet.' There they found civilian clothes laid out for them.

'Rather plain and dowdy, I'm afraid, but it's what French women of the class you are supposed to be are wearing,' said Felicity as she examined the clothes to make sure there were no marks or labels that could identify them as coming from England. She then made sure they carried nothing of a personal nature that might reveal who they were. They were given garments with concealed pockets for revolvers, knives and a compass, to wear under their everyday clothes. 'You'll find these items along with your personal ones in a canister that will be dropped with you. The other things it contains are explosives. You will recognise the type and know what to do, from your training.'

Neither girl spoke but their exchange of glances as good as said, This could be bloody hazardous.

So the day moved on until an evening meal shared with Felicity and the station officers.

When the time came to leave for the aircraft, Felicity accompanied them to the Halifax bomber, modified for ferrying agents and supplies to France. A cool wind blew across the field and whined around the aeroplane, as if protesting against its presence. The waning moon cast an eerie light over the whole scene. Ghostly figures, making final preparations, moved silently around the plane. The pilot briefly acknowledged their arrival and handed them over to the dispatcher who checked that they knew the procedure when it came to the dropping zone. Minutes ticked away relentlessly. The crew climbed on board to carry out their checks. A few minutes later a signal from the cockpit told the dispatcher that they were wanted on board.

'Best of luck.' Felicity shook hands. There was nothing more to be said. She watched as they climbed on board, squeezing through the hatch as best they could with their bulky clothes against the cold overlaid with their parachute harness.

The hatch was closed. Laura and Elise struggled towards the despatch hatch, through a fuselage packed with boxes, parachutes attached, destined to be dropped later in the Halifax's flight. The dispatcher nodded and indicated where they should sit. They settled as best they could in the cramped space. One by one the four engines started, each adding to the noise and vibration that rocked the plane.

'Moving.' Unable to be heard above the noise, Elise mouthed the word at Laura who nodded. They sensed they were taxiing round the perimeter track. They felt the aircraft turning and then it stopped.

'End of runway,' mouthed Laura.

The noise of the engines rose as the throttles were opened. The Halifax moved forward – faster, faster, faster. There came a change in motion.

'Airborne,' Elise formed the word, and Laura nodded her agreement.

Now all they could do was wait and hope the navigator got them successfully to the dropping area and the pilot could quickly identify the field chosen for them.

The drone of the engines became monotonous, seeming to lull them into a sense of security. That was shattered by the crack of bursting shells and the clatter of shrapnel on the fuselage. The aircraft dived, turned and climbed. Elise and Laura braced themselves, but then, almost as quickly as it had started, the sound of shells stopped and the pilot brought the aircraft to fly straight and level again. On they flew, with both girls hoping that this escape was an omen for the rest of their mission.

After a while Elise realised they were banking. They must have reached the dropping zone. She cast an enquiring glance at the dispatcher, who, having seen such queries before, nodded. Now the field needed pinpointing. A few moments later the dispatcher, having received verification over his intercom from the pilot, opened the hatch. A blast of cold air swept through the plane. He nodded to the two young women. They hooked up the static lines to their parachutes, which would open automatically when they fell though the open hatch. Elise sat with her legs dangling into the hole, her back to the front of the aircraft. Laura sat opposite her, ready to swing her legs in once Elise had left. A red light came on. The dispatcher raised his right arm. The red turned to green. Elise shoved herself out. Laura swung her legs into the gap and pushed.

Both girls felt the rush of air from the aircraft's slipstream, then a jerk as their parachutes opened. Elise looked up into the mushroom shape billowing above her. Laura looked down at the white canopy floating below and to her right. The moon still cast a faint light over the rolling landscape that seemed as if it was moving towards them without any sense of danger or urgency. Elise felt swept up in an ethereal moment that she would remember for ever, if she survived. With that reminder she jerked herself back to her immediate situation. She must make a successful landing; injury at this stage could be disastrous.

She made herself small, hit the ground, rolled on impact, grasped her parachute lines and quickly brought it under control, to stop it dragging her across the field. She slapped the harness release and slipped out of it. She scrambled to her feet and, as she pulled the parachute towards her, managed a glance across the field and was relieved to see Laura also had made a successful landing. One more parachute, with canister attached, was still floating down.

With parachutes bundled under their arms, the two girls ran towards each other.

'Okay?' asked Laura.

'Yes. You?'

'Fine. Canister next?'

'Yes. Then the wood to hide all this clobber.'

They ran to the canister and then towards the wood that lined one side of the field.

'Where's the damned reception party?' asked Laura. 'I didn't even see an identifying light as we came down.'

'Nor did I.' They had reached the edge of the wood. 'Let's get rid of this lot then...'

'Mouse and Crow?' The voice, even though it was soft and low, startled them.

'Leopard?'

'Only Mouse and Crow would know my name.' With that a figure stepped out of the darkness shrouding the wood. 'Give me the canister and follow me.'

They did not question this but followed. After a hundred yards Leopard deviated from the track and went deeper into the wood. Another hundred yards on he stopped. Shading his torch, he shone it for them to see they were on the brink of a deep hole. Two men with spades stood on the opposite edge.

'Anything that is not wanted, into the hole,' Leopard ordered.

Elise and Laura discarded their parachutes and harnesses and soon had the canister open; two small holdalls that contained their personal belongings were first out, and the two backpacks they knew contained explosives were quickly made comfortable on their shoulders. The empty canister went into the hole which was already being filled in.

'We have a hut a little further on. We'll stay there the rest of the night,' Leopard explained. 'Tomorrow morning we'll leave for Paris twenty miles away. I will be with Mouse, Tiger here will accompany Crow, and our other companion Rhino will follow just in case we are stopped for any reason. I will do the talking if so and you play along with what I say. If the situation worsens, Rhino will cause a diversion. But you must act implicitly on my orders.'

'We are entirely under your command until we know what we are to do.'

Elise caught his look of surprise. 'I know nothing of that,' he said. 'Yes, we have helped aircrew, and still do when the necessity arises, but we are only a small cog in a bigger wheel. We must have become known in England because we were contacted and asked to continue what we were doing, but to maintain contact with an organisation in England through radios dropped to us. Recently we were asked to accommodate two agents who would eventually receive instructions from England. We were to help them if necessary. That is all I know.' He cast a querying look at the two young women.

'All we know is that we are to await orders,'

Elise explained.

'Then I hope it won't be long before they arrive,' said Leopard. 'I don't like uncertainty, it can lead to danger.'

40

'Wrap up well, there's a bleak wind blowing,' Leopard told them the next morning. 'Get some breakfast. Mouse and I will leave first and Crow and Tiger half an hour later. We will then meet at a night club called La Corinne in Paris, where you will stay.'

'Is that wise?' asked Laura.

'It's as secure as anywhere. Probably safer to be right under the Germans' noses.'

'You mean, they use the night club?' asked an astounded Elise.

'Yes. Because they appreciate our hospitality, they are unlikely to investigate an establishment they frequent and enjoy. Anyone we harbour must obey our instructions implicitly. So far no airman has objected, but this is the first time we have been asked to accommodate agents. That is as far as our instructions go. I was in communication with England last night to report your arrival. It suits us fine to have nothing to do with your mission directly. Our work helping your airmen will not be disturbed, unless you need an escape route when your job is finished.'

'We might be grateful of that.'

'Our help will be readily given. Do you know your target now?'

Elise gave a little smile.

'Do you really think we would tell you if we did?' Laura put in.

Leopard gave a grimace and looked repentant. 'My apologies.'

Elise's smile broadened; she liked Leopard's caution.

'I'm getting fed up with this,' moaned Laura one evening ten days later. 'We are comfortable but I don't like being confined all the time, I need to be doing something.'

'Now you know why Crozier developed those isolation exercises,' commented Elise.

'I think this is worse, knowing we might have to act tomorrow.'

Each evening they had listened to England at the scheduled time, but all they'd heard was the code word for 'nothing yet'.

So it came as a shock, two evenings later, when they did not hear the familiar word; instead their signal was 'Marchtune'. Laura clenched her fist and punched the air. 'Action!'

Elise nodded. 'At last.'

They both concentrated on the message that followed, each making notes so that there would be no mistaking the instructions they received. The transmission ended and they compared notes. The grid references gave them the position of the target, and a code word instructed that it had to be destroyed at all costs. A further code word signified that they must not divulge the

444

target to anyone, not even to the cell that had been sheltering them. They inferred from this that if the Germans got an inkling of the operation they would strengthen their surveillance and a prime target could be lost for ever.

'And we are to take it out on the third night of the next full moon,' Elise pointed out.

'That signifies we are to be lifted out by plane; a full moon makes it easier for the pilot to identify the pick-up point,' said Laura. 'No doubt Leopard will be told where that is to be.'

'We'd better start making our plans,' said Laura. 'Map first.' She was already taking it from a pocket, specially hidden in her holdall and known only to the owner. She spread the map on the table, studied the coordinates she had written down and stabbed a finger on a small group of black rectangles on the map. 'There.'

'Not large,' commented Elise. 'Could be an administrative site ... planning military operations.'

'Or a factory manufacturing small instruments vital to the war effort. Destroy it and German troops could be left unsupplied.'

'Well, whatever it is, we have to destroy it. Will we be able to look it over first?'

'That could be risky, but we might have to. Anything else in that pocket?'

Laura fished inside and withdrew an envelope, from which she took out two sheets of paper and three photographs. The photographs had been taken from the air and gave them a good idea of the layout and which building was the centre of production.

'They'll help,' said Elise. 'I reckon this has all been planned around us from the day we were whisked off to Scotland.'

'You mean, the powers-that-be had this target in mind even then?'

'Yes. Think back to a particular exercise Crozier set up for us.'

Laura looked askance but then her expression changed. 'Of course. Buildings we had to blow up, working only from photographs and some written information.'

'Yes,' said Elise, 'and those we had then were like these; so those buildings in Scotland were based on the photographs.'

'So we were being trained even then for an actual target?'

'It looks like it to me.'

'Oh my God,' gasped Laura. 'We had to get through a very strong guard presence; so, according to your theory, and I believe you're right, we are going to face the same on this mission.'

'Possibly, but Crozier might have exaggerated that aspect to make it easier at the actual target,' said Elise.

'I hope so, but the Germans won't be firing blanks,' replied Laura. 'I bet you wish you were safely tucked up in bed back in England, dreaming of working on the estate with your sister, instead of dicing with death.'

'England and the estate can wait until after we've done this job,' cut in Elise. 'We can't turn the clock back.'

'Margaret, I wish you would receive Oberst Eisberg more amiably,' said Henri, 'I don't want him to misjudge our attitude to any of the occupation forces. Although why we still refer to them as occupation, I don't know. Why can't everyone accept that we have been conquered and the Germans are here to stay? It will be to our benefit in the long run.'

'But don't you and Jacques and his father realise that there has been no talk of the Allies surrendering? There is still a war going on and much of it is beginning to go well for the forces opposed to Hitler; allied success in Africa, in Italy, and now the Russians are having some success.'

'Where do you pick this nonsense up? What you hear is only half the story. It takes no account of German supremacy.'

'That's wishful thinking on your part.'

'Nonsense.' Henri countered. 'If your attitude came to Oberst Eisberg's notice it would bring drastic consequences – arrests and the terrible consequences that would follow them, and the seizure of our factory. Just one wrong word and it could happen.'

'Factory! Is that all that's important to you? What about patriotism?'

'Pah! There's the English coming out in you. I don't mind telling you, I regret bowing to your wishes to send Marie to that convent there and leaving her with her friends when the last war broke out. She came too much under their influence and that shapes her attitudes today. She's often more English than French. I know Jacques doesn't like it. Victor is very conscious of the fact that, if the Germans investigated her and found even a hint of her sympathising with the enemy, it could be disaster for us all.'

'You speak of the English as the enemy!' snapped Margaret with disgust. 'They came to France's help, and you dare to...'

'Where did that get them? Defeated, driven back into the water – and I don't see them making any effort to return. The Germans are in control here and you'd better not sabotage my position with them.' He glared at her, a light in his eyes that sent a shiver down her spine. 'Jacques should be able to keep Marie under control, but you make sure she's careful and doesn't step out of line. Otherwise there'll be more than the Germans to answer to! And you be nice to the German officers ... that's an order!'

'How far does that mean?'

'As far as they want!'

Her face darkened. 'What? I'll certainly not oblige them like you oblige their wives! And don't look shocked that I know – I've been aware of it for long enough!'

He gave her a withering look and strode from the room.

When the door closed on him, Margaret was stiff with rage. So you'd throw us all to the Nazis to save your own skin and your precious factory, would you? she thought. No doubt you've brainwashed Jacques and Victor into thinking just like you. Well, you'll never do that to me or to Marie. Don't you ever threaten either of us again!

Thank God Claude was made independent, she thought. And maybe his wounds from the last war have been a blessing in disguise, a cover for... She pulled herself up short. A cover for what?' Claude appeared to be taking no prominent part in anything except working in his vineyard and driving his wife to La Corinne. But was that enough for him? Supplying the Germans with wine and Corinne entertaining them with songs in the night club could easily be used as cover for obtaining information. Again she clamped down on her own thoughts. She should not let them run wild. But still they persisted.

The next day, knowing that the menfolk would be engaged all day at the factory in discussions with Oberst Eisberg, Margaret paid her daughter an early-morning visit.

Marie was surprised when her mother opened the conversation with, 'I come on a delicate matter.'

'Make yourself comfortable first. I'll make some coffee, and if this matter is as serious as your tone indicates you'd better stay for lunch.'

'Thank you, but I must be away before Jacques comes home. Or anyone else for that matter.'

'Let me get the coffee.'

Once they were settled, Marie looked askance at her mother.

'First, I want your solemn promise not to breathe one word of this to anybody, not even a member of the family, without me knowing.'

Marie's eyes widened. 'As secret as that?'

'It has to be. So I want your promise.'

'You need my help?'

'Advice first.'

'I can see you won't be happy until you have

confided in me.'

'Your promise?'

'Very well, Mother. I promise that what passes between us will remain our secret.' Marie saw her mother relax and was pleased she had agreed.

Margaret quickly related what had transpired between her and Henri yesterday evening. She went on to explain his deep-rooted conviction that the French should now collaborate with the Germans. 'But it all revolves round his obsession with the factory. He would do anything, and collaborate with anyone, if it would preserve his beloved factory. He claims this is all because he is thinking of us and our welfare. But, Marie, he is a collaborator, a man reviled by his fellow countrymen. Have you not seen similar changes in Jacques?'

'To be honest, Mother, I have but I kept quiet about them until now. I agree that collaborating with the Germans is a betrayal of this country. Whenever I say as much to Jacques, he grows angry and defensive, a different person from the man I married. He's also become more and more secretive, especially about his frequent absences.'

'You think he's had affairs?'

'I have never sought proof, but I'm almost certain of it.'

'Have you considered leaving him?'

'Oh, yes, but he wouldn't tolerate it and would do anything to keep me quiet – even to the extent of trumping up evidence that I too had taken lovers. Better to keep quiet than suffer that.'

'Has he ever spoken to you about the Germans?'

450

'He's always hinting I should cultivate friendships with them. There have been times when I've thought he has meant more than friendship. Just like Father, he says I'm too English. Whether he would ever betray me to the Germans, let them know about my connections there, I'm not sure...' She paused and looked questioningly at her mother. 'Where is all this leading us?'

'If our position became more precarious, the obvious answer is to escape. But where to? And we would need help. Anything would be better than being arrested and taken away by the Germans.'

Marie, whose mind had been racing with possibilities, asked her mother bluntly, 'Are you suggesting that you and I should leave?'

Her mother replied just as bluntly. 'Yes.'

Marie stood up. 'I'm going out for a little while, Mother. I want you to stay here until I return. Don't let anyone in. Don't talk to anyone.'

'Where are you going?' asked Margaret with concern.

'You don't need to know, but I hope it will benefit both of us. Just be patient until I come back. Make yourself some more coffee or whatever we call this German stuff.' With that she hurried from the room, prepared to use some of the petrol her father was allowed by the authorities.

Not wanting to attract attention, she drove at a steady speed to reach her brother's vineyard. The sound of the car brought Claude hurrying from one of the sheds.

'This is a pleasant surprise,' he greeted with a

welcoming smile.

She hugged him and kissed him quickly on both cheeks. 'I need your advice, Claude.'

'From your expression this is serious,' he commented, 'and you don't often seek advice from me.'

'I come to you because you broke away from the family business and have no interest in it.'

She quickly told him what had transpired between their mother and father. 'Mother sees danger ahead for her because she is English, and for me because my education made me almost as English as she. Father knows she doesn't approve of his collaboration, putting the factory before all else; I have the same feeling about Jacques and his father.'

'So you are toying with the idea of trying to leave the country? And Mother too?'

'Yes. I have just come from her, but she does not know I am consulting you. That was my idea because I felt you were the only one who could help.'

Claude eyed her with a penetrating expression. 'And what makes you think I can do that?'

'It was a chance remark by Corinne one night, when Jacques and I visited the club. Jacques had wanted to come because he had heard that Oberst Eisberg was likely to be there and he wanted to be seen frequenting the same places as the Germans.'

'Currying favour, no doubt,' commented Claude with disgust. 'What was the remark?'

'It was innocuous at the time. I don't suppose Corinne even realised what she had said.'

'Well, what was it?'

'She said they had guests. That was all. There and then I thought she was referring to Jacques and me, or even the Germans. It was only some days later that I thought it was odd for her to refer to us as guests, and I knew the Germans were regular customers so they would not be classified as guests either. These thoughts were triggered when the Germans announced recently there would be a purge of any organisations in Paris who were aiding escaping RAF airmen – or murderers, as they called them. I decided it was dangerous to harbour thoughts like that and tried to dismiss them ... until today.'

Claude made no comment but merely asked, 'Was it likely that anyone else overheard Corinne's remark?'

'No, Jacques was enjoying a few jokes at Eisberg's table. There was no one else with us. The band was playing, people were dancing.'

He nodded. 'And Mother and you are really uneasy about Father and Jacques?'

'Yes. They have both changed considerably since the Germans took over. They can see no future for France unless we play along with the Germans; become another German state.'

'And you think they would do anything to keep the present status quo?'

'I'm positive.'

'Even betraying both of you, if Eisberg put pressure on them for any reason?'

'Yes,' Marie said emphatically.

She knew he was searching for a way to help them even though it was a difficult decision for him to make. Maybe there was no way he could help; maybe she had posed him an insurmountable problem. Maybe her supposition about Corinne's remark was entirely wrong.

Claude cleared his throat. 'I'm glad you came to me, Marie, and didn't try anything on your own. Ask no questions about anything I say now. I will give you some instructions, which you must follow to the letter. If you don't, it could spell disaster for more people than you and me ... people you have never heard of. Understand?' Marie nodded.

'Go back to Mother and both of you lead your normal lives. No one, and I mean no one, must suspect that anything is different. Both of you pack a small bag with only the minimum of things. It must be easily carried and take up as little room as possible. Get them ready as soon as you are home and be ready to leave at a moment's notice, night or day. You will hear from me when to move. Is that all clear?'

'Yes.'

'Make sure Mother understands the need for absolute secrecy too. One other thing ... if I have to send someone else with instructions, he or she will identify themselves with the word Leopard.' He paused and said, 'Any questions?'

She smiled teasingly. 'You said no questions.'

He laughed. 'Good girl. Now, off you go. I can't promise anything, but I'll do my best. Just pray it will be enough.'

It was a thoughtful Claude who considered his sister's request further. Of course he had been aware of his father's collaboration with the Ger-

454

mans, and Jacques' too, but he had not realised how and to what extent it had affected their family life. Certainly he wanted to help his mother and Elise, but that might put the organisation sheltering stranded airmen in jeopardy. It would be risky to use the same route for the women.

Allowing time for his sister to get away, Claude locked up and cycled as quickly as he dared to La Corinne. Using the back entrance, he went straight upstairs and used his special prearranged knock on the door to the room used by Laura and Elise. It opened and he slipped inside.

'Ah, that is lucky, we wanted to see you,' said Laura, who, at his arrival, had laid the photographs she was studying face down on the table.

'By the look of you it's cold out there,' commented Elise. 'It is,' he said. 'Snow can't be too far off.'

'Well, I hope we don't get it yet. We've had our instructions and were informed that we are to be taken off by an aircraft, a Lysander, and that you would be informed the day before we need it.'

He nodded but made no comment. His mind was already summing up the further uses of a Lysander. His thoughts were interrupted by Elise. 'You wanted to see us?' she asked.

'Er ... yes.'

'Come on, Leopard, you never hold back,' urged Laura.

He gave a wry smile. 'Ah, yes, you are right. Prevarication gets you nowhere.' He went on to explain the situation, saying he needed to get his mother and sister out of France without mentioning the real reason why.

'Naturally we'd like to help,' said Elise, 'but our orders are explicit. We mustn't get involved in anything else that might jeopardise our operation.'

He looked downcast. 'I know; I shouldn't have asked. Forget I ever did.'

Laura cast an anxious glance at Elise. Even though her friend was saying no, Laura could see she really wanted to help. She spoke up. 'Elise, we could bend the rules or even forget them? The authorities back home would be faced with a *fait accompli* if Leopard's mother and sister were already on British soil. We may get torn off a strip, but if we've carried out our mission successfully the powers-that-be can't be too hard on us.'

'I suppose not,' agreed Elise, 'but there is another thing. A Lysander takes only one passenger.'

'I've heard that on one occasion there've been three, cramped but they made it.'

'But there would be four, Leopard's relatives and you and me.'

'I'll stay behind,' said Laura, with no hesitation.

'No, you can't,' said Leopard. 'You are on a planned mission and your report is needed on your return to England.'

'Elise can do that.'

'No,' he said firmly. 'I know my mother and sister would not agree either.'

'We are left with one chance. It might be slim, but it's worth trying,' put in Elise. 'We assemble at the field and leave the decision to the pilot.'

'Then let's try,' said Laura enthusiastically, seeing Leopard was about to object again.

'Agreed!' said Elise. 'Leopard, we'll meet again when we know more about the timing of our mission.'

Though both girls did not voice their thoughts, they realised that with a strong German force in the vicinity, it was likely not everyone would reach the plane; whoever did would be the one to be flown out.

41

Mother and daughter, well wrapped up against the chill, stood on the steps of Rushbrook Hall in the fading light of a clear wintry sky. The sound of aircraft engines starting up, one after the other, had brought them there. They knew it was possible that Terry and his crew were on the final mission of their second tour.

They had come to know what the change in engines' notes meant – testing, taxiing, in position at the end of the runway, then the rising roar signifying take-off. Sylvia slipped her hand into her mother's and silently they offered up a prayer for the safe return of all the squadron.

Sylvia had become closely involved with Flying Officer Philip Pearson. A rapport had grown between them soon after Elise had introduced them; it quickly became a deep friendship that blossomed into love in spite of the danger that hung over aircrew, but it was a danger that brought them closer, reflecting the truism of part of a verse Sylvia had found:

But lovers in wartime
Better understand the joy of living
With death close at hand.

Now, she silently sent Philip her love as one after the other black silhouettes took to the sky.

Veronica fought the tension that gripped her but lost. In spite of knowing Terry was married, she had allowed their friendship to develop, realising that he needed someone to be there for him, to help ease the strain of commanding an operational squadron so far from home.

Mother and daughter stood until the last engine's drone had faded from the sky. Like the ground crews, they waited for their particular plane to return. And like the ground crews, knowing how many had taken off, they would count them on their return.

Knowing even a six-hour trip would have them returning about ten, they decided to eat and doze in their chairs. The first engine sounds brought them awake. By the time they had put on warm clothing the air was filling with the noise of returning aircraft. They knew by the pitch of the sounds when an aircraft was choosing to make its landing at Rushbrook. By the time they stepped out into the cold night air they had counted four back. They stood, adding to the tally until the last reverberation had left the sky.

'One missing,' said Sylvia, a quiet tension in her voice.

'Might not be them.' Veronica tried to reassure her.

They walked slowly back into the house, at a loss to know what to do while they waited for Terry's phone call, something he did whenever he had been on a mission.

The minutes ticked away. There seemed to be no taste to the cup of tea Sylvia made.

'Ring!' she snapped, glaring at the phone. 'Ring!'

Veronica said nothing. If that was the way Sylvia relieved her tension then let her.

Time moved on.

Then a shrill sound startled them. Sylvia left it to her mother as she always did. Veronica grabbed the phone. Sylvia focused intently on her mother's face. She saw her whole body relax and Sylvia too felt the tension drain away.

Veronica put the phone back gently. 'All well,' she said quietly. 'And that's the end of their tour.'

'Thank God,' said Sylvia. 'What happens now?'

'Terry said he will be in touch tomorrow.'

Sylvia came out of sleep, bemused and bewildered by the ringing sound. Realisation brought a moan from her. She reached out, stopped the noise and then pressed the switch on the table lamp beside her bed. Bleary-eyed from getting so little sleep after waiting for the bombers' return, she focused on the clock, though she knew perfectly well the time the alarm went off. She groaned, pushed the bedclothes off, swung her legs out of bed and sat for a few minutes, dazedly wondering why she had ever volunteered for the Land Army. Then the cold caught her. She pushed herself to her feet and hurried to the bathroom.

Half an hour later she was pedalling briskly away from Rushbrook House heading for The Heifer. She found the rest of the girls at breakfast, some cursing the cold, others breezily reliving last night's date, and three especially thankful that Sylvia was able to confirm that Wing Commander Vine's crew was safely back. Banter had brightened all round as they set out on their various tasks, some close by, others on farms a few miles away.

Veronica eased herself in her chair, stretched and then surveyed the papers on her desk with satisfaction; she had managed to re-jig the girls' schedules for next week to accommodate two requests from farmers five miles away. She was considering making herself a drink when she heard a car approaching and slowing down. Anticipating that the door-bell would ring, she was already crossing the hall when it did so.

'Terry! I felt it in my bones you would be flying last night. It's so good to see you back safely.' She held out her arms to him and he sensed there was more to her hug than a welcome home gesture; there was affection there that bordered on love. He was thankful for her presence during a testing period of his life. Now that part of it was over – the squadron had been successful under his command; he would be relieved of that stress, but that did nothing to obliterate the strain of knowing his sick wife was waiting for him in Canada.

'Coffee?' asked Veronica. 'I was just going to

make it.'

He nodded. They walked to the kitchen together.

'Your crew will be relieved?'

'Sure.' He gave a wan smile. 'But it means we'll be splitting up, and there's something sad about that.'

'They were a good bunch. You'll all keep in touch.'

'Why not?' He gave a shrug of his shoulders. 'But time and distance are funny things, and the best of intentions don't always turn out right.'

She sensed there was a personal inference behind his words, possibly involving her.

'Come on, Terry, don't sound so down. You've just completed your second tour successfully. That's an achievement showing great skill and leadership.'

'And a lot of luck.'

'Maybe, but that's only a small part of it.'

He accepted a mug of coffee and said, 'Let's sit at the table in here.'

From the tone of his request she knew better than to suggest the comfort of the lounge.

He warmed his hands around the mug. 'I have a couple of things to say. There will be an end of tour shindig in the Mess tonight, combined with a send off for the CO. Sorry I can't invite you; it's RAF only. I couldn't appease my lot if I allowed outsiders in.'

She laughed at the thought. 'I wouldn't want to spoil their celebrations.'

'But I have told my crew we will have a celebration in the village pub in two days' time. I've

461

asked the landlord to do us a meal, and told the crew and ground-crew to bring a partner, wife, girlfriend, so we'll have a nice mixed gathering for what will be a private farewell party for us all.' Without stopping he added, 'I will be leaving the following morning.'

The stark statement caught Veronica unawares even though she'd known it was coming, but she had thought it might be later rather than sooner.

'Terry.' She reached out and took his hand. 'I'll be sorry to see you go, but ever since I heard your circumstances I've known it was inevitable.'

'You have been good for me; you will never know how much. I owe you a lot for keeping me sane during a testing time.'

'It was nothing, Terry.'

He pressed her hand. 'It was everything. You were there, and you understood.'

'Do you know where you will be posted?'

He nodded. 'Yes, Canada.'

'Oh.' She couldn't keep the disappointment out of her voice but quickly tried to disguise it. 'How wonderful for you.'

He ignored the inference that he judged lay behind her words. 'I am to be part of the aircrew training scheme there that I'm sure you have heard about. The powers-that-be seem to think my operational experience can be useful there.'

'And it will give you the opportunity to see your wife.' Veronica left a slight hesitation before adding, 'Help her recover, Terry.'

He made no comment but his eyes told her that was his intention. He stood up and said, 'I'd better be going. I've a lot to see to. I'll pick you up for our crew party in the village.'

'Thanks.'

At the front door he hesitated, then kissed her on the cheek. 'Thank you, Veronica.'

As she watched him drive away a tear ran down her cheek. She chided herself for letting it appear and brushed it away. The car disappeared but still she stood there staring across a landscape charmed into beauty by a hoar frost. Rushbrook – Canada. So far apart. Here she had beauty and stability; here she had a home. She walked slowly back into the house, wondering about this interlude in her life that had come and gone. Could I have held him, changed his course, if I had had a mind to? Now there was an empty future stretching before her. With that thought came another that startled her. I have not heard from Elise for some time ... I hope she is all right and not letting the revelations about Marie worry her.

'I've heard the pick-up plane will be landing the day after tomorrow at midnight.' Claude had gone to La Corinne immediately he had received word from England.

'We heard it too,' said Elise.

'Will you give us the position of the field that we will use, so we can plan our route after we've carried out the task?' Laura requested.

'Do you want me to show you on a map?' asked Leopard.

'No, that could endanger your cell. Just give us its position, we will work out our route.'

Leopard gave them the information and told them that the next time he would see them would be at the airfield. 'It will be safer if we have no contact between now and then. I will make sure that Corinne announces she is going to do a special show that evening; it should ensure the club is packed with off-duty troops, so fewer of them will be available quickly when the alarm is raised.'

'Good,' said Elise. 'What about our two passengers?'

'If things work out I will be with them, but I will tell them where the pick-up field is in case they have to find their own way there.'

'And they'll definitely know there'll be no waiting? We'll be taking off at the stated time.'

'I'll impress that on them, but with a chance of escape I don't think they'll be late or allow anything to get in their way.'

When Leopard had gone, Elise and Laura meticulously planned their route so that they knew how long it would take them to get from the factory to the airfield, providing everything went well.

With preparations made – explosives with their timers set, revolvers checked, two hand-grenades each and warm underwear donned – they were ready with time to spare so one final time they checked out the tactics they would follow at the factory.

'Time to go,' said Elise.

'To success,' said Laura, and they clasped hands to wish each other good luck.

The personal items they were leaving meant nothing at a time like this. They knew all evidence of their visit would soon be removed.

Music drifted up from the night club and Corinne began the song she knew would raise the biggest cheer from the German soldiers seeking a night off from the rigours of war.

Elise and Laura grinned at each other; it was as if Corinne had engineered a cheer from the Germans to send them on their way.

When they stepped outside they found that snow was just starting to fall. They did not mind; it silenced their footsteps and kept most people indoors. They had soon cleared the outskirts and moved into open tree-dotted countryside. If they had not been on an urgent mission they would have stopped to admire the magical light that silvered the snow and made the falling flakes twinkle like the stars in heaven. Neither of them spoke but they had become so close throughout their training that they knew what each other was thinking – a night like this was not the best for their mission. And both of them also knew that they must shut out its beauty and in its place concentrate on the layout of the factory and the task they must fulfil.

A telephone rang shrilly through a house on the outskirts of Paris. The call from Roland immediately raised concern in Henri.

'There's trouble at the factory,' he said to his wife. 'You'd better drive me there. You said you wanted the car early tomorrow. I don't know how long this will take. Roland will drive me back.'

'What is it?' Margaret asked, anxious as to how this could affect her and Marie's plans.

'Roland had no details. He was about to leave

when the lights went out. Seems like a power cut of sorts, but whatever it is it needs to be right by the morning otherwise production will be halted. I'll give Jacques a ring and get him to the factory too.'

In a few moments Jacques had the news and was on his way.

Marie waited a few minutes and then rang her mother. 'Everything all right?' she asked.

Guarded in her reply, Margaret said, 'I see no reason to alter our plans. I have to drive your father to the factory now. Roland will bring him home. I'll pick you up on my way back. I'll be with you shortly.'

Elise and Laura got themselves into a position they had previously chosen, from which to watch the guards. They checked how long it took a man to walk round half the perimeter and briefly exchange a word there with the man who patrolled the other half.

Laura held her wrist towards Elise, tapped the face of the watch and gave her the thumbs up. The Germans were dead on with their timing; so like them to be methodical in these matters. The parting of the Germans left a short gap in the patrol before they turned to walk towards each other again. In that space of time Elise and Laura went quickly forward to the second position closer to the fence. They watched the guards again and, once they had turned, Elise and Laura were over the wire fence and lying low again.

Their next move took them to the main building where, with a skill learned in Scotland, they speedily placed the explosives to maximum effect, silently thanking Sergeant Crozier for his meticulous preparation in providing a replica of the layout of the buildings. Satisfied, they moved silently to the next block. Once the explosives were in place they quickly made their way to their rendezvous. They waited, watching the guards. With an open space to cross they had to be meticulous with their timing. Braced to move, they were jolted to a halt by the sound of cars approaching at speed. Grateful for the moonlight, they saw the cars come to a skidding halt at the main entrance. A guard had obviously recognised the occupants and hastened to open the gates.

'Damn!' Laura cursed. 'Better move.' She indicated a position in the shadow of the main building. 'What's going on?'

The cars pulled up at the entrance. A man appeared at the door. An older man got out of the first car, paused to have a word with the woman driver who then drove away quickly. A third man sprang from the other vehicle.

'What's happened, Roland?'

'Everything just went off, Jacques.'

'We'd better damn' well get it sorted quickly; Gabin and Martineau have a reputation to uphold.' Their voices faded as the men went into the building, closing the door behind them.

Elise felt numb, yet her mind grappled with what she had just heard. Gabin ... Martineau. Gabin was her family name! Surely there could be no connection; it was a common name in France. But Martineau? Aunt Marie was married to a Martineau and his name was Jacques!

'Come on!' Laura's whisper was urgent as was the tug she exerted on Elise's arm.

'Oh, my God!' Elise gasped.

'What's wrong?'

'My family. The oldest man must be my grandfather ... the one called Jacques my father!'

'What are you blathering about?' snapped Laura. 'Let's go. We've a plane to catch!'

Elise couldn't resist further. With her mind telling her it was the only thing to do, otherwise the hell of training she and Laura had been through, would be for nothing and their mission compromised, they ran.

42

They were over the fence and running fast, but with the guards' scheduled patrol disrupted by the arrival of the cars, Elise and Laura were seen. Siren alarms split the night. The countryside would soon be heaving with searchers. Expecting rifle shots, they urged themselves on through the gently falling snow.

But before any shots were fired an almighty roar split the frosty air, followed by several more explosions in succession. Flames leaped high, contesting with the moonlight to illuminate the destruction caused by two figures who drove themselves onward towards the field that would provide their means of escape.

Margaret had lost no time in leaving the factory and reaching Marie. Ready and waiting, her daughter flung herself into the car and her mother drove away, capably handing the vehicle over the slippery road.

A few minutes later an explosion shattered the air and was followed by others. Marie gasped, 'It's the factory! It's all it can be in that direction. Oh, my... The men!'

Margaret caught an hysterical edge in her voice and knew she had to be strong. 'What's done is done,' she shouted.

'What do we do now?' queried Marie.

'Stick to the plan. We're on schedule. We dump the car as planned to hold up any pursuit, which now is likely to be sooner than expected. We keep alert and do exactly what we're told.'

Reaching the pre-arranged place to leave the car, they pushed ahead on foot, slithering and sliding in the snow. A few moments later shots rang out; their pursuers were nearer than expected.

'Keep going,' yelled Marie. Half turning, she glanced back. Alarm swept through her; her mother, clutching her side, was staggering. Grimacing with the pain, Margaret stumbled. Marie hauled her to her feet, determined to get her to the plane. They staggered a few more yards, then Margaret lurched and fell on her knees.

'Go! Go!' she gasped. 'Leave me!'

'Mama!' screamed Marie, the horror of what was happening tearing at her mind. She crouched beside her mother, who reached for her daughter's hand.

'Go, my love, go. I'm done.'

469

'No!' screamed Marie, cradling her mother's head.

'You must,' gasped Margaret. 'Go!'

Tears streamed down Marie's cheeks. 'I can't leave you!'

'You must! Go, my love.' Her voice was fading. She gripped Marie's hand, then, giving her a smile full of love, let her fingers slip away.

Marie knew this was the end. She kissed her mother, rose to her feet and, choking with grief, ran.

'Do you think the 'plane will get in?' panted Laura when they were about half a mile from the pick-up field.

'If the snow doesn't worsen. The Lysander pilots have developed special skills for these jobs.'

They pushed themselves on. Distant, but audible shots, sent alarm through them.

'The hunt is on,' called Laura. 'Pray our passengers are on time – we don't want to be hanging about.'

'Leopard will be really specific about timing. He won't want to be held to account if anything goes wrong.'

They found their rendezvous point in a corner of the field. Leopard was already there.

Rifle shots drew nearer.

And then the joyous sound of an aircraft engine.

'Right on time,' said Leopard. 'Where are the other two? Hurry up ... hurry up!'

A crashing through the undergrowth brought hope that all was going to be well, but that was disappointed when only one woman appeared.

Leopard was quickly by her side. 'Where's Mother?'

'She was shot.'

'Is she dead?'

'Yes.' The confirmation caught in Marie's throat as she recalled her mother's final smile as she died in her arms, but the situation was too tense for more tears.

The plane was circling.

Claude controlled his feelings; time enough to mourn his mother if they all got away from here. He hastened Marie over to join the agents.

Elise stared in disbelief. 'Aunt Marie!'

'Elise! What...?'

'I'm one of the agents and Laura, here, is the other. We've just blown up that factory.'

'Oh, my God!'

'What...?'

'You'll learn it all later,' said Claude.

'Follow me. The plane will land and turn, the door will open; in as fast as you can, one, two, three.' He pointed at each in turn indicating the order of getting in so that there wouldn't be a split second of delay. He led them forward.

There was a rapid burst of gunfire close by.

Marie staggered and fell.

'No!' screamed Elise. 'No!' She was on her knees.

'Claude, leave me ... see your niece gets away.'

'Claude my uncle? You're Leopard?'

He nodded.

Marie looked into Elise's eyes. 'My darling girl, I'm not going to make it.'

'No! You must. I've just found my real mother!'

'Elise, my…'

'Why did you let me go?'

'Ask Veronica. Tell her I told you she can tell you. And Elise, she brought you up. Let her continue to be your mother.' She gave Elise the sweetest smile of love that would remain with her for ever then turned her eyes to Claude. She could see he was fighting to keep emotion at bay. Nothing must jeopardise getting the agents away.

The plane was landing.

Claude reached down and helped Elise to her feet. 'Come,' he said. 'My niece, a replacement for my sister. Come and see me when this mess is all over.'

'I will. I must bring flowers for my mother.'

'But do as she requested.'

With tears streaming down her face she nodded, grabbed Laura's hand and ran for the plane. The door opened, the pilot urged them on.

Claude jerked, pain ran through his shoulder but he hid it from the others. He helped Laura and Elise into the aircraft. There was no time for more. The door slammed shut. In a few moments the plane was taking off.

Claude, hand clasped to his bleeding shoulder, ran for the edge of the field and his escape route as the Germans turned their rifle fire on the plane but, apart from making a few holes in the fuselage, it was ineffective. The pilot set course for England with the agents he had been scheduled to pick up.

Laura wrapped Elise in her comforting embrace as the aircraft climbed through the silence of the falling snow.

EPILOGUE

Rushbrook House
Rushbrook
North Riding of Yorkshire.

1 January 1950

Dear Terry,
Thank you for your letter. I thought you might do this after a suitable period of mourning. While I am extremely flattered by your proposal of marriage, I feel I must refuse. I am sorry to disappoint you but my family means so much to me. The ties between us are too strong for me to break. To leave them would tear me apart, as would abandoning Rushbrook and Brunton. They are dear to my heart and I would always pine to be back. They are my home; my life.

As I sit here, I look out of the window at snow falling gently on what is already a magical white landscape full of treasured memories. I cannot leave it. My respect for you – no, my love – is not strong enough for me to break free from the roots that bind me to this land, which has always been part of me and always will be. Please understand, and map your own future in the country I know you love.

You will never be far from my thoughts, nor will the time we shared in a deep friendship when we needed solace and found it in each other.

Sylvia and Philip have prospered here with their

473

equestrian business and are expecting their first child. (Another reason for my wanting to stay.)

Elise took some time to settle down after her traumas in France, which I wrote to you about, but she has put them all into perspective now. I am pleased to tell you that life at home suits her. She is a great help to me with the business and financial side of the estate. I am sure she has found peace and tranquillity here and that has helped her desire to become a writer – she has just received a publisher's offer for her first novel! She is dedicating it:

To the mother I have known as my mother all my life;

And to the mother I knew as my real mother for only a few minutes.

I love you both.

Veronica re-read the letter and signed it.

ACKNOWLEDGEMENTS

I am grateful to all those who saw me through to the completion of this novel:

Judith who vetted it as I wrote; Geraldine who read it on its completion and advised some changes;

Anne and Duncan, who have always been supportive of my writing;

Donna Condon and Lucy Icke of my publisher, Piatkus, and the rest of the team who contributed to the final appearance of this novel;

And special thanks to Lynn Curtis who once again has devotedly edited another of my books.

Without them all this novel would not be in your hands now.

My thanks to everyone.

The publishers hope that this book has given you enjoyable reading. Large Print Books are especially designed to be as easy to see and hold as possible. If you wish a complete list of our books please ask at your local library or write directly to:

Magna Large Print Books
Magna House, Long Preston,
Skipton, North Yorkshire.
BD23 4ND

This Large Print Book for the partially sighted, who cannot read normal print, is published under the auspices of

THE ULVERSCROFT FOUNDATION

THE ULVERSCROFT FOUNDATION

... we hope that you have enjoyed this Large Print Book. Please think for a moment about those people who have worse eyesight problems than you ... and are unable to even read or enjoy Large Print, without great difficulty.

You can help them by sending a donation, large or small to:

**The Ulverscroft Foundation,
1, The Green, Bradgate Road,
Anstey, Leicestershire, LE7 7FU,
England.**
or request a copy of our brochure for more details.

The Foundation will use all your help to assist those people who are handicapped by various sight problems and need special attention.

Thank you very much for your help.

THE CYNEFIN MINI-BOOK

Greg Brougham

The Cynefin Mini-Book

© 2015 Greg Brougham. All rights reserved.

Published by C4Media, publisher of InfoQ.com

Production Editor: Ana Ciobotaru
Copyeditor: Professor Laurie Nyveen
Cover and Interior Design: Dragos Balasoiu

Acknowledgements

//

I am indebted to Dave Snowden in his support of this endeavour and his time for reviewing the individual pieces. Mike Burrows and Mika Latokartano have also provided input and comments that have been very helpful, and have corrected me a couple of times. I would also like to men-tion Chris Matts for his comments and for providing the introduction to Shane Hastie of InfoQ, and Clarke Ching for his support and corrections.

Contents

Preface

////////////////////////

This mini-book started out as a series of papers that were experiential in nature, which were intended to provide an introduction to Cynefin, so you won't find discussions about the ontology, epistemology, and phenomenology of the approach (okay, you will: ontology is mentioned once in the third paper when disorder is discussed, but it is an important part of the message). Shane Hastie suggested making them into a mini-book, which also provided the opportunity to add some text on the use of narrative. This discussion provides a bridge between the first paper, which contains the introduction, and the third paper in the series, which is about sense making. It also provided the opportunity to include some writings on Cynefin dynamics, on which there is little written. This deals with the management of groups and moving between exploration (un-order) and exploitation (order).

One of the key messages that comes from complexity is that you should work with fine-grained objects, leverage distributed cognition, and ensure disintermediation. Since this is a new management approach, there are not many stories to reference, but the article about Lotus in The Sunday Times that was published in February 2015 is interesting in that it embodies all of these principles. The new CEO asked for all three existing car models to be broken down into their parts, which were then laid out on tables for inspection. All 900 employees of the company were involved in this exercise and they were asked to tag the components using a traffic-light system. The components were either to be kept, supply renegotiated, redesigned, or discarded. This also ensured that everyone was on the same page and understood why these changes were being proposed. The exercise resulted in saving around 20 kg and £3,000. It also led to the quality of the cars being improved.

One thing that I did not also address in the papers was the derivation of the name Cynefin. It is a Welsh word and the literal English translation is "habit" or "place", but this does not convey its full meaning. Quoting Mike Pearson's In *Come I*: "It is the piece of earth where a community has lived – a community with whom we identify the places that we have lived." Dave Snowden noted in a tweet that its meaning is similar to the Maori word tūrangawaewae, which means "a place to stand". This again falls short in terms of the richness of the word, and Te Ara: The Encyclopedia of New Zealand expands the meaning to "places where we feel especially empowered and connected. They are our foundation, our place in the world, our home."

I hope you find these writings of interest and use.

What is in an InfoQ mini-book?

InfoQ mini-books are designed to be concise, intending to serve technical leaders looking to get a firm conceptual understanding of a new idea, framework, technology or technique in a quick yet in-depth fashion. You can think of these books as covering a topic strategically or essentially. After reading a mini-book, the reader should have a fundamental understanding of the concepts covered, including when and where to apply them, how they relate to other ideas and technologies, and an overall feeling that they have assimilated the combined knowledge of other professionals who have already figured out what these concepts are about. The reader will then be able to make intelligent decisions about the concepts once their projects require them, and can delve into sources of more detailed information (such as larger books or tutorials) at that time.

Who this book is for

This book is aimed specifically at architects, project managers and stakeholders who are interested in a short introduction to the subject of complexity, and Cynefin and its related practices in particular. It is not intended to be a replacement for training, but to demonstrate some of the practices and the value that they offer in dealing with an increasingly uncertain world.

Reader feedback

We always welcome feedback from our readers. Let us know what you think about this book – what you liked or disliked. Reader feedback helps us develop titles that you get the most out of.

To send us feedback, email us at feedback@infoq.com.

If you have a topic that you have expertise in and you are interested in either writing or contributing to a book, please take a look at our mini-book guidelines on http://www.infoq.com/minibook-guidelines.

PART ONE

The Cynefin Framework

Introduction

The Cynefin framework and its practices can be used to address the uncertainty of the modern world. The practices can be used to complement traditional approaches to programme and portfolio management. They provide a more comprehensive approach that reflects the needs of management in an ever more uncertain world.

We have seen a couple of books on the issue of uncertainty appear over the last decade, but neither has a comprehensive framework that allows us to deal with the modern world's increased uncertainty.

If anyone doubts that traditional models are struggling to deal with modern market dynamics, they only need to look at the demise of the Monitor Group. This was the company of Michael Porter (the father of strategic analysis) and used his market-analysis model. He based his approach on rigorous analysis of market forces and the assumption that this leads to a rational, structured approach that would result in a competitive advantage. It became apparent that while it could "help explain excess profits in retrospect, it was almost useless in predicting them in prospect." Matthew Stewart (2009) notes "Most successful strategies emerge through action; they become perspicuous only in hindsight." A.G. Lafley and Roger Martin (2013) also note that market dynamics are not this simple and the world is increasingly complex, global, and competitive. We've learned that there are limits to rationality, but how can we address uncertainty and take advantage of turbulence in the market place?

Limits of rationality

When we are faced with a problem, we assume that all we need to do is elaborate the options, select one, and then execute. This assumes that causality is determinable and therefore that we have a valid means of eliminating options. What we mean by causality is that we can relate cause and effect; if we take a certain action, we know what the effect will be — or

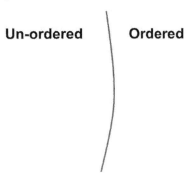

Un-ordered   **Ordered**

given an effect, we can determine what caused it. This is not always the case and we need to acknowledge that there are systems in which we can determine cause and effect and those in which we cannot. We call the former ordered and the later un-ordered[1] systems[2].

can determine causality

In an ordered system, the system is highly constrained, the behaviour is highly predictable, and the causality is either obvious from experience or can be determined by analysis. If the cause is obvious then we have a simple system, and if it is not obvious but can be determined by analysis, we say it is a complicated system as cause and effect (or determination of the cause) is separated by time.

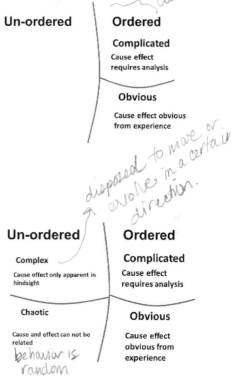

Un-ordered | **Ordered**

Complicated
Cause effect
requires analysis

Obvious
Cause effect obvious
from experience

disposed to move or evolve in a certain direction.

For an un-ordered system, we cannot determine causality. However, we find that some of these systems are stable, and the constraints and behaviour evolve over time through the interaction of the components. They are dispositional in nature — that is, they are disposed to move or evolve in

Un-ordered

Complex
Cause effect only apparent in
hindsight

Chaotic
Cause and effect can not be
related
behaviour is random

Ordered

Complicated
Cause effect
requires analysis

Obvious
Cause effect
obvious from
experience

a certain direction — but causality can only be determined in hindsight, and no amount of analysis will allow us to predict the behaviour of the system. This domain, we call complex. But there are also some systems that are not stable and which we can only described as chaotic: there are few to no constraints, and behaviour is random. There is one additional domain that needs to be considered: systems that we have not yet determined — we put these in the "disorder" bucket.

We can apply another definition to systems that are ordered as we can take them apart and put back together again — for example, a car or an aeroplane; those that are un-ordered can never be deconstructed then put back together. For example, think of making mayonnaise.

---

1 Disordered is a separate state, addressed below.
2 With a tip of the hat to Spencer-Brown.

We also need to acknowledge that systems are not always stable and the state of the system may change over time. A system may be stable and predictable, but its performance degrades over time or it may simply break. In the case of degradation, we may have to involve an expert (say, a mechanic in the case of a car) to analyse what is going on. In the case of breakage — for example, a car that has broken down and we have been thrown into chaos — we may need a rescue service to recover the vehicle and take it to a garage in order for the problem to be analysed. We have moved from obvious (driving the vehicle) to chaotic (the vehicle is broken) to complicated (we need a mechanic) to hopefully return to obvious (the car is again working).

this would be nice to be able to explain the about body

How do we describe the reality of the human body in all of its complexity?

The Cynefin framework

good explanation

These domains of obvious, complicated, complex, and chaos, along with disorder (not yet determined), are the domains of the Cynefin complexity framework. The framework allows us to describe reality, and gives us techniques and practices that can be applied to manage in the complicated and complex domains. These practices complement the traditional approaches that are applicable where order holds. It is not the case that the old practices don't work, but we must realise that they only work within certain boundaries and that if we are not in an ordered space, they are not applicable.

Obvious[3] (known knowns): Here, we know what we are doing and have seen it a thousand times before, so we sense, categorise, and respond (S-C-R). We expect to see best practices employed.

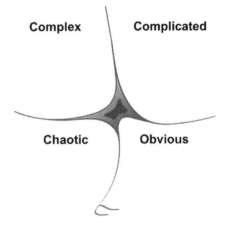

Complicated (known unknowns): We don't know what is going on but we know that we can analyse what has happened and work it out, so we sense, analyse, and respond (S-A-R). This is the domain of good practice.

---

3 This domain was previously called "simple".

Complex (unknown unknowns): We cannot determine what will cause a particular outcome but we can run some experiments to see if they move us in the right direction, so we probe, sense, and respond (P-S-R). This is also the domain of multiple hypotheses: there is no right or wrong answer, so we may want to run a series of experiments or run a number in parallel. This is the domain of emergent practice.

Chaotic (unknowable unknowns): Here, the system is not stable but we need to do something as it is not viable to wait, so we act (do something), sense, and respond (A-S-R). This is the domain of novel practice.

Disorder (not determined): These are the items whose domain we have yet to determine.

These practices are summarised in the following table, which also suggests what we should consider in each domain. This touches on a number of practices such as crews as an alternative to teams or social-network simulation (SNS) — all of which indicate the richness of Cynefin.

	NATURE	RESPONSE	PREPARE
CHAOS	Unkownable unknowns Temporary state - no time No evidence of any constraint High turbulence no patterns Old certainties no longer apply	Act-Sense-Respond Speed of authoritative response vital Follow and enforce heuristics Focus on constraints not solution Use the opportunity to innovate	Establish heuristics & Parables Human sensor networks Crews as crisis management teams Simulation games for key managers Multi-perspective dissent feedback
COMPLEX	Unknown unknowns Messily coherent, patterns discernible Partial changing constraints Flux within stabilities Evidence supports contradiction	Probe-Sense-Respond Monitor safe-to-fail experiments All contradiction within heuristics Flex constraints to manage emergence Agility key to amplification/dampening	Create time and space for reflection Human sensor networks operational SNS & like to create networks Scenario planning (inc. micro) Build and monitor 'requisite diversity'
COMPLICATED	Known unknowns Ordered, predictable, forecastable Constraints evident and enforceable Stable with constraints Evidence susceptible to analysis	Sense-Analyse-Respond Determine experts or process to resolve Manage & enforce process Monitor effectiveness of constraints Focus on exploitation not exploration	Right people & process, right time Process engineering with feedback Diversity of exports in network Sound analytical practice Stand aside but stay in touch
OBVIOUS	Known unknowns Familiar, certain, well worn pathways Constraints self-evident to all Stable within universal constraints Self evident solutions	Sense-Categorise-Respond Ensure sound process in place Monitor for noncompliance & deviance Test for complacency Protect some pet mavericks	Watch for outliers Usable process Right support people for key staff Automate, but not automata Anonymous appeal/whistle blowers

This is a development of the original framework that appeared in the November 2007 Harvard Business Review paper on decision making. Let's look at a situation and see how to use the framework:

The first thing we need to do is to differentiate between order and un-order: have we seen this before or have any experience that can be leveraged? If so, then the problem is ordered. If we haven't seen this before and it is truly novel, then this is something that we may be better off exploring first; therefore, we treat it as un-ordered. If there is no time to consider the domain in which we are operating, then we should consider the worst case, not the most simple — which means that if is ordered, then deal with it as complicated and engage experts and if it is un-ordered, then treat it as chaotic and act in an attempt to stabilise the situation. This avoids oversimplifying the situation and fooling ourselves that we know the answer, only to find that we don't.

Considerations

There are a couple of general points that we need to discuss before we talk specifically about Cynefin practices. These relate to complicated and complex domains.

Groupthink/naivety: The issue with the complicated domain, the domain of experts, is that there is a tendency towards groupthink. There is value in groups as evidenced by the wisdom of crowds, which is based on the average view of a group of experts/experienced people in the area with the key point that the individuals are not allowed to engage each other. The participants may not disclose their guesses to each other and each estimate must be made in isolation to avoid participants influencing one other. This is not necessarily practical on a day-to-day basis so we need an effective strategy to address this and to improve information scanning.

Alfred Sloan said, "Gentlemen, I take it that we are all in complete agreement on the decision here. Then, I propose that we postpone further discussion... to give ourselves time to develop disagreement and perhaps gain some understanding of what the decision is all about."[4] The issue of groupthink can be addressed by engaging diverse groups of individuals and ensuring that some of these come from other domains of expertise and therefore provide a naive view.

The mantra is that there are no dumb questions, but you need people who are willing to ask such questions. Engaging experts from diverse domains can provide this. It is worth noting that President Franklin D. Roosevelt dragged people from one meeting to another if they were bright and he thought that they would provide an interesting point of view (Chip

---

4 Summing up of a GM senior executive meeting – see http://www.economist.com/node/13047099

Heath and Dan Heath 2013). Dave Snowden (Fitzsimmons 2014) tells a story of the engagement of anthropologists to study the management structure of a hotel chain. This gave rise to an interesting chapter in the report on the mating habits of the staff. This should be considered when you engage the experts.

Multi-hypotheses: We have talked about there being no clear answer in the complex domain, which means that we will have competing views. Remember, in this domain, cause and effect are not directly related so we have messy coherence and may be able to ascertain patterns forming over time.

We need to understand and accept that this is not bad in itself and sometimes needs to be embraced. This means that we are not looking for the right answer but for a series of ideas that we can test to find out what works, as more than one idea may be viable. The complex domain is the domain of multi-hypotheses, so aim to run a number of parallel experiments that test these hypotheses and maximise the potential for learning.

> **Conflict resolution**
>
> The use of multi-hypotheses is also a useful technique for conflict resolution. The hypotheses can be outlined and experiments run to determine which are valid and should be progressed. It may be the case that opposing ideas have validity and have benefit. See the portfolio forms in the portfolio-management section for an outline of the experiments.

There is a good example in the Heath brothers' *Decisive* where they discuss the largest direct-car-sales company in America. This started as an experiment to see if people would consider buying cars online and the response was overwhelming. The experiment had to be stopped as the company was losing money because the trial had them purchase cars from traditional dealers to meet the online orders. This type of issue is going to become more common in the future and we need a more flexible and comprehensive model.

Again, naivety has a role to play as we cannot assume that we know what will happen. As long as someone can make a coherent argument, their idea has value and should be explored.

Obliquity: The last point to make is that of the need to recognise the value of obliquity, which is the practice of achieving objectives indirectly. You may know that Apple doesn't focus on traditional management measures but uses net promoter score (NPS) to assess satisfaction from the customer's perspective.[5] It uses NPS to guide its product development and marketing efforts. It does make use of traditional metrics internally but these are not targets in themselves.

To expand on this, I'll use an example from sailing. Whether sailing up-wind or downwind, we are trying to get to the next mark as quickly as possible and the common metric used to indicate progress is VMG (velocity made good). VMG is a direct measurement that doesn't take into account all the other variables that are in play such as wind strength, point of sail, etc., so we typically use an oblique measure, which is that of target velocity. The boat's performance characteristics are used to determine the optimum speed given the wind strength and point of sail. The helm then steers the boat based on this indirect measure, which leads to optimisation of the VMG to the next mark (I would expect the navigator to have VMG on his instruments but not on the main instruments so the helm is oblivious to the direct measure).[6]

What we ideally want to use is an oblique approach, as this avoids the cognitive bias that comes from using a traditional measure that can be gamed. This is explored in John Kay's excellent *Obliquity: Why Our Goals Are Best Achieved Indirectly.*

Closing comments

Cynefin provides an approach and a set of practices for addressing the uncertainty that increasingly faces management today. It provides them with the means to realise that they are facing a messy, intractable problem and with the tools to enable them to make progress in this imperfect world.

This is a significant change from the more traditional approaches, which try to reduce a problem to a set of rational actions and acknowledges that

---

5 Interestingly you cannot optimise for customer satisfaction and shareholder value. See Roger Martin's "The Age of Customer Capitalism."

6 This also allows velocity headers and lifts to be handled, but a discussion of steering to targets is not the focus of this paper. You find dinghy sailors do this intuitively, hence the mantra of ease-hike-trim, and one of the issues that they have when moving to large boats is dealing with the array of information available on a typical race boat. If you are interested in this area, I suggest Will Oxley's recently published *"Modern Race Navigation".*

in some instances we cannot predict the outcomes. Instead of obsessing about predicting the future, we can move to controlling the future, and we therefore don't need to predict everything. This is the value of Cynefin. The portfolio-management section considers the practices related to the running the experiments.

PART TWO

Cynefin and narrative

Words are how we think — stories are how we link.

— Christina Baldwin

Oral narrative is and for a long time has been the chief basis of culture itself.

— John D. Niles

Narrative enquiry is an oblique means of investigation and has wide applicability. This paper uses it as an approach to business architecture but others have used it as an element of structured interventions. We are social in nature and some anthropologists consider *Homo narrans* (storytelling man) a more appropriate name for our species than Homo sapiens as narrative defines us (Niles 1999).

Each of us is embedded in our stories, which provide the context in which we live so we should not ignore them. In a social environment, the stories (Mankell 2011) and anecdotes that people tell act as prompts to others, so one story or anecdote brings other stories to mind and it becomes a virtuous circle: "That reminds me, do you remember when...." The difference between stories and anecdotes are that the latter are the short stories that we would tell around the water cooler or over a drink. They do not have the formal story structure of a beginning and an end with a theme and many subplots. Anecdotes are informal stories that reflect what actually happens versus what people would like to happen.

The practice of narrative enquiry is the use of anecdotes to establish the issues and to help make sense of what is happening. It has a number of advantages over traditional techniques. It is an oblique technique as the user is not asked direct questions, which ensures more openness and honesty. Oscar Wilde said, "Give him a mask, and he will tell you the truth,"[1]

---

1 This is part of the quote "Man is least himself when he talks in his own person. Give him a mask, and he will tell you the truth." from Oscar Wilde, "The Critic as Artist"

and so it is with this approach. Since they are not directed, people will mention things that they would otherwise be uncomfortable discussing. This leads to insights that would not available if we had taken a more direct path. There is also an element of serendipity to the approach, as we may start out with the intention of exploring a particular issue but find that other issues are also raised.

A second advantage of narrative enquiry is that it can exploit self-signification of the stories, which guards against the facilitators or other parties biasing the results (this supports the principle of disintermediation). In a traditional analysis approach, once we have conducted one or two interviews, human biases come into play as we start to look for stories or requirements that confirm the themes that we are seeing (this is confirmation bias at work). This means that the order of the interviews is important, and if we start with senior members of an organisation, the stakeholders, it will bias the other interviews towards their perspective. Cognitive bias, as a result, may make us miss important and relevant details when we then engage the people on the ground floor. For a simple example of mental bias, count the number of F's in the following text: "Finished files are the result of years of scientific study combined with the experience of years." Most people will count around three, but there are in fact six F's in the text. For a discussion of some of the more common cognitive biases, have a look at Jim Benson's excellent book *Why Plans Fail* (2011).

The use of stories allows people to access thoughts and feelings that are otherwise not available to them. This is because some knowledge is tacit in nature, meaning that a person doesn't know it until they need it (Polanyi, 2009). The police do something similar when they interview a person: they will ask what the weather was like at the time of the incident, which then puts the interviewee in the context (Dolan 2014).

Cognitive Edge's approach to this at the group level is the use of anecdote circles, but this can also apply at the individual or community level. In the former case, the core technique is used so the approach remains oblique in nature; for the latter, there is Cognitive Edge's SenseMaker product, which supports collection and self-signification at scale. As noted above, this paper is based on the use of the approach to support the establishment of a business's architecture[2] and is primarily based on individual engagement.

---

2 Some would say enterprise architecture but I'll not go into the difference here.

At the group level, we need to consider the dynamics, and groups should be seven to twelve members large (see the "Shared context and sense making" section for a discussion of group sizes). In addition, we ideally want to record the conversation and transcribe it. We engage at the individual level with an oblique question such as "If a friend was looking to join the company, what would you tell them about the organisation?" We are not directly asking them to tell us about the role or the issues they encounter day to day, but asking for what they would say to a friend. We may need to prompt them to expand on their answers, but we avoid asking direct questions about the challenges and the good or bad. Complex facilitation is lightweight in nature and we should only provide prompts when people seem to be struggling. This rarely happens in a group situation but it may be necessary at the individual level.

As part of the session, we also need to ask them to reflect on what they talked about. This reflection is the self-signification element and helps to establish the issues or points of interest that the anecdotes have raised. We are looking to capture small snippets of story and the self-significance that they gave to these. Write these up later and ask each participant to review them to ensure that the notes accurately represent the discussion and their comments. This means that any question about a specific aspect can be associated with the individual discussions, which supports disintermediation.

This approach was used to help shape an engagement and establish the heat map for a business function (a business capability: see Merrifield, Calhoun, and Stevens 2008). The business capabilities first were established using a form of linear contextualisation and then the narrative piece was undertaken separately. In this case, this helped to reduce the time commitments of the people involved and to provide more flexibility.

The response from the business was supportive. The approach has demonstrated that it can work at the individual level as well as at the more traditional group level and therefore has utility in this mode. I would look to use again as it does not require a large amount of preparation — but it does require that you transcribe the main points of the discussion accurately.

PART
THREE

Shared context and sense making

Knowledge is not determined in advance of our experience; things of strategic and economic relevance are not waiting to be discovered, but are invented as we go.

— Robert Chia and Robin Holt, *Strategy without Design.*

Introduction

The Cynefin framework can be used in different ways: for categorisation, which is useful from a situational perspective; for contextualisation, which is useful in establishing a checkpoint and deciding what we want to do; and from a dynamics perspective – we are here and need to move to here, so this the journey that we need to consider.

With respect to categorisation, we are using the framework to understand which domain we are in, and therefore which approach (act/sense/respond/etc.) is the most appropriate. This is useful to ensure that we don't oversimplify the situation and attempt to address an un-ordered problem using traditional ordered techniques. This is a singular situation, but the exemplar narrative outlined below can help to determine which domain we find ourselves in.

In contextualisation, there is a need to work out where we are, given all the issues that we are facing. We may need to consider where the company is going and the challenges facing a project or programme that is in flight, or we may be looking at starting a new initiative. This is about making sense of the wider situation and, given all the challenges, working out what needs to be done, acknowledging that not everything is obvious.

A dynamics perspective addresses a need to move a part of an organisation or group of people in a certain direction, and we may exploit the dynamic aspects of Cynefin to help. This may involve removing or loosening the constraints to see if we can change behaviours or create novel ones. This is complex facilitated management.[1]

In this section, we are exploring contextualisation, when there is a need to make sense of a situation among a large number of issues. This is the classic situation in which we are in danger of losing sight of the forest for the trees, and we need to pause and reflect in order to understand what needs to be done.

Contextualisation is one of the most useful Cynefin practices as it supports building shared context and purpose within an organisation. Here, the data precedes the model, unlike the traditional pattern of the model coming before the data. This may seem confusing initially but all we are doing in practice is loosening the constraints so as not to bias perspectives; therefore, we don't draw the model beforehand but let the domains and, in particular, the boundaries develop as part of the process. Although the Cynefin framework can be used for categorisation, as noted above, one of its most valuable uses is for development of a model that reflects the context and the uniqueness of each organisation. As English philosopher Gregory Bateson said, "Nothing exists without context."[2]

All of Cynefin's practices are participative in nature. It engages the people of an organisation directly and not via some third party, which ensures that there is no disintermediation. The conclusions come out of the dialogue and are not sprung on people.

It is one of the harder practices to understand, and while it is better experienced than explained, this paper nevertheless outlines the approach and provides some guidance on execution.

It is a lightly facilitated process. The facilitator merely provides an outline then leaves the participants to get on with it, which fosters shared learning. The main thing the facilitator must ensure is to allow the people to learn by doing, providing as little guidance as possible so that the participants freely express their own views. It is not necessary to provide a detailed overview of Cynefin other than to provide some context. This can be combined with the practices for defining and refining the actions that are outlined in the portfolio-management section.

---

1 This leads into ABIDE (attractors; barriers; identities; dissent/disrupt; environment) which is the Cynefin approach to management.

2 Paraphrased from Mind and Nature, A Necessairty Unity, page 14. Gregory Bateson, first edition 1979

Contextualisation

The intent of this practice is to develop a shared understanding of issues that face a project, programme, or organisation, and to make sense of what is going on. It is left to the participants to develop these insights. The approach supports three types of logic:

- Deductive logic — We have a large number of examples and we believe this is the general case.

- Inductive logic — Based on a small sample, we believe this is the general case.

- Abductive logic — Based on a hunch, we believe this is the case.

Most people know deductive and inductive logic as they are taught in most traditional schooling, but few are familiar with the last. Deductive logic is commonly referred to as the only form of pure logic; it takes us from the general to the specific and we can validate it. Inductive logic is case-based reasoning, where we go from the specific to the general. Abductive logic is sometimes called the science of hunches and is typically how most scientific breakthroughs are made.

The term "abductive" is credited to American pragmatic philosopher Charles Sanders Peirce, who introduced the term to mean "guessing". "Ab" means back and "duct" comes from the Latin *duco* (to lead), so the word means "to lead backwards". We need relevant experience to be able to make such leaps. Gary Klein's writing on the power of intuition (2004) explores how we use intuition in the workplace and is well worth reading.[3] Not everything is based on analysis, which is an underlying theme in Cynefin.

Most external agents can apply deductive and inductive reasoning to a problem, but abductive logic requires deep understanding of the domain. The participative nature of Cynefin is important as this leverages the knowledge and insights of the people who are part of the organisation. These people have developed this deep knowledge over time.

This also touches on tacit and explicit knowledge. Michael Polanyi (2009) said, "We know more than we can tell," and it is the engagement in the exercise that allows this tacit knowledge to be accessed. By definition, this

---

3 There is also an interesting discussion on intuition in the Heath brothers' *Decisive*. They reference Hogart's work and note that this is only likely to develop where there is a learning environment.

means that any approach that attempts to extract or gain access to this knowledge by questions is limited as it makes the assumption that you know which questions to ask. This is basically a Catch-22 situation: if we knew what the questions were, don't you think we would know what to do? So don't look to over-constrain the situation, and if other issues arise as part of the exercise then they should also be included.

Please note that when we talk of disorder, we need to acknowledge that we are making an ontological error, but it is where we are most of the time. This is an inauthentic state, and the value of sense making is in learning how we can move towards an authentic state. However, this is dynamic, so we need to acknowledge that we will never achieve true authenticity. This also exists within each of the Cynefin domains, as the boundaries are not hard. Therefore, we should note that Cynefin is a dynamic sense-making framework. I am indebted to Mika Latokartano for providing the breadcrumbs.

Shared context

A shared context is developed by contextualisation — that is, establishing the issues that exist in this environment and how they relate. We are using Cynefin to develop this understanding of the issues so we are assuming that we are largely aware of the issues; there may be an issue log or list of questions that we are looking to make sense of. Note that I would not advocate the use of brainstorming as this constrains people (if you are in any doubt

Linear contextualisation and value-stream mapping

One of the issues I have with VSM is that it looks to optimise an existing process and therefore focuses on doing the thing right without asking whether or not we are doing the right thing.

As an alternative, I prefer to use linear contextualisation, which starts from the client perspective and works backwards to establish what would be appropriate. The advantage this has over VSM is that it allows us to consider changes to the process as part of the mapping process. This use of linear contextualisation came from Mike Burrows.

about this, read Klein). If we don't have time, then we ask people to prepare their own lists of issues/concerns beforehand and to bring them. We could also consider running a narrative exercise to establish the issues as part of the exercise.

Remember that diversity and naivety are key tenets of Cynefin, so it is desirable to engage other parties as they bring different perspectives to bear. If we are doing this in the context of a department, we should think about engaging those we see as our clients and suppliers, those that depend upon us and those that we depend upon, to ensure that we are taking a holistic view. We may want to keep this exercise internal to avoid washing our dirty laundry in public, but if this is the case then see if we can get people to act as surrogates for these external parties.

The ideal group size for this exercise is seven to twelve.[4] Nancy Kline (1999) mentions that twelve is as large a group as we want, as this is the size of group in which people are still comfortable expressing themselves. Similarly, we don't want a lot of small groups as we want to encourage diversity; don't form groups any smaller than seven members as a general rule. If the group is too large, consider splitting it into a few smaller groups. We need not be too concerned about ensuring the diversity within these groups, as this will emerge when we review the different groups' interpretations.

There are three approaches that we can use to support contextualisation: four tables, four corners, or linear. Of these, I prefer four corners. In the four-corners method, we start out with a large, blank piece of paper or a wall. For a typical group of around ten people, we will get away with a piece of A0. Don't try to create an A0 out of four sheets of A3 unless there's no other option as the edges of the individual sheets make boundaries that people will subconsciously exploit when placing the issues on the paper.

In each of the four corners, we place an exemplar, a sample narrative, of each of the four core domains of the Cynefin framework. These can be:

- Obvious — Have seen it before and you know what to do.

- Complicated — Know someone who could work it out with some analysis.

---

4 Jeff Sutherland in his last book maintains that the best group size is five to nine, but this is a different context. What he is looking at is the smallest group that has all the skills necessary to do development.

- Complex[5] – There are competing hypothesis about what is happening.

- Chaos — There is no structure and everything is chaotic.

The outline below shows how this should look:

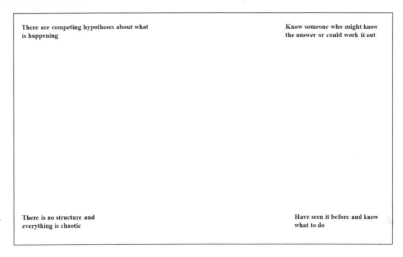

There are competing hypotheses about what is happening

Know someone who might know the answer or could work it out

There is no structure and everything is chaotic

Have seen it before and know what to do

The process is to write each issue on a small piece of paper (for example, Post-it notes) and then place these on the piece of paper one at a time based on where they sit between the exemplars. Remember that there is fifth domain called "disorder" for items whose domains we have not yet determined. Place these in the middle for now.

There is no right or wrong position for an issue, as the placement should be based on the individual's opinion of where each sits relative to the exemplars — for example, "It was not completely obvious but if we undertake a bit of analysis, I'm sure we can find an answer so this fits around two-thirds of the way from the bottom to top on the right hand side." Issues fit not only between any two of the exemplars but among all four. We may need to remind people of this until they get the hang of it (we only advise if we think this problem may be compromising the group).

We are emplying an oblique practice here, so although we are looking at developing a shared understanding of the issues that we face, we are also managing for emergence and insights that may help establish the

---

5 The original text here was "We have no idea but in hindsight it was obvious what was going on." I've noted that Dave Snowden had changed this in a comment on a blog post and thought the new text more relevant as it focuses on the now, not the past.

direction in which people want to progress.[6] These are the "Aha!" moments when we realise something and a lot of the little pieces fall into place. This is why it is important to engage our people. They are the ones who have the deep understanding, as they are immersed in what is going on and therefore are capable of these insights. Few consultancies will have this level of knowledge of our organisation's operations and certainly won't have a deep understanding of our organisation's context. Since the approach is participative in nature, the buy-in to any ideas will be more straightforward, as the group has been involved in developing and refining them.

The process is summarised in the following steps.

Position the issues on the wall based on association with the exemplars. This is not an absolute position but based on how we think each issue relates to each of the exemplar narratives. I must stress that we should not allow people to place an issue directly on any corner — for example, in the bottom right corner if an issue "is just obvious". Nothing is ever as simple as we think. There may be complications, and therefore we may want to see it placed a bit towards the top to indicate this.

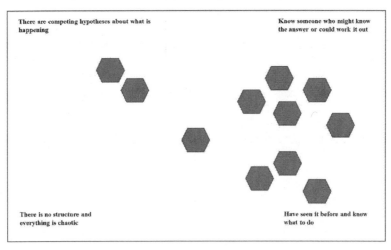

After placing all the issues, we want to draw the domain boundaries, which are defined by where the issues have been grouped. We ideally do this with tape that we can move until people are happy with the placement (remember the fifth domain that can hold issues that are not yet determined). If people cannot agree whether an issue sits on one side of a

---

6   Direction is not the same as strategy. Strategy is the means that you use to move in the direction and fulfil the purpose.

boundary or other, then we ask them to consider if there are in fact two issues, and whether they could be split into two with one placed inside either associated domain.

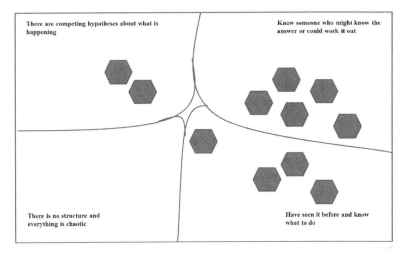

The borders give us a set of contextualised issues that we can start to work on. Remember to keep an ear open for insights that come out of this exercise, which are instances of abductive logic.

Each business is unique so the solutions that have worked for other organisations may not be ones that work in this context. Beware the adage "If I have a hammer then everything looks like a nail," and beware of people who have quick fixes or who believe that they have an answer that worked for them in some other context.

The next phase is the development of a series of initiatives that start to address the key issues that we have identified, embracing the insights that have come out of the exercise.[7] Remember that there may not be a strong justification for an idea, but as long as there is a coherent argument it should be considered. This approach to development and refinement of the initiatives is covered in the portfolio-management section. It discusses the use of portfolio forms and ritualised dissent to review and formalise these initiatives.

---

7   Do make sure you keep the maps as these are a useful source of other initiatives. Once, we were discussing initiatives after finishing an exercise when I turned around to find one of the programme managers removing and grouping the stickies from the wall. Fortunately, I had taken a photo!

Closing comments

We can use these techniques when considering direction to help inform strategy, when starting a new project, or when forming a new team and wanting to accelerate the gelling process by developing a shared context and to ensure alignment of purpose. The linear-contextualisation approach is also useful if we need to review workflows, and provides an alternative to the lean practice of value-stream mapping.

The technique is scalable and we need not limit involvement to twenty or thirty people. It is possible to run this for whole departments or organisations and involve large groups of people —which makes for some interesting discussions.

Note: these practices are the registered property of Cognitive Edge and are covered by the following user agreement: http://cognitive-edge. com/user-agreement/. If you register as a member of the Cognitive Edge Network, you can use them for personal use or within an organisation, but to use them commercially, you need a "rights to use" licence, which you can obtain by becoming a premium member of the network. See http://cognitive-edge.com/join-network/.

Resources

Hexagon stickies are available from http://www.logovisual.com/shop/ lvt-products/hexagon-sticky-notes/. Go for the small ones. These have two glue lines and are more durable and stay flatter when attached than any with a single line. Cognitive Edge also has these in stock. But we can also use traditional Post-it notes.

PART
FOUR

Portfolio management

Failure is instructive. The person who really thinks learns quite as much from his failures as from his successes.

— John Dewey

It was an idea, and ideas stood (or fell) because they were strong enough (or too weak) to withstand criticism, not because they were shielded from it. Strong ideas welcomed dissent.

— Salman Rushdie, *Joseph Anton: A Memoir*

Introduction

One of the core ideas of Cynefin is the use of safe-to-fail experiments to determine how we want to evolve the system. This needs to be done within the context of the direction in which we want to develop, which is the subject of this section. As Seneca the Younger said, "If one does not know to which port one is sailing, no wind is favourable." This approach supports the use of the scientific method (see below) to determine what works and has value.

Since another of Cynefin's key tenets is the exploration of multi-hypotheses, and there will be a number of experiments and portfolio forms to control these tests. The term "portfolio" is well understood in organisations, which typically have processes for organising and managing them. There are different templates for the complicated and complex domains: these need to be treated differently since one is the domain of good practice and the other the domain of emergent practice.

An alternative view holds that these small experiments should serve to pre-qualify the portfolio options and ensure that there is a balance to the portfolio. This has a number of advantages — the first being that it validates initiatives before there is any large commitment or expenditure. It also clarifies what constitutes success and allows exploration of multiple ideas when this traditionally could not be accommodated. Additionally, it allows for the development of a balanced portfolio that can deliver some business value, and is not only focused on hygiene-driven change such as system maintenance, upgrades, or regulatory or legislative change.

Cynefin also includes a practice for rigorous review of the proposals before presenting them to senior management (here meaning managers with authority for budget approval). This ensures that the ideas are well developed and the success criteria are well understood.

This is a lightly facilitated process, which means that the process is outlined and then the participants are left to get on with it, fostering shared learning. We run multiple, small, parallel, safe-to-fail experiments to maximise organisational learning. The facilitator must leave the people to learn by doing, providing as little guidance as possible, so that they express their own views and the facilitator does not bias the outcomes. Once a number of people have exposure to these practices, they can perform them with no external facilitation in an on-going basis.

Background

We need to distinguish between ideas and options. Ideas are what Martin, in *Playing to Win*, calls "possibilities", and he stresses the need to explore all the possibilities to establish the options. In Cynefin, we talk of hypotheses, which are basically ideas, and the exploration of these as long there is messy coherence — that is, someone can make a coherent argument for a particular hypothesis. We are not trying to establish if a hypothesis is right or wrong, only that there is enough coherence to support an experiment. The implication is that we remove the need for a formal justification for an idea as we are looking to validate them as part of the establishment of options.

The key to the validation process is the application of the scientific method as advocated by Karl Popper:

> We never argue from facts to theories, unless by way of refutation or "falsification". This view of science may be described as selective, as Darwinian. By contrast, theories of method which assert that we proceed by induction, or which stress verification (rather than falsi-

fication)… are typically Lamarckian[1]: they stress instruction by the environment rather than selection by the environment.

We are looking to maximise learning and invalidate an idea, not substantiate an idea. In this way, what we are doing is in fact similar to what Lean Startup does, but unlike it, we are looking at multiple ideas to accelerate learning. If you are struggling for ideas then a future backwards or contextualisation exercise may be worth running but most organisation typically already have a list of ideas or problems that they would benefit from addressing.

You will recall from the first section that complex systems are dispositional in nature, meaning that they are disposed to move or evolve in a certain direction, but we cannot determine causality so the only way we can manage this type of system is by probing, sensing, and responding. That is, we run a series of experiments to see if we can move the system in a direction that is desirable or beneficial to us.

In the complicated domain, in comparison, we manage by sensing, analysing, and responding. Here, we are looking for someone or a group of people who could determine what is desirable based on sensing and analysing the environment. The sensing may be based on existing data or we may need to undertake an experiment to collect the data to support analysis.

For each of the ideas, we are looking to outline an experiment that will invalidate the proposal as quickly and as cheaply as possible. As the management approaches to the two domains are different, there is a template for each domain. Note that there are no templates for the obvious domain, which only requires us to get on and do it (conventional project management works fine), and for the chaotic domain, which needs action that is novel. Since the complex domain is non-linear, we also need to consider an appropriate dampening strategy as stopping the experiment may not be sufficient.[2] There is also the domain of disorder, which provides a placeholder for items whose position we have yet to determine.

In summary, this is how we approach the initiatives in each of the domains once they are identified:

---

1 Lamarckism is the idea that an organism can pass on characteristics that it acquired during its lifetime to its offspring.
2 Sometimes referred to as the "Mail effect" in the UK, because if an issue is published, just denying it is not normally sufficient!

Obvious — Just do it, as you have seen it before and it should be obvious what needs to be done (this is after all the criterion for it being classified as obvious). It should just be a case of what resources are needed and whether you have them.[3]

Complicated — You need to involve a group of experts or knowledge-able individuals to undertake the analysis. Remember to engage related experts to honour the principle of requisite diversity and to bring naive views to bear to avoid groupthink.

Complex — What are the viable (that is, coherent) hypotheses and therefore what are the experiments that we are proposing? Remember, this is the domain of messy coherence and therefore we cannot predict the outcome, so we need to undertake a series of experiments to see if we can move in a desired direction (this being where you want to move or at least start to progress towards).

Chaotic — This is not often encountered during planning as this is normally a dynamic state that doesn't exist for long. We want to do something to move the problem into the complex or complicated domain so that we can start to get a handle on it.[4] Remember, we approach this domain based on act-sense-respond, so someone just needs to propose an action and then we go from there.

We then need to rigorously review these safe-to-fail experiments to ensure that the ideas are fully developed before presentation to senior management for sponsorship and funding. As noted in the introduction, we should explore any idea for which there is a coherent argument as the ideas are not necessarily mutually exclusive and there may be value to be gained from progressing more than one. This can be thought of as establishing the options, as an option is something that provides a choice.

The Cynefin practice of ritualised dissent is used here to review and validate the initiatives and this is something that most organisations are not good at. It is all too common, due to the siloed structure of most organisations, for the initiative of an individual or a small group to go without wide review or support. This technique ensures a wide review and therefore that the idea is more likely to be complete and supported.

---

3   There may be a need for capability building, but that is not the subject of this paper.

4   The term "management" can be taken to be "man handling", as manage is derived from the Italian word *maneggiare*, which means to handle, which in turn derives from the Latin *manus* (hand).

The ideas behind the practice are similar to neuroscientist Vincent Walsh's idea of trashing, in which a proposal is rigorously critiqued to ensure that it is fully formed. This practice ensures an objective review of the idea and removes the subjectivity.

It should also be noted that this leads to more centralised control than is typical within most organisations. Some people will not see this as desirable but it has the benefit of breaking down barriers both horizontally and vertically within an organisation.

Complicated portfolio template

This is the domain of experts, so the focus is on establishing who needs to be engaged — but with a twist. To improve information scanning, we want to ensure requisite diversity by engaging people who are not familiar with the domain. This brings a degree of naivety and ensures that different views are brought to bear (before execution and not as an afterthought!), so consider other groups that may have value in addition to the groups that traditionally exist. These can be acknowledged experts from other areas of the organisation that would typically not be engaged or they could be external agents. What they should not be are other people in the function/department in question, as there may be a conflict of interest and you are not increasing diversity. The outside experts do not need to know the field we're working on but should be knowledgeable in the area in which they work. Remember President Roosevelt, who dragged bright people from one meeting to another to learn their perspectives.

The complicated portfolio form is composed of four sections: three boxes on the left that describe the initiative, two boxes on the top right that cover the approach to be taken, two boxes on the middle right that cover the resourcing, and two boxes below those that cover expected completion date and formal review (sign off).

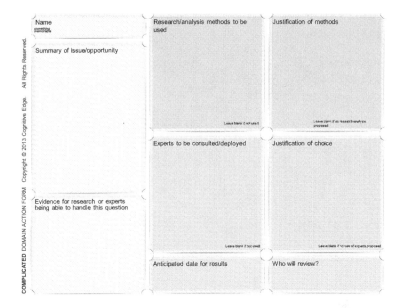

Name: This should describe the initiative distinctly and resembles what is done in A3 reports (Shook 2010).

Summary: This needs to detail the problem or opportunity in complete, standalone sentences. Remember, we are trying to establish the problem and not the solution here.

Evidence: This is a sense check to indicate why we think we can resolve this problem. If we cannot answer this, we may be operating in the complex domain and may need a different approach. Do not use tautologies such as "the sky is blue because it is blue." This may demand some thought.

Research approach: Since this is the domain of the experts, how do we expect them to undertake the necessary analysis to determine causality? It may be necessary to talk to people with related knowledge to establish a possible approach.

Research justification: In addition to outlining the approach, we need to justify it to ensure that we are being realistic. Why do we believe that the approach is valid?

Experts required: Remember that we want diversity in the people engaged so we need to not only consider which experts we would typically involve but also who else could provide a naive or original view. They can be experts in associated fields to ensure that groupthink does not become dominant.

Experts justification: This is why we think that the people we have suggested are appropriate and should be involved.

Anticipated date: This is the date by which we will complete the proposal. We may want to think about the prerequisites and the associated lead time when determining this. Note that this box doesn't say "expected" or "planned" as this is intended to be indicative — this is a portfolio and not a project document. When we get into the detailed planning then we may need to revise this.

Reviewer details: Who will review the outcomes and approve the subsequent steps? This may be the management team or head of department who will approve the funding to implement the initiative.

Complex portfolio template

This is the domain of multi-hypotheses so we expect there to be more than one by the nature of the domain. Remember that any idea that appears coherent may have value and should be evaluated. The objective is not to determine what should be done but what probes (experiments) would help clarify the situation.

The structure of this template is similar to the complicated portfolio template with four sets of boxes: three on the left define the initiative, the top two on the right hold the signs of success, the middle two are for signs of failure, and the bottom two list additional attributes that we should consider. Note that there is no date on the form, but we should have a view of how long the experiment will take.

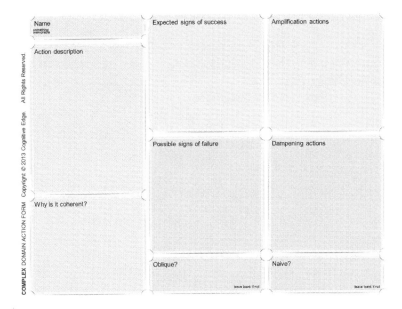

Name: Again, this should accurately describe the proposal.

Action: This describes the proposed probe or experiment.

Why is it coherent?: This is the justification. We are not trying to say that it is right, but explaining why we think it makes sense. If we can't justify it then we don't really have a basis for the proposal.

Signs of success: These are the things that we think indicate success. We may express these as some impact that we believe we would see, such as less defection of clients.

Amplification actions: What actions would we take if we start to see signs of success and want to increase the benefits?

Signs of failure: These are signs that the probe is potentially not successful, and may not simply be the opposite of the signs of success.

Dampening action: How would we deampen the action if we detect a failure? In the complex domain, stopping the experiment may not be enough and there may be other actions that we need to undertake to achieve this.

Obliqueness[5]: Have we considered the obliqueness of the probe and how have we exploited it?

---

5 Obliqueness and naivety are discussed in the introductory section.

Naivety: If we are embracing naivety, how are we leveraging it?

The last two boxes serve to remind us to consider these criteria. Note that the actions are necessary but should be seen as an adjunct to the act of portfolio management itself. Portfolio management is about determining what experiments we are willing to fund, while the action forms relate to the management of the experiments themselves.

Portfolio initiatives review

One of the most useful simple practices is that of ritualised dissent, which is used to review and refine the proposals. If we do want to use this practice to review proposals, we can do it as part of a workshop or establish a review body with members drawn from each of the teams or functions to ensure diversity.

The quality of ideas that can come out of such a session is amazing. It can also lead participants to buy in to the plan. Often, the more difficult people, who are always questioning proposals, provide useful comments. It engages these people, who therefore will not later stand on the sidelines throwing rocks; it fosters what Russell Ackoff called "agreement in practice and not just agreement in principle"[6]. If we have the opportunity, we can ask people what would need to be true to support the hypothesis. This moves them away from thinking of barriers and allows us to start looking at what we need to invalidate an idea, as these are just the opposites of what it would take for it to be true. This also brings focus to the discussions.

In this practice, one person from each team, or the person who is making the proposal, presents it to an alternative team or a panel of reviewers. A panel of reviewers requires us to ensure that a wide range of interests is represented. We may want to consider selecting one person from each of the different functions and rotating the membership on a regular basis.

The presenter has a few minutes to outline the initiative during which no other person is allowed to speak. They can take notes for later discussion but they must allow the presenter to speak without interruption. Once finished, the presenter disengages from the group by hiding their face — donning a mask, if available, or turning their chair so that their

---

6   Russell L. Ackoff, The Democratic Corporation, pages 81–83

back faces the group. This prevents personality from becoming involved in the review, keeps the presenter from feeling personally criticised, and ensures focus on the presentation.

The group members may now express their views of the idea, particularly what is wrong with it, and they should not hold back as this is about ensuring that all aspects are covered. There are no guidelines here but you could consider the clarity of details, the value proposition, whether dampening has been considered, etc. Again, this is not a debating forum so only one person at a time should speak until each has voiced all their concerns. People may find that comments made by others raise more concerns, which in turn should be voiced. During this, the presenter takes notes of the points raised for consideration in a revision of the initiative. We are trying to ensure that the initiative is reviewed objectively and the individual is not involved.

When the group has finished expressing concerns, the presenter takes the ideas back to the original group or goes off to revise the proposal to address the points that have been made. In a workshop setting, we can pass through a series of cycles to refine the initiatives that have been documented.

This simple practice takes advantage of the expertise and knowledge of the organisation to ensure that any initiative is well formed and has been objectively reviewed before presenting it to management for sponsorship. It is not the function of the reviewers to reject proposals, which is the prerogative of management, but to improve them. When you see this done, it's interesting how quickly an idea can be substantiated and formed. As noted above, it is similar to the trashing sessions that Vincent Walsh advocates.

Portfolio management

The outcome of the initiative review is likely to be a series of robust initiatives that should be considered for implementation. It is down to management to approve and fund these, but it is unlikely that all of them can be supported, due to resource and cost constraints. Therefore, before the workshops, or before presentation of ideas, we should think about the criteria for funding.

We may have to address a series of strategic themes, business priorities, and ensure that the initiatives are balanced and not biased towards one particular area. Also, if we are dealing with complex issues, we want to have multiple initiatives. In the complicated domain, it may be more straightforward as there is likely to be only a single initiative within a theme, but there may be multiple competing ideas from different teams or areas of the business, and we should explore these. These are only elements that need to be considered as part of each organisation's approach to exploiting Cynefin.

Closing comments

The practices are simple in nature, but allow us to start to embrace complexity and not avoid it. After experiencing one of these types of engagement, anyone can run it. This means that once an organisation has experience, it can use them internally for other initiatives without external facilitation. This is one of the strengths of Cynefin: the practices are simple and easy to exploit once we have basic knowledge of the techniques, and we don't need a deep understanding of the underlying theory of complex systems.

Note: these practices are the registered property of Cognitive Edge and are covered by the following user agreement: http://cognitive-edge.com/user-agreement/. If you register as a member of the Cognitive Edge Network, you can use them for personal use or within an organisation, but to use them commercially, you need a "rights to use" licence, which you can obtain by becoming a premium member of the network. See http://cognitive-edge.com/join-network/.

PART
FIVE

Cynefin
dynamics

We would expect that introducing additional constraints into a complex environment will make it ordered but, paradoxically, over-constraining a complex situation leads to chaotic behaviour. People introduce constraints that don't always fit the situation because they are attempting to treat a complex problem as one that is ordered and arbitrarily use traditional management approaches that are not applicable.

Remember that Cynefin is about bounded applicability, and we can use exemplars to determine the context to ensure that we respond in an appropriate manner. Kim Ballestrin (2015) uses simple language to assess whether the problem is simple or complicated (remember, chaotic is transitional), and if there is a need to approach the situation as if it is complex. I like this but think that the same exemplars used for contextualisation (see the section on sense making) can be used. These are "Is it obvious?", "We know what to do," or "We know someone who can probably provide an idea with some analysis." Otherwise, the problem is complex in nature and traditional practices shouldn't be used.

There are also times when it is useful to be able to move a problem from one domain to another. We may start out in complex, establish what needs to be done via safe-to-fail interventions, and move into the complicated domain in terms of execution. There are other situations where we find ourselves in a highly constrained, ordered situation and may benefit from moving to enable exploration. The analogy that I find useful is that of gybing of a boat, in particular a dinghy. When sailing, we are trying to keep the dynamic forces in balance to head in the direction we desire. We do this by small changes to the direction of the boat via the tiller and trimming the sails. When the boat is in a stable state, its direction is predictable. When it comes to gybing around a mark of the course, we want the boat to turn quickly so we intentionally put the dinghy into an unstable state as this increases its rate of turn. The trick in a dinghy is to control the initiation of the gybe. We do this with a short, sharp reversing of the tiller so that it happens when we want it to. Once we have completed the gybe, we move to put the boat back into a stable state as quickly as possible.

Some books advocate operating on the edge of order at all times as this increases the agility of the organisation, but as the authors point out in *Simple Habits in Complex Times* (Garver Berger and Johnston, 2015) people don't like ambiguity. We all require some degree of certainty, which means that causality needs to apply; therefore, we are better to think of this as a shallow dive into chaos (note that in Cynefin, chaos is regarded as a transitional state as it does not persist for long). This is basically what we want to do to support exploration and this is the area of Cynefin dynamics. We may be able to use an existing crisis or, as advocated in the introduction of *Learning to See* (Rother and Shook 1999), create one.[1]

This gives rise to two situations where moving between domains is of value: one where we want to move from exploitation to exploration and the other where we want to increase the organisational agility (rate of change).

In the first case (marked A in the diagram to the right), we have encountered a problem that is messy in nature.[2] We may or may not realise that this is complex in nature but we would benefit from dealing with it as complex as we can use probes to see if we can move the situation in a desirable direction. The point to remember is that this should

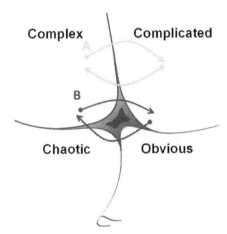

not be about a single experiment (probe). If there are competing hypotheses, we should explore all of them, so the path from complicated into complex may split into multiple paths of exploration. The resulting series of safe-to-fail probes will then lead to a series of options that may be then exploited in an ordered domain.

In the second case (B), where we want to create a change in an organisation, we can move the issue intentionally (or let it collapse) into a chaotic state. This is more a challenging art than a science, but we are looking to enter a shallow dive through chaos to invoke a change of direction for the organisation. The path in this example may be from complicated through chaos and complex back into an ordered domain. The first step is creating the crisis or letting it develop, and this is not addressed here. The thing to realise is that the chaotic element needs to be contained and we need to look to move out of this domain as quickly as possible. What I find useful is to use this to explore the direction that we want to take and then

---

1   The American politician and mayor of Chicago Rahm Emanuel told a Wall Street Journal conference in 2008, "Never let a serious crisis go to waste."

2   What Ackoff called "a mess" — see http://en.wikipedia.org/wiki/Wicked_problem

use complex domain practices to explore the competing hypotheses. This means that the cycle can be executed quite quickly if there is management support. Without such support, the organisation may drift into a chaotic state and linger there, which is not at all desirable (we sometimes hear of companies in crisis, and I think this describes them well).

These are just two examples of Cynefin dynamics — there are other patterns that we may observe over time. The use of Cynefin to explore these should allow us to understand what is happening and how we can exploit that to achieve desirable change.

Further reading

///

Although not referenced directly, the following books have influenced the development of the Cynefin framework, are listed on http://cognitive-edge.com/resources/influential-books/, and are well worth reading.

Cilliers, P. (1998) *Complexity and Postmodernism: Understanding Complex Systems.* Routledge.

Paul Cilliers wrote, "If something really is complex, it cannot be adequately described by means of a simple theory. Engaging with complexity entails engaging with specific complex systems." He thinks we can model complex systems, but I believe most models are inadequate and time is never on our side. Jamshid Gharajedaghi (2005) relates an anecdote:

> A minister of economy in my native country once asked me to help him assess the impact of a certain decision on three important factors he was concerned with. I told him it would take me a month to develop the proper model. He replied, "The decision is going to be made without you. If you want to have any influence on this one, be in my office with your model at 7:00 a.m. Monday morning. Otherwise, get the hell out of the way."

One of the main advantages of Cynefin is that it provides a set of simple practices that allow us to engage directly with a complex system and avoids the need for modelling.

Juarrero, A. (2002) *Dynamics in Action: Intentional Behavior as a Complex System.* Bradford Book.

Alicia Juarrero puts forward that causes can be considered dynamical constraints — that is, constraints not only constrain but also give rise to action. This means that we have two types of constraints, those that she refers to as context-free and those that are context-sensitive. The latter are the enabling constraints that lead to higher-order behaviour: emergent behaviour that can't be predicted and is therefore complex in nature.

About the Author

Greg Brougham is a systems and technical architect specialising in card and payments systems. He has worked on the renewal of the main UK domestic clearing and settlement system and a similar system for one of the major card companies. It was while working on the latter that he thought that there must be more effective means of delivery than the prevailing approaches, which were preoccupied with utilisation. This led to a review of the prevailing management literature and an interest in the theory of constraints, systems thinking, lean, and, more recently, complexity (in particular Cynefin) and the cognitive sciences.

References

Ballestrin, K. (2015). "Navigating Project Uncertainty — An Explorers Toolkit." LeanUX NYC (presentation). http://brooklyn.leanuxnyc.co/.

Benson, J. (2011). *Why Plans Fail: Cognitive Bias, Decision Making, and Your Business.* (1.1 edition). Modus Cooperandi Press.

Chia, R. C. H. and Holt, R. (2009). *Strategy without Design: The Silent Efficacy of Indirect Action.* Cambridge University Press.

Collingridge, J. (2015). "Lotus turns its back on the big league." *The Sunday Times, 8 February.* http://www.thesundaytimes.co.uk/sto/business/Industry/article1516483.ece. [Accessed June 2015]

Denning, S. (2012). "What Killed Michael Porter's Monitor Group? The One Force That Really Matters." *Forbes, 20 November.* http://www.forbes.com/sites/stevedenning/2012/11/20/what-killed-michael-porters-monitor-group-the-one-force-that-really-matters/. [Accessed June 2015]

Dolan, P. (2014). *Happiness by Design: Change What You Do, Not How You Think.* Hudson Street Press

Fitzsimmons C. (2014). "How to win from uncertainty: four tips for entrepreneurs." *Business Review Weekly, 29 January.* http://www.brw.com.au/p/entrepreneurs/how_to_win_from_uncertainty_four_MrOzgB-CrFEXzzoc3yeir5L. [Accessed July 2015]

Garvey Berger, J. and Johnston, K. (2015). *Simple Habits for Complex Times: Powerful Practices for Leaders.* Stanford University Press.

Gharajedaghi, J. (2005). *Systems Thinking: Managing Chaos and Complexity: A Platform for Designing Business Architecture* (second edition). Butterworth-Heinemann.

Heath, C. and Heath, D. (2013). *Decisive: How to Make Better Choices in Life and Work.* Cornerstone Digital.

Hodgson, P. and White, R. (2001). *Relax, It's Only Uncertainty: Lead the Way When the Way Is Changing.* Pearson FT Press.

Kay, J. (2011). *Obliquity: Why Our Goals Are Best Achieved Indirectly.* Profile Books.

Klein, G. (2004). *The Power of Intuition: How to Use Your Gut Feelings to Make Better Decisions at Work. Crown Business.*

Kline, N. (1999). *Time to Think: Listening to Ignite the Human Mind. Cassell Illustrated.*

Lafley, A.G. and Martin, R. L. (2013). *Playing to Win: How Strategy Really Works.* Harvard Business Review Press.

Mankell, H. (2011). "The Art of Listening." *The New York Times,* 10 December. http://www.nytimes.com/2011/12/11/opinion/sunday/in-africa-the-art-of-listening.html. [Accessed June 2015]

Martin, R. L. (2010). "The Age of Customer Capitalism." *Harvard Business Review,* January-February. https://hbr.org/2010/01/the-age-of-customer-capitalism. [Accessed June 2015]

Merrifield, R., Calhoun, J., and Stevens, D. *(2008).* "The Next Revolution in Productivity." *Harvard Business Review,* June. https://hbr.org/2008/06/the-next-revolution-in-productivity. [Accessed June 2015]

Niles, J. D. (1999). *Homo Narrans: The Poetics and Anthropology of Oral Literature.* University of Pennsylvania Press.

Pearson, M. (2007). "In Comes I": Performance, Memory and Landscape. University of Exeter Press.

Polanyi, M. (2009). The Tacit Dimension (reissue edition). University of Chicago Press.

Rother, M. and Shook, J. (1999). *Learning to See: Value-Stream Mapping to Create Value and Eliminate Muda* (1.3 edition). Productivity Press.

Shook, J. (2010). *Managing to Learn: Using The A3 Management Process to Solve Problems, Gain Agreement, Mentor, and Lead.* Lean Enterprise Institute.

Skillicorn, N. (2014). "'Creativity is not a team sport': Interview Vincent Walsh, Prof Neuroscience UCL." *Improvides* (blog), 24 March. http://www.improvides.com/2014/03/24/creativity-team-sport-interview-vincent-walsh-prof-neuroscience-ucl/. [Accessed June 2015]

Snowden, D. (2012). "Cynefin: Revised leadership table." *Cognitive Edge* (blog), 1 December. http://cognitive-edge.com/blog/cynefin-revised-leadership-table/. [Accessed June 2015]

Snowden, D. J. and Boone, M. E. (2007). "A Leader's Framework for Decision Making." *Harvard Business Review,* November. https://hbr.org/2007/11/a-leaders-framework-for-decision-making. [Accessed June 2015]

Stewart, M. (2009). *The Management Myth: Debunking the Modern Philosophy of Business. W. W. Norton & Company.*

"Story: Papatūānuku — the land." *Te Ara: The Encyclopedia of New Zealand* (webpage). http://www.teara.govt.nz/en/papatuanuku-the-land/page-5. [Accessed June 2015]

Syrett, M. and Devine, M. (2012). *Managing Uncertainty: Strategies for Surviving and Thriving in Turbulent Times.* Wiley.

Made in the USA
Columbia, SC
20 January 2019